SECRETS OF THE TUDOR COURT

→ *The Pleasure Palace* ←

Secrets

of the

TUDOR COURT

❖ *The Pleasure Palace* ❖

KATE
EMERSON

POCKET BOOKS
New York London Toronto Sydney

Pocket Books
A Division of Simon & Schuster, Inc.
1230 Avenue of the Americas
New York, NY 10020

First Pocket Books trade paperback edition February 2009

POCKET and colophon are registered trademarks of Simon & Schuster, Inc.

For information about special discounts for bulk purchases, please contact Simon & Schuster Special Sales at 1-800-456-6798 or business@simonandschuster.com.

Designed by Ruth Lee-Mui

Manufactured in the United States of America

10 9 8 7 6 5 4 3 2

Library of Congress Cataloging-in-Publication Data

Emerson, Kate.
Secrets of the Tudor court : the pleasure palace / Kate Emerson.—1st Pocket Books trade pbk. ed.
p. cm.
ISBN-13: 978-1-4165-8320-2 (alk. paper)
ISBN-10: 1-4165-8320-3 (alk. paper)
1. Popincourt, Jane—Fiction. 2. Mistresses—Great Britain—Fiction.
3. Henry VIII, King of England, 1491–1547—Fiction. 4. Great
Britain—Kings and rulers—Paramours—Fiction. 5. Great Britain—Court
and courtiers—Fiction. I. Title.
PS3555.M414S43 2009
813'.54—dc22   2008030455

FOR MEG AND CHRISTINA

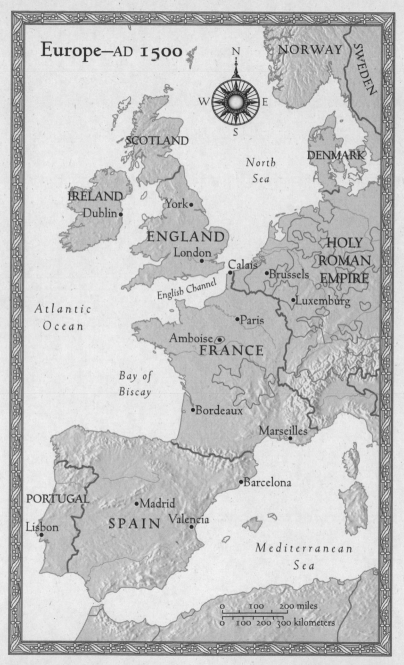

Europe—AD 1500

NORWAY

SWEDEN

SCOTLAND

DENMARK

North
Sea

IRELAND

York

Dublin

ENGLAND

HOLY
ROMAN
EMPIRE

London

Calais

Brussels

English Channel

Luxemburg

Atlantic
Ocean

Paris

Amboise

FRANCE

Bay of
Biscay

Bordeaux

Marseilles

PORTUGAL

Barcelona

Madrid

SPAIN

Valencia

Lisbon

Mediterranean
Sea

0   100   200 miles
0   100 200 300 kilometers

Map by Paul J. Pugliese.

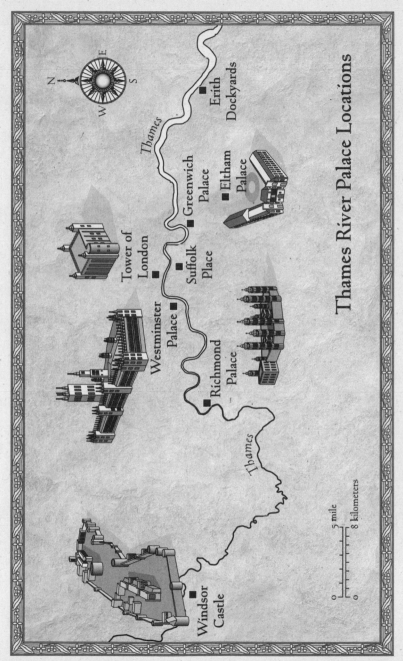

Thames River Palace Locations

Erith
Dockyards

Thames

Greenwich
Palace

Eltham
Palace

Tower of
London

Suffolk
Place

Westminster
Palace

Richmond
Palace

Thames

Windsor
Castle

5 mile
8 kilometers
0
0

Map by Paul J. Pugliese.

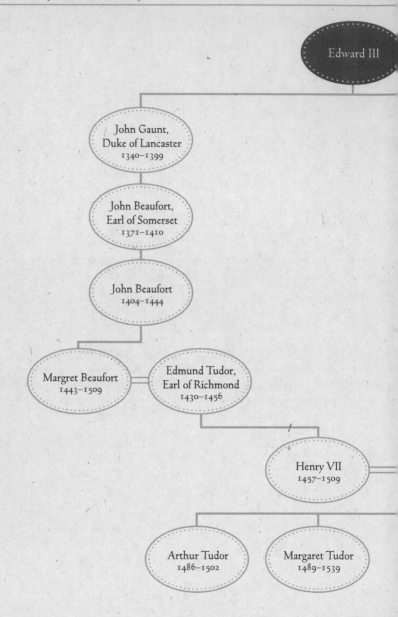

Edward III

John Gaunt,
Duke of Lancaster
1340–1399

John Beaufort,
Earl of Somerset
1371–1410

John Beaufort
1404–1444

Margret Beaufort
1443–1509

Edmund Tudor,
Earl of Richmond
1430–1456

Henry VII
1457–1509

Arthur Tudor
1486–1502

Margaret Tudor
1489–1539

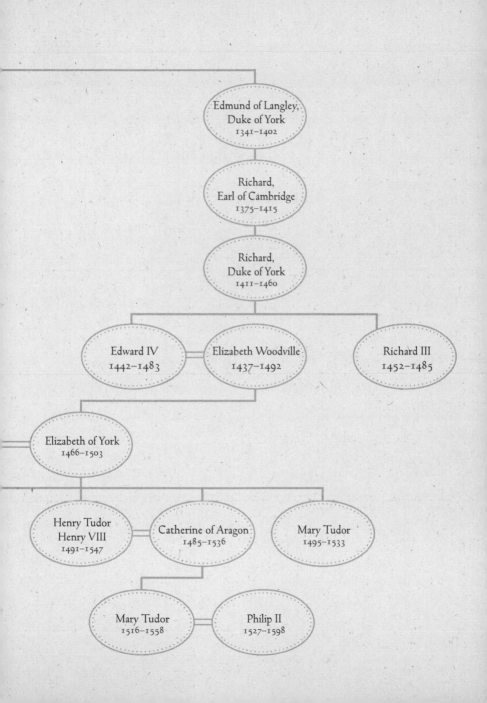

Edmund of Langley,
Duke of York
1341–1402

Richard,
Earl of Cambridge
1375–1415

Richard,
Duke of York
1411–1460

Edward IV
1442–1483

Elizabeth Woodville
1437–1492

Richard III
1452–1485

Elizabeth of York
1466–1503

Henry Tudor
Henry VIII
1491–1547

Catherine of Aragon
1485–1536

Mary Tudor
1495–1533

Mary Tudor
1516–1558

Philip II
1527–1598

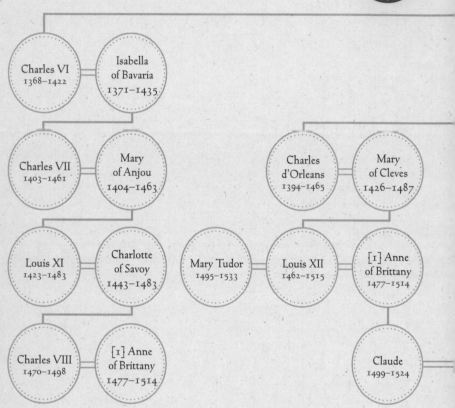

Charles V
1337–1380

Charles VI
1368–1422

Isabella
of Bavaria
1371–1435

Charles VII
1403–1461

Mary
of Anjou
1404–1463

Charles
d'Orleans
1394–1465

Mary
of Cleves
1426–1487

Louis XI
1423–1483

Charlotte
of Savoy
1443–1483

Mary Tudor
1495–1533

Louis XII
1462–1515

[1] Anne
of Brittany
1477–1514

Charles VIII
1470–1498

[1] Anne
of Brittany
1477–1514

Claude
1499–1524

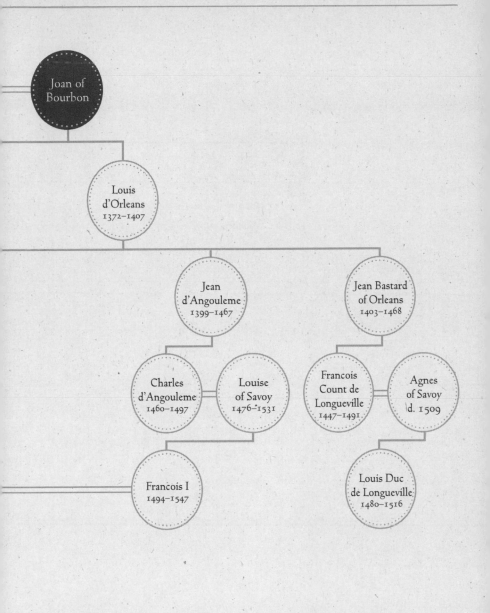

Joan of
Bourbon

Louis
d'Orleans
1372–1407

Jean
d'Angouleme
1399–1467

Jean Bastard
of Orleans
1403–1468

Charles
d'Angouleme
1460–1497

Louise
of Savoy
1476–1531

Francois
Count de
Longueville
1447–1491

Agnes
of Savoy
d. 1509

Francois I
1494–1547

Louis Duc
de Longueville
1480–1516

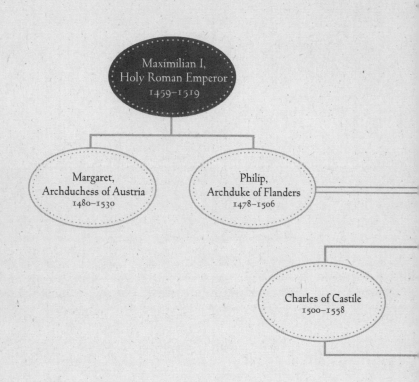

Maximilian I,
Holy Roman Emperor
1459–1519

Margaret,
Archduchess of Austria
1480–1530

Philip,
Archduke of Flanders
1478–1506

Charles of Castile
1500–1558

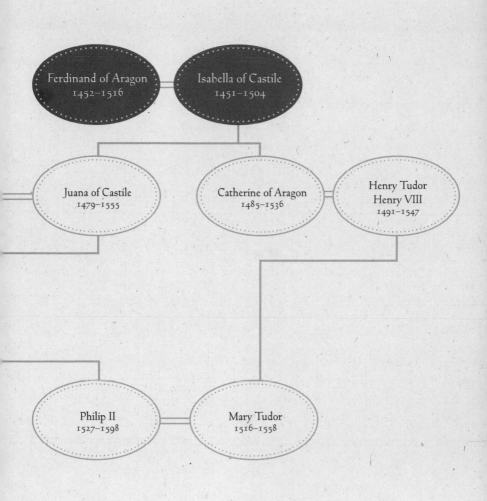

SECRETS OF THE TUDOR COURT
✣ *The Pleasure Palace* ✤

1

I was a child of eight in April of the year of our Lord fourteen hundred and ninety-eight. I lived in a pretty, rural town on the south bank of the Loire River, where a fortified château faced with white stone graced the hill above. This castle had been much restored by France's King Charles VIII, and his court spent a good part of every year in residence there. Both the town and the château were called Amboise.

My mother, Jeanne Popyncourt, for whom I was named, served as a lady-in-waiting to the queen of France. My father, until his death six months earlier, followed the court from place to place, taking lodgings in nearby towns so that Maman could visit us whenever she was not in attendance on Queen Anne. We had a modest house in Amboise and several servants to see to our needs. After Papa died, Maman added a governess to the household to look after me.

I was so often in Amboise that I had become friends with some of the neighborhood children. I spent a great deal of time with one in particular, a boy of my own years named Guy Dunois. Guy taught me how to play card games and climb trees, and he made me laugh by crossing his eyes. They were a bright blue-green and always full of mischief.

Then everything changed when King Charles died. When word of it spread throughout Amboise, people went out into the street just to stare up at the château. Some had tears in their eyes. Madame Andrée, my governess, told me to stay in my bedchamber, but from my window I could see that she and everyone else in the household was outside. Guy and his mother were out there, too. I was just about to disobey Madame's orders and join them when a cloaked and hooded figure burst into the room. I let out a yelp. Then I recognized my mother.

"We must leave at once on a long journey," Maman announced.

Surprised by my mother's disguise, I was nonetheless elated by the prospect of a great adventure, I clapped my hands in delight. I treasured the hours I spent in my mother's company, the more so since the loss of my father. For the most part, Maman and I could only be together when she did not have duties at court. As she was one of Queen Anne's favorite ladies, she was rarely free.

"Where are we going? When do we leave? What shall I pack?"

"No questions, Jeanne, I beg you."

"But I must say farewell to Guy and my other friends, else they will wonder what became of me."

"There is no time." She had already stuffed my newest, finest garments into the leather pannier she'd brought. "Don your cloak, and change those shoes for your sturdiest pair of boots."

When I'd done as she asked, I held out a poppet I treasured, a cloth baby with yarn for hair and a bright red dress. Maman looked sad, but she shook her head. "There is no room."

She left behind my comb and brush and my slate and my prayer book, too. With one last look around the chamber to assure that she'd packed everything she thought necessary, she grasped my hand and towed me after her to the stable.

A horse waited there, already saddled and carrying a second bulging pannier. I looked around for a groom, but no one was in sight, nor had Maman hired any guards to escort and protect us.

Many people were leaving Amboise in the wake of the king's death. "Where are they all going in such a hurry?" I asked as I rode on a pillion behind Maman, clinging tightly to her waist.

"To Blois, to the new king."

"Is that where we are going?"

"No, my darling. Please be silent, Jeanne."

She was my mother, and she sounded as if she might be about to cry, so I obeyed her.

Once free of the town, she avoided the main roads. When I'd made journeys with my father in the past, we'd spend our nights in private houses, mostly the country manors belonging to his friends. But Maman chose to take rooms in obscure inns, or lodge in the guest quarters of religious houses. It was not as pleasant a way to travel. The beds were often lumpy and sometimes full of fleas.

Maman said I must not speak to anyone, and she rarely did so herself. We both wore plain wool cloaks with the hoods pulled up to hide our faces. It was almost as if she feared being recognized as a lady of the French court.

Our journey took two months, but at last we reached the Pale of Calais, on the north coast of France. Maman reined in our horse and breathed an audible sigh. "We are on English soil now, Jeanne. This land belongs to King Henry the Seventh of England." I was puzzled by her obvious relief at having left our country, but I dared not ask why.

A few days later, we had a rough sail across the treacherous body of water the English called the Narrow Seas, finally arriving in the town of Dover. It was the twelfth day of June, two days after Trinity Sunday, and the English port was in an uproar. The authorities were searching for an escaped prisoner who had been held under light guard at the English king's palace of Westminster. His name was Perkin Warbeck—and he was a pretender to the throne.

My mother was much troubled by this news. She had met Perkin Warbeck years before when he visited the French court of King Charles. At the time he claimed to be the true king of England and had been seeking help from our king to overthrow England's Henry VII.

Although I was by nature a curious child, I had little interest in the furious search for Warbeck. I was too caught up in the novel sights and sounds of our trip as we traveled overland to London. Everything was new and different—the language, the clothes, even the crops. We traveled for the better part of three days through the English countryside before we reached the city.

In London, we took a room at the King's Head, an inn in Cheapside, and Maman sent word of our arrival to her twin brother, Rowland Velville, whom she had not seen in many years, not since he had left home to serve as a page for an English exile named Henry Tudor. That done, we settled in to wait for him.

Our chamber looked out upon the innyard. To pass the time, I watched the arrivals and departures of guests and the ostlers at work. Servants crisscrossed the open space dozens of times a day on errands. Deliveries were made. Horses were led to stabling. Once I saw a young woman, cloaked and hooded, creep stealthily from her room to another. It was a noisy, busy place, but all that activity provided a welcome distraction. We had no idea how long we would have to remain where we were.

On the third morning of our stay, the eighteenth day of June, I was awakened by the sound of hammering. I slipped out of bed, shivering a little in my shift, and went to the window. From that vantage point I had a clear view of a half dozen men constructing the oddest bit of scaffolding I had ever seen. It was made entirely of empty wine pipes and hogsheads of wine.

When it was completed, the men secured a heavy wooden object to the top. I blinked, bemused, but I was certain I was not mistaken. I had seen stocks before. Even in France, those who committed certain crimes were made to sit in them while passersby threw refuse and insults their way.

"Jeanne, come away from there!"

I turned to find my mother sitting up in bed, her face all flushed from sleep. I thought her surpassing beautiful and ran to her, clambering up beside her to give her a hug and a kiss. I loved the feel of Maman's skin, which was soft as flower petals and smelled of rose water.

"What is all that hammering?" she asked.

"Some men built a scaffold out of wine pipes and hogsheads and put stocks on top of it. Is the innyard like a marketplace? Do you think it is the custom to punish criminals at the King's Head?"

"I think only very special prisoners would merit such treatment. We must dress, and quickly." Her face, always pale, had turned white as the finest parchment. I did not understand what was wrong, but I was afraid.

We had to play tiring maid to each other, having brought no servants with us from France. I laced Maman into a pale gold bodice and kirtle and helped her don the long rose-colored gown that went over it. We did have fine clothing, and Maman had taken special pains to pack our best. The fabrics were still new and smelled sweet and the colors were rich and vibrant.

By the time we dressed and broke our fast with bread and ale, a great to-do had arisen in the innyard. Together, as the bell in a nearby church tower rang out the hour of ten, we stepped out onto the low-railed gallery beyond the window and looked down.

A man had been placed in the stocks. His long yellow hair was dirty, and his fine clothing rumpled and soiled, but he still had the look of someone important. It was difficult to tell his age. He slumped like an old man and, since I was only eight, almost everyone seemed ancient to me. In fact, he was no older than my mother, and she was just twenty-four.

The crowd, noisy and jostling, swelled as we watched. They jeered at the prisoner and called him names. He had been put on public display as punishment for some crime. I understood that much. What continued to puzzle me was the strangeness of the scaffold.

"Who is he?" I asked. "What did he do?"

I spoke in French, in the high, ringing voice of childhood. A man in a lawyer's robe looked up, suspicion writ large upon his swarthy, ill-favored countenance. Those few words had drawn attention to us. Worse, they had marked us as foreigners. Maman hastily retreated into the chamber, pulling me after her, and closed the shutters.

"Who is he?" I asked again.

"Perkin Warbeck," she answered. "The pretender the soldiers were looking for in Dover."

The noise outside our window increased as the day wore on until finally, at just past three of the clock, Warbeck was taken away under heavy guard. A scant quarter of an hour afterward, my uncle arrived.

"You have grown up, Rowland," my mother said as she hugged

her twin hard. "But I would have known you anywhere. You have the look of our father."

She had not seen her brother since they were nine. Within three years Rowland's leaving home, Henry Tudor had become King Henry VII of England.

"And you, my dear sister," Rowland Velville said courteously, "have a most pleasing countenance."

"Jeanne," she said, turning to me, "this is your uncle, Master Rowland Velville."

"Sir Rowland," he corrected her, sparing one hard stare for me.

I studied the two of them while they talked quietly together, fascinated by their similarities. Both were blessed with thick brown hair and large, deep-set brown eyes. I shared their coloring, but my eyes have golden flecks. I was extraordinarily pleased with that small difference. I did not want to be just like anyone else, not even my beloved mother.

My uncle's nose was large, long, and thin. My mother's, too, was thin, but much smaller. Mine was the smallest of all—a "button," Maman called it. Uncle was of above-average height. Maman came up to his shoulder. Both of them were slender, as was I.

Having given her brother a brief account of our journey, Maman described the scene we had witnessed in the innyard. "Poor man," she said, meaning Perkin Warbeck.

"Do not waste your sympathy!" Uncle sounded so angry that I took a quick step away from him. "He is naught but an imposter, a commoner's son impersonating royalty."

Maman's brow furrowed. "I know that, Rowland. What I do not understand is why he would try to escape. The rebellion ended months ago. We heard about it at the French court, including how King Henry forgave Warbeck for leading it."

"Your information is remarkably accurate."

"Any tale of the English court soon reaches the ears of the king of France. No doubt the English king has similar sources who report on every rumor that comes out of the court of France."

"If he does, I am not privy to what they tell him. He has never confided in me."

Maman looked relieved to hear it.

"King Henry does not always reward those who deserve it."

"He has been generous to you. You have been made a knight."

"An honor long overdue." He sounded bitter. "And there were no lands to go with it. He takes more care for the future of this fellow Warbeck! As soon as the pretender admitted that he was an imposter, the king gave him leave to remain at court. He was under light guard but was treated like a guest. Warbeck's wife fared even better. She has been appointed as one of Queen Elizabeth's ladies and is accorded her full dignity as the daughter of a Scottish nobleman."

"Lady Catherine Gordon," Maman murmured. "Poor girl. She thought she'd married a king and ended up with a mere commoner."

"Warbeck will be lodged in the Tower of London from now on. He'll not find life so easy in that fortress, nor will he have any further opportunity to escape."

"The Tower of London? It is a prison?" Maman sounded confused. "I thought it was a royal palace."

"It is both, often at the same time. Prisoners accused of treason and those of noble birth are held there. And kings have kept lodgings within the precincts from the earliest days of the realm."

I tugged on my uncle's dark blue sleeve until he glanced down with the liquid brown eyes so like my mother's. "How could a commoner be mistaken for a prince?" I asked.

"He was well coached by King Henry's enemies." My uncle

went down on one knee so that we were face-to-face and caught me by the shoulders. "You are a clever girl, Jane, to ask me this. It is important that you know who people are. The court much resembles a small village. If you do not know that the butcher's wife is related by marriage to the blacksmith, you may do yourself much harm by speaking against him within her hearing. So, too, with plots and schemes. A family's enmity can—"

"Rowland!" My mother spoke sharply, cutting him off. "Do not continue, I beg of you. She is too young to understand."

He gave a curt nod, but kept hold of my shoulders and looked me straight in the eye.

"Listen well, Jane. I will tell you a cautionary tale now and save the other story for another day. Many years ago, the two sons of the English king Edward the Fourth were declared illegitimate upon King Edward's death by Edward's brother, Richard the Third. Richard then took the throne for himself. Thereafter the princes disappeared. No one knows what happened to them, although most men believe that Richard the Third, now king, had them murdered. Henry Tudor then defeated King Richard in battle at a place called Bosworth and became King Henry the Seventh in his stead. To end civil war, Henry Tudor married Elizabeth of York, Edward's eldest daughter, even though she, too, had been declared illegitimate by Richard's decree."

My uncle glanced at my mother. "King Henry the Seventh is especially sensitive just now on the subject of the royal bastards."

"That is understandable," Maman replied. Her expression was serene, her voice calm, but sadness shone in her eyes.

My uncle turned back to me to continue his history lesson. "But King Henry's throne is not yet secure. He has been plagued by imposters claiming to be one of the missing princes. So far, his grace has always been able to discover their true identities and expose them, taking the heart out of the traitors who support them. But many rebellious souls still exist in England, men all too ready to rise up again, even in the cause of a royal bastard."

My brow puckered in confusion. "I know what a bastard is, Uncle. It means you are born outside of marriage. My friend Guy Dunois is one. But if these two boys—who may or may not be dead—are bastards, why would anyone try to impersonate them? They cannot claim the throne even if they are alive."

Uncle gave me an approving look. "I would not be so certain of that. Before marrying their sister, King Henry the Seventh reversed the royal decree that made her and her brothers illegitimate. So, dead they are and dead they must remain—for the good of the realm."

My curiosity led me quickly to another question. "Why was Warbeck's scaffold made of wine pipes and hogsheads?" I asked.

The briefest hint of a smile came over my uncle's face. "Because the popular belief is that the king's navy came close to capturing Warbeck before he ever landed on these shores. He eluded them, it is said, by hiding inside an empty wine barrel stowed in the prow of his ship."

My mother's fingers moved from her rosary to the silk sash at her waist. Her voice remained level, but the way she twisted the fine fabric around one hand betrayed her agitation. "With so much unrest in his land," Maman said, "it is good of the king to take an interest in us."

"Your future is not yet secure, Joan."

"She is Jeanne," I protested. "Jeanne Popyncourt. As I am."

"No longer. You are in England now, my dear niece. Your mother will be known as Joan and you will be Jane, to distinguish between the two of you."

"I do not understand," I said.

"I will explain everything in good time, Jeanne," Maman said.

"Jane," Uncle insisted.

"Jane, then," she continued. "Be patient, my child, and all will be revealed. But for the present it is best that you do not know too much."

"And in the meantime," my uncle interrupted, "you will both be provided for. Come. I am to take you to the king."

"Now?" The word came out as a hoarse croak. Maman's eyes widened in alarm.

"Now," he insisted.

At my uncle's urging, we gathered up our possessions and soon were aboard a wherry and headed upriver on an incoming tide. I sat between him and my mother in the pair-oared rowing boat.

The vessel's awning kept the sun out of our faces, but it did not obscure my view. Attempting to see everything at once, I twisted from side to side on the cushioned bench. We had boarded the wherry just to the west of London Bridge and so had a good distance to travel before we passed beyond the sprawling city of London with its tall houses and multitude of church steeples. When at last we rounded the curve of the Thames, the river broadened to reveal green meadows, riverside gardens, and a dazzling array of magnificent buildings that far outshone anything the city had to offer.

"That is Westminster Abbey," my uncle said, pointing. "And there is the great palace of Westminster, where the king is waiting for us."

Once we disembarked my uncle escorted us to the king's privy chamber. I caught only a glimpse of bright tapestries and grand furnishings before a liveried servant conducted us into the small complex of inner chambers beyond.

"Why is it so much darker here?" I whispered, catching hold of my mother's sleeve.

"Hush, my darling."

"Show some respect," my uncle snapped. "Do you not realize what a great honor it is to be allowed to enter the king's 'secret' lodgings?"

We moved briskly through one small chamber and into another. There the servant stopped before a curtained door.

"Make a deep obeisance," my uncle instructed in a harsh whisper. "Do not speak unless spoken to. Address the king as 'Sire' or 'Your Grace' when you do speak to him. And do not forget that you must back out of the room when you are dismissed."

My eyes wide, my lips pressed tightly closed, I crept farther into the room. Like a little mouse, I felt awed and terrified by the prospect that lay before me—my first meeting with my new liege lord.

In those days, King Henry did not stoop, as he would toward the end of his life. He was as tall as my uncle, a thin man but one who gave the impression of strength. His nose was long and thin, too. He was dressed most grandly in cloth-of-gold and crimson velvet. His black velvet bonnet, sporting a jeweled brooch and pendant pearl, sat atop reddish brown hair. It was just starting to go gray. Beneath was a clean-shaven face so exceedingly pale that the red wart on his right cheek stood out in stark contrast.

I stared at him, my mouth dropping open, as fascinated as I was awestruck. King Henry regarded us steadily in return. For a considerable time, he said nothing. Then he dismissed his servants and sent my uncle away, too.

"You have your mother's eyes," he said to Maman, speaking in French.

"Thank you, Sire," she said. "I wish I could remember her more clearly, but I have always been told that she was a most beautiful woman."

This was the first that I had heard of my grandmother's beauty. Maman rarely spoke of her parents. I knew only that her mother had died when she was a very young girl and that afterward her father had sent her to the ducal court of Brittany to enter the service of the duke's daughter, Anne.

"I was sorry to hear of the death of your husband," the king said.

"Johannes was a good man, Your Grace."

"A Fleming, was he not?"

"He was. A merchant."

There was a small, awkward silence. Maman was of gentle birth. She had married beneath her. I knew a little of the story. Maman had wed at fifteen and given birth to me the following January. Then she had returned to the Breton court. The following year, when Duchess Anne married King Charles, she had become part of the new French queen's entourage. Papa had often shared the houses she found for me near the court, but sometimes he had to go away to attend to business. He imported fine fabrics to clothe courtiers and kings.

"Plague?" the king asked, suggesting a likely cause for my father's death.

Maman shook her head. "He had purchased a new ship for a trading venture. It proved unseaworthy and sank when he was aboard. He drowned."

"A great pity. Did he leave you sufficient to live upon?"

Maman's reply was too low for me to hear. When they continued their conversation in quiet voices, I heard their words only as a gentle whisper in the background.

My gaze wandered around the room. The chamber boasted no tapestries and had no gilded chests or chairs, but it did contain a free-standing steel looking glass. I longed to peer at my own face, but I did not dare move from where I stood. On a table next to the looking glass, a coffer overflowed with jewels. I also noticed books. I had never seen so many of them in one place before.

The restless movements of King Henry's fingers, continually twisting the fabric of the narrow silk scarf he wore knotted around his waist, brought my attention back to the king. I strained to hear what he and my mother were saying, but I could only catch a word or two. The king said, "my wife" and then, "my protection."

King Henry glanced my way and deliberately raised his voice. "It is well that you are here. I give you my word that you will have a place at court as long as you both shall live." A slow smile overspread his features. For some reason, he seemed mightily pleased that my mother and I had come to England.

"On the morrow," the king said, addressing me directly, "you will be taken to the royal nursery at Eltham Palace. Henceforth you will be one of the children of honor. Your duties will be both simple and agreeable—you are to engage my two young daughters, the Lady Margaret and the Lady Mary, in daily conversation in French so that they will become fluent in that language. Margaret is only a few weeks older than you are, Jane," the king added. "Mary is just three."

"I will do my best to serve them, Your Grace," I promised.

"I am certain that you will," he said, and with that the audience was over.

We spent that night in the great palace of Westminster, sharing a bed in a tiny, out-of-the-way chamber. I was certain good fortune had smiled upon us. I believed Maman and I would be together, serving in the same royal household. It was not until the next day, when I was about to board one of the royal barges for the trip downriver, that I learned the truth. Maman could not accompany me to Eltham. King Henry had made arrangements for her to remain at Westminster Palace. Like Lady Catherine Gordon, she was to be a lady-in-waiting to his wife, Queen Elizabeth of York.

"We will see each other often," Maman promised as she kissed me farewell. "Queen Elizabeth is said to be devoted to her children. I am told she pays many visits to Eltham and that her sons and daughters regularly come to court."

I clung to this reassurance as I was sent off on my own, speaking no English and knowing no one. My uncle, who had his own lodgings at court, escorted me to my new home, but he did not tarry. As quickly as he could, he scurried back to Westminster Palace.

AT THE TIME I entered royal service at Eltham Palace, the king had four children. Arthur, the Prince of Wales and the heir to the throne, lived elsewhere. He was not quite twelve years old. Shortly before I arrived, King Henry's second son, also Henry, who was seven and held the title Duke of York, had been given his own household staff within the larger establishment at Eltham. Nurses and governess had been dismissed. Male tutors had taken charge of the young prince's education.

The two princesses, Margaret and Mary, shared a household staff. They also shared some of Prince Henry's tutors, so that all the children of honor, boys and girls, came in daily contact with each other. That was why, within a few days of joining their ranks, I was one of a dozen students being taught how to dance the pavane.

"Is all your dress fastened in place?" the Italian dancing master asked.

For my benefit, he repeated the question in French.

Most of the boys in Prince Henry's entourage had been taught French and spoke it fairly well, if with a peculiar accent. I turned to a boy named Harry Guildford, who had been assigned as my partner, and whispered, "Why is he so concerned about our clothing?"

Harry Guildford was an affable lad a year my senior. His round face was remarkable for its large nose, the cleft in his chin, and his ready smile. The twinkle in his eyes reminded me of my friend in Amboise, Guy Dunois, except that Harry's eyes were gray instead of blue-green.

"All manner of clothing can drop onto the floor in the course of a dance, if the movements are too energetic. That is why we must always check our points before we begin."

By points, he meant the laces that tied sleeves to bodices, breeches to doublets, and various other garments to each other. I could not imagine why anyone would be careless in fastening them in the first place, but I tugged at my sleeves and skirt to make sure all was secure. I had been given a white damask gown with crimson velvet sleeves, as well as gold chains and a circlet—a sort of livery.

"It is particularly vulgar for a lady to drop a glove while dancing," our tutor continued, "as it causes gentlemen to bestir themselves and run like a flock of starlings to pick it up."

"Do starlings run?" I whispered to Harry. "I should have thought they flew."

He thought my remark amusing and translated it for those who did not understand the French language. I had begun to pick up a little English, but I only realized that I'd said something clever when Prince Henry smiled at me.

At seven he was a chubby child with small, blue-gray eyes and bright golden curls. He had a very fair complexion, almost girlish, and he already knew how to be charming. I smiled back.

The dancing master clapped his hands to signal the musicians to play. Then he watched with hawklike intensity as we went through our paces. Most of his attention was on Prince Henry and

Princess Margaret, but as soon as I began to dance backward, he shrieked my name.

"Mademoiselle Jane! It is bad manners for a lady to lift her train with her hands. You must sway in such a way as to shift the train out of the way before you step back."

Frowning in concentration, I tried to follow his instructions, but there was so much to remember. What if I tripped on my own gown and tumbled to the floor? Everyone would laugh at me.

My heart was in my throat as Harry and I continued to execute the gliding, swaying steps of the pavane. I felt a little more confident after he squeezed my hand and gave me a reassuring smile. Somehow, I managed to finish the dance without calling further attention to myself.

"*Merci*," I said when the music ceased. "I am most grateful for your help."

Harry executed a courtly bow. "My pleasure, mademoiselle."

By AUGUST, WHEN I had been at Eltham for some six weeks, I could converse much more easily in English, although I still had trouble with some words. I spent several hours every morning in the nursery, playing with the Lady Mary and speaking with her in French. She was an exceptionally pretty child with blue eyes and delicate features. Slender, she gave promise of being tall when she grew to womanhood. Her hair was golden, with a reddish tinge.

In the afternoons, I attended the Lady Margaret, conversing with her in both French and English. Unlike her little sister, Margaret was dark eyed, with a round face and a thick, sturdy body. Her best features were her fresh complexion and her auburn hair.

Both royal princesses seemed to like me, although the other girls among the children of honor regarded me with suspicion because I did not speak their language. Margaret was sometimes temperamental and had a tendency to pout, and Mary was prone to tantrums. But I quickly learned how to avoid being the object of their wrath. The other girls resented me for that, too.

I also learned to play the lute and the virginals and to ride. One day we rode as far as another of King Henry's palaces on the Thames. It was only a few miles from Eltham.

"What is this place?" I asked, looking across an expanse of overgrown gardens to a huge complex of buildings. Scaffolding rose up in several places. Busy workmen swarmed like bees over one tower.

"It is called Pleasance," the Lady Margaret said.

"Pleasure Palace?"

My innocent mistake in translation produced immoderate laughter, especially from the two oldest children of honor, Ned Neville and Will Compton, and from Goose, Prince Henry's fool.

"It was named Pleasance because of its pleasing prospect," Will said, "but there is pleasure to be had within those walls, too, no doubt of that."

"I was born here," Prince Henry said. "It is my favorite palace. I wish Father and Mother had not gone on progress. If they had come here, we could visit them."

"They cannot stay at Pleasance until the renovations are finished," Margaret said.

Translating this exchange, I frowned. I had not seen my mother since we parted at Westminster on the morning after our meeting with the king. "What does going on progress mean?" I asked, unfamiliar with the English word.

"The entire court moves from manor house to castle to palace, visiting different parts of the realm," Harry Guildford explained.

"Sometimes they take us with them." The Lady Margaret sounded wistful.

"Not this year," Prince Henry said. "And they will not be back at Westminster Palace until the end of October."

That meant I would not see Maman again for some time. Resigned, I dedicated myself to perfecting my English and mastering music, dance, and horseback riding. In September we all moved to Hatfield House, a palatial brick manor house in Hertfordshire, so that Eltham Palace could be cleaned and aired.

On a crisp, cloudless day a week later, when I had been one of the children of honor for nearly three months, the Lady Margaret and I strolled in the garden while we held our daily conversation.

"I was frightened for my life," she confided, speaking of her reaction to the great fire at Sheen, another of her father's palaces, the previous Yuletide. The entire royal family had been in residence at the time. They had been fortunate to escape unhurt.

"Fire is terrifying," I agreed. "A house burned down in Amboise once when I was living there. Everyone was afraid that the sparks would ignite the entire town. All the men formed a line and passed buckets of water along to douse the flames. My friend Guy helped, too, for all that he was only a very little boy at the time."

It had been weeks since I had thought of Guy, or any of my other friends in France. A little ripple of guilt flowed over me. Had they forgotten me, as well?

Deep in thought, I rounded a bit of topiary work trimmed to resemble a dragon, one of King Henry's emblems. A few steps ahead of me, the princess stopped in her tracks. "What man is that?" She squinted at a figure just emerging from a doorway, her vision hampered by the distance.

My eyesight being more acute, I immediately recognized my uncle, Sir Rowland Velville. He strode rapidly toward us along the graveled path.

"Your Grace," he greeted the Lady Margaret, bowing so low that his nose nearly touched the toe of her shoe. "I beg your leave for a word in private with my niece."

"You may speak with her, but in our hearing," Margaret said in an autocratic voice.

My uncle bowed a second time. "As you wish, Your Grace." He turned to me, still as formal as he had been with the Lady Margaret. "Your mother, my beloved sister, has died, dear Jane." He showed not a trace of emotion as he delivered his devastating news. "It happened suddenly, while she was on progress with the court."

Stunned, I gaped at him, at first unable to form words, almost unable to think. The enormity of what he'd said was too much for me to grasp.

As if from a great distance, I heard the Lady Margaret speak. "Of what did she die, Sir Rowland?"

"A fever of some sort. I cannot say for certain. I had gone on to Drayton, in Leicestershire, with the king, while the women remained where they were for a few days longer."

Fighting a great blackness that threatened to swallow me, I sank down onto a nearby stone bench. I suppose that the sun shone as brightly as ever, but for me its light had dimmed. "No," I whispered. "No. She cannot be dead. You must be mistaken."

"I assure you, I am not. I was present when she was buried at Collyweston."

Tears flowed unchecked down my cheeks, but I scarcely felt them. I was only dimly aware that the Lady Margaret had left us. "No," I said again.

"The king himself bade me bring this news to you, Jane." I could hear a slight impatience in his voice. "Why would I lie to you?"

"You . . . you would not." I accepted the handkerchief he proffered.

"I brought you this." He gave me the small, enameled pendant that had been Maman's favorite piece of jewelry. Like the topiary work, it was in the shape of a dragon. I sobbed harder.

"She had little else. She sold most of her jewels to pay for the journey to England. But you need not be concerned about your future. You are one of the king's wards now. He'll look out for you." I suppose Uncle meant to be comforting, but his words did nothing to lessen my sense of loss.

Having discharged his duty, my uncle left me sitting alone on a stone bench in the garden at Hatfield House. I do not know how much time passed as I cried my heart out. But when I had no more tears to shed, I looked up to find Will Compton leaning against a nearby tree.

At sixteen, Will was the oldest of Prince Henry's children of honor. He had been sent to the royal nursery at Eltham when the prince was still a baby. He was a tall, lanky lad with friendly hazel eyes. They were dark with concern.

"I am sorry for your loss, Jane. I know what it is to be orphaned."

"My mother's mother died when she was younger than I am now." I do not know why I told him that, and I realized as I spoke that I had no idea when my mother's father had died. I'd never known any of my grandparents and, except for my uncle, had never met another Velville. If the rest of them, unlike Maman, were as unfeeling as he was, I did not want to.

"My father died when I was eleven." Will sat down beside me on the bench and took my hand in his. "After that I became one of the king's wards."

"One of the king's wards," I repeated. "That is what my uncle said I am to be. What does that mean?"

"That the king will look after you, manage your estates if you have any and, one day, arrange your marriage. You need never worry about having a roof over your head or food in your belly. You will always have a home at court and a place in the royal household."

"With the Lady Margaret?"

"Or with the Lady Mary. In a year or two each of them will have her own household and you will have to choose."

A terrible thought came to me. "What if they should die?"

His grip tightened painfully on my fingers. "Why would you think such a thing?"

"Anyone can die. Even princesses."

He nodded, his expression solemn. "You are right. King Henry and Queen Elizabeth had another daughter, born between Prince Henry and Princess Mary. She died when she was the same age the Lady Mary is now."

Fresh tears made my vision blur.

"But the Prince of Wales lives and is healthy, as is Prince Henry. There is nothing sickly about the Lady Margaret or the Lady Mary or anyone in this household."

Sniffling into my uncle's handkerchief, I tried to embrace Will's optimism, but it was no easy task.

Maman is dead. I will never see her again.

As if he sensed my thoughts, Will stood and pulled me to my feet. "Come, Jane. No one can take the place of a mother, but here you have brothers and sisters, in spirit if not in blood. The children of honor look out for each other."

His words did make me feel a little better. "Are the prince and princesses our brother and sisters, too?"

Will slung an arm around my shoulders and steered me toward the palace. "Indeed they are, Sister Jane . . . except that they must be catered to at all costs."

2

King Henry VII rebuilt Pleasance during the first two years I lived in England, facing the whole in red brick and renaming it Greenwich Palace. My "brothers" and "sisters" at Eltham, however, had already taken to calling it "Pleasure Palace" in private.

By the time I reached my ninth birthday, during my first January in England, I was fluent in English and no longer had any trace of an accent. This pleased me very much, for I did not wish to call attention to my foreign birth. The English, by nature, are suspicious of anyone who is not a native of their island. That may be why I never became close friends with any of the other girls among the children of honor. Little Princess Mary, however, took to me from the first and tagged along after me, chattering in French, even when I wished she would not.

In February of that same year, a new prince was born—Edmund

Tudor. Queen Elizabeth of York gave birth to him at Pleasure Palace, but soon after, he was sent to join his siblings at Eltham, while the queen continued to live at court with the king.

The court never stayed in one place long. Sometimes it was at Richmond, which King Henry built to replace Sheen, sometimes at Windsor Castle. It was often at Westminster Palace and Greenwich. In the summer, it went on progress.

In late November, Perkin Warbeck, pretender to the throne, was executed. He had involved himself in one too many plots and had to pay the price for it. I felt sorry for his wife, Lady Catherine Gordon. I had never spoken to her, but she was one of Queen Elizabeth's ladies and I had seen her once or twice when I was at court with the princesses. I did not see much of Queen Elizabeth either, although she always spoke kindly to me and brought me gifts of clothing when she visited her daughters at Eltham.

When I was ten, the Lady Margaret and the Lady Mary were given separate household staffs. Harry Guildford's mother, who until then had been one of Queen Elizabeth's ladies, was appointed as Mary's lady governess. Princess Mary took to calling her "Mother Guildford," and soon we were all using that name behind her back. To her face, we addressed her as Lady Guildford or madam.

I was nominally assigned to the Lady Mary—she refused to be parted from me—but I still conversed with the Lady Margaret, in both French and English, on a daily basis. All four households—Prince Henry's, the Lady Margaret's, the Lady Mary's, and Prince Edmund's nursery—continued to live, for the most part, at Eltham. But we were all at Hatfield House again in June that year when Prince Edmund died. He was only sixteen months old. I was saddened by his death, but I would have been much more upset to lose one of my princesses, Prince Henry, Harry, or Will.

I was always happy to go to Pleasure Palace when the court was there. It lived up to its name as a place where we could indulge in pleasant pastimes. We were allowed to watch the disguisings and the dancing, and we had games of our own. Harry Guildford was always the cleverest at devising those. He was the one who set prince and princess against each other in a contest with hoops.

One day in my tenth year, Prince Henry, the Lady Margaret, Harry, and I eluded the tutors, governesses, and five-year-old Mary to meet in the passageway that ran beneath the king's apartments. Above us, King Henry's rooms were stacked one above the other in the five-story keep.

"The goal," Harry explained, "is to be the first to roll these hoops from the chapel to the entrance to the privy kitchens."

The passage, newly floored, was long and level and perfect for the purpose, but I regarded the metal barrel hoops and sticks Harry had "found" for us with a sense of dismay. I did not see how I would be able to keep control of such an unwieldy thing.

The Lady Margaret had no such doubts. She sent her younger brother a superior smile and was off, deftly spinning the hoop at her side. Prince Henry followed an instant later and nearly overtook his sister near the royal wardrobe; but for all her stocky build, the princess was fleet of foot.

My hoop toppled over at the first uneven bit of flooring. Harry completed the course, but was wise enough to move much more slowly than his young master.

"I was faster!" Prince Henry complained. "If you had not started before the signal to begin, I'd have reached the finish sooner."

"Is it a race, then?" Margaret asked, eyes aglow with anticipation.

"It is. Let us see who takes the best two out of three."

"Agreed. We will go back the way we came." Margaret kilted up her skirts and ordered Harry to count to three.

Prince Henry was off at "two," but his sister still passed him halfway to the chapel and beat him handily.

"Best three out of five," the prince said, panting.

"Done."

This time when Margaret won, they had an audience. Servants had come out of various household offices and courtiers had trickled down from the king's apartments, drawn by the commotion.

"You cheated!" Face red, eyes bulging with anger and humiliation, Prince Henry threw his hoop against the wall. When it bounced back, the sharp metal rim nearly struck Harry. He barely jumped out of the way in time.

The spectators made themselves scarce. I eyed a nearby tapestry, wishing I could duck behind it and hide. I stiffened my spine. It was my duty to remain at Princess Margaret's side, but I dearly wished she would wipe that smug expression off her face. Seeing it only heightened her brother's anger. He glared at her, saying not a word, but if thoughts could kill she'd have burst into flames.

"Cheat!" With a snarl, the prince stalked off. Harry trailed after him, shoulders slumped.

WHEN I WAS eleven, a fifteen-year-old Spanish princess named Catherine of Aragon arrived in England and married Prince Arthur. She was greeted with elaborate processions and festivities. I had to laugh at my first sight of the Spanish ladies. They rode on mule chairs instead of saddles, two to each mule, back-to-back. The arrangement made them look as if they had quarreled and were refusing to speak to each other.

A little more than two months after that, the Lady Margaret was betrothed to King James of Scotland and married to him by proxy at Richmond Palace. She was twelve. There was a tournament to celebrate, the first I was allowed to attend. My uncle was one of the competitors. Although he lived at court and was master of the king's falcons, I rarely saw him after my mother's death. If he noticed me in the crowd of spectators, he did not give any sign of it.

In April of that year, tragedy struck. Prince Arthur died. Prince Henry, who had been intended for the church, became the new Prince of Wales and heir to the throne. He went to live at court, taking all his household with him—Harry Guildford and Will Compton and Ned Neville and the younger boys, like little Nick Carew, who had come to Eltham well after I'd arrived there.

We were reunited at Westminster toward the end of that summer, and to entertain us King Henry paraded his collection of curiosities. He kept a giant woman from Flanders and a wee Scotsman, a dwarf. There was a man who ate sea coal—a very strange sight! But the oddest curiosities of all were the newest additions. Certain men of Bristol who had sailed to the New World that lies across the Western Sea had brought back three natives of that distant land and given them to King Henry as a gift.

The sight of these savages both frightened and fascinated me. They wore the skins of beasts as clothing and ate raw flesh. No one was able to understand their speech.

"You must keep them locked up, Father," Princess Mary told the king. "Otherwise they might eat us."

"They are not cannibals, Mary, and we mean to civilize them. I have assigned them a keeper. He will look after them, just as keepers watch over the more simpleminded of our royal fools."

Distracted by this idea, she frowned. "Goose does not have a keeper."

"Goose is not simple, so he does not need one," King Henry said with an indulgent chuckle. "He is the *other* kind of fool—the sort who has a wit sharp enough to cut and the cleverness not to use it to slice into the wrong person."

QUEEN ELIZABETH DIED shortly after I turned thirteen. She'd just given birth to another child, a daughter, but the baby also died. The loss of his wife affected King Henry VII even more than the death of his eldest son. I think he truly loved her.

A few weeks after the queen's funeral, the king came to Eltham. He dismissed the Lady Margaret's other attendants but bade me remain. Then he seemed to collapse onto a window seat. He indicated some cushions on the floor in front of it with a listless gesture, inviting his daughter to sit. I remained standing.

The king was a pitiful sight. Hair that had once been reddish brown had gone gray and was uncombed. His pale coloring had gone sallow, and the skin around his jowls sagged, as if he'd lost all interest in food or had forgotten to eat. He was almost fifty years old, but he had never looked it before. Now he seemed to have aged a decade in a single month.

As if he felt my gaze upon him, he looked up, peering at me for a moment without recognition before he gathered himself and motioned for me to come closer. "Sit, Jane. This concerns you, too."

"Your Grace?" Hesitantly, I settled myself on the cushion to the right of the Lady Margaret.

"My dear," he said, turning to Princess Margaret. "You must set out for Scotland as we planned. You will leave from Richmond Palace in late June."

Margaret frowned but did not argue. She had been married to King James IV more than a year earlier and plans for her departure had been well advanced before her mother's death.

"Jane, Margaret asked that you go with her. I had intended to permit it, but no longer. I wish you to remain in England."

We both stared at him. I had not known about the Lady Margaret's request. Now I did not know what to say. Indeed, I hesitated to say anything at all.

"Jane *must* accompany me," Margaret objected. "I cannot do without her."

"You will have to," her father said. "Your sister needs her more. Mary is eight years old, the same age Jane was when her mother died. If I could keep you here, Margaret, I would, but you needs must go to Scotland. In your place, Jane must stay."

"In my *place*?" Margaret looked offended. "Jane is no princess!"

The king sighed and glanced again at me. A crafty look came into his pale eyes. "What say you, Jane? Do you wish to go to Scotland with Margaret or stay here with Mary?"

He could command that I stay, no matter what I said. I thought of Mary. I'd heard her crying for her mother in the night and my heart had gone out to her. I looked at Margaret—solid, sturdy Margaret who knew her own mind even at the tender age of thirteen. She did not need me . . . and Mary did.

"I will stay here," I said.

"You will not regret your decision." The king looked pleased.

After he left, the Lady Margaret stared at me with cold, unforgiving eyes. With a wrenching sense of loss, I knew our friendship was at an end.

"I always knew our father loved Mary best," she said when I started to speak, "but I thought you would be loyal."

"The king of Scots may not permit you to keep any of your household," I reminded her. Although James IV had agreed to let her bring a goodly number of English men and women with her, she had been warned of the possibility that he would dismiss most of them after she arrived in Scotland.

"I am a princess of England," Margaret declared. "I shall do as I like."

After Margaret Tudor left England for Scotland, I tried not to think about her. My "sister," as Will Compton would have it, had stopped speaking to me—in either English or French—well before her departure.

I devoted myself to the Lady Mary and was pleased when, over the course of the next two years, she began to turn to me for advice. I became her "dearest Jane," but I never let myself forget how quickly that might change. When she asked for honesty, I gave her only as much as I thought she wanted to hear.

I CELEBRATED MY sixteenth birthday at Pleasure Palace in January of the twentieth year of the reign of King Henry the VII. By then I had lived in England for some seven and a half years and, while the Lady Mary feared thunderstorms, I had developed a liking for the wild weather that sometimes battered the English Isles at that time of year.

For three long days and nights in the middle of the month, a gale that had swept across the Narrow Seas and into the south of England raged unchecked. It uprooted trees and sheered tiles off rooftops. From the Lady Mary's apartments, which looked out upon a garden with a fountain, an apple orchard, and part of the two-hundred-acre park her father had enclosed for hunting, I was able to watch branches waving madly but could see little else.

Curiosity finally drew me to the opposite side of the palace, to the passageway beneath the king's apartments where we had once rolled hoops. There the windows overlooked the rapidly rising waters of the Thames. From that vantage point I had a clear view of a surface that had been frozen solid only a few days earlier. Now the river had overflowed its banks, flooding the lowest-lying areas. In awe, I watched stairs designed to give access to Greenwich Palace at any stage of the tide vanish beneath the roiling water.

I was so intent upon the sight that I did not at once realize I was no longer alone. I heard footfalls approaching and then a man spoke.

"Why, it is Mistress Popyncourt," said Master Charles Brandon, stopping beside me.

I recognized him at once. He had been taking prizes in tournaments for the last four years, ever since one held at Richmond Palace to celebrate the betrothal of Princess Margaret to the king of Scots. He was also the most handsome man at court. All the Lady Mary's ladies thought so. Tall and broad shouldered, he had hair of such a dark red it sometimes looked black and eyes the color of agates.

I was a little surprised that he knew me by name. My features were not sufficiently distinctive to make me stand out in a court filled with beautiful women. I could boast of nothing more than a trim figure, medium height, brown hair and eyes, a pale complexion, and a small, thin nose.

Master Brandon wore livery—clothing of a particular dusky brown-orange called tawny that was decorated with a badge that featured a silver falcon crest. He was master of horse to the Earl of Essex, but his demeanor was not that of any man's servant. His bearing betrayed a proud, independent spirit. I had heard that he was a man who liked to have his own way and I had no trouble believing it.

"What brings you to this part of the palace, mistress?" he asked.

"I wished for a better view of the storm."

"It is a fierce one." The wind still howled and rain lashed the windows, although the thunder and lightning had passed on. "I am told that in London the gale ripped the brass weathercock out of its socket atop the spire of St. Paul's and blew it clear across the churchyard. It struck the sign over the door of an inn three hundred paces away and smashed it to bits."

"Some might call that an evil omen," I murmured.

"Do you believe in signs and portents?" He chuckled. "Then mayhap it is good luck that brought me here at this hour."

When he slipped his arm around my waist, I belatedly realized that the gleam in his eyes was desire. He had warm feelings toward me and was happy to have found me alone in this secluded place. I responded by sending him an encouraging smile.

In common with every other young woman at the royal court, I had read the tales of chivalry and romance. Sometimes I daydreamed of being swept off my feet by a bold knight and carried off to his castle. I imagined marriage and children and a return to court when my "brother," Prince Henry, took the throne as Henry VIII and had likewise wed. I saw myself taking charge of his nursery, for surely such a big, strapping lad would produce a goodly number of sons and daughters.

Charles Brandon, I thought, might make a very suitable husband. He had no fortune yet, but he was a favorite of both King Henry VII and the Prince of Wales. Brandon seemed destined for a successful career at court. And so I did not protest when he lowered his head and kissed me.

The experience was not what I had been expecting. He gave me a wet, sloppy kiss and seemed to be trying to slide his tongue into my mouth. I allowed this, out of curiosity, but I found it unpleasant when he began to press small, smacking kisses on my cheek and throat. Over his shoulder, I could see the river. When something on the surface of the water caught my eye, I stiffened and made a little sound of surprise and consternation.

Brandon released me with unflattering speed. "Do you hear someone approaching?"

I ignored his question, leaning closer to the window until my nose almost touched the expensive glass pane and my palms rested flat against the casement. A wherry was approaching the submerged water stairs. The fitful light of several lanterns on land and one aboard the tiny craft itself revealed a heroic struggle as the boatman attempted to make a landing.

My breath caught as the boat's single passenger stood up, waving his arms about. This made the boatman's task even more difficult. One of the oars he'd been using to steer his small craft disappeared beneath the water. At any moment, I expected to see the passenger follow. It did not look as if the boat itself would stay afloat long enough to reach the safety of the shore. I clutched my rosary.

At my side, Master Brandon also watched the drama unfolding on the riverbank. "There! The boatman has managed to catch hold of something."

"And look—help is coming." A detachment of the king's yeomen of the guard had appeared, all in their livery and carrying halberds. They pulled the wherry onto the shore. The passenger scrambled out, still waving his arms about in an agitated fashion, but I lost sight of him when the guards surrounded him. A moment later, they were marching him toward the palace.

Charles Brandon was no longer beside me. He was sprinting down the passageway toward the stairs that led to the king's apartments, no doubt hoping to be the first to bring news of the stranger's arrival to the king. No one, I realized, would have been so foolish as to risk life and limb on the swollen river unless he had urgent business at court. The king might well look favorably upon the courtier who gave him advance warning.

Certain I would eventually learn who the man was—it was difficult to keep secrets at court—I returned to the Lady Mary's apartments. The warmth of her rooms was welcome after the chill damp of the passageway. Although nothing could successfully ward off winter's icy grip on Greenwich Palace, woolen tapestries covered the interior walls of the princess's privy chamber. A fire blazed in the hearth. In addition, two green-glazed ceramic stoves on wheels had been placed close to the half circle of women seated on the floor in front of the Lady Mary. Bay leaves and juniper added to the sea coal made the smoke fragrant, and the heat from these stoves warmed busy fingers as they plied their needles.

I moved to join the others, but Mother Guildford intercepted me. She seized my arm and pulled me into the relative privacy of a window alcove, out of earshot of the ten-year-old princess and her ladies.

There was a striking family resemblance between Lady Guildford and her son. Like Harry, his mother had a round face dominated by a large nose and a cleft in the chin. Unlike him, she had a caustic tongue. Her voice was low and stern and as icy as the cobblestones in the courtyard. "What have you been up to, Jane? Your face is most unbecomingly flushed."

"I went to look at the river."

Her eyebrows shot upward. "And where, pray, did you find a window that overlooks the Thames?"

"In the passage beneath the king's lodgings."

Servants had closed the green-and-white-striped satin curtains to conserve the heat in the Lady Mary's chambers, but even curtains lined with buckram could not keep out the bitter, penetrating iciness of a severe frost. The oak flooring was covered with fitted rush mats, making it considerably warmer than stone or tile. But inside my shoes and two pairs of stockings my feet felt like blocks of ice. I glanced with true longing at the thick footcloth on the floor in front of the long, padded bench where the Lady Mary sat. As befit her station, she had the hearth to heat her back and the braziers to warm her front.

"You should not have been in that wing of the palace," Mother Guildford said.

"Why ever not?" I asked, distracted by my desire to move closer to the heat. "We often played there as children."

Mother Guildford's face hardened. Her displeasure was an almost palpable force in the confined space. "We?"

Suddenly wary, I nodded. "The Lady Margaret and Prince Henry and some of the children of honor." There had been games of blindman's buff and shovelboard as well as that memorable race with hoops.

"Then my son was among them," Mother Guildford said. "Were you with Harry today?"

"No, madam." But I felt heat creep into my face as I remembered the time I had spent with Charles Brandon in the deserted passageway.

"Harry's not for you, mistress." Mother Guildford's sharp reproof made me jump.

"And I do not want him!" I replied. Indignant, I drew myself up straighter and thrust out my chin.

The idea of a romantic attachment between the two of us was laughable. Harry was a friend. Nothing more. Still, it annoyed me that Mother Guildford thought she could do so much better for her son. I was as gently born as he was, even if my father *had* been a merchant. More to the point, given what *Harry's* father had been up to, Lady Guildford and her son were fortunate to still be at court.

The previous July, Sir Richard Guildford had been arrested over irregularities in the accounts he controlled as master of ordnance.

He'd spent five months in Fleet prison awaiting trial. Just before Christmas, without explanation, the king had ordered his release, but everyone at court knew that he had not been cleared of wrongdoing, nor had he been pardoned. He had retreated to his country estates, where he still awaited His Grace's pleasure.

"You worry me, Jane."

The hint of genuine concern in Mother Guildford's voice diffused my irritation, but then I had to fight the urge to roll my eyes heavenward. I did not need anyone to look out for me. I had been fending for myself from a very early age.

"You have grown into an attractive young woman. You have been noticed."

"What is wrong with that, madam?" I preened just a little. "Everyone comes to court in search of advancement, if not for themselves, then for their families."

Her lips twisted into a wry smile. "True enough. We all look to marry higher than we were born. But marriage is a business arrangement, best negotiated by one's father."

An all too familiar ache settled into the center of my chest at the reminder that I had neither mother nor father to look out for me. Squaring my shoulders, I stared the Lady Mary's governess straight in the eye. "Lady Guildford, I have no desire to wed your Harry, but if I did, I do not see why we would be such an unsuitable match."

Mother Guildford did not enlighten me. Instead she said, "You are sixteen, Jane. That is a dangerous age."

"Dangerous to whom?"

Her eyebrows shot up at my tone. "To you, my dear. You must not wander about the palace alone. It is neither wise nor safe."

I blinked at her in genuine surprise, unable to imagine what danger could possibly escape the notice of the king's guards.

Mother Guildford sighed and patted my arm. "You are young in many ways, Jane, and innocent, but you are old enough to marry. That you have no one to make arrangements for you to wed concerns me deeply."

"I am one of the king's wards."

"You are His Grace's dependent. His servant." Voice even, words blunt, Mother Guildford gave no quarter. "You inherited nothing when your mother died, because she brought nothing of value with her when she left France. This places you in an awkward position, Jane. Gentlemen seek a rich dowry when they contemplate taking a wife, and you have none save what the king decides to give you."

Already well aware of these hard facts, I resented her all the more for reminding me of them. I preferred to concentrate on the pleasures of life at court.

"If you are to remain in the princess's household unwed, then you must have a care for your virtue. Any man, even the most honorable, will take advantage of a woman if he's given half a chance."

I made a small, involuntary movement before I managed to hold myself still again. What Mother Guildford said was true enough. Master Brandon's kisses were proof of that, and he was not the first courtier to show an interest in me.

"I am always careful of my reputation," I lied. "And no courtier would dare accost one of the princess's ladies."

"You were observed kissing Master Brandon."

For a moment I thought someone had seen us together earlier that day. Then I realized that she meant the kiss Charles Brandon had given me when we'd encountered each other in the garden the week before. I had been with several of the princess's ladies. Brandon had been accompanied by his constant companions, Tom Knyvett and Lord Edward Howard. He had not singled me out. He'd kissed all of us in greeting, as had the other two men.

"It is the custom to exchange kisses upon meeting," I protested. It had taken me years to adjust to this peculiarly English habit. In France, etiquette forbids kissing on the lips in public, but in England these light touches of mouth to mouth are nothing more than a symbolic gesture of welcome, not unlike bowing before royalty.

"There are degrees of kisses." Mother Guildford's face was set in hard, uncompromising lines and her voice vibrated with disapproval.

I had begun to suspect that the kisses given to a woman by a man who desired her were quite different from those exchanged in casual greeting. In truth, that was why I'd been so willing to let Charles Brandon kiss me in the passageway beneath the king's lodgings. In spite of Mother Guildford's dire predictions, opportunities were few for the Lady Mary's attendants to meet in private with handsome men.

"Drunkenness and lechery go hand in hand," Mother Guildford continued, "and not all the king's courtiers are temperate men. Many of them have sired bastards, both before and since coming to court. Others are simply uncouth louts. I cannot count the number of times I have come upon some gentleman relieving himself in a corner rather than bothering to walk to the nearest garderobe. And once I saw a maidservant emerge from behind an arras, her skirts rucked up and her bosom exposed."

I had seen such sights myself. "I would never allow myself to be treated with such disrespect."

"Not even if it were the Prince of Wales himself who showed an interest in you?"

Taken aback, I required a moment to adjust to this notion. "Prince Henry is not yet fifteen."

"He takes after his grandfather, King Edward the Fourth, in appearance. I warrant he shares Edward's appetites as well. Queen

Elizabeth's father had a great many mistresses and fathered a number of bastards, starting when he was just a boy. And at fourteen, even Prince Henry's father had—"

She broke off, appalled that she'd very nearly criticized the present king's behavior. It was never a good idea to do that, and most particularly unwise when that same king could send your husband back to prison on a whim.

"No matter," she said brusquely, recovering. "What you need to remember, Jane, is that you must not encourage the prince or any of his friends."

"Prince Henry behaves toward me as he does to his sisters. When we were younger, he regularly put frogs in my bed and pulled my hair, and he still trounces me soundly at chess." The chubby little boy I'd first met at Eltham had grown into a big, golden-haired lad. He was already taller than his father. He drew every eye the moment he strode into a room. I suppressed a smile, thinking it likely he *had* already seduced a willing wench or two, but the idea that his amorous interest might fix on me seemed as remote as the possibility that Harry Guildford and I would fall into each other's arms and tumble into bed.

Mother Guildford did not look convinced. "Henceforth when you leave the princess's lodgings, take another female with you—a maidservant or one of the other gentlewomen. I will have your promise on this, Jane. You must not take foolish chances."

I agreed, but grudgingly. It seemed to me most unfair that she should restrict my movements solely because I was female and of marriageable age. Satisfied at last, Mother Guildford released me to return to my duties.

I'd barely had time to warm my hands at the brazier before a messenger arrived to summon the Lady Mary and her women to the king's presence chamber. An explosion of excited whispers and titters greeted this news. We'd been confined indoors by bad weather for days and the prospect of some new entertainment delighted everyone.

The king squinted in our direction when we entered his presence chamber but did not acknowledge his daughter in any way. I wondered if he recognized her. Although his eyesight had been failing for years, he refused to wear spectacles.

The rise and fall of voices filled the crowded room. Following close behind my mistress, I advanced toward the dais. On the far side of the presence chamber, I caught sight of Charles Brandon. He noticed me, too, and sent a smile my way that made me think I might let him kiss me again. Perhaps I would like it better the next time. As I felt heat creep into my cheeks, I quickly shifted my attention back to King Henry.

He looked down on us from a raised dais, a morose expression on his face. As was his custom, since he set great store by appearances, he sat beneath a cloth-of-gold canopy and upon a braided and tasseled cushion. Both were symbols of his authority. The ceiler and tester were trimmed and tasseled with Venice gold, and the section hanging down the wall behind him was embroidered with the royal arms.

Whatever chair the king's cushion was placed upon became the chair of estate, even though the principal chair of estate was the one he now occupied in his presence chamber. No one but the king of England could sit on that one. Courtiers newly arrived in the royal household were taught that even if they entered this room when His Grace was not present, they must still doff their caps and bow as they passed the chair.

It *was* impressive to look at, upholstered in cloth-of-gold studded with gilt nails. It was also the only chair in the chamber. No one was allowed to sit unless His Grace gave permission. He did not ordinarily do so, but for those rare occasions when he did, the room was furnished with settles for those of the highest rank and stools for men and women of lesser importance.

A duke outranked all other noblemen. Then came marquess, earl, viscount, and baron. Most courtiers, however, were only knights, or gentlemen like Master Brandon.

When the Lady Mary reached the dais, the king spoke quietly to his daughter, then acknowledged my presence with a nod. "Bring the messenger in," he ordered.

The room abruptly fell silent. All eyes shifted toward the door through which we had just entered.

A man stepped through from the great watching chamber. He was clad entirely in black. He twisted his cap in his hands, and the smell of wet wool emanated from his clothing. Narrowing my eyes, I studied him. This appeared to be the same fellow I'd seen earlier, taken into custody during the storm by the king's guards near the submerged water stairs.

After much hesitation and throat clearing, he addressed the king in French, the language common to every royal court. He introduced himself as a secretary to the king of Castile, which explained his odd accent and provoked a stir of interest in the crowd. There were exclamations of surprise and excitement when he announced that King Philip, driven ashore by the storm, had taken refuge in England and begged King Henry's leave to remain.

The babble of voices almost drowned out the messenger's next words. I moved nearer in time to hear him say that he had brought a letter from his master. King Henry accepted it and in the hush that descended, he perused its contents.

A loud chattering sound broke the silence. The Lady Mary and I shared an amused glance. Jot, the king's pet monkey, was loose . . . again. A stir in the crowd of courtiers marked his progress from the door of the privy chamber to the dais. Still reading, King Henry absently held out one arm. A streak of brown fur flashed along it to settle on His Grace's shoulder and sit up.

The little spider monkey, a mischievous creature whom the late queen had named Jot, wore a decorative collar of velvet and kid adorned with the king's arms. Still chattering softly, he reached out one small paw and tugged on a lock of white and thinning royal hair. King Henry reached up to stroke the creature's small head.

Anticipation bubbled in the presence chamber with palpable force. Thoughts were plain to read on every courtier's face. Visiting royalty was no common occurrence. Such events ordinarily required months of preparation. Even at short notice, however, a display of hospitality must be made. That meant tournaments and disguisings, hunting and hawking, and games of all sorts.

My heart beat a little faster at the prospect. There had been few celebrations at court after the festivities surrounding Princess Margaret's departure for Scotland, and even those had been steeped in sadness because of Queen Elizabeth's death.

I thought of Margaret sometimes. It was unlikely I would ever see her again. Princesses who married foreign princes rarely returned to the land of their birth. Catherine of Aragon, who had so briefly been married to Arthur, Prince of Wales, remained in England. She was styled the princess dowager, but she was rarely at court.

When King Henry looked up from the letter, his deep-set blue eyes were alive with an enthusiasm I hadn't seen in them for a long while. "King Philip and Queen Juana, on their way from Flanders to Castile by sea, encountered the same storm that has wreaked such havoc here in England. It scattered their fleet. The ship carrying the royal couple and their courtiers made landfall at Melcombe Regis, in Dorset. King Philip begs our hospitality until he can make such repairs to his ships as are necessary to continue the journey."

The king gently lifted the monkey down from his shoulder and placed him on the arm of his chair. Only then did he address the messenger directly.

"Our fellow monarchs are most welcome in England. They will be entertained during their stay as befits their station. Return to your master and invite him to meet us at Windsor Castle in two weeks' time."

"Will the entire court go to Windsor, Father?" Princess Mary placed one hand on her father's arm and extended the other to Jot.

She and her brother were the only people at court permitted to show such boldness before the king. I edged closer to the dais, but was careful not to place myself beneath the royal canopy.

His Grace's rare, slow smile appeared, somewhat brackish and gap toothed. "We will stage amusements fit for a princess."

"Will there be dancing, Father?" His ten-year-old daughter all but bounced up and down with excitement at the prospect, every movement accompanied by the tinkling of dozens of tiny bells that had been sewn onto her sleeves. "Please say there will be dancing."

"Just to please you, Mary," the king promised, "there will be dancing."

3

In a generous and expansive mood, King Henry sent gift after gift to the travelers stranded in Dorset at Wolverton Manor—clothing suitable to their station first of all, then horses and litters. Closer to home, he also spent with a liberal hand, determined to impress his royal visitors. Carts full of tapestry, plate, and furniture were sent ahead to Windsor to decorate the castle in the grandest style possible. More was purchased new, to add to the display of England's wealth and prosperity. Then the king proclaimed that everyone at court should have new clothes at his expense.

The richness of the fabrics varied according to one's position in the household, but even the lesser servants were given plain cloth livery in green and white, the king's colors. Catherine of Aragon, the princess dowager, received enough velvet to make new kirtles and gowns for herself and all five of her ladies.

The rains and stormy weather of mid-January were followed by a cold snap, leaving the waterways impassable and the roads icy and even more treacherous than usual. It was foul going for a journey of any length, but the Lady Mary, the princess dowager, and their attendants all arrived safely at Windsor Castle. We rode in litters, protected from the elements but jounced about unmercifully every inch of the way.

On the day King Philip was to arrive, a few of us went out onto the battlements of the Round Tower, the oldest part of the castle, to watch for him. The view was spectacular, encompassing the countryside for miles around as well as both the upper and lower wards of Windsor Castle itself.

"They will be here soon." The Lady Mary pointed toward the southwest. "See—they are coming this way."

The king had ridden out to meet his royal guest, who had been escorted for the last part of his journey by the Prince of Wales. From my tower perch, I had a clear view of King Henry in miniature, mounted on his favorite bay mare, surrounded by the greater part of the nobility of the realm. Colorful as peacocks, they made a bright splash on the landscape. At a distance of a half mile, the figures of the two kings and the Prince of Wales were tiny, but I could see them move through the formalities of greeting.

Queen Juana had been left behind at Wolverton Manor. She was to join her husband at Windsor, but not for a week or more. It was cruel to make her wait, I thought. Juana of Castile was Catherine of Aragon's sister, and they had not seen each other for many years.

I was distracted by a harsh wind that whipped our cloaks hard against our ankles and threatened to carry away our headdresses. It seemed to gust around me with malevolent intent. I burrowed deeper into my fur-lined cloak, pulling the collar up to cover my nose, and tried not to think about the frost forming on my toes.

Francesca de Carceres, one of Catherine of Aragon's Spanish ladies, sidled up to me. Curious, I slanted a glance in her direction. We both wore new headdresses, but while the black velvet of mine was decorated with pearls, hers was unrelieved by any light touches. The ebony hue of headdress and cloak combined made her olive complexion look sallow. There would be no improvement in her looks when she removed the outer garment either. Beneath it was more black, and despite a contraption of hoops called a *verdugado* that all the Spanish ladies wore to make their skirts fall from waist to toes in the shape of a bell, she was extremely thin. I'd often heard the expression "all skin and bones," but until I met Francesca I'd never met anyone who personified that description.

"They are riding this way," she said.

After their brief exchange in the open air, the two kings had remounted. They approached the castle with King Henry in the middle, between his son and heir and King Philip of Castile, who was also archduke of Flanders. They led a huge contingent more than five hundred strong. Trumpets and sackbuts sounded as the cavalcade reached the gatehouse.

The yeomen of the guard were lined up just outside the castle. They had been the first to receive new livery. Ordinarily they wore their own shirts with sleeveless white-and-green-striped tunics made of plain cloth. For the occasion of King Philip's visit, however, King Henry had given them shirts, hose, and bonnets, all in a particular shade of rose vermillion. He'd supplied new sword belts, scabbards, and shoes of black leather. Their new tunics were of damask, with stripes that counterchanged at the waistline. Embroidered on both front and back were round garlands of vine branches, decorated with silver and gilt spangles. In the middle of the design was a red rose beaten in goldsmith's work. When each man was armed with halberd, bow and arrows, and sword, they looked very fine indeed.

I strained to see King Philip. I had heard him called "Philip the Handsome," and sometimes "Philip the Fair," and in French, "Philippe le Beau." At first glance, he did not impress me as particularly imposing. He was only of medium height and heavily built. He was also shrouded in black—hood, gown, even harness, were all of that color, as were the garments of the dozen or so noblemen he'd brought with him.

"So that is the king." I let my disappointment show.

"He is a very important man," Francesca protested. "He is heir to the Holy Roman Empire and ruler in his own right of many Austrian possessions along the Danube and of the lands he inherited from his mother in the Netherlands. He is not just king of Castile, but Archduke of Austria, Duke of Burgundy, and Count of Flanders."

Then he should dress in a more regal fashion, I thought. In contrast to King Philip's unrelenting black, King Henry wore a purple velvet gown and hood. His heavy gold chain had a diamond pendant that reflected the pale winter light.

"I wonder what courtiers he has brought with him," Francesca murmured, leaning out at a precarious angle in an attempt to see them better.

"What does it matter who they are? They will not stay long." King Henry had many entertainments planned, but even if King Philip attended every event, the festivities were unlikely to go on for more than a few weeks. If nothing else stopped them, they would cease at the beginning of Lent. This year, Ash Wednesday fell on the twenty-fifth day of February.

Francesca lowered her voice. "Have you ever suffered misfortune, Mistress Popyncourt?"

I frowned. "Have you?"

Her nod was so vigorous that it almost dislodged her headdress. "Like you, I was chosen to serve royalty and my family was glad of it, thinking that a rich marriage would be sure to follow."

I did not disabuse her of the notion that we shared this particular background.

"The death of Prince Arthur was a great blow to my mistress."

"As it was to us all."

Francesca directed a wary glance at Catherine of Aragon, who stood next to the Lady Mary to watch the spectacle below. Catherine and Mary looked more like sisters by birth than sisters by marriage. Catherine, too, had red-gold hair and was no taller than ten-year-old Mary. Black velvet flattered her rosy complexion and gray eyes.

Reassured that the princess dowager was paying no attention to us, Francesca leaned so close to me that I could smell the lavender scent she'd used to perfume her body. "Her Grace cannot provide for her ladies as she should. Her father, King Ferdinand, refuses to release the remainder of her dowry to King Henry, and your king has been so miserly with our upkeep that we have been forced to live in poverty. We wear rags on our backs and have no hope of escape back to Spain."

"You are scarcely in rags now." I gave Francesca's headdress and cloak a significant look. Although the gown beneath might be plainly cut, it was made of expensive velvet.

But I could not help but feel sorry for her. Under my cloak— pale gray with rabbit-fur trim—my velvet gown was a flattering peach color with close-fitting undersleeves, cut and slashed at the wrist, and long, wide oversleeves decorated with bands of embroidery. The skirt was long and loose, with a comfortable kirtle and chemise beneath, and it flattered my waist and hips as one of those stiff *verdugados* could never hope to. It was the most beautiful garment I had ever owned, and I knew I looked very fine in it.

"Our good fortune will not last," Francesca predicted with gloomy certainty. "I know what will happen to Princess Catherine when King Philip goes away again. She will be forgotten. She and her ladies will be worse off than before."

"Why do you confide in me?" I asked, afraid she was about to criticize King Henry again. It was dangerous to speak so frankly and almost as unwise to listen to such sentiments.

"You have the king's ear," Francesca said. "You can persuade him to treat us better."

"I have no influence over King Henry. I am like a poor relation, tolerated in a gentleman's home out of charity." Unsettled, I pretended great interest in the scene below, hoping she would say no more of this.

"Ah," Francesca murmured. "Not unlike the princess dowager." To my great relief, she walked away.

In the lower ward, minstrels played as gloriously attired courtiers rode into the castle. They'd spared no expense to make a grand display. There were splendid jewels and bright colors—gold and crimson and blue predominated. The members of the king's household added to the sparkle. Livery badges with golden letters hung suspended from their long green-and-white-striped sleeves and reflected the sun almost as brilliantly as did the jewels.

My eyes narrowed when I recognized a familiar face among them. Charles Brandon had traded his old livery for the king's colors. I had not seen him, not even at a distance, since the night the messenger from King Philip arrived at Greenwich. But his distinctive garments told me he'd joined the king's spears, that group of gentlemen who were charged with protecting King Henry's person on an even more intimate level than the yeomen of the guard.

I saw Charles Brandon next, again at a distance, at the first of the festivities King Henry had arranged to entertain his guest. Pretending to ignore him, I stared at King Philip instead.

The king had the blond hair so common among the Flemish. My own father had had the same coloring. I wondered if Philip dressed entirely in black to emphasize this feature. His face was handsome, but there was a hard, calculating look in his eyes when his gaze swept over the assembled English courtiers. Those same eyes acquired a lascivious gleam when he looked at the ladies, all except his sister-in-law, Catherine of Aragon.

The princess dowager was seated near her brother-in-law, but Philip for the most part ignored her presence. So did King Henry. Only the Prince of Wales paid attention to her. In fact, he stared, a look of adoration on his face.

The king of Castile's minstrels performed, followed by the antics of John, King Philip's French fool, and the Prince of Wales's fool, Goose. Then the princess dowager performed a Spanish dance with one of her ladies. It was not Francesca, for she was too tall to look well dancing with a woman as petite as the princess dowager.

When they had finished, King Henry called upon the Lady Mary to dance. I was her partner, so it fell to me to take the gentleman's part. As a man would, I removed my glove and offered her my hand. After all the years of lessons at Eltham, we fell easily into the familiar slow and stately steps of "The King's Pavane."

"Well done, Mary," King Henry said as the last strains of music faded away. "Well done, Jane. Sit, my dears. Both of you. There, Jane." He gestured toward a stool just outside the area covered by the cloth of estate. "Rest yourself."

This unexpected consideration was most welcome. Now that the performance was over, my limbs had begun to tremble in reaction. I was no novice at the pavane but never before had I danced in front of two kings and the entire court. For the next few minutes I simply sat, letting my heart rate slow and trying to catch my breath.

It was the sense of being stared at, long after everyone should have lost interest in me, that made me suddenly self-conscious. I surveyed the gathered company and caught sight of Charles Brandon just turning away. Had it been his gaze I'd felt?

Then I realized that someone else was watching me. Goose, Prince Henry's fool, waggled his fingers in greeting and I smiled back at him. The man standing next to him glanced my way, too. At first I thought him a stranger. Dark skinned and wearing court dress, I supposed he was one of the Spaniards in King Philip's retinue. Only after he sent a second, almost furtive look in my direction did I suddenly recognize him.

Seeing my start of surprise, the man ducked his head and walked swiftly out of the hall. I left my stool and circled the chamber until I reached Goose's side.

Goose doffed his hat and bowed. "I fear you arrive too late, Mistress Popyncourt. Your secret admirer has fled." For once, his odd, high-pitched voice did not make me want to laugh.

"Was that one of the king's savages?"

"Bless me! It has eyes to see!" I took his answer to mean yes.

"How astonishing. Are the other two here, as well?"

"One died," Goose reminded me. "Oh, woe is me."

I remembered then that the keeper King Henry had assigned to care for the savages from the New World had dressed the remaining two in gentlemen's attire and attempted to teach them English. Instead of learning the language, they had stopped speaking entirely. Everyone assumed their silence was because they were little better than dumb animals, incapable of being educated. But unless I was much mistaken, I had just seen the gleam of intelligence, as well as a hint of amusement, in the eyes that had been watching me.

"After so many years at court, both men must understand English tolerably well," I mused aloud. "No doubt they can speak it, too . . . if they want to."

"Hard to learn a foreign tongue," Goose said.

"Not so very difficult." A laugh caught in my throat. Like the dwarf and the giantess and the rest of the king's curiosities, those savages had been taken from their homeland, brought to a foreign country where they did not understand the language, and kept at court to serve at the whim and pleasure of the royal family. For the first time I realized that the same could be said of me.

Pondering this revelation, I slowly made my way back to my stool and resumed my seat. The king had just announced that his daughter would perform on the lute. I welcomed the distraction.

The tune she played was familiar to everyone at the English court. It had been written to celebrate Henry Tudor's marriage to Elizabeth of York and the end of civil war. The lyrics asked what flower was most fragrant and colorful and followed that question with a host of possibilities, each with their attributes—marjoram, lavender, columbine, primrose, violet, daisy, gillyflower, rosemary, chamomile, borage, and savory. It the end, the rose was declared to be above all other herbs and flowers, the "fair fresh flower full of beauty," whatever its color. The song concluded with the words "I love the rose, both red and white."

As the courtiers applauded both the sentiment and the princess's performance, Princess Mary handed her lute to me and signaled for a manservant to bring in a rectangular box with a keyboard and thirty-two strings.

"Do you know why that instrument is called a virginal?" King Henry asked his guest. "It is because, like a virgin, it soothes with a sweet and gentle voice."

King Philip smiled appreciatively. Prince Henry looked bored.

He grew restless whenever he was not the center of attention and fidgeted throughout his sister's rendition of "The Maiden's Song." As soon as she lifted her hands from the keyboard, he leapt from the dais and called for the musicians to play a canary—a pavane designed to demonstrate a dancer's skill. Then he turned to me.

"Come, Jane. Let us show them how it is done."

He did not give me time to think, but caught my hand and pulled me to my feet. As the music began, he danced me to the far end of the hall, then withdrew to the point he'd started from, so that we were left facing each other from opposite ends of the room.

Panic swamped me. I swallowed hard. What should I do next? I'd memorized dozens of complicated floor patterns, from pavanes to *passamezzos* to *salte vellos*, but in that moment I could not remember any of them.

In the canary, first the gentleman and then the lady perform solo variations on the steps, dancing toward each other and then retreating. I had a choice between using steps I'd been taught by our dancing master or inventing new ones. Most people favored the latter course, priding themselves on the ingeniousness of what they created. Watching Prince Henry caper, clearly showing off, I realized that relying on learned steps was better. The simpler I kept my dance, the more my partner's skill would shine.

The Prince of Wales was as enthusiastic a dancer as he was an archer, a wrestler, and a tennis player. He excelled at all sports. In dancing, he had been known to throw off his gown and perform in doublet and hose, the better to execute high leaps. He did not go that far on this occasion, but his energetic capering was both skilled and athletic.

Everyone applauded when the performance drew to a close. Afterward, I was in great demand as a partner and the prince asked his sister-in-law to dance. He had been showing off for Catherine,

I thought. It was an open secret among those of us who had been raised with the royal children that he was enamored of his late brother's widow.

They made an attractive couple. Catherine was some six years older than Henry, but she was so tiny that she looked younger. His attitude toward her was both loving and protective.

Later, after the two kings withdrew, taking the prince with them, the dancing continued. By the time another hour passed, I was on the brink of exhaustion. I retreated to a secluded corner to rest, and it was there that Charles Brandon found me.

"Mistress Popyncourt," he said.

"Master Brandon." I expected him to ask me to dance. Instead he suggested that we go out for a breath of fresh air and to talk awhile.

When a servant had fetched my cloak, Charles wrapped it closely around me, tying the laces with his own hands. Then he took my arm and guided me along one passage and through another with the sureness of one who knew Windsor Castle well. We emerged in one of the smaller courtyards.

I shivered. It was much colder out of doors than it had been inside. Charles chuckled and slipped an arm around my waist to guide me over an icy patch.

"Prince Arthur once remarked that it was a great pity there were no galleries or gardens to walk in at Windsor," he said. "I fear there has been little improvement in that regard since his death."

Each step we took on the frozen cobblestones produced a crunching sound as a thin layer of ice cracked under our weight. A pale sun still lit the sky, but its beams held no warmth. I was powerfully tempted to burrow against Charles's side to absorb his heat.

"Did you go into Wales with Prince Arthur after his marriage to Princess Catherine?"

He shook his head. "My uncle, Sir Thomas Brandon, believed I would do better to stay at court. He is the king's master of horse, you know. He trained me to participate in tournaments. My very first performance in the lists brought me to the attention of the Earl of Essex and secured me a post in his household."

That joust had also brought him to the attention of every lady at court. "I remember," I admitted.

"You noticed me?"

"How could I not?" I teased him. "It was *my* uncle, Sir Rowland Velville, that you unhorsed so spectacularly."

"Is that how you came to be in Princess Mary's household?" he asked. "Did your uncle sponsor you at court?"

I nodded.

"Sir Rowland came to England with King Henry, I believe, although he was only a boy at the time."

"You are surely too young to remember that!" He was no more than twenty-one. That was one reason his performance in the tournament had been so startling. Boys did not even begin their training in the lists until they reached their sixteenth year.

"Both my father and uncle were in exile with the king," he said. "My father died in the Battle of Bosworth, where King Henry won his throne."

"I am sorry."

"I do not remember him. I was a babe in arms when he died."

"I lost my father when I was young, too, and my mother, as well."

We had circled halfway around the small courtyard and come to another door. Charles led me inside and along a corridor, and when we came to the end, he ushered me into a chamber tucked in beneath a stair.

"Whose lodgings are these?" I asked as he lit a candle. My nose twitched at the musty odor that clung to the bedding. There was no window to let in fresh air.

"The room is assigned to a friend of mine, but he is not at court at present. He will not mind if we borrow his accommodations." He helped me out of my cloak, and before I could think better of it, caught me by the waist and lifted me onto the bed. A moment later he was sitting beside me and leaning in for a kiss.

I put a hand out to stop him. His chest felt like iron beneath my palm. "You invited me to walk and *talk*, Master Brandon."

"So I did. But is that what you really want, Jane? Just to talk?" He ran one hand along the curve of my cheek. His touch made me shiver.

"It would be prudent to do no more than that." Greatly daring, I added, "Charles." I placed my hand over his and moved it from my face to the coverlet between us.

This seemed to amuse him. "Well, then, Jane, what shall we talk about?"

"You could tell me your intentions, for if you mean to court me, Charles, you should know I have no dowry."

"But you are much beloved by the king. I know that to be true."

I frowned. First Francesca and now Charles seemed to have the mistaken notion that I could somehow influence the king. "I serve his *daughter*."

He slid an arm around my shoulders. The embroidery on his sleeve scratched the underside of my chin. "Mayhap you have more value than you know."

Uncertain how to respond to this statement, my lips parted slightly in preparation for speech. Before I could form words, he took advantage of my hesitation to steal a kiss. This one was not as sloppy as the ones in the passageway at Greenwich. I liked it better. I would have kissed him back had someone not chosen that moment to rattle the latch on the door.

We sprang apart. Charles cursed.

"Jane?" Harry Guildford called, his voice muffled by the thickness of the oak door. "I saw you go in there. My mother is looking for you. If you have any sense you will take yourself back to your own lodgings before she finds you."

CANDLEMAS, THE SECOND day of February and the traditional beginning of spring, dawned to fresh snow on the ground and an icy wind whipping up the newly fallen flakes. After freezing them into stinging pellets, it flung them into the face of anyone foolish enough to venture outside.

The interior of Windsor Castle was little better. Cold drafts crept right through the walls to chill every chamber. The maidservant I shared with two more of the Lady Mary's gentlewomen went out early to fetch glowing coals for the brazier and a bowl of washing water free of ice. A quick splash was sufficient for my ablutions.

With King Philip and all his retinue in residence, the castle was crowded. The most favored courtiers, together with their servants, occupied double lodgings—two rooms, each with a fireplace and a stool chamber. Those less important resided in single lodgings—one room with a fireplace—and were obliged to use the public latrines. Others shared cramped quarters and were fortunate if they had a brazier and a bed instead of pallets on the floor.

I wondered if the little, windowless room Charles Brandon had taken me to had been his own poor lodging. That would explain how Harry had known to look for me there. I did not believe for a moment that he'd just happened to see us as we entered the chamber.

My two bedfellows and I had a slit for a window but scarcely space enough to house the bed and the truckle for the maid to sleep on and our traveling chests. I lost no time dressing in my warmest clothing. As I adjusted my headdress, I wished I had some excuse not to go to the Candlemas ceremony, followed by Mass in St. George's Chapel. The hall and chapel would be even colder than this bedchamber and I had seen the ritual designed to drive out evil spirits many times before. The only difference this year was that two kings instead of one would carry lit tapers, hallowed by the archbishop of Canterbury, in procession around the great hall.

Just as we were leaving, one of my garters came loose. "I will follow directly," I promised, and stopped to retie the ribbon holding up my stocking.

Left alone, I found myself gazing with real longing at the bed. A lump marked the location of the spaniel one of my bedfellows kept as a pet. Braveheart, she called him. I usually ignored the annoying little creature, but I envied him the warmth of those blankets and fur coverlets.

The Lady Mary would not miss me, I thought. She had a bevy of young women surrounding her. Unfortunately, the same could not be said of Mother Guildford. Nothing escaped her notice, and of late she had paid particular attention to my comings and goings. Resigned, I left the chamber and slowly made my way along the deserted passageway.

I had not gone far when I saw a gloved hand emerge from behind a tapestry. When I stopped and stared, it beckoned to me. The thought crossed my mind that the hand might belong to Charles Brandon. Was he waiting there, in an alcove just large enough to hide two people from passersby?

I had not forgotten Mother Guildford's warnings about

lecherous courtiers. I was curious to know who might be lurking behind the arras, even if it was not Charles Brandon, but this could be some unknown man waiting for any court damsel who might happen along.

"Come out where I can see you," I called, careful to stay more than an arm's length distant.

"Are we alone?" The words were muffled but I recognized the voice.

"Harry Guildford, what are you playing at?" A trace of disappointment colored my question.

"Are we alone?" he repeated.

"Yes!" I stepped closer, reached around the side of the arras, grasped him by the arm, and pulled him out of hiding.

It had been a great game, when we were younger, to conceal ourselves behind a convenient hanging or piece of furniture, then jump out and startle one another into shrieking aloud. Prince Henry in particular used to do this. Now, however, we were much too old for such foolishness. I saw at once, by the earnest expression on Harry's face, that he knew it, too. He had not been in hiding simply for the fun of frightening me.

"I must talk with you, Jane."

"Now?"

"We will not be missed." The desperation in his voice suggested that whatever troubled him was no small matter.

"Come to my chamber, then," I said. "No one will bother us there."

We were in luck. There were still coals in the brazier that sat in the small square of open floor between the bed and the chests full of clothing.

Harry hesitated. "Your maid—"

"She has gone to break her fast, and then will attend the

Candlemas ceremony along with everyone else." Except, it seemed, for Harry and me.

A few minutes later we had tugged pillows off the bed and were ensconced on the floor next to the firebox. Its heat dispelled some of the chill, but not enough that we were willing to remove our cloaks or gloves. I allowed Braveheart to climb onto my lap, happy to absorb the warmth from his small, wriggling body.

"What troubles you, Harry? Has the prince thrown you out? I cannot keep you here, you know." I indicated the spaniel burrowing deep into my skirts. "I am allowed either a lapdog or a singing bird, but you are neither."

My teasing failed to cheer him. He sat tailor fashion, hunched over the brazier, elbows on knees and shoulders slumped. I had never seen him look so wretched.

"Why is it so important that we speak in private?" Now that he had my full attention, he seemed loath to confide in me.

"I did not want anyone to overhear what I have to say to you."

"Well?"

"This is not easy for me, Jane." He stared at the glowing coals.

I narrowed my eyes. "You are not about to ask me to marry you, are you?"

"By the saints, I swear I am not!" The shock of my suggestion jerked him upright. His eyes all but popped out of his head. "How came you by such a mad notion?"

"From Lady Guildford."

"My mother thinks I want to wed you?"

"Your mother thinks I might try to trap you into marriage." I waved a dismissive hand. "What she believes is of little importance so long as you and I know better. But if that is not why you wished to talk to me, then what is it that troubles you, Harry?"

"Not my mother, but my father." Heaving a great sigh, he

reached inside both cloak and gown to fumble at his doublet. At length he produced a piece of paper folded in thirds and handed it over. "Read this. Then you will understand."

"It is from Sir Richard to you." I hesitated to peruse the private words written by a father to his son, in part because Harry and I had never spoken openly of his father's disgrace.

Sir Richard Guildford's letter stated that he wished to make a pilgrimage to the Holy Land. He wrote that he had a great sin on his conscience he hoped to have absolved through this penance. This notion troubled me not at all until I realized that Sir Richard wanted Harry to go with him. Suddenly, I felt a giant fist clench around my heart at the thought of losing yet another person I cared for. I could barely find breath to speak. Wordlessly, I returned the missive.

Harry tucked it away inside his doublet. "I do not know what to do, Jane. It would be a great adventure to travel to foreign lands."

"If you desire to visit shrines, there are plenty right here in England. Surely you do not *want* to go on a pilgrimage?"

He gave a rueful laugh. "Can you not see me in a pilgrim's cloak?"

"I cannot imagine that you would want to give up the pleasures of the prince's household. All your life, you have been trained as a courtier."

"My father was once accustomed to those same luxuries."

"Perhaps your father has reason to seek forgiveness!"

"You think his mismanagement of crown funds is the 'great sin' he refers to in his letter?" Harry did not seem convinced.

"What else could it be? But whatever sin it is that he carries upon his conscience, *you* have nothing to atone for. If he wants his own flesh and blood with him on this journey, let him take Edward." Harry's brother was the son of Sir Richard's first wife and fifteen years Harry's senior. "You cannot go to the Holy Land."

"Because you say so?" Harry gave a short, humorless bark of laughter. "Careful, Jane, or I will think you do have designs on me after all."

I stuck my tongue out at him as I shifted position on my cushion. Roused from a nap, the little dog yawned, stretched, and abandoned me for a spot on the truckle bed.

Harry sighed again and seemed to fall into melancholy.

Clasping my knees to my chest, I buried my face in my arms, pulling the cloak more tightly closed around me on the pretext of being cold. In truth, confusion enveloped me, relentless as an incoming tide. Our childhood was over, but the old bonds were strong. I yearned to keep Harry at court but knew not how.

The silence between us stretched until it was pulled taut as a bowstring. At last Harry stirred and spoke. "I am bound to serve the prince, but my father is . . . my father."

"The first loyalty is stronger than the second," I said slowly, thinking the matter through as I spoke, "for your father, in his turn, serves the Crown." As I obeyed the Lady Mary, Harry was Prince Henry's to command. I added, carefully, "The Prince of Wales depends upon you, Harry. He *listens* to you."

"He has others to—"

My head shot up. "He needs *you*, Harry! You have known him almost longer than anyone. When he loses his temper, everyone relies upon you to calm him down."

"What of Will Compton?"

"Oh, yes. Will can also restore Prince Henry to his better self, but it takes him twice as long."

"Do you ever wonder what he will be like when he becomes king?" Harry asked, his face pinched with worry. "You know Prince Henry lacks his father's self-control."

Snaking one hand out from beneath my cloak, I reached across the brazier to touch Harry's forearm. "As long as he gets his own way, or thinks he has, all will be well," I said.

Another humorless snort of laughter answered me.

"*Use* that, Harry. Prince Henry won't want you to go to the Holy Land. Let that be your answer to your father."

For a long time we sat listening to the wind howl outside the chamber window. I could say little more. I consoled myself with the thought that it would be weeks yet, perhaps even months, before anyone could set sail. The destruction of King Philip's fleet was proof enough of the foolishness of travel by sea at this time of year.

"He has never asked anything of me before," Harry murmured.

Scrambling to my feet, I circled the brazier and fell to my knees beside him and hugged him tightly. "Stay here, Harry. You belong with Prince Henry. You cannot abandon a brilliant future for an uncertain fate."

My face was so close to his that I could see the agony of indecision in his eyes.

"Someday Prince Henry will be king. He'll make you a knight, if his father has not already done so. Serve him well and you'll end up a baron at the least, or perhaps even a viscount. Kings reward loyalty, Harry."

He still did not look convinced, so I searched harder for an argument that would convince him.

"Prince Henry will need you beside him when he passes his sixteenth birthday and begins training for the lists. With your jousting experience, you'll know how to keep His Grace safe from injuries while he learns how to fight in tournaments."

Like dawn breaking, relief flooded into Harry's face. "I knew I could count on your good sense!" He leaned over and squeezed me so tightly that I let out a squeak of protest. Grinning, he released me and stood. "That excuse is one my father will understand. He will see that I have no choice but to stay with the prince."

To ENTERTAIN KING Philip there was more dancing, as well as hunts and tennis matches, bear baitings and horse baitings. Then, a week after Candlemas, Queen Juana arrived.

The very next day, the Lady Mary and her household and the princess dowager and her attendants left Windsor to go ahead to Richmond Palace. King Henry was to follow with King Philip in a few days.

"Such a pity," the Lady Mary murmured as we set out aboard one of the royal barges. The Thames was open again and our journey would be far easier and far swifter than it had been by road.

"What is, Your Grace?"

"That Queen Juana remains behind at Windsor when she and the princess dowager have only just been reunited."

"They will be able to spend time together at Richmond."

But the princess shook her head. "No, they will not. By the time King Philip and my father join us there, Juana will be on her way to Plymouth, where their ships are being repaired."

"But they cannot hope to sail for many weeks yet."

Mary looked more solemn than her years. "It is a ploy, Jane, to keep Catherine and Juana apart. Do you not remember who their father is?"

"King Ferdinand of Aragon," I said slowly, comprehending at last. At the time of the marriage between Princess Catherine and Prince Arthur, King Ferdinand had been England's ally. But now, no doubt because he had refused to pay the remainder of Catherine's dowry after Arthur's death, King Ferdinand and King Henry were at odds. King Henry feared that the two sisters might somehow conspire against him to aid their father.

A tournament was held at Richmond to entertain King Philip. Charles Brandon acquitted himself well. During the next weeks, Charles continued to pay court to me and even stole the occasional kiss, but he made no further attempt to spirit me away to some secluded chamber. I convinced myself that he was being careful of my reputation.

KING PHILIP TOOK his leave of the English court in early March. In early April, Sir Richard Guildford, newly pardoned by King Henry, sailed from England for the Holy Land—without Harry. By then, Charles Brandon seemed to have lost all interest in me. I consoled myself by flirting with Harry, and with Will Compton, neither of whom took me seriously.

Then in September word came that King Philip had died suddenly during his visit to Spain. Rumors flew. Some said his wife, Queen Juana, had poisoned him in a fit of jealousy. Others suggested King Ferdinand was the villain, since it was Ferdinand who would not govern Castile for Philip and Juana's six-year-old son, Charles.

I pitied Queen Juana. She had lost her beloved husband and was said to have run mad with grief. But I felt much greater sympathy for Harry Guildford. The news arrived in England in October that Sir Richard had reached Jerusalem only to die there.

I was never certain how Mother Guildford felt about her husband's fate. She did not permit her emotions to show. When she asked me to step into her lodgings on a fine, sunny morning in mid-November, murmuring the name "Charles," I assumed she wished to discuss plans for the Lady Mary's betrothal to Charles of Castile.

King Henry and King Ferdinand were friends again. They had agreed that King Henry's daughter Mary would marry King Ferdinand's grandson Charles and there was even talk that King Henry himself might marry King Ferdinand's widowed daughter Juana.

The ceremony to bind Mary to Charles was scheduled to take place in a few weeks. She would not leave England for several years, but as soon as she was officially betrothed, she could call herself queen of Castile even though Queen Juana was still alive. Everyone in her household would also be elevated in importance.

"Sit, Jane," Mother Guildford said, indicating a wooden stool. She had the luxury of a chair with a plump cushion to pad the seat. Her lips were pursed tight and she had a look of disapproval in her eyes.

"Is something amiss, madam?"

"I could not help but observe, Jane, that you showed a marked interest in Master Charles Brandon during the king of Castile's visit and afterward."

I folded my hands primly in my lap and said, "He is a handsome man, madam. Few women could avoid noticing him."

"Was your heart engaged, Jane?"

I thought about that for a moment before I answered. "No, madam."

"I am relieved to hear it." Her posture relaxed a fraction. "Still, better you hear the news from me than elsewhere. Master Brandon has wed a wealthy London widow, Lady Mortimer."

I sighed. "I suppose, if I'd had a large dowry, he might have made an offer for me."

"Consider this a lucky escape. Master Brandon's treatment of gently born young women leaves much to be desired."

I started to defend Charles, but she cut me off, wagging a finger at me. "Remember this, Jane: What happens away from court is not always known to us here until much later. Nor do we always hear the whole story behind some of the rumors that do reach us. Charles Brandon was betrothed to another young woman at the same time he was courting you. Mistress Anne Browne was once a maid of honor to Queen Elizabeth. He kept her as his mistress for years after the queen died, and she bore him a child."

"If he was betrothed to her, why did he not marry her? Indeed, how *could* he marry someone else?" Betrothals were supposed to be almost as binding as marriages.

"An excellent question, and one for which I have no answer." Mother Guildford looked thoughtful. "I do not believe we have heard the last of this matter."

Shortly after that conversation, Charles Brandon returned to court. He did not bring his new wife with him. He continued to be one of Prince Henry's boon companions, along with Tom Knyvett, Lord Edward Howard, Ned Neville, Will Compton, Harry Guildford, and Harry's older half brother, Edward.

In THE SPRING following King Philip's visit, King Henry was seriously ill. I was seventeen and horribly afraid that he, too, might die and leave behind a son too young to rule for himself. The king recovered, but he was sick again the following year. His physicians said it was only gout, and he was well enough by the end of February to receive two envoys from King Ferdinand. One was Francisco di Grimaldo, an elderly Italian banker. The other was the new Spanish ambassador, Don Gutiene Gomez de Fuensalida. They had come to discuss Catherine of Aragon's still unpaid dowry.

The princess dowager seemed doomed to live out her life in poverty in England. Her father would not take her back and King Henry refused to permit her to marry Prince Henry, the most sensible solution. Francesca de Carceres, having had no better offer, escaped by eloping with old Master di Grimaldo.

In the summer of my eighteenth year, King Henry collapsed while out hunting. This time one of his doctors, John Chambre, a man already made memorable by his extremely large nose, dared speak the truth—the king had consumption and was likely to die of it.

Prince Henry accompanied his father on pilgrimages to Walsingham and Canterbury to pray for a cure. The Lady Mary went, too, taking me with her. It did no good. We watched the king grow steadily weaker and knew that before long the disease would kill him.

King Henry VII did not want to die, especially not before his son was eighteen and of full age to inherit. That day would come on the twenty-eighth of June in the year of our Lord fifteen hundred and nine. King Henry was determined to hold out until then.

That January, I turned nineteen. Over the next weeks, the king's health continued to deteriorate. He had acute pains in his chest and difficulty breathing. He asked that the Lady Mary come and sit by his side and told her to bring me with her.

A few days later, we were joined in the sickroom by the king's mother, Lady Margaret Beaufort, Countess of Richmond. The countess was a small, birdlike woman who dressed like a nun and wore a hair shirt under her habit. She was only fourteen years older than her dying son, but seemed likely to outlive him by a good many years.

She did not speak to me. She never did. I was not certain why she'd taken a dislike to me, but over the years she had gone out of her way to ignore my presence in her granddaughter's household.

At the end of March, King Henry made a new will. On the twenty-first day of April, he once again sent for the Lady Mary and for me.

"She has no business here," the countess said when she saw me enter her son's bedchamber.

"I asked for her," King Henry whispered. He was so weak that his voice carried only as far as the foot of his bed.

The countess allowed me to stay, but only until the king fell asleep. Then she sent me away.

I met Prince Henry just arriving at his father's sickroom door. "Is he any better?" he asked.

I shook my head and felt tears well up in my eyes.

"I want to be king someday," the prince said, "but not yet." He seemed reluctant to enter the bedchamber.

"Your presence will comfort him, Your Grace."

"A pity you cannot stay in my stead, Jane," Prince Henry said with a rueful laugh. "I hate the sight and stink of illness." But he went in and I went away and the king died the next day.

Since Prince Henry was not quite eighteen, his grandmother proposed that she serve as regent. Henry refused. He did not intend to be governed by anyone. He sent the countess to Cheyney Gates, a house adjoining the palace of Westminster but not actually a part of it, and arranged for his father's lying-in-state and burial himself. He also set the date for his coronation as King Henry VIII. And then, in the chapel at Pleasure Palace, he quietly married Catherine of Aragon.

On the twenty-fourth day of June, they were crowned together as king and queen of England. I watched the procession that preceded the ceremony from the windows of a house in Cheapside in London. It was quite near the inn in which my mother and I had stayed when we saw Perkin Warbeck put in the stocks. How different this was! I was still a spectator, but now I stood beside Mary Tudor, princess of England and queen of Castile.

Nearby was Mary's grandmother, the Countess of Richmond. As usual, she pretended not to notice my presence. I shed no tears when, a few days later, word reached us at court that the Countess of Richmond had choked to death on a bone while eating roast swan.

4

In the first year of the reign of King Henry VIII, the court spent Yuletide at Richmond Palace. We were still there when I passed my twentieth birthday and stayed on a few days more for a tournament. It ended badly. Will Compton was almost killed jousting against Ned Neville. He broke several ribs, his arm, and his nose and was unconscious for hours.

Leaving Will behind in the care of Dr. Chambre, we moved on to Westminster Palace on schedule. I worried about him. Even a cut could be fatal if it grew inflamed, and I did not want to lose anyone else to death, especially not one of my "brothers."

"It does no good to fret," Harry Guildford said when I asked if he'd heard any news of Will's condition. "Either he'll recover or he will not. It is in God's hands."

I knew he was right, but his words offered little comfort. I sighed.

Harry looked thoughtful. "You need something to distract you from gloomy thoughts," he said. "Will was to have played a role in a disguising I am planning." The new king had appointed Harry his master of revels. "You could take his place."

"I look nothing like Will Compton," I said, pointing out the obvious.

"Ah, but Will would not have resembled himself in the least. He was to have been our Maid Marian."

As a lad, Prince Henry had loved the Robin Hood stories above all others. We had often acted out tales of the famous outlaw and his Merry Men. I'd portrayed Maid Marian once or twice, but it was more common among companies of players for boys to take on the women's roles, wearing long skirts and wigs.

"Is this a masque for the court?" I asked.

Grinning, Harry shook his head. "It is a private performance." He held one finger to his lips. "And it is a secret. Are you with us?"

"Can you doubt it?"

Harry provided a costume—green gown, yellow wig, and a mask that concealed my features—and told me to be ready at first cockcrow on the morning of the eighteenth day of January. We met in the king's secret lodgings, and from there, through a passage I had not known existed till then, entered the queen's bedchamber. There were a dozen of us in all, the king as Robin Hood, ten of his companions as the Merry Men, and myself as Maid Marian. Our sudden appearance was met by shrieks of surprise and alarm.

Sweeping back the hangings that enclosed his wife's bed, Robin Hood found Catherine still half asleep. "Rise and dance with me, madam," he said. "I vow we will not depart until you agree to this demand."

The queen was a tiny woman and looked even smaller in her

nightclothes. The king towered over his wife, but his manner was gentle. Even as he delighted in teasing and embarrassing her, his stance was protective. She was expecting their first child.

As was the custom, the queen and her ladies pretended not to know who the intruders were. I had no doubt that Catherine had recognized her husband. She'd never have allowed the assault on her dignity otherwise, and she must have realized that her guards would never let strangers into her chamber.

"You give me no choice, sirrah," she said. "I yield." Catherine had a deep, throaty voice at odds with her small stature and, in spite of the many years she had been in England, retained the hint of a Castilian lisp. She permitted the king to lift her out of her bed and set her on the rush matting in her bare feet.

One of the Merry Men produced a lute and soon there were several couples dancing. I joined in the merriment with Harry for a partner, and amused myself by trying to identify the other revelers. Even with a visor hiding his face, the king was impossible to mistake. For height and breadth of shoulder, only Ned Neville was his equal, and Ned lacked that shock of bright hair.

Ned was also easy to pick out, but the others were more difficult. They all wore identical coats of Kendall green. I decided that the one who seemed a bit aloof was Harry's half brother, Sir Edward Guildford, who was older than the rest of us and a bit stodgy. I could tell Charles Brandon by his demeanor, and if Brandon was one of the party, so were Tom Knyvett and Lord Edward Howard.

At first I did not realize that my identity, too, was the object of speculation. Several of the queen's ladies stared openly at me as I danced. I'd forgotten I was supposed to be pretending to be a man pretending to be a woman.

I tried to change my movements, to make my steps bigger and less graceful, but it was too late. A glance at Queen Catherine told me that she, too, had recognized me as a female. When King Henry was not looking, she glared at me with venom in her eyes.

My heart sank. The queen had set ideas about what sort of women were permitted to live at court. She disapproved of lewd behavior and clearly thought me a creature of low station and even lower repute. I was grateful the visor concealed my face.

The dancing continued for another hour. I was relieved to be allowed to depart still unmasked but I spent the next few days expecting at any moment to be banished from court. Nothing happened. As far as anyone knew, the queen never asked who had played Maid Marian. She did, however, take a renewed interest in the morals of the court.

A short time after our morning invasion of her chamber, Queen Catherine convinced her husband that the reputation of his inno-cent young sister—Mary was then not quite fifteen—must be pro-tected. He agreed. Henceforth, he decreed, Mary was to be shielded from the bawdier aspects of court life. He had no intention of restricting the antics of the high-spirited young men who were his boon companions, but it cost him nothing to put the Lady Mary's household out of bounds. Not just the princess, but all the ladies who served her were, therefore, protected from temptation.

I told myself I should be grateful that we had not been sent away to rusticate at some distant country manor. At least we were still at court and able to attend all the pageants, tournaments, dances, and hunts.

JUST BEFORE MY twenty-first birthday, Queen Catherine gave birth to a son. Her first pregnancy had ended in a miscarriage, but now King Henry had an heir, yet another Prince Henry.

As master of revels, Harry Guildford was responsible for pro-ducing a pageant to celebrate the christening and, as he often had during the year and a half of the reign, he asked me for suggestions. The result was a great success, but Harry had another reason to be pleased with himself. He confided his news to me as we were supervising the removal of the pageant wagons afterward.

"The king has approved my betrothal to Meg Bryan, Jane. We are to wed sometime next year."

"I am happy for you, Harry." I knew Meg only in passing, but she seemed pleasant enough. She was eighteen, a slender girl of middling height with thick, dark brown hair and widely spaced, deep brown eyes. Her mother was one of the queen's ladies and her father was the vice-chamberlain of Queen Catherine's household. Meg and her younger sister, Elizabeth, had no official standing at court, but they had shared their parents' quarters since the beginning of the reign and attended all the dances and tournaments.

"I feared her father might object. Because of what mine did," Harry confessed.

"Sir Richard was pardoned," I reminded him. "Besides, it is how you are regarded at court that matters now and everyone knows that you are one of the king's oldest and dearest friends."

"Oldest, mayhap, but no longer his favorite. Charles Brandon has usurped that honor. It is a good thing Brandon has no interest in Meg or he'd have had her instead of me."

"I should think any father *would* object to that!" Harry's mother had been right all those years ago. We had not heard the last of Charles Brandon's irregular matrimonial history. Because of his earlier betrothal to Anne Browne, his marriage to Lady Mortimer had been annulled. After that he'd finally married his longtime mistress, but Anne Browne, poor lady, had died soon after giving birth to Brandon's daughter.

"Will you befriend Meg, Jane?" Harry asked. "Talk to her about me while I am gone so she will not be tempted to flirt with any other man?"

I stared at him, perplexed. "Gone? Where are you going?"

He grinned at me. "Did I not tell you? I am to leave for Spain at the end of next month on an embassy to King Ferdinand."

I had to force myself to smile. "That is a great honor, Harry." One that would take him away from England for many months.

"Say rather a great challenge. Queen Catherine's father is a treacherous man. Sometimes he has been England's friend and other times he has plotted against us. I do not think he can be trusted at all and yet I must treat with him to maintain our alliance."

"You have had a great deal of practice dealing with difficult monarchs," I reminded him.

"Indeed I have," he agreed. "But you have not given me your answer. Will you spend time with Meg while I'm gone? I have already told her that you are one of my closest friends."

"I will be happy to," I said, although I had my doubts even then. For some reason the other girls among the children of honor had never taken to me, and I had always felt more comfortable spending my free time with the boys. That preference had not changed over the years. The only female confidante I had ever had was the Lady Mary.

I had every intention of keeping my promise, but only a few days after Harry left for Spain, the infant Prince of Wales suddenly died. The entire court went into mourning, eliminating all entertainments at which I might encounter Meg Bryan by chance. Eventually, I sought her out in her lodgings, but only her sister, Elizabeth, was there.

"Will you tell your sister I would like to speak with her about Harry Guildford?" I asked.

Elizabeth paused between stitches in her needlework to smile sweetly at me. She was fifteen and the beauty of the Bryan family. She had bright, chestnut-colored hair, delicate features, and an air of innocence about her. "Meg does not want to talk to you, especially about Harry."

"Why not?" I blurted out, too surprised by the young woman's blunt statement to be any more subtle than she was.

"You are Harry's . . . friend." Her tone insinuated that we were more than that. Elizabeth was not so innocent as she appeared.

"He is like a brother to me."

Her eyebrows lifted in disbelief.

If Elizabeth thought I was Harry's mistress, clearly Meg did, too. I was at a loss as to how to convince either of them otherwise. "Harry and I have spent many long hours together," I said, "planning masques and pageants."

"Why would he want your help?" Elizabeth asked.

"We are old friends."

"So you said." She jabbed her needle into the cloth and I had the uneasy suspicion that she'd have liked to stab me with it. I admired her loyalty to her sister, but it was both frustrating and insulting to be condemned without a hearing.

I never did manage to have a conversation with Meg. In the end I gave up trying.

AFTER A LONG sojourn in Spain, Harry came safely home. On the twenty-fifth day of April in the year of our Lord fifteen hundred and twelve, he wed Meg Bryan. The king himself attended the ceremony and so did his sister. Meg would no doubt have preferred that I not be there, but I came as the Lady Mary's waiting gentlewoman and she could hardly send me away.

Harry's embassy to Spain resulted in an alliance to invade

France and reclaim territory there that had once been ruled by England. The English fleet sailed a week after Harry's wedding. He went with it as captain of the *Sovereign*.

For the first time in years, I found myself remembering France and my life there. I knew that the French were not the monsters the English believed them to be. Guy Dunois had been a sweet, amiable boy, every bit as much my friend as Harry Guildford later became. My governess, although I had by then forgotten her name, had been kind to me. Even Queen Anne of Brittany, the one time I had been presented to her, had kissed me and made much of me. Anne was still queen of France. She had taken King Louis XII, King Charles's successor, as her second husband.

I did not voice my opinions about the French. I did not want to remind anyone of my foreign birth. This proved to be a wise decision when the ships England sent to war were routed. Harry had a close brush with death when a ship blew up right next to the *Sovereign*. Tom Knyvett, another of the king's friends and one of our band of Merry Men, was killed in the sea battle.

King Henry swore to avenge Tom's death. So did Tom's closest friends, Charles Brandon and Henry's lord admiral, Lord Edward Howard. Tom was a man they'd jousted with and reveled with. He was a man with whom I had danced and flirted, but I was very glad that if someone of our circle had to die, it had not been Harry or Will Compton or Ned Neville.

In March, less than a year after Tom Knyvett's death, a second fleet set sail. This time it went without Harry, who was busy helping the king ready a land army. A few weeks later, I was on my way from the Lady Mary's apartments to my own lodgings when I came upon him standing in the middle of an otherwise deserted corridor. His face was devoid of color.

I touched his arm. "Harry?"

He started and stared at me. He did not seem to recognize me.

"Harry, what is it?" Alarmed now, I tightened my grip and shook him.

"Lord Edward Howard is dead." Harry looked like a corpse himself.

"A battle?"

He nodded. "The news came an hour ago. They fought a great naval battle off the coast of Brittany near Brest." I thought he might start to cry.

"What else, Harry?" I could sense there was more.

"Lord Edward captured a French vessel. He and his men boarded it, thinking that the French crew had been disarmed, but something went wrong. The ship was cut free of its captor and some fifty Englishmen were trapped onboard. The French dispatched some of them with pike thrusts and threw others into the sea."

"Lord Edward, too?" I was appalled. As King Henry's lord admiral, he should have been taken prisoner and held for ransom.

"Lord Edward was pinned against the rails by a dozen Moorish pikes. Then the French admiral, Bidoux, ordered him killed. And worse." I did not want to hear the rest, but Harry could not now be stopped. "Bidoux!" He spat. "The one they call Prior John. He desecrated Lord Edward's body. Oh, he ordered that it be embalmed and sent home, but first he cut out the heart. He has kept it as a trophy!"

ON THE THIRTIETH day of June, King Henry landed on the continent at Calais with an army at his back. Leaving Queen Catherine as regent in his absence, he took courtiers and soldiers alike to exact revenge upon the French.

Those of us who remained at court with the queen were at

Richmond Palace when word arrived that the two armies had met on the sixteenth day of August. This time England had emerged victorious.

On into September, we busied ourselves sewing standards, banners, and badges for the king's army. The battle had been won, but not yet the war.

I was engaged in hemming yet another banner showing the red dragon of Wales when I heard the rustle of brocade and caught a whiff of a perfume made with marjoram. I looked up to find Mistress Elizabeth Blount, Queen Catherine's newest maid of honor, standing beside me. She had been at court all of a week.

Bessie Blount was a pretty creature with fair hair and sparkling blue eyes. She was fifteen to my twenty-three and had never before been away from her father's country estate. She had a puppy's eager friendliness, anxious that everyone think well of her.

"Mistress Popyncourt," she said in a low, sweet voice, "the queen wishes to speak with you."

"With me? Are you certain she did not send you for her sister-in-law?" We both looked toward my eighteen-year-old mistress Mary Tudor, who sat on a padded window seat, engrossed in the badge she was embroidering. With her head bent over her work, all I could see of her face was an inch of pale forehead and the narrow band of red-gold hair that showed at the front of her elaborate headdress.

"The queen wants you," Bessie insisted.

The Lady Mary gave me leave to go and even suggested that we use the privy stairs to the queen's apartments, the most direct route. In actual fact, the rooms in question were the king's. As regent, Queen Catherine had installed herself in King Henry's apartments and given those she usually occupied on the floor below to the Lady Mary.

Once in the stairwell, I took the lead, speeding upward with footfalls so nearly silent on the stones that the yeoman usher stationed on the next landing did not hear my approach until I was almost upon him. With a yelp of surprise, he lowered his halberd, leveling the point at my chest. Only a hasty step backward saved me from being pinked by the spear end of his weapon.

"Your pardon, Mistress Popyncourt," he stammered. "I did not mean . . . that is, I—"

"No harm done," I assured him.

Bessie Blount, who had fallen behind, reached the landing. Her face becomingly flushed and her eyes wide, she stared at the halberd. The guard's cheeks also flamed. He was new at court as well, since all the experienced men had gone off to war with the king.

Moments later, I entered the royal bedchamber where the queen was being dressed. The air was thick with mingled scents—musk and rosewater, jasmine and civet, rosemary and lavender. Queen Catherine stood beside the bed wearing only her chemise and a *verdugado*. The undergarment was made of canvas into which bands of cane had been inserted at intervals from the waist downward. The bands gradually widened as they approached the hem.

As I made my obeisance, one of the ladies of the bedchamber put a linen petticoat over the queen's head. It fell into place, masking the lines of the *verdugado*'s ribs. I was obliged to wait while other highborn tiring maids added an underdress and overskirt and arranged the queen's long, thick, red-gold hair atop her head. Queen Catherine did not acknowledge me until her gable headdress was firmly anchored in place.

"Come forward, Mistress Popyncourt."

I obeyed, casting a surreptitious glance at the royal bed as I passed it. It was a massive structure fully eleven feet square and positioned beneath a gold and silver canopy suspended from the ceiling by cords. The hangings were of the finest silk, drawn back to reveal lawn sheets, wool blankets, feather bolsters and pillows, and coverlets of silk, velvet, and fur. Across the one made of crimson velvet lay a sinfully luxurious black night-robe trimmed with sable.

One of the tiring women reached for it, but the queen commanded that she leave it be. Then she sent everyone away save for myself and Maria de Salinas, her most trusted lady-in-waiting.

Uneasy in my mind, I watched them go. The queen had never singled me out for attention before and I could not think why she should now unless—could it be that she had recognized me as Maid Marian after all this time?

"Where were you born, Mistress Popyncourt?" the queen asked.

"In Brittany, Your Grace, of a Breton mother and a Flemish father." I was surprised she did not know that, but perhaps she had never bothered to ask about me before.

"Not France?"

As the queen's hatred of all things French was well known, my nervousness increased. "No, Your Grace. At that time, the duchy of Brittany was still independent."

I refrained from adding that when Brittany had been absorbed into the kingdom of France, I had gone there to live. In the earliest days I could remember, I'd thought of France as my homeland.

"Is it true that you are a . . . *huérfana?*" At times, unable to remember the correct English word, the queen still expressed herself in Spanish.

"Orphan," Maria de Salinas supplied. The queen's favorite lady spoke better English than her mistress.

"Yes, Your Grace. My parents died when I was a child."

Queen Catherine used both hands to adjust her headdress, wincing as if the weight of it made her head ache. Although no official announcement had been made, it was widely speculated that she was again with child. I prayed that was so. As of yet, King Henry had no heir for his throne.

"How old were you when you came here?" the queen asked.

"I arrived in England in the summer of my eighth year." With each question, I breathed more easily.

"And then?"

"I was installed in the royal nursery at Eltham for the purpose of speaking French in daily conversation with the Lady Mary and the Lady Margaret, the king's daughters."

"Margaret," the queen muttered, scowling.

I said nothing. Margaret's husband, King James, had allied himself with Louis of France. There were rumors that he was about to cross the border from Scotland into England at the head of an army.

"You will have heard of the king's great victory over the French," the queen said.

"Yes, Your Grace. The French troops fled before our greater English force."

Moving toward a nearby Glastonbury chair, the queen waited for Maria de Salinas to plump the cushions before she sat. Relief suffused her features, making me more certain than ever that she was with child.

"His Grace has sent me a gift," the queen said. "A French prisoner of war. He bids me treat this man, a duke, as our honored guest. In all, seven prisoners arrived here this morning, the duke and his six servants. I must meet with him and inform him that he is to be held in the Tower of London until both Scotland and France are defeated. He will be treated well. He will have the use of the royal apartments there. But he cannot be allowed to live at court while we are still at war." Her eyes, which had gone unfocused as she spoke, suddenly fixed on my face. "You must tell him this, Jane. My French is better than it was, but I must be certain of everything—what he learns from me and what he says in return. I rely upon you to translate every word, each . . . nuance. You will be my ears, Jane, and my voice."

"It will be my pleasure, Your Grace."

"Come, then." She rose and walked toward the door to the privy chamber. Maria de Salinas made little shooing motions, urging me to hurry after her.

The privy chamber led into the presence chamber. The rise and fall of voices ceased at the queen's entrance. Courtiers made a leg and ladies sank into their skirts as she made her way to the dais and the chair of state that sat under a canopy of cloth-of-gold, just as it had in old King Henry's day. Seating herself with a rustle of stiff, jewel-encrusted fabric, the queen gestured for me to stand just behind her.

"Bring the prisoners in," she commanded.

Expectant, everyone waited, eyes on the door to the great watching chamber.

A yeoman of the guard stepped through first. "Louis d'Orléans, Duke of Longueville, Marquis of Rothelin, Count of Dunois, and Lord of Beaugency."

I stared. I could not help myself. The duke's hair, blue-black as a raven's wing, glistened in the sunlight pouring in through the chamber windows. His face was sculpted in bold, hard lines—a strong jaw and a noble nose. He was ten years older than I, thirty-three when I first saw him that day, and in prime physical condition. He entered the presence chamber with long, confident strides, all hard, lean muscle and flowing movement.

Following him came his servants, but I paid them no mind.

Although the duke carried his bonnet in his hand and bowed to the queen, there was nothing servile about him. He approached the dais with as much presence as any monarch, his back held straight and his shoulders squared. He commanded the attention of every person in the room.

For just a moment, as he stopped in front of the queen, his gaze slid sideways to focus on me. His eyes were a bright, metallic black, as striking in color as his hair. A shiver racked my entire body. In an instant my accustomed composure shattered.

Even after the duke looked away from me to make a second, lower obeisance to the queen, I continued to stare at him. A curious sensation began to make itself felt deep inside me.

When he spoke, it was in a resonant rumble that fell pleasantly on the ear.

"The Duke of Longueville," I heard a courtier whisper.

"He will command a rich ransom," came an answering voice.

Since I was there to serve as translator, I forced all other considerations from my mind. Yet I could not stop myself from smiling at the duke as I conveyed the queen's wishes. And when I had told him where he was to be lodged, I felt compelled to reassure him.

"The Tower of London is a palace as well as a prison, my lord. You will be housed in great comfort. You will be lodged in the very rooms the king and queen occupied on the night before their coronation."

When the audience was over, the guards were told to escort the prisoners to the barge that would transport them downriver from Richmond to the Tower of London. The queen dismissed me at the same time and I exited the presence chamber just behind the Frenchmen, passing with them into the great watching chamber where yeomen of the guard stood at attention at regular intervals along walls hung with tapestries and furnished with carpet-covered sideboard tables and many-tiered buffets.

It was a room designed to inspire awe. The guards were an impressive sight all on their own. Each of them wore a sword and carried a fearsome-looking gilt halberd, both blades glittering almost as brightly as the gleaming cups, dishes, and goblets set out on the tables and buffets. Gold and silver, jeweled and enameled, every item had been selected to proclaim the wealth and importance of King Henry VIII of England.

I noticed none of it. All my attention was on the duke. I did not want him to leave. Was this lust, one of the sins the priests warned us about? I had certainly never felt such a powerful attraction to any man before.

My musings were cut short when a voice beside me spoke in French. One of the duke's servants had turned back. Although he now stood only inches away, I had not been aware of his approach.

"The queen called you Mistress Popyncourt," he said in a low voice almost as deep as his master's. "Is your Christian name Jeanne?"

"I am *Jane* Popyncourt." I corrected him without thinking. To insist upon the English version of my name was ingrained in me by then.

"Jeanne. Jane. It is all the same, I think." His eyes, a distinctive shade of blue-green, twinkled at me.

Frowning, I stared at him, taking note for the first time that he was a man about my own age. His hair was a light chestnut color, his features regular, and his face clean shaven. Something was familiar about his smile.

"Guy? Guy Dunois?"

"At your service, mistress." He sketched a bow.

It was indeed the friend of my youngest days in Amboise. A rush of warmth filled me at being so unexpectedly reunited with him.

"Move along now." One of the yeomen of the guard chastised him with a clout on the arm. "You're not to be bothering the ladies."

I drew myself up as I had so often seen my mistress do and looked down my nose. "A moment, sirrah. It is the queen's bidding that I translate everything these prisoners have to say."

Since he had plainly seen me perform this service for Queen Catherine, he could scarcely argue. I let him fume, returning my full attention to Guy. "I cannot believe you are here."

"I came with my brother."

My gaze shot to the doorway, but the duke had gone. Only a brown-haired, blue-eyed youth in Longueville's livery remained, anxiously shifting his weight from foot to foot as he tried to decide whether to stay behind with Guy or hurry after his master.

Guy, I remembered now, was the bastard son of the Count of Dunois and Longueville. I had a vague recollection of Guy telling me he hoped to enter his half brother's service when he was older. It had been a reasonable ambition. Bastard sons often went on to serve their fathers or half brothers in positions of trust, as stewards and secretaries and the like.

"I never expected to see you again," I told Guy.

"Nor I, you. Especially after word reached Amboise that you were dead."

Guy's stark words had me gaping at him, jaw slack and eyes wide. "Dead?"

He nodded. "You and your mother both. How came you to be here in England?"

"My mother wished to join her brother, Sir Rowland Velville, at the court of King Henry the Seventh."

That was the same answer I always gave, the answer I believed to be the truth. But for the first time, seeing the doubtful look on

Guy's face, I wondered if there might have been more to our hasty departure from France than a sudden desire to be reunited with my uncle.

"Who told you we had died?" I asked.

"It was a long time ago. What does it matter now?"

"Do you mean you do not remember, or that you would rather not say?"

"No one person told me, Jeanne. Everyone in Amboise said it was so. And there was other talk, too."

"Of what sort?"

He shrugged. "Gossip. Nothing more."

"Master Dunois," the boy interrupted. "His Grace cannot go to the Tower without us."

Guy barely glanced at the lad. "Go and tell my lord the duke that I will be with him in a moment, Ivo. Will we be allowed visitors?" He addressed the question to me.

"The king has given orders that his prisoners are to be treated as honored guests. I will find a way to speak with you again. I have so many questions."

"So do I, Jeanne," Guy said, and bade me farewell.

I wanted to call him back, to ask about this "other talk" he had mentioned. I did not like the sound of that. But guards were waiting to take the duke and his servants to the Tower and I had no choice but to let Guy go.

5

Rumors also flew in the days following the arrival of the French prisoners of war, but most had to do with Scotland, not France. A Scots army had invaded England. It was variously reported to be forty thousand, sixty thousand, even one hundred thousand strong.

However great the Scottish force, it had to be stopped. Queen Catherine was spurred on by the memory of her late mother, Queen Isabella of Castile, who had personally led the army that drove the Moors out of Spain. Catherine set herself to rally the people to defend the realm. She rode north at the head of a band of citizens of London and gentlemen and yeomen from the home counties to join the army already defending northern England. The cannon from the Tower went with her.

The Lady Mary and her household stayed behind, taking up residence in the royal apartments in the Tower of London for safety. The duc de Longueville and the other French prisoners were thus temporarily displaced and reassigned other quarters nearby. Our move to the Tower pleased me greatly. I was eager to question Guy further. And I had no objection to seeing more of the handsome duke.

"It is difficult to remember that you have not always lived here at court, Jane," the Lady Mary remarked when I asked her permission to visit Guy Dunois, "but how do you know one of the duke's men?"

"We were children together before I came to England. Guy's mother's house was but a stone's throw from the one my mother leased whenever the French court was at Amboise." No royal court stayed in one place long. The French king moved from château to château along the Loire and made occasional visits to Paris and other cities.

Mary pondered for a moment, then sent one of her quick, sunny smiles in my direction. "It is only polite that I entertain the duc de Longueville in the queen's absence. I will invite him to walk with me after dinner in the gallery my father built. And I will bid him bring Master Guy Dunois, his servant, so that you may spend time with him."

I said, "As you wish, Your Grace," but inwardly I sighed in frustration. Although the Lady Mary treated me as a friend and confidante, I could never forget that she was a king's daughter and I was not. Mary took for granted that she would be obeyed. She did not always take other people's feelings into consideration, not even mine. That is the way it is with royalty.

I had hoped to converse with Guy in private. The presence of both the princess and the duke would make it difficult to ask questions. I was not certain why I did not want the Lady Mary to hear about those false rumors of my death, but anything to do with

France while we were at war was sensitive and I thought it wise to be cautious.

The timber-framed gallery to which we repaired that afternoon had been built less than a decade earlier atop the curtain wall that ran from the King's Tower across a gateway to Julius Caesar's Tower. It had been designed to give a splendid view of the privy garden below—rampant lions and crouching dragons fashioned out of shrubbery; roses and woodbine growing on trellises; and several unusual species of tree, each planted in the center of a raised bed. I had been told one was a fig, one a mulberry, and one a Glastonbury thorn, but I did not know which was which.

In September, the garden was not as colorful as in summer, but in any season the shapes were pleasing to the eye. The center of the garden was filled with turf, and stone benches were scattered here and there around the perimeter of this expanse of green. The view should have instilled a sense of peace in the beholder. Instead, as we waited for the two French prisoners to join us in the gallery, it provoked the disconcerting realization that, like those trees, I had been transplanted on a royal whim.

It was not the first time I had been plagued by such thoughts. Usually, I managed to suppress them. I was happy at court. I had a busy, fulfilling life. I had friends. Unlike that Glastonbury thorn, I was not just decorative.

I was, however, still an oddity. I winced, remembering how I'd once wondered if King Henry VII had collected me, as he did his curiosities. I found consolation in reminding myself that at least I did not require a keeper!

My position at the English court *was* out of the ordinary. I had always known that, although I did not like to dwell on the subject. I told myself that there was no reason to be troubled by it. I was fed and clothed and entertained and all I had to do in return was wait on a girl-child of great beauty—and only a few unpleasant habits.

I glanced at the Lady Mary. She had the family temper and a self-centered outlook—those were drawbacks, indeed. But she rarely unleashed her fury on me. There were times when I thought that she looked upon me as the next thing to a second older sister.

But I was *not* her sister. I was not her maid of honor or one of her ladies-in-waiting either. Mary had appointed me "keeper of the princess's jewels," but the title carried no stipend. Unlike others in the royal household, I was paid nothing for my services. I had a small annuity, granted by the seventh King Henry, but it was not enough to live on.

As we waited in the gallery, I thought back to my first meeting with the late king. Henry VII had made me welcome and assured me that I would always have a home at court. But now a long-buried question had come back to haunt me: Why had I, of all the French-speaking girls in the world, been the one selected to join the children of honor at Eltham?

Everyone around me knew exactly who they were and where they belonged. Family connections and marriage alliances—some going back many generations—defined them. All I had was an uncle, Sir Rowland Velville, who barely acknowledged my existence. At the moment, he was off fighting the French with King Henry, but he had never been part of my life. Watching him compete in tournaments over the years had been as close as I'd ever come to spending time with him.

"Those clouds look most threatening," the Lady Mary murmured.

I heard the edge of fear in her voice and promptly banished other considerations from my mind. Even as a small child, the princess had been deathly afraid of thunderstorms.

"Do you wish to retire to your chamber?" I asked. Among the relics she kept there was a small gilded box, a reliquary that contained a saint's tooth reputed to have the power to ward off lightning strikes.

She made a visible effort to steady herself. "You have been looking forward to speaking with your former countryman. I would not wish to deprive you of the opportunity."

"That is most considerate of you, Your Grace, but another time will serve as well."

I could sense her inner struggle as she cast another nervous glance toward the lowering sky. "I have women enough to wait on me without requiring your services, Jane. Stay and make my excuses to the duke."

Ignoring my expressions of gratitude, she sped away, delaying only long enough to give orders to the yeomen of the guard that the prisoners had her permission to enter the gallery.

Left alone, I turned again toward the windows. It was not yet twilight, but the world beyond the panes was already murky. Eerie shadows played on the expensive imported glass.

In an instant, a blinding glare of lightning flashed so close that I jumped. Then thunder crashed, pulsing like a living thing. I pulsed, too.

In normal circumstances I would have been alert for the sound of leather shoes slapping against the stone floor. This time the only warning I had was the smell of ambergris. The expensive scent emanated from the duc de Longueville, wafting out from the pomander ball he wore at his waist to block out disagreeable odors. Both Guy and the boy Ivo followed a few paces behind him.

"Have I come too early to my rendezvous with Her Grace?" The duke's expression was somber and his voice grave. He squinted to see me in the dimness. Only a few candles illuminated the gallery, but that was sufficient for him to recognize me. "You are Mistress Popyncourt, I believe."

I made the obeisance due to one of his rank. I spoke, as he had, in French. "Yes, My Lord. I am Jane Popyncourt."

"I had thought to find your mistress here."

He did not sound disappointed by her absence, which secretly pleased me. Keeping my gaze firmly on the juniper and wormwood-laced rushes at our feet, I explained that the princess had a fear of storms.

The duke made a *tsking* sound. He seemed amused, but I was at a loss to know why. "Are you not afraid?" he asked.

"No, Your Grace." Although my heart was racing, I was determined to appear composed. I'd had a good deal of practice at this in fifteen years of living at the English court.

Then Longueville unleashed the full force of his smile. I felt heat rise in my cheeks and had to fight the urge to stare at my toes again. He was, as I had thought from my first good look at him, a most well-favored man.

The next bolt of lightning bathed his face with an eerie glow, giving it an almost demonic cast. I told myself it was the storm that made me shiver, but in my heart I knew better. It was a different sort of thrill that shot through me as the rumble of thunder followed a few seconds after the flash. The full fury of the tempest would soon begin to fade, but inside the gallery a new kind of storm was brewing.

"I admire bravery in a woman, Mistress Popyncourt, especially one so beautiful as you." The look of approval on the duke's face made my heart race. I barely noticed that Guy and Ivo had retreated to the far end of the gallery, or that the guards, too, had moved out of earshot.

"Storms fill the air with excitement, Your Grace." My voice

sounded a trifle unsteady. We stood side by side at the south-facing window and watched a distant bolt of lighting streak across the sky.

"And danger?"

"And danger," I agreed.

"It is the violence," he said, and slid an arm around my waist.

Over the tops of trees and bushes bent by the wind, we could just glimpse the choppy waters of the Thames. I smiled to myself, remembering another storm and another man. I had stood just this way at a window in Pleasure Palace, looking out at the Thames with Charles Brandon. Then I had been driven by curiosity to sample my first real kiss. Now something more intense stirred in me, generated by nothing more than the touch of the duke's hand resting on my hip.

The river was so roiled up by the storm that the few boats fool-ish enough to be out on its surface were tossed about as if they were no heavier than bits of kindling. At the sight, another shiver ran through me.

"Are you cold, mistress?" Longueville whipped off the velvet cloak he wore and wrapped it around my shoulders. "We might retire to a less drafty spot." His intense gaze left me in no doubt that he had somewhere much more private in mind.

The heavy, richly embroidered fabric enclosed me in a protec-tive cocoon, but I was already much too warm. "I am quite com-fortable as I am," I assured him, shrugging out of the garment and handing it back to him.

He flung it carelessly behind him, trusting that one of his ser-vants would be there to catch it before it landed. The duke's faith was justified, and for just a moment my eyes locked with Guy's in the dim light. The message was unmistakable—beware the duke!

I knew the dangers well enough, but never before had a man

attracted me so strongly. The sight of him, the smell of him, the sound of his deep, resonant voice—all these drew me to him. For the first time ever, I wanted to experience this fascinating man with all my senses.

"I have been lonely in my captivity," he murmured, dipping his head close to mine.

"Mayhap you need a pet," I teased. He had said he admired bravery. I would be more than brave. I would be bold. I had been at ease with kings and princes since childhood. What did I have to fear from a mere duke?

His laugh charmed me. "What do you suggest, Mistress Jane? A bird, perhaps? A dog?"

"Oh, no, Your Grace. Only a monkey will do."

The startled expression on his face made me smile. He did not seem to know whether to laugh or be insulted.

"The late King Henry had a spider monkey," I explained, remembering Jot with fondness. "He loved the creature dearly. Why, once His Grace even forgave it for destroying a little book full of notes and memorials, writ in his own hand."

"That cannot be true," Longueville protested. "A king's rage at the loss of such an important possession should have been exceedingly great."

"So one would think, Your Grace. And the members of the royal family are far from temperate when something displeases them. But in this instance the king only laughed."

He still looked skeptical.

Anxious to convince him that I spoke truly, I added more, something no one had dared speak of at the time. "It is said a groom of the king's privy chamber egged the creature on. The courtiers all hated His Grace's habit of recording their every failing in that little book."

Longueville's laughter burst forth again. "Animals can be the very devil. I once had a hunting dog that could track any game, but he developed an unfortunate addiction to tallow candles."

"You do not mean—?"

"Oh, yes. He ate all he could find. We feared there would not be a light left in the castle if he continued as he was."

"What did you do?" I feared I was about to hear that he'd had the dog put down, but the duke surprised me.

"He was the best hunter I had. I ordered extra candles made for him, with drippings from the game he'd caught himself."

"I fear I am not fond of dogs," I confessed. "Some of the Lady Mary's women keep spaniels and I cannot abide their yapping."

"Lapdogs. They can scarcely be considered dogs at all. Why, such creatures are as annoying as ferrets, and less useful." He winked, surprising a laugh out of me. We both knew why some people wore pet ferrets wrapped around their necks like a ruff—ferrets ate lice.

While we had been talking, the storm had passed. Pinpoints of light now dotted the early evening sky as stars began to come out. "I should have returned long since to the princess," I murmured.

"It is early yet. Stay awhile. Do you ride, Mistress Popyncourt? Last year I purchased a splendid courser and two brood mares from Francesco Gonzaga, Marquis of Mantua. He is famous as a breeder of horses. Never have I owned better-trained animals."

"I enjoyed riding when I was younger," I told him, "but now Queen Catherine insists that we ladies use Spanish sidesaddles." I made a face. Shaped like chairs, these saddles did not permit much freedom of movement.

His voice deepened. "King Henry treated me well when I was brought to him as a prisoner, but his queen seems disinclined to follow his lead."

"She is Spanish. She is suspicious of anyone born in France."

"Except for you, Mistress Popyncourt," he said. "Why is that, do you suppose?"

"I was born in Brittany, not France."

"Ah," he said, understanding the distinction at once.

A nearby candle guttered, throwing the gallery into deeper shadow. I sensed the duc de Longueville bending toward me and felt a delicious prickle of anticipation at the center of my being. His lips—soft, full lips—lightly brushed my mouth.

From behind us came the sound of a throat clearing. Loudly. It was Guy. The yeoman of the guard would not have dared hint that a nobleman had overstepped the bounds of propriety. Longueville stepped back so abruptly that I felt chilled.

"Your Grace?"

"I have kept you here far too long, Mistress Popyncourt, but I am certain we will meet again . . . if you so desire." He lifted my hand to his mouth and I felt the imprint of his lips through the thin leather of my glove.

I stared blankly after the duke until he and Ivo had gone. Guy stayed behind. Belatedly, I remembered that my original intention had been to speak privately with him. I frowned, recalling the look my childhood friend had given me.

"You are not my keeper, Guy Dunois," I said.

"That does not mean you do not need one."

"I have lived at court for many years. I am accustomed to flirting with courtiers, noblemen and gentlemen alike."

"Not French noblemen," Guy muttered.

I saw no reason to be alarmed by the duke's interest in me. Neither did I want to quarrel. "It was you I wanted to talk to, Guy."

"You have an odd way of showing it."

The sound of shuffling feet told me that the remaining guard grew impatient. He had waited to escort Guy back to his quarters. The prisoners of war were confined in considerable luxury, but they were still prisoners.

"It is late." More time than I'd realized had passed while I engaged in pleasant conversation with the duke. "Mayhap we should talk another time."

He sketched a mocking bow. "As my lady wishes."

THE FOLLOWING DAY, I sought Guy in the duc de Longueville's lodgings in one of the many towers that made up the Tower of London. I encountered Ivo first. A gangly youth not yet grown into his feet, he directed me to a small inner chamber. When his voice broke halfway through this short speech, splotches of color stained his pale face.

In the room Ivo had indicated, I found Guy hard at work scribbling numbers in a ledger at a writing table. Papers were strewn across the table's surface along with a scattering of quills and bottles of ink.

"Are you a clerk, then?" I asked.

Guy looked up in annoyance. Tiny spectacles slid down his nose. He removed them, closed the account book, and set the spectacles on top of it. "I serve as His Grace's steward. I manage his estates when we are at home. And my own."

"You have done well for yourself?"

"Well enough. What is it you want, Jeanne?"

"Jane."

"His Grace is at the tennis play," he said. Then he lapsed into a disapproving silence.

"I did not come here looking for the duke."

I glanced around the antechamber. Ivo had left and no one else had come in. If I wanted to learn more about the rumors Guy had heard of my demise, this was the time to ask. Yet now Guy seemed strangely unapproachable.

"Are you wroth with me?" I blurted out.

He shrugged. "I have seen too many women enthralled by an excellent physique and a surfeit of charm. My half brother has a wife and children back in France. He has naught that is honorable to offer you."

Nettled by his words, I spoke without thinking. "Have you not heard of courtly love? A woman may derive great pleasure simply from being in a man's company."

"That is not the kind of pleasure the duc de Longueville has in mind. Be careful, Jane, lest you end up as his plaything."

I scowled at Guy, pretending to be insulted. At the same time, my heart beat a little faster and a heady excitement began to build inside me. Had the duke spoken of me? One part of me knew I should heed Guy's warning. Another urged me to seize the chance, mayhap my only chance, to step out into a storm of passion.

For years I had avoided engaging in anything more than mild flirtation with the men of King Henry's court. Charles Brandon's abrupt loss of interest in me had been proof that none of them would take me to wife without a dowry, and I'd had no interest in becoming some English courtier's mistress.

This was different. Longueville was a nobleman, his rank high enough to protect me from the scorn that might otherwise come my way. That he had a wife did not trouble me. I was never likely to meet her. What mattered was that I was drawn to him, as I had not been to any other man I'd met. And he, if Guy's intimations were to be believed, returned my interest.

Curiosity and lust are a potent combination. I started to speak, then thought better of it. Longueville was England's enemy, a prisoner of war. He would return to France as soon as he was ransomed.

So would Guy.

If I wanted answers about my past, I must ask my questions while I had the chance. I placed both hands on the table and leaned forward until we were quite close. "I want to speak to you of days gone by."

His expression gave nothing away. "As you wish."

I cleared my throat, still oddly hesitant to begin. "Have you all you need to be comfortable here?" I asked instead.

"All save the duke's ransom." He indicated the closed ledger. "We are housed in luxury but your king allots us only forty shillings a week to live on."

I was surprised by the paltry amount and said so.

He shrugged. "Prisoners are expected to augment that sum from their own funds, but the duke's only recourse would be to sell off his wardrobe and jewels, and that he will not do. We are reduced to living on pottage, brown bread, and cheese."

"When the king returns, you will be given accommodations at court until the duke's ransom is arranged. That will entitle you to three cooked meals a day."

"You will pardon me if I remain skeptical."

"The duke has been permitted to keep six servants," I reminded him.

"With funds barely sufficient to keep one in food and candles. The constable of the Tower tells me that stipends for prisoners have not been increased in decades."

Guilt assailed me. As one of the Lady Mary's attendants I regularly had my choice among dishes of beef, mutton, veal, capon, cony, pheasant, pigeon, lamb, and chicken, not to mention a plentiful supply of butter and fruit and pastries. "I wish I could help, but

I receive no stipend at all, only a tiny annuity scarce sufficient to purchase New Year's gifts for the members of the royal family."

That silenced Guy's complaints about money and all else. He rose and offered me his stool. I shook my head and we stood facing each other.

I met his steady gaze with my own. "Do you wish that the duke had left you behind when he went off to war? You might be free now. If not for your half brother, you might be riding through your own fields, supervising the harvest."

Guy smiled slightly. His sea green eyes lost their forbidding look. "I was the one who persuaded Longueville that he should take me along on campaign instead of another of our father's bastards, our brother Jacques. I wanted an adventure. Still, I cannot regret coming here. How else should I have found you again?"

"Was I truly supposed to be dead?"

"I fear so." He took both my hands in his and his eyes twinkled in a way I remembered well from our shared childhood. "But I am beyond pleased to have found you alive and well."

Tentatively, I smiled back. "It is a great mystery to me why anyone should have thought my mother and I had died."

"That was the story on everyone's lips. There was no reason to doubt it. You and your mother had gone off without a proper escort. No guards. No servants. I supposed that you had been killed by outlaws bent on robbing you."

"You said there were other rumors."

Guy released me to move to the window and stand staring out at the White Tower, the oldest part of the castle, and the temporary buildings erected in front of it to house court officials in need of work space after a fire the year before at Westminster Palace had destroyed their offices.

I crossed to him and placed my gloved hand on his arm.

"Maman died shortly after we arrived in England. She never told me why we left France."

I remembered her words to me that day at the inn in London: *I will explain everything in good time.* But she had not lived long enough to keep that promise.

For the present it is best that you do not know too much. She had said that, too. I had not known what she meant then and did not now. But now it seemed important that I find out.

"Tell me what people said about us, Guy. I have a right to know."

"I do not want to upset you." Turning, he placed his hand over mine. His grip was firm and somehow comforting, even if his words were not. "I remember how you adored your mother."

I felt queasy but ignored the sensation. "Nothing you tell me will change my love for her or erase my fond memories."

Reluctance writ large upon his face, he stared at our joined hands, thus avoiding meeting my eyes while he gathered his thoughts. "On the day after you disappeared, members of the royal guard—the *gens d'armes*—came to the house where you lived in Amboise."

Inhaling sharply, I felt as if I had taken a blow. This news did not bode well.

"When they found only your servants in residence, they took your governess away with them."

I struggled to recall the woman, but she had only been employed to look after me for only a short time. I could not bring to mind either her name or her face. "Why did they arrest her? And where did they take her?"

"No one knew. That is why there was so much speculation. Coming so hard upon King Charles's death in the château above the town, there were some who said the two events must be connected."

I stared at him, not only unwilling but unable to form the words to ask the next logical question.

Guy took pity on me. "That was sheer foolishness, I am certain. The king's death was sudden, but it was an accident. He struck his head on a lintel. He was surpassing tall and the doorway was very low."

I blinked at him, confused. I had never thought to ask how the king of France had died . . . or why my mother had left court immediately after his death. "He died of a blow to the head?"

Frowning, Guy released my hand and turned away. He stared out at the White Tower again, his thoughts clearly far away. "The accident brought on an apoplexy, or so I have been told. King Charles did not collapse at once. It was several hours before he fell unconscious and could not be revived."

I was certain there was more to the story but I was hesitant to ask outright. I waited in an agony of suspense for him to continue. After a few moments, he did, his voice so low I could only just make out his words.

"He had eaten an orange that morning. Some said it was poisoned."

My breath hitched. "P-p-poison?"

Of a sudden, I felt light-headed. I did not need to hear the words to know that the *gens d'armes* might have come looking for Maman because they thought she'd had something to do with the king's death. She had been there in the château, in attendance on Queen Anne. I could not imagine why suspicion would fall on her, but clearly it had. Then an alternate explanation occurred to me.

"Mayhap Queen Anne sent the guards because she was concerned for Maman's well-being."

"I do not think so, Jane. Remember that it is the custom in France for a royal widow to lie in bed for six weeks in a darkened room lit only by candles, cut off from the rest of the world. Queen Anne was already in seclusion on the day after King Charles's death and in no position to give orders."

"Then perhaps it was the governess they sought all along and not Maman."

But Guy shook his head. "They asked all the neighbors if they had seen your mother. She was the object of their search, Jane. There is no doubt about that."

"But why? Maman was a good person. She'd never have harmed anyone." Whatever I had thought to learn from Guy, this was not it.

He glanced at the curtained doorway to make certain there was no one in the next room before he spoke again. Even though we were alone, he kept his voice low. "You know what royal courts are like. Ambition and intrigue abound. I cannot say for certain, but it is likely your mother had some connection to Louis d'Orléans."

"Louis d'Orléans? The duc de Longueville?" I was truly confused now, and again felt light-headed.

"Two men bore that name in those days."

Guy guided me to the stool and left me there while he went to a nearby cabinet. The screech of hinges in need of oiling made me jump, and I gave a nervous, embarrassed laugh. When Guy produced a cup and a bottle of wine, I accepted a drink without demur.

"The Louis d'Orléans I mean is not the duc de Longueville, but rather Louis the Twelfth, king of France. Shortly before King Charles's death, Charles was investigating his cousin Louis d'Orléans for certain actions he took as governor of Normandy. They were at odds, too, because Louis had refused to lead Charles's army to Asti in a renewal of the French campaign against the Italian city-states. It seemed as if Louis was waiting for Charles to die, as if he remained close so he could more easily seize the throne."

"Was he not the rightful heir?"

"He was one of them. François d'Angoulême had as good a claim, but he was a child of three at the time and no one wanted another regency."

A few sips of wine had revived me and helped me think more calmly. "How do you come to know all this?" I asked. "You were scarce older than I was back then."

"I kept my ear to the ground." His gaze locked for an instant with mine. "And I wanted to know what had happened to you."

"My mother had naught to do with King Louis, and naught to do with King Charles's death."

"Are you certain?"

"Did rumors suggest my mother acted on behalf of Louis d'Orléans?"

Guy winced at my sharp tone of voice. "I've told you as much. All manner of stories were bandied about. Most died away as fast as they sprang up, but Louis *was* nearby, at Blois." He shrugged.

In my agitation, I stood and began to pace. Maman must have known Louis would be the next king. When she fled from court, had she been running from him? Had she somehow known *he* poisoned King Charles?

But no. That made no sense. Queen Anne had gone on to marry her late husband's successor. She was married to him still.

"When did word come to Amboise that Maman and I were dead?"

Guy ran one hand over a face that suddenly looked more weary than his years. The dark stubble shadowing his jaw made him seem more soldier than courtier and his eyes were sad. "It was perhaps a month after you disappeared."

"Where did the rumors say we died? And of what cause?"

Guy shook his head. "No one knew any details. Although I was still a child, I asked. Then I grieved for you . . . as my friend." Another shrug. "Soon afterward I left Amboise to enter the service of my half brother."

Pressing my fingers to my brow, I tried to think, tried to remember the details of our departure from Amboise and our journey to Calais. Those weeks of travel remained a blur, although I knew we had avoided the main roads and waterways. But my first clear recollections were of Calais and crossing the Narrow Seas and arriving in England.

"Maman must have feared pursuit," I murmured. "We did not stay with friends. And I had to promise not to speak to anyone on the journey. She would not even let me say farewell to you, Guy."

I tried to tell myself that Maman had been frightened away by the fear of *false* accusations, that she'd fled because she could so easily have been blamed for something she had not done. Mayhap she had started the rumors of her death herself. There was irony in that, seeing as she did die not many months later.

"I want to know the truth, no matter how terrible it is."

"That may never be possible." Guy's arms came around me. "It was all a long time ago," he whispered. "Fifteen years. What can any of it possibly matter now?"

WHEN KING HENRY VII was alive, he enjoyed no sport better than tennis, not even a good tournament. He built tennis plays at all his principal residences and until a few years before his death was as enthusiastic a player as he was a spectator. A game was already in progress when the Lady Mary's entourage arrived at that freestanding structure in the Tower of London.

Once the princess was settled in the upper gallery, furnished with cloth-of-gold cushions and a chair under a canopy of estate, I approached the window overlooking the covered tennis court and peered down at the players.

The duc de Longueville looked up at me, his black eyes alight with pleasure. He acknowledged the Lady Mary's presence by sketching a bow before the game resumed. The duke served a small, hard, white-kid-covered ball, sending it winging across the fringed cord that divided the court in two.

I could not stop myself from staring at him. His shirt, dampened by perspiration, clung to his broad chest. As was common with most men when they played tennis, he wore only silk drawers ornamented with gold cord. From their hem to his soft, square-toed shoes, his excellently shaped legs were bare.

So absorbed was I in assessing his figure that I barely recognized Longueville's opponent as Guy Dunois, similarly attired. To return a ball, Guy threw himself into the air, nearly crashing into a wall. The ball flew straight into a window frame on the opposite side of the court.

Although I had watched tennis matches for years, I still did not understand the game. The rules are complicated—a deliberate attempt, I suspect, to assure that only educated men can play. I did know that when one player failed to return the ball, points were scored according to how far from the center cord that ball had come to rest.

I leaned forward in order to see better. When the ball struck the wire mesh directly in front of me with a resounding twang, I jumped back.

The Lady Mary whooped with laughter. She was in a jovial mood that put me in mind of her brother the king. "Shall we wager on the outcome?" she asked when she had her mirth under control. That, too, smacked of King Henry.

I held my hands spread wide. "I have no money with which to gamble, Your Grace."

"Risk something you value, then. Your pendant." She pointed to the tiny enameled dragon I wore suspended from my waist.

Most people did not notice it alongside my rosary and my pomander ball. But the Lady Mary knew it was there, and she knew what it meant to me. The bit of jewelry was one of the few things I had by which to remember my mother. I clasped a protective hand around the little dragon, feeling the edges bite into my palm through my glove.

Caught up in the match, Mary did not notice my distress. "I wager ten pounds against your bauble," she said, "on the duc de Longueville to win."

A sudden tightness in my chest left me fighting tears. Certain that I would lose, I ran one finger over the small keepsake, caressing the smoothly cold surface of the tiny dragon body, feeling the protuberances of its head and wings and feet. Then my hand moved to the rosary beside it and I murmured a brief prayer.

Since my conversation with Guy, I had been unable to stop thinking about my mother and how little I knew of her. She had married at fifteen. I remembered her telling me that when Papa died only a few months before we left France. And she had married for love. She had told me that, too, for Papa was not a Breton, nor even a landowner, but rather a Flemish merchant who did business in both Brittany and France.

Maman had been raised in the household of Duchess Anne of Brittany, later Queen Anne of France, after her own mother died. If she ever spent much time with relatives on either side of her family, she had never spoken of it to me. After I met my uncle, Sir Rowland, I pictured the rest of the Velvilles as distant as he was.

As play continued, I focused on Guy. If he had been

Longueville's companion for fifteen years, surely he would have received training in jousting, hunting, hawking, and all other sports. The duke had been the captain of a company comprised of a hundred gentlemen of the French king's horse at the time he was taken prisoner. Since Guy was here with him, he must have been one of that hundred. A soldier, then.

He was shorter than the duke—only a few inches taller than I—and had a slighter, more wiry build than his half brother. As I watched, Guy leapt halfway across the court to return the ball, scoring a point. For a moment I let myself hope he might prevail, but despite Guy's considerable athletic prowess, the duke far outshone him.

Longueville handled his racquet as if he had been born holding one. Moreover, he was a nobleman and Guy's master. I knew too well how unwise it was to try to outshine the sun. No matter how much energy Guy exerted, he was unlikely to win the match. In the end, he would not even try to emerge victorious. He would give the duke a good game but make certain Longueville won.

When the match reached its inevitable conclusion, the Lady Mary beckoned to me, commanding my presence at her side. She looked well pleased with the outcome until she glimpsed my face. She caught my hand before I could finish unclasping my pendant.

"This wager was a foolish impulse on my part. I would never deprive you of something you treasure so dearly."

"Then I am in your debt, Your Grace."

I might have said more, but her attention had already shifted to the court below. "He is a most well-favored fellow," she murmured.

Following her gaze, I felt again the fierce pull of desire. To prevent taking a chill, the duc de Longueville had donned a rumpled crimson velvet tennis coat decorated with strips of dark blue satin.

His face, sweat streaked and glowing with health and vitality, lifted toward the royal box. Once again, he bowed to the Lady Mary.

The princess sent a sidelong glance my way. "I vow," she murmured, "he is almost as toothsome as Charles Brandon."

A mischievous little smile played around her mouth. Two years earlier, when Mary was sixteen and had admired Brandon's prowess in a tournament, I had confided in her, telling her of his brief courtship of me when I was her age. I also told her I thought myself fortunate to have escaped the entanglement heart-whole.

She'd been fascinated by her brother's friend ever since.

Longueville and Guy had just left to wash and change their clothing when a great shout went up outside the tennis play. A messenger in the queen's livery appeared a moment later, bearing a letter to the Lady Mary from Queen Catherine. She did not have to read it to know there had been an English victory. All around us people were cheering as the news spread.

"Our army engaged the Scots at a place called Flodden," Mary said as she skimmed the letter. "Queen Catherine herself was not on the battlefield, but she claims the triumph as her own."

We'd heard already how Catherine had inspired the troops. Soldiers had joined her cavalcade all along the way north, swelling ranks that had once been outnumbered by the Scottish invaders. Pride in my countrymen and my queen filled me with a fierce joy . . . until I saw Mary's face change. Tears welled in her eyes, although she did not permit them to fall.

"What is it?" I stepped closer, shielding her from prying eyes.

"King James the Fourth of Scotland is dead."

I thought at once of Margaret, Mary's sister and my one-time playfellow. The king of Scotland was her husband. His death left her a widow at twenty-three. Would she grieve for him? Given what I knew of Margaret, and the reports that had come out of

Scotland over the years, she would be as upset by her loss of influence as by James's death. Scotland had a new king now, James V, Margaret's son. The boy was still an infant. The country would have to be ruled by a regent for many years to come.

Mary's breath caught as she read on. "Catherine lists half the nobility of Scotland here."

"Prisoners?"

"Dead. Killed in the battle."

I stared at her in shock. Noblemen were supposed to be captured and held for ransom. I'd believed that the French admiral who had butchered Lord Edward was an exception, but it seemed the English generals could be just as brutal.

"Catherine has ordered James's body embalmed and sent to Richmond Palace," Mary whispered. "She writes that she plans to send James's blood-stained coat to Henry as proof of how good a steward she has been for his realm in his absence."

I could imagine King Henry's reaction to that. He'd think she was trying to belittle his own accomplishment. She'd killed a king—his sister's husband. All he'd done was capture a duke.

Sickened by the reports of carnage, and by the pleasure most people seemed to take in them, I wanted nothing more than to retreat from public view. It was not to be. The Lady Mary was expected to speak to the crowd gathered within the Tower precincts. She and all her household had to appear to rejoice at the news of England's great victory over the Scots.

6

The night after we received word of the Battle of Flodden, the Lady Mary suffered from nightmares. The next night, she ordered me to keep her company. It was not uncommon for one of her ladies to sleep with her for warmth, but what she wanted from me was distraction.

Closed into the high, curtained bed, the covers pulled up to our chins, we were as private as anyone could ever be at court. In the room beyond, several more of her women slept on pallets on the floor. If we spoke too loudly, we would be overheard.

"I do not wish to think of blood and battle," the princess said. "Tell me what you have learned from your French friend."

I hesitated, uncertain it would be wise to admit that my mother had been thought capable of killing a king. I did not believe for a moment that she had done so, but the royalty of any country are bound to be sensitive about such matters.

Mary pouted. "I thought we were friends. You can trust me to keep your confidences."

I lay on my back, staring up at the brocade ceiler over our heads. "It appears that my mother wished to disappear. She spirited me out of France and somehow the rumor started that she and I had both died after leaving Amboise. In truth, we came here to England to begin a new life."

"Anyone would prefer England to France." Mary sounded smug.

"What troubles me is that I do not know why we had to hide where we were going. Maman promised me that she would explain, but she died before she could keep her word."

"Is there no one else you can ask?"

"My uncle must know something of her reasons, but he is with King Henry. It could be months yet before I have the opportunity to talk to him."

As we'd had reports of the war with Scotland, so, too, had we received news of King Henry's campaign against the French. After the battle in which the duc de Longueville had been captured, the English had gone to Lille, where they were entertained by Archduchess Margaret, the regent of the Netherlands. Diplomacy had replaced combat, and among the matters being discussed was a date for the Lady Mary to consummate her marriage to Charles of Castile. His title might come from a Spanish kingdom, but Charles himself had been raised by the Archduchess of Flanders. She was his aunt, the sister of that same King Philip who had once visited England. Charles had another aunt, too—our own Queen Catherine.

"Is there no one else who knew your mother when she first arrived?" Mary asked. "She was one of my mother's ladies, was she not?"

"Yes, for a few months before she died." My voice was flat, hiding the turmoil inside me.

"A few weeks is long enough to make friends. Oh! I know! You must talk to Mother Guildford. Do you not remember? Before she took charge of my household, she was in Mother's service. She must have known your maman."

I grimaced, thinking my expression hidden, but Mary knew me too well.

"Stop making faces. Mother Guildford is exactly the person you need. She has an excellent memory and she knows *everyone*. She should. Before she was in my mother's household, she served my grandmother."

"Which one?"

"Father's mother, the Countess of Richmond."

Perhaps, I thought, that was where Mother Guildford acquired her sour temperament. I remembered the countess as being irascible on her best days, and she had always seemed to go out of her way to make me feel inferior . . . when she took notice of me at all. But Mary was right. Mother Guildford was the most likely person to remember who had befriended a newcomer at court some fifteen years earlier.

Two days later, accompanied by a groom, I set out on horseback for Mother Guildford's little house near the Blackfriars' Priory, in London. She lived there in strained circumstances. Her husband's death in Jerusalem on pilgrimage had left her deep in debt. Her only income, so her son Harry had told me, came from fifty marks a year in dower rights and the rent Charles Brandon paid to live in what had once been his uncle's house in Southwark, the London suburb on the south side of the Thames. No one seemed to know why, but Sir Thomas Brandon had willed the property to the widow of his old friend Sir Richard Guildford. Perhaps he had felt sorry for her.

Mother Guildford received me in a small parlor at the upper end of the hall. It smelled of cedar and the strong, unpleasant odor of gout wort. "Why have you come now?" she asked. "It cannot be for the pleasure of my company or you would have found time to visit me long since."

Time had wrought few changes in the former lady governess. She was more irascible, it was true. And her hair that had once been brown had more gray and new lines had appeared around her eyes and mouth. Otherwise she was still the same forceful woman I remembered from my youth. She had just entered her fiftieth year.

"I thought you might wish to hear the news from court," I said from my perch atop a low Flemish chest. She was ensconced in the room's only chair.

"I am not without friends! And I have eyes to see and ears to hear." She gestured toward an open octagonal window that took up most of the gable end of the room. "No one could have missed the shouts and huzzahs and ringing bells that celebrated England's victory over the Scots."

Nodding, I allowed that the celebrations would have been difficult to miss. "I have news for you of Queen Margaret."

"Poor chit." Mother Guildford's voice abruptly softened. For a moment, I thought she shared my own conflicting feelings of joy and sorrow. "There will be another battle now," she continued. "This one political. The nobles will fight over who keeps control of the new king's person while he grows to manhood."

"Not so. Queen Catherine took a hand in arranging matters. That is my news. As the king's mother, Margaret Tudor will serve as regent."

"How long will that last? The Scots will not take to being ruled by a woman. Like as not, Margaret will soon find herself shunted aside to live out the rest of her life bereft of both husband and children."

"I do not think I would care to be a queen," I murmured.

Mother Guildford gave a snort of laughter eerily like the sound her son Harry was wont to make. "On that we can agree. Now tell me why you really came to visit me."

"Because you know everyone of any significance in all of England."

"True enough." Mother Guildford preened a bit.

"Do you remember my mother, Joan Popyncourt? She joined the household of Queen Elizabeth of York about fifteen years ago."

A hint of wariness came into Mother Guildford's expression. "She was not with us long."

"Mid-June until early September."

I thought I detected a flash of sympathy in her steel gray eyes. "Your mother came to England with you because she had family here. Talk to your uncle if you wish to know more. He is still alive, is he not?"

"Sir Rowland is abroad with the king. I will speak with him when he returns to England, but in the meantime there must be others I can ask about her."

"What is it you wish to know—and why now?"

Why did we leave France in such a hurry? Why did we bring nothing with us but our clothing? I thought to myself.

Aloud, I said only, "I have found myself remembering her of late and wondering about her last days. I thought perhaps she might have confided in you, mayhap told you what her reasons were for leaving France."

"I did not know her well enough to inspire confidences."

"Did anyone?" I held my breath.

"No."

I hid my disappointment. My gaze shifted to my hands, folded in my lap. I clasped them together so tightly that the seam on one glove popped.

I could feel Mother Guildford's gaze boring into me. She waited until I looked at her to say, "She was already dying by the time she reached England."

"That is not possible! Surely if there was something wrong with her when we left France I would have noticed."

"You were a child, Jane. Your mother took pains to hide her illness from you. A wasting sickness, as I recall." Sitting stiffly in her leather-backed chair, Mother Guildford's expression was set in grim lines. "No doubt *that* is why she came to England. She hoped her brother would provide for you, as he did by finding you a place at Eltham."

She could have found me a place at the court of Anne of Brittany, I thought. Besides, Mother Guildford's explanation did not mesh with my memory of that first meeting between my mother and King Henry.

"My uncle cares little about me. Indeed, he has gone out of his way to avoid me since my mother died."

"He did his duty by you. Upon her death, you became a royal ward."

"Maman talked privately with the king when we first arrived. I was in the room with them. He promised to look after us both." That, too, now that I thought about it, seemed strange. Why had he taken responsibility for me?

"Underage children of the gentry and nobility almost always become wards of the crown when their parents die. Do not think yourself anything out of the ordinary."

But I was, I thought. I'd had no wealth or property to be used for the king's benefit during my minority. Why had he bothered to assume responsibility for me? And why, since I *had* been his ward, had he not found me a husband? In the ordinary way of things, that was the first duty of a guardian. There had to be more to the story.

"Who was with my mother when she died? If not a friend or confidante, then what servant had she? Which of the queen's other ladies was her bedfellow?" Few at court had the luxury of a bed to themselves. I could not remember ever sleeping alone. I usually shared both chamber and bed with one or two other gentlewomen.

Reluctantly, Mother Guildford said, "We were on progress."

"I remember. That was the reason Maman could not come to Eltham to visit me." King Henry VII, Queen Elizabeth of York, the Countess of Richmond, and their households had all traveled together, first into Essex and then north. Along the way they'd visited numerous courtiers and stayed at an assortment of castles and manors.

"She died at Collyweston," Mother Guildford continued. "That was the king's mother's principal residence. When it was clear that your mother was dying, the countess ordered her removed to a small room of her own for fear of contagion."

"She was left alone?" Horrible thought!

"One of the royal physicians was likely sent to her. She'd have had a servant to see to her needs."

"Who?"

"How should I remember? It was many years ago."

"What physician, then?"

"I do not know." Mother Guildford held up a hand, palm toward me, to stop me from asking more questions. "I have an excellent memory, Jane, but I cannot recall every detail, nor can I tell you something I never knew."

"Did Maman have a confessor? Surely a priest must have given her last rites."

"I am certain one did, but again I have no idea who he might have been."

"Someone must know. Who might I ask?"

"The queen's household was broken up when Elizabeth of York died. By then I had been placed in charge of the Lady Mary's household at Eltham. I do not know where anyone went. They are scattered, if not dead, by this time. It would be most difficult to track them down and I do much doubt they could tell you any more than I have. No one knew your mother well, Jane. She was not with us long enough and she kept to herself."

In my agitation, I could no longer be still. I stood and began to pace, my steps taking me to the cold hearth, then across the room to a window hung with curtains of green say. It overlooked a small garden, ill tended. "If she was ill . . . dying . . . why did no one do anything to help her?"

"Shall I tell you what I recall of your mother's illness?" Her voice sounded reluctant.

"Yes, if it please you."

"It does not particularly, but I can see you will not let the matter rest until you have satisfied your curiosity." Her tone was the same one she'd used to quell childish rebellions in the nursery. "With each passing day on progress, your mother seemed to grow weaker and more listless. She never ate much. I suppose she had difficulty keeping food down, but she did not complain. She did not ask for physic. Then, near the end, she collapsed. That is when she was separated from the other ladies. I am told she lay on her bed like a dead woman, only the movement of her eyes showing that she still lived. And then she did die."

"And no one cared."

"People sicken and die all the time, Jane. It is God's will. You must be satisfied with that."

No, I thought. *I cannot be.*

I had lived too long questioning nothing. It was past time I dug further into my own background. There *were* answers to my questions, all of them, and I was determined to find them. When my uncle returned from the French war, I would be waiting for him.

IN THE ABSENCE of both King Henry and Queen Catherine, we remained in the Tower of London. The queen, having managed things to her liking in the matter of Scotland, all without the need to travel farther north than Woburn, went on to Walsingham to visit the shrine of Our Lady. This was a popular pilgrimage for women who wished to pray for the safe delivery of healthy children.

The Lady Mary and I passed our time agreeably enough. King Henry VII's library was housed in the tower he'd built adjacent to the royal apartments. It contained French romances as well as religious tomes and histories. The Lady Mary enjoyed being read to. Still more, however, she liked to be active and she preferred to include gentlemen in her activities. The duc de Longueville accompanied us when we went to visit the royal menagerie.

"Kings of England have kept lions and leopards here at the Tower of London for as long as anyone can remember," the Lady Mary told him.

The three of us peered into the pit where one of the great cats was confined. He had a golden mane and many sharp teeth and roared when the Lady Mary threw a rock in his direction.

"In my father's reign," Mary said, "a lion just like that one mauled a man to death."

I was surprised she remembered hearing about that incident,

for she'd been no more than three at the time. It was before I came to court. Her brother Henry had been old enough that when he'd been told what happened, he'd vowed never to go near the beasts again. To the best of my knowledge, he never had.

"In France, lions are used for sport," the duke said. "Once I saw a mastiff pull down first a huge bear, then a leopard, and finally a lion, one after the other."

"My father," Mary countered, "once ordered a mastiff hanged because it presumed to fight against a lion. The lion, he said, was king and had sovereignty over all other beasts, therefore it was treason for a dog to attack it."

"Let us go look at the porcupine," I suggested.

Before we parted company with the duke, the princess invited him and the other French prisoners to dine with her the next day.

"What do you mean to offer for entertainment after we dine?" I asked as we watched Longueville walk away.

Mary's smile faded. "It was most unfair of Henry to take the King's Players away with him to war, and his fools and minstrels, as well. How am I to provide a lavish display with only a few musicians?"

"They will do well enough to provide music for dancing. And I am not without resources. I did help Harry Guildford devise some of his masques and pageants. Thanks to Harry, I know how to procure the services of tumblers, jugglers, and Morris dancers. I also know where to find John Goose."

"Henry's Goose?"

"The same." The elderly fool, once part of the young Duke of York's household at Eltham, had retired years before, but he lived in London.

I made all the arrangements. Less than twenty-four hours later, Goose was taking his final bow and the Lady Mary, wearing a new gown of carnation-colored brocade, claimed the duc de Longueville as her partner for a dance.

I found myself facing Guy Dunois as the musicians struck up a lively tune. "You look tired, Jane," he said.

I made a face at him. "You are supposed to tell me my beauty surpasses that of a rose and give me other flowery compliments."

We parted, as the dance demanded. When we faced each other again, his eyes were full of mischief. "You were never the rose, Jane, and these days, I vow, you are more like the thorn."

"How wicked of you to say so."

"I do but tell the truth. If you prick me, I will bleed."

When we danced apart again, I frowned, trying to make sense of his banter. I had never purposely hurt Guy. Was he only teasing me, or had I inadvertently caused him pain? Or did he mean that I was about to?

As we once more joined hands, he begged my pardon for his harsh words. "You are, it is certain, no English rose, nor yet a French lily, but mayhap you are one of those new blossoms from the East that now grow in the Low Countries. They call them daffodils."

For the second dance, Guy partnered the Lady Mary and I found myself facing the duc de Longueville. Rational thought fled. He paid me all the pretty compliments I could desire, making me feel like a princess myself.

He was a superb dancer, even better than King Henry. When he partnered the Lady Mary for a second time, I retired from the floor and gave myself leave to stare at him with unabashed appreciation.

Small shivers of excitement passed through me as I watched him caper and cavort. There was no question but that he was toothsome and that I was physically attracted to him. I told myself he was not for me, but I could not stop myself from imagining what skills he might bring to the bedchamber.

I repressed a sigh and chided myself for my wanton thoughts. When he was eventually ransomed, he would return to France to his wife. If he took me for a mistress now, where would I be then?

Tearing myself away, I slipped into the antechamber where the hired entertainers had gathered. It was my responsibility to make sure all of them had been fed and had received payment for their services. I stopped before the fool. "Master Goose," I said. "Well played."

"Mistress." Age had lowered the pitch of his voice, but not by much.

Some fools are innocents, in need of a keeper to make certain they are fed and clothed. Others live by their wits, daring to be outrageous but seeing far more than they ever speak of. John Goose was in the latter category. "Did you know my mother, Goose?" I asked on an impulse.

"No, mistress. She was part of Queen Elizabeth's household. I belonged to young Henry."

I might have left it at that, but if Goose knew my mother had been one of the queen's ladies, he might also recall other names. "Who else was there then?" I asked. "Can you remember?"

His brow furrowed in thought. "Before the great fire at Sheen that were, and after the great scholar Erasmus came to visit the royal children."

"No. After the fire and before the visit."

Goose thumped the side of his head with one fist. "Long ago. Long ago." Then he brightened. "Lady Lovell. She were there!"

"Sir Thomas Lovell's wife?"

"Aye, that's the one. She yet lives. She serves the new queen now."

My breath came a little faster at this news. Not only was Eleanor, Lady Lovell, in service to Queen Catherine, but so was her husband. Sir Thomas Lovell also held the post of constable of the Tower. Although he had gone north with the army to repel the Scottish invasion, he should return soon. The soldiers who had defeated the Scots were expected home well before the larger force that had gone with King Henry to France.

"Do you wish to hear the names of the others?" Goose asked.

"There are more? Ladies who served Queen Elizabeth and now serve Queen Catherine?"

"Oh, aye." His head bobbed up and down. "Lady Weston. Lady Verney. Mistress Denys. Lady Marzen. Lady Pechey, too. Some not yet married in the old days, but they were at court."

I recognized the names. I knew all these women by sight, although I was not on intimate terms with any of them. At present, five were with the queen at Walsingham. The sixth, Lady Marzen, was a member of the Lady Mary's household.

That was not entirely good news, for it revealed a flaw in Goose's memory. I had no doubt that everyone he'd named had once served Elizabeth of York, but the queen had outlived my mother by some five years and the composition of any royal retinue was wont to change with great frequency. Lady Marzen had been a minor heiress from Hertfordshire when she'd married Sir Francis, a groom of the privy chamber to King Henry VII . . . but they had not wed until well after my mother's death.

"Died, did she?" A bemused look on his face, Goose seemed to be struggling to remember something.

"My mother? Yes. At Collyweston, on progress."

Instantly, he brightened. "Skyp would have been there then. Ask Skyp."

"Alas, I cannot." Skyp, the Countess of Richmond's fool, was long in his grave.

"Always wore high-heeled shoes, did Skyp," Goose said. "Reached above his ankles."

Boots, not shoes. Poor Goose could not even keep articles of apparel straight. And yet, in spite of my doubts about the fool's memory, I asked another question. There was always a chance he would recall what I wished to know. "What priest would have given her last rites, Goose? What physician would have attended her?"

"Master Harding, clerk of the queen's closet, was a priest." Goose put both hands on his head. "Black round cap and black gown. A dull fellow."

"What happened to him?"

"Went on pilgrimage and died in the Holy Land."

Dumbfounded, I stared at him. I had heard of only one other Englishman who'd gone on pilgrimage in all the years I'd been at court. "With Sir Richard Guildford?"

"Aye. Aye. That's the one. Reached Jerusalem only to die there."

I felt as if I'd taken a blow to the midsection. Had Mother Guildford deliberately tried to mislead me? If Harding had traveled with her husband, she must have known his name. Could she have forgotten he tended my mother? It seemed unlikely. She remembered other things well enough. And she must also have known the names of all those ladies who'd returned to court to serve the new queen.

Goose picked up his pack and started to wander off, but at the door he turned back to me, eyes bright with curiosity. "If she died at Collyweston, would she not have been attended by the Countess of Richmond's servants?"

"Who was the countess's physician? Who was her confessor?"

But Goose's moments of clarity had been flashes of lightning in the dark of night. Even as I watched, he went dull eyed and slack jawed. His wits dimmed by age, he could recall no more, not even my name.

It was left to me to puzzle out who among the ladies still at court might remember my mother and be able to tell me what physician and priest were with Maman when she died.

SINCE I COULD do nothing to pursue my inquiries until we left the Tower of London and rejoined Queen Catherine's court, I set aside my questions for the nonce. The queen, sadly, had suffered another miscarriage shortly after leaving the shrine at Walsingham. She had sent word to the Lady Mary that Mary was to stay where she was. In the king's continued absence, Catherine's word, as regent, was law.

It was no hardship to remain in the Tower of London. The duc de Longueville's company amused Mary and delighted me. The princess gave orders that he be allowed to go anywhere he chose within the Tower, save for her privy lodgings, without a guard. He gave her his parole not to try to escape.

After that, we spent a great deal of time in his company. The Lady Mary laughingly called me her duenna, charged with guarding her reputation while she dallied with the well-favored duke.

Afternoons and evenings passed quickly, filled with laughter and fine food, good music, and, because the princess commanded it, dancing. The duke often chose me as his partner, although I danced with Guy, too. It was from Guy that I learned that the duc de Longueville was King Louis' distant cousin.

"I wonder if King Henry knows that," I mused as we whirled in a circle with the movements of the dance. "Prisoners' ransoms are set according to kinship as well as rank. The amount should be much higher for a king's cousin."

"*Distant* cousin," Guy repeated. The steps of the dance took us apart, then brought us together again. "And even more distantly related to King Charles."

"Then you must be, too," I said without thinking.

"I do not count." He chuckled. "Although it was through a bastard line that the Longuevilles descend from kings." I could see he was well aware of the irony of that.

When I danced with Guy, we talked and sometimes joked.

When I danced with the duc de Longueville, the mere touch of his hand created a subtle longing to be held more closely in his arms, to be alone with him.

I took care never to be out of sight of the princess. Although she did not know it, she also served as my duenna.

Then came the evening when another strong thunderstorm blew in. The princess took to her bed, and I slipped away from her lodgings to let myself into the privy gallery. Within moments, the duke joined me.

"Mistress Popyncourt. I thought I might find you here." The duke's voice was deep and smooth, and when his hands came up to caress my shoulders I abandoned myself to the sensation. We were quite alone. No guards. No princess. No Guy.

In silence we watched until the storm passed. His hands slid from my shoulders to my waist, but he made no further overtures. In the eerie quiet that followed the noisy display of flashes and bolts, I felt him sigh.

"In that direction, far to the south, is our homeland," he said.

"I was born in Brittany, not France," I reminded him, and reminded myself that Brittany had been a separate entity at the time. Only after losing a war with France had Duchess Anne agreed to marry King Charles and unite the two.

"Brittany is part of France now," the duke said, following my thought. "That makes you French."

"I am English," I insisted. *Jane, not Jeanne.*

"Are you?" The duke's lips twitched, as if my assertion amused him. "I am not certain one can change one's heritage."

"I do not remember much about France," I said. "I was only eight years old when I left. My mother brought me to England because my uncle was already here. He had come to this country with Henry Tudor, after King Henry's exile in Brittany. The Lady Mary's father," I added, lest he should confuse the two King Henrys.

For a long time, I had avoided thinking about my earliest memories. It had been too painful to dwell on what I had lost. My father had died. My mother had died. I'd been taken away from everyone else I knew and cared for. And since it hurt to remember, I had lived entirely in the present. I had turned myself into a complete Englishwoman and a loyal servant of the Crown.

Longueville turned me in his arms till we faced each other yet kept a respectable distance between our bodies. His eyes were in shadow in the dimly lit gallery, but I could see his mouth most plainly. "A pity your mother did not take you to Brittany instead. We might have met sooner."

"I suppose her family there had all died."

"And your father's family?"

"He came from Flanders. I know nothing of his kin."

More questions. I wondered if I would ever answer them all.

"Are there many Bretons at the English court?" the duke asked.

"Fewer than in the last reign. My uncle remains, as does Sir Francis Marzen." At that moment, I could think of no others.

Longueville's thumb brushed my cheek. "Such a serious

expression. Do you wish you might return someday?" He toyed with a lock of my hair that had somehow come loose from beneath my headdress.

Caught off guard by the suggestion, I took a step away from him.

He chuckled. "England and France will not always be enemies, Jane. You could return to Amboise." He touched a fingertip to my lips. "You must forgive me. I asked Guy about you. My country seat is not far from Amboise, at Beaugency. Dunois Castle has been ours since my ancestor, the Bastard of Orléans, gave his support to Joan of Arc against the English."

"Yet another time when England and France were at war. I do not think it would be wise for me to visit your homeland, my lord."

"Will you go with your princess when she marries Charles of Castile?"

I nodded. I felt no great enthusiasm at the prospect. Charles of Castile had lands in Spain and in the Netherlands. I could not imagine living in either place.

"That is a great pity," Longueville murmured. "Charles is a mere boy, not yet fourteen, with a great ugly beak of a nose."

I turned to stare out at the darkness again. I could make out dozens of darting lights—lanterns carried by boats on the Thames. "I would like to see Amboise once more," I admitted, "but I have no more choice about where I go than the princess does."

"How long has her marriage been arranged?"

"Nearly seven years now. When she marries, she will be obliged to leave her homeland forever, as her sister, Margaret, did when she married the king of Scots. Mary has already said she wants to take me with her." That would mean I'd most likely never see England again, but the alternative was even less to my liking—a pension and genteel poverty for the rest of my days. In my mind's eye I saw myself living out my life in a little house in Blackfriars, slowly turning into another Mother Guildford.

"You might return to France instead."

"I lack the wherewithal to travel, even if a peace were to last long enough to make such a thing possible."

"You might come home with me," Longueville whispered.

The flutter in my stomach, the sudden race of my heart, had me turning, lifting my face toward him. "You already have a wife."

He smiled. "She is an understanding woman. She will not object to sharing me with you."

"I do not wish to be . . . tolerated."

His smile broadened, creating deep lines around his mobile mouth. "If she finds you even half as delightful as I do, she will befriend you."

I felt my eyes narrow. "How many of your mistresses has she taken to?"

He laughed aloud at that. "You, my dearest Jane, are unique. You will enchant her, but not, I hope, in quite the same way I wish you to please me."

Slowly, giving me every chance to evade him, he lowered his head toward mine. Our lips touched. He kissed me with exquisite, gentle thoroughness. Heart racing, skin hot as fire, limbs atremble, I kissed him back.

When he took my arm, I went with him through one torchlit passage, down a stairway illuminated by lanterns, and along another corridor, this one redolent with freshly changed rushes and crushed woodruff. I knew where we were headed, but I did not demur. At that moment, I wanted to lie with him more than I wanted my next breath and it had little to do with his offer to take me with him to France.

"Shall I serve as your tiring maid?" he asked when we were alone in his bedchamber. The only light came from the hearth, bathing the chamber in a rosy glow.

Without waiting for my answer, he put his mouth on mine again and set quick, clever hands to untying the laces at my back. He freed me from my clothing with a skill and a rapidity that left me almost as dazed as the magic in his kiss.

Caught up in myriad pleasurable sensations, I never thought to protest. Everywhere he touched, I tingled. It was like being caught out in a furious storm—thrilling, exhilarating, and just a little dangerous.

When he had stripped me of all but my shift, discarding my body stitchet by tossing it halfway across the room, he started on his own clothing. I touched the place his mouth had been with the tip of my tongue and tasted him there—sweet Spanish wine and something darker and more heady still.

Doublet and hose soon lay in a disorderly heap atop my bodice and kirtle, and he was edging me backward toward the curtained bed. Laughing, he reached out to catch me by the waist and lift me up onto the mattress. With a lithe movement, he positioned himself beside me and began kissing me again.

I put a hand out to stop him. "I have not . . . I do not—"

"I know," he said. "I will be gentle with you."

His kisses were soft, his breath sweet. He knew just how to dispel a maiden's fears. The sensual aroma of ambergris surrounded us, a subtle, mossy, musky scent drifting up from the bedding.

I shook my head to clear it. "This is not wise," I murmured, more to myself than to him.

"No harm will come to you for being with me, my dearest Jeanne. I swear it."

"Jane." I corrected him without thinking, then froze, remembering that he was the duc de Longueville. He was the next thing to royalty and not to be contradicted.

He surprised me by laughing again. "I believe I shall address you as 'sweeting,' as the English do their paramours." The way he said the word, in English with a trace of a French accent, made the endearment sound as if he had coined it just for me.

I melted against him, tentatively joining in the love play. I touched my tongue to the side of his neck and tasted him.

We were lying inside the drawn curtains now, shielded from the rest of the world. Only enough light filtered through the gaps in the hangings to allow me to see the admiration in his gaze. That his glittering black eyes also contained a hint of amusement gave me pause, but only for a moment.

"Shall I call you sweeting in return?" I whispered, suddenly unsure how to address my lover. "Your Grace" seemed impossibly formal in private and I could not bring myself to call him by the Christian name he shared with the king of France.

"But I am not sweet," he protested, and tumbled with me across the wide, wool-stuffed mattress until we sank together into the dip in the middle of the bed.

"Shall I choose a spice, then?" I teased him. Greatly daring, I ran my hand over his cheek. He turned his face into my palm and kissed it.

"I have always been partial to coriander."

The name suited him, I thought. The ripe seeds had a pleasantly citrus smell.

I would willingly have played like that for hours, but with an eagerness that stirred my blood he turned his attention to making short work of my shift and his shirt. When they were gone, I had but a moment to revel in the experience of being naked in a man's arms. Enjoying every delicious new sensation, I was just beginning to learn his body and to savor his first intimate touches on mine, when he abruptly rolled me onto my back and plunged inside me.

The building pleasure was replaced by sharp, searing pain.

He begged my forgiveness, but he did not stop.

Afterward, when his breathing had calmed and the sweat had nearly dried on our still entwined bodies, he declared that he must rest awhile. "Go and wash yourself," he instructed, "but then come back to bed. The next time will please you better."

He was already snoring by the time I located the basin and ewer.

7

I could assume my chemise without difficulty, but the remainder of my clothing required lacing. That made me wonder how great court ladies managed to take secret lovers. Their tiring maids, at the least, must know every intimate detail.

Struggling to keep from tripping on my skirts, I bundled my garments in front of me and crept out of the duke's bedchamber. Young Ivo was stretched out on a pallet in front of the door. He woke with a start, stared at me in alarm, and scurried away before I could ask him to tie the points that held the back of my bodice together.

Stifling a sigh, I continued across the outer chamber. I had almost reached the door to the passageway when Guy appeared. We stood staring at each other for a long moment. Although I expected him to make some disparaging comment, he said only, "Turn around."

With deft fingers, he laced me back into my clothes. I could sense his disapproval, but he did not utter a single word of reproach.

I bore myself proudly as I left the duke's lodgings and made my way to my own small bedchamber, but halfway there a sob escaped me. It had begun so well. There had been such a fine building of excitement, of anticipation, and then . . . messy seemed to sum up the situation best.

That the duke had derived pleasure from the encounter, I knew. I suspected that I had missed out on something. I was not naive. I had heard married women talk about their lovers. The duke had taken his own release and given me none.

Resolved never to visit his bed again, I confessed my sin to the Lady Mary's chaplain the next day and went about my duties to the princess with my head held high. It was early afternoon when young Ivo, bearing a small, ornate box, sought me out in the presence chamber.

"Gifts, Jane?" The Lady Mary appeared at my elbow, eager curiosity radiating from every pore.

"I do not know, Your Grace."

"You will once you open that box."

Inside was a brooch I had last seen pinned to the duc de Longueville's bonnet. It was a pretty bauble made of three stones— peridot, garnet, and sapphire—framed in a gold border designed to resemble acanthus leaves. The Lady Mary's eyes widened when she saw it, and a short time later she spirited me away into the privacy of her bedchamber and shut her other women out.

"Do you wish to rest?" I asked when she removed the Venetian cap she wore over her long, loose hair.

The scent of lavender wafted up from the coverlet as I pushed aside the bed curtains. I offered to unlace her outer garments, that she might lie down in comfort, but she waved me away. Her expression was as serious as I'd ever seen it.

"I wish to talk. I fear for you, Jane." She kept her voice low even though we were alone.

"For me, Your Grace?" I stared at her, amazed. "Why, what have I done to displease you?" I did not see how she could possibly know what had transpired the previous night. No one save Guy Dunois had seen me leave his master's lodgings, and I had told no one save my confessor.

"Only God and your conscience know," said the Lady Mary, "and mayhap the duc de Longueville."

I felt my face blanch.

"He has bedded you, has he not?" The Lady Mary held my gaze with an uncompromising stare that put me uneasily in mind of her brother.

"Say rather that we have bedded each other." It had been my choice to lie with him. He had not coerced me.

Although she frowned, a gleam of curiosity appeared in her light blue eyes. After a moment's struggle, she gave in to it. "What does it feel like to have a man's yard inside you?"

Heat rose into my cheeks. "It is not my place to tell Your Grace such things."

"If you do not, who will?"

She was a royal princess, but I had been her friend and companion and sometime bedfellow, as well as her servant, for many long years. When her first woman's courses came, it had been to me she turned, not her lady governess, for sympathy and a distillation of poppy to ease the pains. When she'd had questions about what passed between a man and a woman, she had likewise come to me. In the past, I had been able to tell her only what I'd heard at secondhand.

"It hurts the first time," I blurted out.

"Was there pleasure after?"

I looked at the brooch I still held tightly clutched in one hand. Was this payment for my services? Or did he mean his gift as an invitation to spend more time in his company? I could not say for certain, but my foolish heart fluttered with hope. "There can be."

"Is the pain very bad?" the Lady Mary asked.

I shook my head. "And what leads up to that moment is most pleasurable." Remembering made my breasts ache and my loins soften. My breath soughed out, full of longing.

Still curious, the Lady Mary settled herself in the middle of the feather bed, curling her legs beneath her. She patted the coverlet next to her. "Come and tell me more."

"It is not meet."

"I command it!"

Moments later I sat facing her, my knees folded tailor fashion. Accompanied by a good deal of giggling and several exclamations of disbelief, I told her everything.

"You left him?" she exclaimed. "After he had promised there was more?"

I nodded. Perhaps that had been foolish, but I had not known what else to do.

The princess's soft sigh echoed mine. "It must be a wondrous thing, to be with a man after the first time, else why would women do it so often? But, Jane, he is a Frenchman." She named his nationality as if the word was synonymous with "devil."

A snort of laughter escaped me as an image of Longueville in horns and a long tail—and naught else—flashed through my mind. "He is a man like any other. Better than many." Most of King Henry's courtiers did not bother to send love tokens to their conquests.

"Most women at court who acquire lovers take the precaution of first finding husbands," the Lady Mary ventured. "If you should conceive, if you bear the duke's child, it will be a bastard."

"In the duc de Longueville's family, bastard children are well treated. You have only to look at Guy Dunois to see that it is possible for a by-blow to find success."

"He is his half brother's steward," Mary agreed, "and the duke mentioned once that Guy had been able to amass a respectable fortune of his own." She giggled. "He should not have said that. I might tell Henry, and then he'll set their ransom higher."

I smiled, but my thoughts had already circled back to my own dilemma. If the duke should get me with a child, I would be banished from court. *That* was a risk I was reluctant to take. Until Longueville's ransom was paid and he was free to return to France, he lacked the power to protect me. He did not even have the funds to support me.

Had he really meant his offer to take me with him to France? I avoided looking at the Lady Mary. It felt disloyal to consider leaving her and yet that possibility, more than any words of love, more than the promise of physical pleasure, was the lure that tempted me most strongly to return to the duke's bed. The answers to my questions about my mother were in France, but that was not the only reason I wanted to go there. I wanted to know why she'd left, but I also had a vision of what my life might be like separate from the English court, free of obligation to princess or king. It danced like a will-o'-the-wisp, just out of reach, a fanciful notion impossible to ignore.

I sighed. It would be months yet before any ransom was paid. In the meantime, England was still at war with France, and I was still dependent upon my mistress and her brother for everything I had. If I went to the duke's bed again, I must take measures to protect myself.

There are ways to deter conception. I'd heard married women talk of them. I did not speak of such things to the princess. It was her duty to produce children when she wed. She had no need to know she had a choice, but my case was different. I resolved then and there to make another trip into London to procure a bit of sponge and some lemons. That was the combination reputed to be most effective.

"It must be a wondrous thing to have a lover." The Lady Mary leaned closer to me and placed one hand over mine. "But have you given thought to what my brother will say when he returns? For all that Henry may lie with whatever woman he chooses, he does not approve of lewd behavior at court any more than our father did. You must take great care, Jane. The king could banish you for wantonness, and I do not want to lose you."

"I will be careful. And circumspect."

She was right about King Henry. He had no objection to tupping a willing woman in private, especially when the queen was great with child and unavailable to him. But under that same queen's influence, he'd come around to the point of view that courtiers should behave with great propriety in public.

"It makes matters more difficult that your lover is our enemy. No matter how gallant or courtly he is, he is still a Frenchman."

"Now you sound like the queen." I struggled to keep my tone light, but I took her point. To consort with an enemy of the Crown could all too easily be misconstrued as treason.

ENEMY OR NOT, when the duke danced with me that evening, my desire for him returned tenfold. As he took my hand to lead me away from the crowd, I went willingly.

The second time was much more pleasurable.

The third was even better.

Soon, coupling with the duke became so passionate and intense I found myself slipping away to his bed every moment I could spare from my duties with the princess. He was always glad to see me. In truth, we were finding it hard to be apart.

With the king still in France and Queen Catherine occupied first with repelling the Scots invaders and then recovering from her miscarriage, no one troubled to inquire how one of the princess's ladies passed her time. The prisoners of war were all but forgotten by the outside world.

The intensity of my dear Coriander's attentions made me happier than I had ever been. In spite of my best efforts to remain heart-whole, I fell under his spell, enthralled by how he made me feel and what he seemed to feel for me in return.

A picture of our future together began to emerge. I would travel with him to France as his beloved mistress, accepted even by the wife who had already given him four children. Since their alliance had been arranged by their families, it had nothing to do with either liking or passion. He convinced me that she would have no objection to my presence in their lives.

Then, on a crisp October afternoon, just as I was contemplating slipping away to the duke's lodgings for an assignation, a messenger arrived. The Lady Mary read the letter he brought, then gave us all orders to pack our belongings.

"Queen Catherine is in residence at Richmond Palace. She has sufficiently recovered from her miscarriage to desire my company."

Excited chatter broke out among the princess's ladies. We had been living in the Tower of London since early September and were ready for a change. It was rare we stayed in any one place so long. It was best to move every few weeks so that the buildings we vacated could be thoroughly cleaned before our next visit.

"What of the prisoners of war?" I asked, already suspecting what this summons would mean.

The princess's gaze was rife with pity when she looked up from the queen's letter. "They must remain in the Tower."

ONCE WE WERE settled at Richmond Palace, I seized the opportunity to resume my search for answers about my mother. Queen Catherine had no objection when I offered to lend my hand at embroidering an altar cloth, and I managed to position myself in the sewing circle between Lady Pechey and Lady Verney, two of the women Goose had named as former members of Queen Elizabeth of York's household. I knew who they were, even though I had rarely spoken to either, and then just pleasantries.

Lady Pechey, like Lady Marzen, had not married until after my mother's death, but unlike Lady Marzen, she had been at court before she wed. Nervously, I cleared my throat. "I wonder, Lady Pechey, if you knew my mother?"

She looked down her high-bridged nose at me, sniffed, and continued stitching—tiny, perfect stitches that would never need to be redone. Honing that skill had left her with a marked squint. "Why would you think so?"

"Her name was Joan Popyncourt. You were at court when she entered Queen Elizabeth's service."

"I do not recall." Back stiff, demeanor unfriendly, she avoided looking at me.

"Joan Popyncourt," Lady Verney mused on my other side. She had been listening to the conversation, as I'd hoped she would. An older woman, in her fiftieth year with a deeply lined countenance and hands disfigured with age, she had reportedly been one of Queen Elizabeth's favorites.

"Perhaps you remember my mother, Lady Verney?" I could not keep the eagerness out of my voice.

"She died soon after she joined us," Lady Verney said. Deep in thought, she stared up at the ceiling studded with Tudor emblems: gold roses, portcullises, the red dragon of Wales, and the greyhound of Richmond. After a few moments, she shook her head. "No, I do not believe I recall more than that."

"I had hoped she might have had time to make friends with some of the other ladies in the queen's court."

Lady Verney did not know anything about that either.

On subsequent days, I asked the same questions of the others Goose had named. Lady Weston could tell me nothing. Mistress Denys said it was a great pity I could not ask her husband.

"He was King Henry's groom of the stole," she reminded me with a wink. "He had an intimate knowledge of everything that affected His Grace."

I had to smile at that. The groom of the stole attended the king when he used the royal close stool—a glorified chamber pot!

Lady Lovell was my last hope. A buxom woman with blunt features and a round face, she had a brusque manner but she heard me out. "You wish to know about your mother's days at the English court?" she said when I had stuttered out my questions. "Why?"

"Because I never saw her again after I was sent to Eltham. No one even told me she was ill."

"You were a child."

"I am not a child now. I should like to know if she had friends, if she was well cared for, if—"

"Queen Elizabeth would not have let a dog suffer. She was all that was good and kind. I am certain everything possible was done for your mother."

Walking together in the great hall at Richmond, we passed under the eyes of kings. A series of large portraits had been painted in the wall spaces between the high windows by Maynard the Fleming in old King Henry's reign. Two lines of these, showing Brutus, Hengist, King William Rufus, King Arthur, and others—all depicted wearing golden robes and brandishing mighty swords—led up to the dais and a similar portrait of King Henry VII.

"He sent my mother to the queen," I said, indicating the painted monarch. "Maman knew no one else in England save her twin brother, Sir Rowland Velville."

"Yes. I remember hearing that she was his sister. A ferocious jouster, Sir Rowland, but that's the best I can say for him." My uncle's short temper was almost as legendary as the king's.

Lady Lovell stopped in front of one of the big bay windows that overlooked a courtyard. Beyond the turrets and pinnacles and a profusion of gilt weather vanes and bell-shaped domes, I could just glimpse a part of the deer park that completely surrounded Richmond. Everything had been built to old King Henry's specifications after the old palace on this site, a place called Sheen, had burned to the ground the Christmas before I arrived in England.

"There was one person who befriended her," Lady Lovell said. "Or, rather, they befriended each other. She is no longer at court."

"Is she still living?"

"Oh, yes. She's plain Mistress Strangeways now, but she and her husband own considerable property in Berkshire."

I felt my eyes widen as I realized whom she meant: Lady Catherine Gordon, the daughter of a Scottish earl, who had once been married to Perkin Warbeck, the notorious pretender to the throne. She'd been captured along with her husband when Warbeck invaded England. He'd been executed, after making a second attempt to escape, but she had remained at court as one of Queen

Elizabeth's ladies. A few years ago, I'd heard that she had remarried. Her second husband, James Strangeways, was one of King Henry's gentlemen ushers.

That she and my mother should have been friendly made perfect sense. What more natural than that two newcomers, two foreigners, be drawn to each other? When I left Lady Lovell's company I felt more optimistic than I had since I'd begun asking questions about my mother. Berkshire was not close enough to reach on my own, but eventually the court would travel to Windsor Castle. I should be able to slip away and visit Lady Strangeways then.

My high spirits were short lived. I'd no sooner reached the Lady Mary's lodgings than she declared herself in need of exercise and swept me off with her to the timber-framed, two-story galleried walks built around Richmond's gardens. They gave a splendid view of knots, wide paths, statues of the king's beasts, and fountains, but the princess was intent on speaking privily with me and paid no attention to her surroundings.

"Why do you ask so many questions?" she demanded.

"I wish to know more about my mother." She knew this already.

"She has been dead almost as long as I have known you. What can you possibly expect to learn now?"

There was no simple answer to her question. I did not know myself. I only knew that there had been something secretive about our coming to England, and about the way we had been treated once we arrived. Why had we left? Had the *gens d'armes* been looking for Maman, or only for the governess they'd taken away with them? But most of all I wanted to know why the king should have shown us favor. My uncle was only one of many knights at court. He was expert in the lists and in falconry, but beyond those skills he had nothing special to recommend him.

I could scarce explain all that to the Lady Mary, even if I possessed a greater understanding of events than I did. Instead, I offered the only crumb I had. "I have been thinking a great deal of late about my early days here as well as my years in France."

"That was all very well when we were on our own in the Tower," the Lady Mary said, "but here, showing an interest in anything French, even your own mother, is not at all wise. We are still at war."

"But my mother was a Breton," I reminded her.

"That hardly matters. When you ask these questions, you remind everyone that you are not English. If people should also learn that you have become close to the duke, you risk being branded a traitor."

A little silence fell. I knew she was right. I silently cursed all rumor-mongering, small-minded courtiers.

"You must cease badgering the queen's ladies with your questions," the Lady Mary said.

I sighed. "Next you will say I must give up the duc de Longueville. I miss being in his bed more than I ever imagined I could."

The princess gave me a curious look. "Do you think that perhaps it is not *him* you miss. Oh, do not look so shocked, Jane. Answer me this: If the king and his favorites were here at court, could you be tempted by any of them?"

My smile was rueful. "They are well favored to a man, and lusty, too, but I have known most of them too long and too well. I was never tempted before."

"Mayhap it will be different now that you have discovered the joys of being with a man."

I could not help but be amused by her naive logic. "But, Your Grace," I said lightly, "would that not be far worse, not to mention much more difficult to keep secret?"

I expected her to laugh, but of a sudden she looked very serious. "It would be better for you, Jane. At least then your cater-cousin would be an Englishman!"

ON THE TWENTY-SECOND day of October, the king rode hard from Dover to surprise his wife at Richmond Palace. He burst into her privy chamber, followed by his closest companions, all noise and laughter. They were cock-a-hoop about their first venture into war, even though the battle they had won had been far less significant than the one fought at home at Flodden in their absence.

Henry Tudor was the largest man at his own court, well over six feet in height, with proportions to match. There was not an ounce of fat on him, for he kept trim with jousting and wrestling and other manly exercises. He was well favored, with pleasant facial features—not always the case with royalty—and broad shoulders and long, muscular legs. Those who had long memories always said he had the look of his mother's father, King Edward. Edward himself had been big and blond and lusty.

After greeting his queen, King Henry moved into the crowd of courtiers, demanding kisses from every gentlewoman and lady in lieu of the bows he received from the men. When he reached his sister, he lifted her right off her feet and swung her around in a great circle, to the delight of everyone watching.

"By St. George, it is good to be home!"

The cheers and applause that greeted this sentiment were so loud that I did not hear the Lady Mary's reply even though I stood right next to her. The king set her back on her feet and turned to me.

"And we are most pleased to have you back, Your Grace," I said, prepared to greet him with a kiss.

The next moment, I gave a squeak of surprise as he swept me into the same embrace he had given the princess. Holding me with my feet still dangling a foot above the floor, he kissed me soundly, full on the lips.

Laughing, he set me on my feet again a moment later. I smiled up at him and said the first thing that popped into my head. "Your Grace has acquired some new finery at the Burgundian court."

The king beamed at me. He had no modesty when it came to his apparel. He was garbed in the newest knee-length bases from Italy, heavily embroidered with vines and flowers. His brocade doublet had puffed and slashed sleeves. A dagger, purse, and gloves hung suspended by golden laces from a cloth-of-gold belt, and, following the current fashion, he had padded his codpiece and decorated it with jewel-encrusted points. It thrust out from the center opening of the bases, impossible to ignore.

Before becoming intimate with Longueville, I had never given much thought to that part of a man's body, save when I came across some gentleman urinating in the corner of a courtyard and was forcibly reminded that men and women are differently made. Now I caught myself staring at the gaudy, ornate covering. Like everything else about the king, his yard was both oversized—or at least overstuffed—and blatant.

His Grace moved on, indiscriminately dispensing kisses until he came to young Bessie Blount. The maid of honor Queen Catherine had sent to fetch me to her on the day the French prisoners first arrived at court had gone north with the queen, but I had spoken with her several times since I had been at Richmond. She was a sweet-natured girl still growing accustomed to life at court.

The terrified expression on her face reminded me that she had not previously met King Henry. She had arrived after he left for France. She froze, uncertain whether to make an obeisance or go up on her tiptoes to kiss him in greeting.

His voice boomed out, audible in every corner of the presence chamber. "Here's a pretty new flower since I went away to war! What is your name, sweeting?"

"Elizabeth Blount, if it please Your Majesty."

"It does indeed!" He picked her up, as he had his sister and me, and kissed her soundly.

Bessie stared after him in bemusement as he moved on to another of the queen's damsels. Had I looked like that, I wondered, the first time I beheld the duc de Longueville?

By the time the king resumed his place by the queen's side, busy servants had the royal furniture in place. The king's cushion had been placed upon the chair of estate and a canopy had hurriedly been erected over it. Queen Catherine, having lost her status as regent from the moment of her husband's return, was relegated to a smaller chair with a lower canopy.

"Your Grace," she greeted him in her low, throaty voice. And then, in tones even lower and more husky, she murmured, "My Henry."

In spite of all the flirtation and the indiscriminate kissing, Henry Tudor had eyes only for his Catherine. She glowed, basking in his undivided attention. Their desire for each other was a palpable force in the presence chamber and no one doubted that the king would visit his wife's bed come nightfall.

At court, however, ceremony surrounds every royal action. Music and dancing and games would come first, for the king rarely retired before midnight. After that, if he wished to lie with the queen, he would summon his grooms of the bedchamber. They would bring his night-robe, help him into it, and escort him through the private connecting stair or gallery—which one it was depended upon the palace—to the door of the queen's bedchamber. The grooms would then wait outside that door until the king was ready to return to his own bed.

On this evening, however, King Henry departed from protocol. Halfway through the festivities, he abruptly rose, took Queen Catherine's hand in his, and led her from the room. The attendants on duty scurried after, more than one of them aghast at the breech in etiquette. I hid a smile behind my hand as I heard a distant door close. Ceremony, it seemed, would for once take second place to desire.

I wondered if the king would understand my longing for my Coriander. I sighed deeply. Understanding and acceptance were two different matters. In spite of his obvious affection for his wife, His Grace no doubt shared the Lady Mary's conviction that any partner would do to provide physical release. The king was quick enough to turn to other women when he could not go to the queen.

To give and receive pleasure was a marvelous thing. In his own way, I thought, Longueville had come to care for me. In spite of the princess's warnings, I had no intention of giving him up.

To take my mind off missing the duke, I surveyed the chamber, in search of familiar faces. Everywhere I looked, courtiers and ladies were exchanging pleased and knowing glances. The queen's miscarriage had been a blow, but it had taken place almost a month earlier. Another attempt to beget an heir was not only desirable, it was necessary.

With the king and queen occupied, we were granted an additional boon. We were left to our own devices. It was at that moment that I belatedly recalled there was someone with whom I had been anxious to speak. I scanned the crowded room, looking for my uncle, sure that he must be somewhere in the sea of bright colors and noisy chatter. At last I would have the opportunity to ask him about his twin sister. I would insist he tell me all he knew of my mother's last days in France and of her brief life in England.

Sir Rowland Velville, however, was nowhere to be found.

Harry Guildford was there. So were Will Compton and Ned Neville from our old band of children of honor. Will had completely recovered from his tiltyard accident three years earlier, except for a small bump on the bridge of his nose to remind him of the place where it had been broken.

Charles Brandon was also present. The Lady Mary had already made her way to his side, heedless of the speculation that might arise from her obvious preference for his company. I had to admit he looked exceedingly fine, even in boots and a cloak that were mud spattered from hours of rapid travel over bad roads.

In contrast with the energy that seemed to radiate from Brandon, Harry Guildford lounged with one shoulder propped against a window casement. The bored and slightly melancholy look on his face reminded me that, although his mother-in-law, Lady Bryan, had remained with the queen, his wife had been sent to Staffordshire to visit friends. After all, neither Meg nor her sister, Elizabeth, had any official post at court. That meant it would be some days yet before Harry could retire to his marital bed.

I brushed a kiss of greeting across his lips. No sparks flew. I hadn't expected any. I would have linked my arm companionably with his had I not noticed the condition of his doublet. The fabric was so stiff from the ill effects of traveling that it would have abraded my skin right through my sleeve. He carried the faint stench of the road, too. I took a small step away from him.

"Have you seen my uncle?" I asked.

"Sir Rowland is still in Calais."

"Why?"

"He'll sail from there direct to Anglesey. At long last he's to take up his post as constable of Beaumaris Castle."

"He is going to *Wales*?"

Harry laughed at my expression of disbelief. "It is not exile, although given Velville's uncertain temper, there are some who'd think that a fine idea. He was appointed constable just before the old king died, but he did not receive a grant of denization until last year. Then the war came. This is the first chance he's had to claim his prize."

I frowned. I was surprised that King Henry—both of them— had waited so long to grant my uncle the same rights as an Englishman born and bred. He had, after all, lived in this country since he was a boy of eleven.

"Come, Jane," Harry chided me. "Forget Velville. You never liked him anyway. We are home. We have won. I've pageants to plan, masques to prepare. Will you assist me?"

Glad to see him more cheerful, I agreed.

"The king intends to bring his French prisoners to court," Harry informed me, unaware of how much pleasure his news gave me. "We must devise an entertainment suitable to welcome them."

Linking my arm through his, I assured him that I would be able to help him with that.

MY REUNION WITH my lover did not take place for some time. The king fell ill only a few days after his arrival at Richmond, delaying matters. Then the queen, who had nursed her husband herself, objected to the idea of the French prisoners living at court. To make matters worse, an outbreak of the plague in London prevented us from moving closer to the city. I was too far away to make clandestine visits to the Tower.

It was late November before the king fully recovered and at last persuaded the queen that the noble duc de Longueville must be invited to live at court until his ransom was paid. Resigned to the inevitable, Queen Catherine changed tactics. She would personally welcome the duke by inviting him to her own manor of Havering-atte-Bower. As soon as the court took up residence at this huge, rambling estate in Essex, she commandeered the services of the king's master of revels, Harry Guildford, to produce a disguising to entertain the duke.

I was assisting him with his preparations—supervising the decoration of a miniature castle—when word reached me that my lover had arrived at Havering. I abandoned my task without a backward glance, unable to wait another moment to see him again. We had been separated for nearly six weeks.

I caught a glimpse of Longueville as soon as I left the barn Harry had appropriated for the construction of pageant wagons. The duke was walking with Guy toward the bower that had given the manor its name. It was a beautiful spot, a garden atop a hill that boasted a stunning view of the valley of the Thames.

I took a secondary path, climbing rapidly. My heart raced as much from anticipation as from the exertion. It had been so long since I had seen my lover, touched him, pleasured him, and had him pleasure me. It seemed an eternity.

A deep, booming laugh—the king's laugh—brought me to an abrupt halt just before I crested the hill. Longueville had not gone to the bower for the view. He had gone there to meet in private with King Henry.

I knew I should retreat but I feared to step on a twig or dislodge a stone, attracting their attention. No good could come of that! I hesitated, unable to decide what to do.

"You are good company, Longueville," I heard the king say. "Did I not tell you that when we met in France?"

"You did, Your Grace, just before you set my ransom at an exorbitant sum."

The king chuckled. "I would be inclined to pay half of it myself, save that would more quickly deprive me of your presence."

"You flatter me, Your Grace."

"You must consider yourself my honored guest while you are in England. A member of my family. Have all your needs been seen to?"

"All, Your Grace." Longueville lowered his voice so that I could hear nothing of what seemed to be a lengthy speech . . . except my name.

Still as a deer scenting danger, I waited, barely daring to breathe. The king might not object to the duke's acquisition of a mistress, but he had always been adamant that not the slightest taint of corruption come in contact with his sister, not even at secondhand.

I heard only the low murmur of the king's voice, his words too faint for me to catch. I crept closer, sheltered by an evergreen hedge, until I could see the king and the duke sitting companionably together on the long stone bench in the bower. Guy stood nearby, within earshot, as did the courtier who had accompanied the king to this rendezvous—Charles Brandon.

The king's amused chuckle drew my attention quickly back to him. Even seated, King Henry was a giant among men. The top of Longueville's head only came to the level of His Grace's broad shoulders. The midday sun had made a halo of the king's bright hair, picking out both the red and the gold. He wore his locks trimmed short, in the French fashion. The same barber who kept him clean shaven regularly used curling tongs to make the ends curve under all along the line of his strong jaw.

I squinted to see more clearly—the reflection from the jewels sewn onto the collar of the royal cloak glittered in the sunlight— and stretched my ears to hear better. The two men appeared to be engaged in friendly conversation. If the king was angry that I had become Longueville's mistress, he gave no sign of it.

"Indeed, she is most delightful," I heard the duke say, "and an excellent diversion for a poor captive."

I felt my skin grow hot.

"She is a pretty piece," the king agreed. "I wonder how it is that I never noticed she had grown into such a beauty."

"If you want her for yourself," Longueville said, "it would please me greatly to cede her to Your Grace."

Shock rocked me back a step, hands pressed to my lips to prevent me from crying out in protest. The chill that went through me had naught to do with the cold of that late November day.

The lover of my imagination, the one who cared deeply for me, would never offer my favors to another man, not even a king.

"Keep her for the present, my friend," King Henry said. "Enjoy her as part of our good English hospitality. Time enough for me to take another look at her after you return to France."

8

I never thought the duc de Longueville loved me. I was not such a fool. Nor did I love him, except in the carnal sense. I had known all along that he would not be mine to keep. But I had believed that the man I'd called my Coriander had a certain fondness for me, as I did for him. I had thought the intimacies we shared meant more to him than a convenient means of physical release.

I should have known better.

Had I learned nothing in more than fifteen years at court?

Men took their pleasure where they found it. One woman was the same as another. Even when they married where they wished, choosing mutual affection over a rich dowry or a powerful alliance, it was the rare husband who remained faithful.

The king himself was proof of that. He had wed Catherine of Aragon because he had panted after her like a puppy dog for years.

They'd been enraptured with each other at first, but less than a year had passed before he'd betrayed his wedding vows with one of his wife's married ladies. He had certainly not been faithful to her while he was away at war. According to Harry, King Henry had found himself a Flemish mistress named Étienne de la Baume during his visit to Archduchess Margaret's court at Lille.

I made my way back toward the barn in a state of mingled anger and distress. Longueville's words had hurt me beyond measure. How dare he offer me, like a bauble or a joint of beef, to another man, even if that man *was* the king!

At first I tried to pretend nothing was amiss. I joined Harry Guildford and Richard Gibson, his deputy master of revels, in a discussion of how best to make our small version of the White Tower of the Tower of London more impressive. Carpenters and painters had devoted the better part of the last three days to constructing the lightweight wooden frame of a castle that resembled the keep. With my own hands, I had helped cover it with gilt paper that would shimmer in candlelight. At the time, I had thought to create a spectacular setting in which to show myself off to my lover.

That hope aside, we were all painfully aware that the spectacle would fall far short of the usual court masque. "It is no *Golden Arbor of Pleasure*," Harry lamented, citing one of his greatest successes, a masque performed some two or three years back.

"Aye, that was most memorable." Master Gibson chuckled to himself. "Do you recall? We constructed that pageant wagon at the bishop of Hertford's place in London and it was so heavy that it broke right through the floor. I was obliged to apply for additional funds to make repairs."

Master Gibson, a tall, lanky fellow with thinning straw-colored hair, had been leader of the King's Players in the last reign. A yeoman tailor by profession, he'd become principal costume designer and producer of court entertainments under Harry Guildford. Whenever a disguising was to be staged, it was Gibson who requested material from the wardrobes, rented houses to serve as workshops, and hired carpenters, scene painters, and tailors. For the last Twelfth Night pageant he had built the Rich Mount, a set piece that had taken nearly a month to construct.

I had first come to know Master Gibson when he made my costume to play Maid Marian in the king's dawn raid on his wife's bedchamber. He had not had much notice beforehand and had coped surpassing well, but presenting a masque at Havering-atte-Bower on the spur of the moment presented a far greater challenge, one that could not be overcome with a few yards of green cloth.

The queen's manor was located inland, making it difficult to transport set pieces and machines to the location. They were customarily conveyed by barge from workshop to palace along the Thames, roads being unsuited to the movement of such large objects. Deprived of easy access to existing structures, we were left with no choice but to build our own scenery.

It was some time after my return from the bower before I became aware that both Harry and Master Gibson were staring at me. "What ails you, Jane?" Harry demanded. "I have asked you the same question three times over."

"I do beg your pardon, Harry. I-I was thinking." I squared my shoulders, prepared for opposition. "I do not wish to participate in the disguising."

"But there is no time for anyone else to learn your part," Master Gibson objected. "And Purity is an important role in the masque."

A hand clamped down hard on my arm. As Master Gibson shook his head, no doubt lamenting the flightiness of waiting gentlewomen, and resumed work on the pageant wagon, Harry pulled me aside.

"This is not like you, Jane. Why have you changed your mind?"

"I do not wish to call attention to myself tonight. Do not fret. I will find someone else to wear my costume. Mistress Blount is about my size." She was also the most lively of the queen's younger maids of honor, quick witted and agile. She would have no difficulty mastering my part in the evening's entertainment.

"But why?" Confusion and concern warred with irritation in Harry's voice.

I looked away, reluctant to explain that the substitution would allow me to avoid dancing with the duc de Longueville at the end of the masque.

After a moment, he released me. "Go on, then. Teach her the lines and the steps and pray she is a quick study. Both the king and the queen expect this entertainment to run smoothly."

COLOR AND NOISE assaulted me as I moved through the crowd that evening. Courtiers and ladies garbed in white, green, and yellow satin engaged in spirited conversations while musicians added to the tumult. I caught a glimpse of the queen at the far side of the room, brilliant as a jewel in silver damask. Her ladies drifted like bright flowers around her feet, some in white cloth-of-gold and others in violet satin. The Lady Mary was in popinjay blue.

Nearby were the king and the Duke of Longueville. Having no desire to come to the notice of either of them, I sought the very edge of the crowd. The rich crimsons, yellows, and greens of a Venetian tapestry showing St. George defeating the dragon gleamed dully in the light cast by hundreds of wax tapers. Wearing pale green slashed with yellow myself, I attempted to blend into that background.

A fanfare sounded and the room stilled. The doors at the far end of the great hall opened and six burly yeomen of the guard, presently out of uniform and dressed as wild men in saffron kilts and braided hair, towed in the pageant wagon on which our castle had been built.

This set piece was far smaller than the scenes and machines constructed for disguisings at Greenwich or Windsor or Westminster Palace, but it seemed surpassing large in the hall at Havering-atte-Bower. I studied the structure with a critical eye and was pleased with what I observed. No hint showed of what, or rather who, was concealed within.

On the outside, four veiled women clad all in white perched on little ledges around the sides of the towers. Once the pageant wagon was in position, the first woman spoke, revealing that each of them represented a virtue. She was kindness. I suppressed a smile. Kindness was portrayed by Meg Guildford, Harry's wife, who had become almost as notorious for her sharp tongue as his mother was.

At least she was fond of him, I thought, and he of her. She still did not greatly care for me. Harry said she was jealous of my long friendship with him. I suspected she still believed we'd been lovers.

When Meg finished her speech, Patience, Temperance, and Gentleness took their turns. Then there was a stir in the crowd. Several people gasped and one woman giggled as four black-cloaked men emerged from hiding places scattered around the hall. They stormed the castle, flinging off their outer garments when they reached it to reveal apparel of crimson satin embroidered with gold and pearls. Even their caps and visors matched.

Murmurs rose from the audience as people tried to guess the identity of this veiled lady or that masked man. "That tall one on the far left does much resemble the king," said a woman standing near me.

"The king is over there, with the queen and that French duke," her companion replied, "so the gentleman laying siege to the castle must be Ned Neville."

From a distance, Ned did bear a strong resemblance to King Henry, but I knew him too well ever to be deceived. When he'd been a young boy and one of the children of honor at Eltham, his likeness to his royal master had been so marked that some speculated he might be King Henry VII's by-blow. Speculation was all it was. Unlike the eighth Henry, the seventh had been faithful to his queen.

After many calls for the ladies to surrender, each of the four lords made an impassioned speech in which he revealed his identity. One was Nobility, another Loyalty, one Honor, and the last, predictably, Pleasure.

They were rewarded with a rain of dates and oranges thrown down from the towers. When the ladies had done pelting their besiegers with fruit, they sent a shower of rose water over their heads. A hail of comfits came next. I joined in the laughter and applause echoing through the hall.

The show of resistance by the castle's defenders over, the lords scaled the pageant wagon. Each lifted a lady down from her perch. Some lords were welcomed more exuberantly than others. Meg Guildford tumbled happily into Harry's embrace, greeting him with kisses.

To exclamations of surprise and delight, the front of the castle now began to open. When it stood wide, yet another lady in white was revealed. Unlike the others, Bessie Blount's features were not hidden by either visor or veil. Her golden curls tumbled free, long enough to reach her waist, and her own sweet innocence shone so bright that she was instantly recognizable as Purity.

I smiled wryly to myself. Bessie and I might have been able to fit into the same costume, but I would never have been able to appear so innocent.

I held my breath as she began to speak. Her part in the disguising, which I had written for myself, was short but crucial. Sweet, loud, and clear, the words rang out. Her flawless delivery commanded everyone's attention as she explained that virtues united were stronger than those kept apart.

The masque ended with a ceremony that joined the participants together in the service of His Most Gracious Majesty, King Henry of England. The lords and ladies, now allegorically wed, assisted Bessie from her castle. As the wall closed behind her, she called for music. Everyone who had participated in the disguising went forth to select partners from among the spectators. Meg Guildford approached the duc de Longueville, while her younger sister Elizabeth boldly asked the king to partner her.

I saw Harry Guildford look around for me just as the pageant wagon passed by on its way out of the room. Its bulk obscured me from his view, but only for a moment. In Harry's second sweep of the chamber, his lynx-eyed gaze picked me out against the background of the tapestry.

"Hiding, Jane?" he asked as he made a leg. "By the saints, that will not do."

He was right. I would only make myself more conspicuous if I tried to avoid being seen. We danced.

"Another success, Harry. You are a superb master of revels."

"Wait until you see what I have planned for Christmas at Pleasure Palace."

We exchanged a private smile at his use of the name I had coined so long ago. Then his expression changed to one of consternation, but it was already too late to avoid the other couple bearing down on us. With as deft a maneuver as I have ever seen, Meg executed a trade, dancing off partnered by her husband and leaving me to finish the pavane with the duc de Longueville.

"Sweeting, I have missed you," he murmured close to my ear.

We stepped apart, but that low, sensual tone had already had an effect. In spite of everything I had heard at the bower, in spite of the hurt and anger that had simmered inside me in all the hours since, I still felt a flutter of desire deep within.

I forced myself to smile when the dance brought us face-to-face once more. Even if I dared reveal that I had been listening when he offered me to the king, I could scarce berate him for what he'd done. Even in private it would be folly for a mere gentlewoman to take a duke to task.

Each casual brush of his hand against mine weakened my resolve to avoid him. In spite of his betrayal, my traitorous body longed to lie with him.

Unpalatable as it was, I could not deny the truth: I still craved his touch.

A daring thought came to me. He had used me for his pleasure. Could I use him for mine? I needed time to think. Forcing my lips into a smile, I parted from him at the end of the dance. "There are others who would claim you as a partner, my lord," I told him, and all but shoved him into Elizabeth Bryan's arms.

Meg's sister was happy to have him. He was an excellent dancer and his skill would allow her to show off her own agility. While they capered, I retreated into a window alcove, one shielded by a curtain partway drawn across to keep out drafts. There I hid, catching my breath and gathering my composure while I contemplated stealing away to my lodgings.

When a shadow fell across my skirts, I looked up, bracing myself to meet Longueville's black-eyed gaze. Instead King Henry stood there, so big and solid that he blocked all the light from the hall, and at the same time cut off any hope of escape.

"Your Grace!" I tried to make an obeisance, but there was no room for the maneuver.

He stayed my pitiful effort with a gesture and moved closer. The smell of musk, rose water, ambergris, and civet, the combination he preferred as a scent, was nearly overwhelming in the confined space.

"An excellent entertainment, Jane. Harry tells me you wrote some of the speeches."

"I am glad my poor attempts pleased you, Your Grace."

"You always please me, Jane."

My heart stuttered in my chest. For one terrible moment I was afraid the king's talk with Longueville had piqued his interest in me. He had said he'd "take another look" after the duke had been ransomed and returned to France. What if he had decided not to wait?

"Do you fancy yourself in love with the duc de Longueville?" The king posed his question casually, but I was certain it was not prompted by idle curiosity. King Henry did nothing without purpose.

It came to me in that moment that what I'd felt for Longueville all along had been exactly what I'd thought it was when I'd first seen him—lust. If I'd been a man, I would not have hesitated to say that to His Grace. How unfortunate that the king held those of my sex to a different standard. By royal decree, "lewd women" were not permitted in the royal household.

"I was intrigued by him, Your Grace," I said carefully, "and interested to hear his stories about life in France."

The king's round, almost cherubic face knit into a frown, but it vanished almost as quickly as it had appeared. "You are Velville's niece. I had forgot."

"Yes, Sire."

"He's sworn allegiance to England. Can you say the same?"

"I have always been loyal to the Crown, Your Grace, from the moment your father first took me in." I did not remind him that I had been his father's ward and now was his. As my guardian, he might decide to exercise even more control over my actions.

He pondered my statement, his blue-gray eyes as serious as I'd ever seen them.

Although the king's big body obscured most of my view, I caught a glimpse of the queen when he shifted his weight from one foot to the other. She did not look pleased to see her husband conversing with me. If we remained in the alcove much longer, she would think the worst.

"I cannot say I was pleased to learn you had become Longueville's mistress," King Henry mused aloud. "When I sent orders to make him welcome in England, I did not intend to go so far."

At his comment, my stomach tied itself into knots, but I forced myself to offer an excuse. "I was swept away by passions I did not understand."

The king nodded, as though I had said something profound. "Would you end it with him if I asked you to?"

"Your wish is my command, Sire."

"I said ask, Jane, not order."

"My loyalty is to you and the queen and the Lady Mary. No other will ever come before you in my heart or in my mind."

"A pretty speech, but I believe you are sincere. I am pleased, Jane, and will be even more so if you will allow me to take advantage of the situation."

"In what way, Your Grace?" Grateful as I was to have been spared either anger or censure, something about the purpose of this conversation eluded me.

"I want you to continue to bed the duke for the duration of his stay in England. During that time, as my loyal subject, you will report to me anything Longueville confides in you, no matter how trivial it seems."

"You . . . .you want me to *spy* on him?"

"I do. You are a clever creature, Jane. Persuade him to talk to you of French troops, French politics, even old King Louis himself. We are still at war with France. If Longueville plots against me, I must know his plans." He put one heavy hand on my shoulder. "I am generous with my rewards for loyal service, Jane."

"It is enough reward just to serve you, Your Grace." And it would scarcely be a hardship to do as he asked.

AFTER THE MASQUE at Havering there could be no more such entertainments until Christmas Eve. Advent, encompassing the four Sundays before Christmas, was a time for fasting and prayer, and for forsaking all frivolity.

That did not include entertainments of a private nature. With the duke and his entourage now living at court, I came into daily contact with both Longueville and his half brother, Guy. It was difficult at first to make myself smile and laugh, flirt and entice, to pretend I did not know how little my lover thought of me. But I was so often in his company and he was so constant in his attentions to me, that it was not long before I was on the verge of forgetting everything I had overheard him say to the king.

"I have missed you, Jane." He whispered the words in my ear as we strolled together toward a table set up for card play. His warm breath sent a rush of heat straight through me. "Will you not visit me later tonight?"

"I must remain with the Lady Mary, my lord."

His chuckle was low and sensual. "It is not your turn to be on duty, my sweet. Others are assigned to see her off to bed and guard her through the night."

I did not ask how he knew what schedule the princess's attendants followed. Such information was not difficult to come by in a place where everyone accepted bribes. Instead I sent what I hoped was an enigmatic smile his way and busied myself arranging my skirts as I sat down.

The game was honors, which I had played since childhood. With pleasure, I saw that Longueville and I were matched against Harry Guildford and his wife. My smile faded at the hostile look in Meg's dark brown eyes.

"You shall teach me this game, yes?" The duke's tone made it obvious to all three of us that this was a command, not a request. As usual, he spoke in French, and Harry and I replied in that language. Meg Guildford, having only English, had to rely on her husband for translation. The necessity did not make her look any more kindly upon my presence.

"In honors, forty-eight cards are dealt," I explained, trying hard to ignore the glares from the other side of the gaming table. "All the twos are discarded."

When Harry had dealt twelve cards to each of us, he turned over the last one he'd given himself, revealing the five of spades. "That is trump," I told Longueville and gave a little cry of delight when I saw that I had the ace. "I have the honor," I said, producing it. "Have ye?"

He blinked at me in confusion. I switched to French. "You are my partner. I am asking if you have any of the other honor cards in spades. If we have three of the four—ace, king, queen, or jack—we score one point. If we have all four, we score two points."

"Ah," he said, sending me a smile so intimate it turned my insides liquid. "Alas, I have none."

"Then play commences with you, since you sit to the dealer's left. You must lead a card and the rest of us will follow suit, if we are able. A player who cannot may play any card. We win the trick by playing the highest card, either the highest in the suit that is led or the highest trump. The winner of each trick leads the next. One point is awarded for every trick taken over six tricks. The first team to score nine points wins the game."

He frowned at me over his cards. "But if I understand you correctly, it is only possible to score eight points in a single hand."

I beamed back at him, pleased that he'd caught on so quickly. "And so we must play at least two hands. Lead a card, if you please, Your Grace."

By the time we had bested the Guildfords three times, we were in charity with each other. We were also considerably richer, as it was the custom to wager on the outcome of every game. And because the duke's servant, young Ivo, had refilled our cups with wine before ever they could be emptied, I felt deliciously light-headed when we left the card table.

I made no protest when the duke steered me toward the spacious lodgings King Henry had assigned to him at court. The rooms were very grand. To the casual observer, these would seem the lodgings of an honored guest rather than an enemy prisoner of war.

I told myself I was returning to Longueville's bed only out of a sense of duty, but in the one small section of my mind not fogged by wine I knew that was not entirely true. The duke was a skilled lover and I wanted to enjoy his embraces again. When we were both naked, I opened my arms, welcoming him into my eager embrace. Enraptured by the heat of our passion, I put out of my mind the insulting offer I had overheard him make to the king.

But I never again called him Coriander.

Hours later, I lay awake, sated but unable to sleep. My conscience had begun to trouble me. If I was in the duke's bed on the king's orders, should I have enjoyed myself so thoroughly? The only one I could ask was my confessor, and I did not think I wanted to hear his answer.

It was not as if I had any choice in the matter, I told myself. Had I not already considered using the duke to bring me pleasure?

Would he also bring me information? That was a more complicated question. We had talked together, laughed together when he was a prisoner in the Tower, but he had rarely spoken of military matters or of posts he'd held in King Louis' government. He had not even told me how he'd come to be captured.

What if the king was not satisfied? If I was no use to him as a spy, would I be banished from court after all? I would starve to death if I had to survive on nothing but my tiny annuity.

Troubled, I rose and dressed as best I could without a tiring maid, anxious to return to my own room before my bedmates became too curious. No doubt they'd already guessed I had a lover. Secrets were nearly impossible to keep at court.

I slipped out of the duke's bedchamber and almost tripped over Guy. He lay stretched across the doorway on his sleeping pallet. He rose at once and I saw that he was fully dressed.

"I will escort you."

"There is no need." I backed away from him, more anxious than ever to be gone.

"There is every need. There is much drunkenness and lechery at any royal court and this one is no exception. I will see you safely to your door."

I accepted his wise advice and his company, but we did not speak. The scene in the bower at Havering came back to me in a rush. Guy had heard the duke's offer, just as I had. That he might now regard me as little more than Longueville's whore, a commodity to be given away on a whim, distressed me out of all proportion.

Why, I wondered, did it matter so much what Guy Dunois thought of me?

I HAVE ALWAYS loved Yuletide, the more so because the king customarily spends part of the season at Greenwich. As night fell on Christmas Eve, the entire court gathered to help decorate the palace with holly, ivy, and bay, and whatsoever else the season afforded that was green. The distinctive smells of those plants filled the palace.

As soon as an enormous Yule log was set to burning in the presence chamber, King Henry officially appointed William Wynnsbury as his Lord of Misrule. Wynnsbury had held the title every year, going back into old King Henry's reign. For the whole of the Yuletide season, the Lord of Misrule would be accompanied everywhere by a train of heralds, jesters, acrobats, dancing children, and men who did conjuring tricks.

"As Master of Merry Disports," the king declared in ringing tones, "you are charged to produce goodly and gorgeous mummeries."

Under cover of cheers and applause, Will Compton came up beside me and took my arm, tugging gently. His sharp-sighted hazel eyes and the nose that had been broken during that fall in the tournament dominated a face given to frequent smiles. But his expression now was grim. "Come with me, Jane."

He gave me no choice in the matter, sliding his hand from my forearm to my waist and tightening his grip. He steered me out through a service door while everyone else was distracted by the Lord of Misrule's antics.

Sudden panic had me digging in my heels on the rush matting. This pitiful effort to slow Will down did nothing but make him more irritable. He stopped, but only to lift me right off the ground until my face was only inches from his. "Cooperate or I will shake you till your bones rattle!"

"Where are we bound in such a rush?" I meant to sound annoyed, but my voice did not cooperate. I sounded as frightened as I felt.

"God's bones, Jane! Stop fighting me. I have been sent by the king." For all the frustration behind them, his words were no more than a whisper of sound.

"Then stop hauling me about as if I were a sack of grain!"

Slowly, he lowered me, holding me so tightly against him that I could feel the bulge of his codpiece against my belly, even through the many layers of my skirts. His hands slid from my waist up to my shoulders. "His Grace awaits your report."

Fear replaced, momentarily, by fury, I stomped hard on his foot, then kicked him in the shin.

He released me and stepped back. His face was still set in a scowl, but a hint of amusement lit his eyes. "I assure you, Jane, that you do not in the least resemble a sack of grain."

Frowning, I started to speak, but he held one finger to his lips. "Not here. Follow me."

In silence, I did so. I had no doubt that Will was telling the truth. As the king's chief gentleman of the bedchamber and groom of the stole, he was the most trusted of royal servants. He was also the one who escorted women to the king's bedchamber, should His Grace wish to bed someone other than the queen. He was the king's keeper of secrets. It made sense that he should be the one sent to question me.

Unfortunately, I had nothing to tell him.

In a small private closet fitted out as a study with a stool, table, and shelf for books, he paced while I sat. "You are the duke's mistress, that we know."

I nodded. Although our coupling remained most enjoyable, the sense of magic that had always been present when we were in the Tower of London was absent. After the first few nights back in Longueville's bed, it had been determination that had kept me returning to lie with him. If not for the king's command, I'd have weaned myself of my craving for his lovemaking ere now.

"Well?" Will sounded impatient.

I spread my hands wide. "I cannot help it if he is more interested in pleasure than policy. He talks about the color of my eyes and the softness of my skin. He does not prattle of battle plans in bed."

"You are a clever wench. Convince him that you are fascinated by such things." Will reached down to pinch me on the cheek. "You can cozen secrets out of him if you put your mind to it. Be subtle, but persist. You should have no difficulty. You are comely enough. I have always thought so."

"You never paid the slightest bit of attention to me at Eltham," I shot back, annoyed. When he reached for me again, I slapped his hand away. "Go home to your wife, Will Compton!"

"Whatever for?"

I looked pointedly at his codpiece, one nearly as gaudily decorated as the king's. He laughed and gave up what had been, after all, only a halfhearted attempt on my virtue. "Come along, Jane. The king has arranged a surprise for you, an early New Year's gift."

More puzzled than wary, and no longer fearful, I accompanied him through passages and along corridors lit by torches. I knew Greenwich so well that I had no difficulty recognizing the way to the duc de Longueville's apartments. Will led me to a nearby double lodging in which a wax taper in a latten candlestick had been left burning and a fire had already been lit in a fireplace of the sort built flush with the wall.

This outer room was furnished with an oak chest carved with panels that showed various sorts of foliage, a table with two stools, and a cabinet for storing food. A small but attractive tapestry showing a hunting scene adorned one wall. Lavender had been added to the rushes on the floor to make the place fragrant.

"Should you, or a guest, feel hungry late at night, as His Grace sometimes does," Will said, indicating the food press, "you have been provided with a few provisions."

I opened the pierced door to find not only comfits and suckets but also a supply of aleberry, the bread pudding flavored with ale that the king himself favored as a treat. I did not share his taste for it, but thought it politic not to say so. "His Grace is most kind," I murmured, and then was struck by a sudden thought. "Does *he* plan to visit me here?"

"I do much doubt it." Will parted the curtains that had hidden the inner room from view.

Plucking up the candle, I went through the doorway. Here, too, a welcoming fire had been lit in the hearth, and all my belongings had been moved to these, my new quarters. My traveling chest sat next to a tester bed with a heavy wooden frame and wooden boards to support the mattress. It was richly furnished with pillows, bolsters, and blankets.

"And who is to occupy that?" I asked, pointing to the truckle bed tucked beneath the larger one. "I have no maid of my own."

"You do now. The girl whose services you have been sharing with your bedfellows, if you want her. She packed for you and can be sent for to take up her new duties tonight."

I winced. "Then no doubt she has already carried stories back to the servants' hall." I worried my lower lip. "Are you certain the king wishes to call so much attention to me?"

He looked at me askance.

"Your pardon. I should have known better than to ask." None of the king's men did anything unless it was at His Grace's express command. For whatever reason, King Henry now wished the entire court to know that the duc de Longueville had taken me for his mistress.

A mirror lay upon a small table, next to a coffer meant to hold jewelry. I picked it up and stared at my reflection in the polished steel surface. I looked the same as I always had—pale skin, brown eyes, brown hair, and a small nose set in a narrow face. I was no great beauty. How was it that I had suddenly become the object of so much male interest?

Abandoning the looking glass, I moved on to my traveling chest, reaching down to run one hand over the familiar curved top. It was a sturdy piece with a leather exterior that had been soaked in oil to make it waterproof. The iron fittings included a lock. I frowned. The key still hung from my waist, as it always did, even though I kept nothing more valuable than my clothing and a few bits of jewelry inside the trunk. That had been no barrier when the king wanted my possessions moved. There was a lesson there, I thought. A warning.

Will's hand settled on my shoulder. "Discover useful information, Jane, and His Grace will be in your debt. He can be most generous. If the information you provide has sufficient value, you will be able to name your own reward."

I AWOKE ON Christmas morning uncertain where to go or what to do. Was I still to attend upon the princess? I knew she would hear

Mass in private with the king and queen, then walk in procession with them to the chapel for Matins. The entire court would join them there, both to worship and to watch the king participate in the service. I doubted that anyone would notice if I was absent. Except, perhaps, Will Compton.

I sighed and wrapped myself more tightly in the sinfully thick and warm coverlet that graced my bed. I ran my hand over the soft fur from which it had been made and wondered what animal's pelt I stroked. That made me think of the spaniels some ladies in waiting kept at court. Although in general I detested the little beasts, I thought perhaps I should acquire one. I was not accustomed to sleeping alone.

Always before I had shared my bed with someone. I was not certain I liked having the entire expanse of mattress to myself. On the other hand, I did not miss my most recent bedfellows, two of the Lady Mary's attendants who thought themselves my betters simply because their fathers had been knighted.

I tried to imagine the expressions on their faces when they heard about my luxurious new quarters. They would speak disdainfully of my morals, but secretly they would envy me.

Drowsing in my warm little cocoon, indulging myself in pleasant fantasies, I was startled by the sound of the outer door opening. I cowered behind the bed hangings, uncertain what to do. A moment later, two servants entered the inner chamber. They seemed surprised to find me peering out at them from the gap in the bed curtains.

"What do you want?" I was relieved to hear no tremor in my voice.

"We come to collect all the unfinished candle stubs and the torches, mistress."

"Why?" Genuinely curious, I pulled the coverlet around myself and leaned out into the chamber. They had a large basket with them, into which they'd put the remains of candles.

"They are melted down and made into new, if it please you, lady."

"You collect these every day?"

Two heads bobbed in unison. "Aye, mistress." They looked anxious, as if they feared I would call a guard.

"Away with you, then. Go about your business."

They scurried out like mice pursued by a cat and left me to wonder what else went on in the royal household that I had never noticed. Even on Christmas, I supposed, close stools must be emptied, candles replaced, and meals cooked.

That made me wonder where Nan was. Nan Lister, the maidservant who was now all mine to command, should have brought washing water to the chamber by now. It was her job, too, to keep the brazier—the fireplace, I corrected myself—fueled, in addition to mending tears in clothing and serving as my tiring woman.

What else did she do, when her work was done? Was she well compensated for her services? A wry smile made my lips quirk at the thought that her wages per annum might be greater than my paltry stipend. It was fortunate indeed that I was not responsible for paying her.

She should have slept on the truckle bed. Stepping through the hangings, still wrapped in my coverlet, I almost tripped over the narrow, wheeled bed, but of Nan there was no trace. I shoved it into place beneath the larger bed, noticing as I did so that a bunch of mulberry twigs had been tied to the underside to keep fleas at bay.

Had Nan declined to serve a French nobleman's mistress? That seemed an unlikely explanation. What servant would dare refuse an order from the king? But why else did I have no one here to wait upon me?

I was alone.

Abandoned.

I shook off the sense of disquiet that shivered through me. I told myself I should be glad of the privacy, a rare and precious thing at court. In truth, I could not remember ever being so completely solitary before, save for once when, as a child, I wandered off into the woods near Amboise and was lost for the better part of an hour. I had been terrified then. Now I was merely ill at ease.

Trailing the coverlet, I approached the clothes press. It contained new garments in the Flemish fashion. Unfortunately, I would need help to assume any of them. Every piece—sleeves, bodice, kirtle, and partlet—required fastening together with points. It was a physical impossibility to dress myself.

Would anyone notice if I did not attend one of the greatest feasts of the year? My stomach growled at the thought of all that food. To begin the first course, a boar's head was always carried in on a platter decorated with rosemary and bay. Seethed brawn made from spiced boar was a traditional Christmas treat. There would be roast swan, as well. Dozens, perhaps hundreds, of other dishes would follow. The best never reached the lower tables, but there was plenty enough for all to dine well, and no sooner would dinner be complete, than we would sup. This year the king had planned a banquet, too, a rich offering of sweets and fruits after supper.

The whole court would feast, I thought miserably, while I starved to death for want of a maid to lace me into my clothing. Would *anyone* notice I was missing? Harry Guildford might, but only if he needed my help. For weeks he had been preoccupied with organizing the revels to be presented for Twelfth Night, neglecting both wife and friends to supervise every detail. I sighed. Even if he realized I had vanished, he would have no notion where to look for me.

I was dressed only in a chemise and half in and half out of a new kirtle when my rescuer arrived. The tentative scratching at the outer door was accompanied by a soft voice calling my name. Guy's voice.

Clasping the sleeves and bodice to my bosom, I let him in.

"Jesu, Jane!" His eyes widened as he took in my disheveled state.

Heat flooded into my face, and with it, no doubt, high color. I did not dare glance at my reflection in the looking glass. My loose, uncombed hair was better suited to the role of wild woman than waiting gentlewoman.

"Compton sent word to the duke only this morning of your new accommodations. When I noticed you were not in chapel, I thought I should come and find you."

"It is well you did. I appear to have lost my new maidservant." I made a helpless gesture with one hand, almost losing my grip on my clothing as I did so.

Guy hesitated. "I will go in search of her."

"Far simpler to tie my laces yourself." Straightening my spine, I turned my back on him, dropped the sleeves, and hoisted the kirtle. "The points at my waist first, if you please."

Once again, Guy proved more than adequate as a tiring maid. I began to suspect that, in common with the duke, he might have had considerable practice dressing—or rather, undressing—women in court dress.

When I was suitably attired for the Christmas Day festivities, we went together to the great hall. We separated there, Guy to sit with the duke's men, while I joined the Lady Mary's other attendants. I pretended not to notice the intense scrutiny I received.

That day seemed interminable. I held my head high and ignored the countless conversations that abruptly ended as I approached and the whispers that began as soon as I'd passed by. That it was Christmas made it a little easier to endure the snubs. Rank perforce gave place to revelry, and there was a good deal going on to distract the court's attention from speculation about me.

Master Wynnsbury was in rare form. In common with the king's fools, the Lord of Misrule could say what he would to anyone, even the king. He was wise enough not to abuse the privilege, but he knew King Henry's taste. He kept up a steady stream of ribald tales and jokes about bodily functions, fare that would not ordinarily have been approved of in the presence of the queen and princess. Both royal ladies showed great forbearance and endured the tasteless jests without demur. The king roared with laughter at every one.

The king's banquet was the last event of a long day. There was only one table, set up in the shape of an inverted U with Longueville, the queen, the king, and the Lady Mary seated at the top. A select group of courtiers occupied the two long sides, each man paired with a lady. To my relief, I was seated between Guy Dunois and Ned Neville.

"Your maidservant has been located," Guy whispered as we were served the first of twenty different sorts of jellies sculpted into the shapes of animals and castles. It was more common at banquets to dismiss the servants and serve ourselves, but I suspected King Henry was attempting to impress the duke.

"I am in your debt." I waved the jelly away, knowing there would be more delectable selections ahead.

"She says she became lost among the passageways."

"That is more than possible. Pleasure Palace is a maze if one does not know it well."

He lifted his eyebrows at the name and I found myself flushing as I explained why I'd called it that.

"She was a child and knew no better." Already well on his way to being cup-shot, Ned leaned in front of me to grin at Guy.

My color deepened. He made it sound as if I had been some-one's mistress even then. I covered my embarrassment by biting into a sweet biscuit.

Out of consideration for me, Guy ignored Ned's comments as well as his boisterous behavior. He seemed set on putting me at my ease—a good thing, since we sat at table for hours. Every sort of wine from Burgundy to Canary was served, along with confections in animal shapes, marchpane, "kissing comfits" of sugar fondant, fruits dipped in sugar and eaten with special sucket spoons, and the mounds of syllabub called Spanish paps. Servants brought in bowls of water in which to wash our hands between courses, but after enough wine, it was more fun to lick the excess sugar off our fingers.

At last the hippocras and wafers were served, signaling the end of the banquet. Scarcely a caraway-seed-covered apple was left by the time the king finally rose to call for dancing. Stifling groans, the members of his court joined in. The musicians played tune after lively tune, and it was dawn before anyone escaped to bed.

By then, I welcomed the solitude of my lodgings. I slept the whole day through, and if servants crept in to collect the candle stubs that morning, I was blissfully unaware of their presence.

9

The court made frequent moves from one palace to another even in winter. We were at Richmond again in time for the New Year's Day giving of gifts. Some said the tradition went back to pagan days. It did not, in spite of the name, mark the start of the new year. The year of our Lord fifteen hundred and fourteen would not officially begin until Lady Day, the twenty-fifth of March.

On the morning of the first of January, I was on duty as one of the Lady Mary's attendants. My first task was to deliver her New Year's gift to the king. Members of the royal household crowded the presence chamber, waiting for their names to be called, but as the representative of the second lady in the land, I was passed directly through to the privy chamber. Only Sir Thomas Bryan, the queen's vice-chamberlain, was ahead of me. He had brought Her Grace's gift to the king, her husband.

Sir Thomas glanced at me then quickly away, but not before I caught a glimpse of his disapproving expression. I repressed a sigh. He knew. And if he knew, so did his daughter, Meg Guildford, and Meg would have lost no time in telling Harry. I had no idea how my old friend would react to the news that I had given myself to a French prisoner of war, but I suspected he would not be pleased.

A fanfare sounded, breaking in on my gloomy thoughts. The usher of the chamber waved Sir Thomas forward and called out the customary words: "Sire, here is a New Year's gift coming from the queen. Let it come in, Sire."

When the door to the royal bedchamber opened, I caught a glimpse of the king. Fully dressed, he sat at the foot of his bed. His father had followed the same practice, waiting there to receive gifts from every member of the court. They were presented in order of rank, from the queen through the noblemen through the lords and ladies of lesser titles. Even those courtiers who were away from court sent gifts through representatives.

My own present for King Henry would be a pair of gloves I had embroidered myself. The gift was similar to those I had given him in years past. He always seemed pleased. I was the one who wished I could afford better. This year in particular, I regretted that I did not have the funds to give him a truly memorable gift.

A clerk stood to one side of the bedchamber, writing down the description and value of each offering. All the gifts would afterward be displayed in the presence chamber—jewelry and money, clothing, and gold and silver plate. And, after each gift had been presented with due ceremony, the king's servants handed out gifts of plate in return. Cups and bowls chased with the royal cipher were each weighed according to rank. Each person at court, even the most menial kitchen wench, received something.

When the usher of the chamber announced the Lady Mary's gift, I entered the bedchamber and walked toward the enormous royal bed. I felt unaccountably nervous, in part because there was a strange look on the king's face as he watched me approach. When I stood directly in front of him, His Grace waved the clerk out of earshot.

"Come closer, Jane."

Obeying, I made a deep obeisance and held out a jeweled and enameled pin for the king's hat, together with a matching ring.

King Henry barely glanced at them. His voice low and intense, he demanded to know why I had learned nothing of importance as yet from the duc de Longueville.

A chill went through me at his tone. When I dared peek at his face through my lashes, I wished I had not. His small eyes had narrowed to slits. There was no affection, no benevolence in that expression. He was angry . . . at me.

"Sire, I cannot conjure intelligence out of nothing. The duke does not speak to me of such things. I doubt he knows what King Louis intends. He tells me he has never spent much time at the French court."

The king's growl cut me off. My head bowed, I held my silence, hoping this storm would pass. After a moment, King Henry gave a gusty sigh. "The war with France continues, Jane. Persuade Longueville to talk to you of the battle in which he was captured. Mayhap that will loosen his tongue about other matters."

"There may be another way," I said hesitantly, "but I am loath to try without Your Grace's permission."

"Explain." I could hear the eagerness in his voice as he leaned closer.

We were surrounded by his attendants. I could only hope no one was close enough to catch my whispered words. "If I were to express a desire to return with him to France when he is ransomed, he might believe it safe to confide in me."

Scarcely daring to breathe, I waited for a reaction. I had lied to the king before, but never to this degree. What if he should guess my real reason for making such a bold suggestion? I had restrained myself for weeks . . . months, asking no more questions about my mother, but that did not mean I had given up my quest to learn all I could about her. I wanted to go to France with the duke and stay there long enough to discover the truth about Maman's sudden decision to flee with me to England.

Pondering my suggestion, the king hesitated so long that I wondered if he was building up steam to boil over. I did not dare look at him. The volatile temper of the Tudors was legendary.

"It is a good plan, Jane."

If I had not been holding myself so stiffly, I would have sagged with relief. "I have leave to deceive him, then? Your Grace will not believe the tale if there are rumors of my disloyalty?"

"Do and say whatever you must. Your sovereign can tell truth from lies."

Dipping my head again, I prayed he could not, but I left the royal bedchamber with a lighter heart.

AT YULETIDE MORE than any other time of year, the households of the king, the queen, and the princess mingled at court. The twelve days of Christmas began at sundown on the twenty-fourth day of December and continued until the beginning of Epiphany on the sixth of January. The period from sundown on the fifth through the day of the sixth was Twelfth Night and celebrated with a banquet and mumming.

We were all in our finest apparel, even the liveried servants, who had been given new garments for the new year. The queen's pages wore gold brocade and crimson satin in checkers while her adult male attendants were dressed in gray broadcloth and gray, white, and scarlet kersey. The king's yeomen of the guard had new scarlet livery, replacing the green and white coats they had worn in the old king's reign.

The gentlewomen and ladies of the court vied with each other to dress in their finest. That they were exempt from the sumptuary laws meant their excesses knew no bounds save the good sense not to outshine the king and queen. In honor of Twelfth Night, the duc de Longueville wore a short doublet of blue and crimson velvet slashed with cloth-of-gold.

I sighed as I looked around the great hall.

"What is it, my pet?" Longueville asked.

"Alongside all this splendor, I look very plain indeed." I wore the best that I had—dark green velvet, the sleeves puffed and slashed to show yellow silk beneath. In any other company, I would have looked very grand.

His eyes sparkled as he flashed me a smile. "Perhaps this will help."

I felt him slide something onto my finger and when I looked down, I was wearing a ruby ring. I wondered how he had obtained it, knowing as I did the state of his finances, but I did not ask. I held my hand out, admiring the way the stone reflected the light from the candles.

"It is beautiful, Louis. You are most generous." I was not too proud to accept the expensive gift. Indeed, if I did not live up to the king's expectations and was not allowed to return to France with my lover, the sale of such a bauble might be all I had to provide for myself.

He lifted my fingers to his lips and kissed them. "I would shower you with such jewels if I could."

The ring was soon remarked upon . . . in whispers. Such an expensive gift proclaimed louder than words that the duke had staked his claim on me. Anyone who had not previously suspected that I was his mistress would know it now.

As the evening wore on, one after another the queen's ladies snubbed me. Even the princess's gentlewomen pointedly avoided my company. Only young Bessie Blount, naturally friendly as a puppy, braved the censure of the others to exchange greetings with me.

If I had not had the Lady Mary's friendship and the king's support, I might well have kept to my lodgings. As it was, I knew I must be brazen and pretend nothing had changed. I lifted my chin, pasted a smile on my face, and attempted to enjoy the festivities. I was saddened, but not surprised, when Harry Guildford also stayed well away from me.

Everyone rose as the lord steward carried a cup full of spiced ale into the torchlit presence chamber. He called out the traditional greeting: "Wassail, wassail, wassail!" and then presented the cup to the king. King Henry sipped and handed the cup to the queen, who looked fine indeed, wearing her long hair loose over her shoulders, as only queens and unmarried girls are permitted to do. The king's blue-gray eyes sparkled as he watched her pass the wassail cup to his sister. After that, all the courtiers in attendance took their turns while the Children of the Chapel sang.

As soon as the wassail cup had made its rounds, confections and spices of all sorts were served, first to the king and queen and then to the rest of the court. In the past there had been as many as a hundred dishes at a Twelfth Night banquet. Last to be served was always the cake made of flour, honey, spices, and dried fruit. By that time, I no longer had any appetite. I toyed with the slice in front of me, mangling the pastry.

"*Qu'est-ce que c'est?*" Guy gestured toward the cake. Once again we had been seated together, as befit our station. To sit next to Longueville, given his rank, would have been a breach of protocol.

I looked down and there, lying in the ruins of the cake, was a bean. *The* bean. I stared at it in horror. Whoever found this prize became King or Queen of the Bean for the rest of the evening and the last thing I desired was more notoriety.

Nick Carew, seated on my other side, had not touched his cake. He was preoccupied with sending longing glances at Elizabeth, Meg Guildford's beautiful, chestnut-haired sister. I plucked the bean from my crumbs and shoved it into the center of his portion of cake. Moments later, Nick discovered the prize. He made a most excellent King of the Bean. His first act was to call for the evening's entertainment to begin.

There were no great set pieces required for this revel, although Master Gibson had made the costumes and sent them to Richmond from London by barge. He'd dressed six gentlemen in white jackets and black gowns and minstrels and a fool in yellow sarcenet painted with hearts and wings of silver. But the centerpiece of the spectacle consisted of two women clad in silver—Meg and her sister—who represented the goddesses Venus and Beauty.

There was less story than usual to this piece, but the servants and ordinary folk seated on benches around the outside of the chamber were enthralled when the gentlemen performed a Morris dance. There followed an interlude performed by the Children of the Chapel and then Venus and Beauty sang to the accompaniment of a lute. By the last verse, everyone was familiar enough with the chorus to join in, even Guy, who did not understand a word of it.

" 'Bow you down,' " we sang, " 'and do your duty, to Venus and the goddess Beauty. We triumph high over all. Kings attend when we do call.' "

Bowing down to kings, I thought, was a much wiser course for the rest of us.

A second interlude was performed by the King's Players, but it was overlong. There were restless stirrings in the crowd and the king left before the end of it. The queen departed soon after.

Nick Carew, as King of the Bean, and Master Wynnsbury, who was Lord of Misrule for this one last night, called for dancing. I looked wistfully back over my shoulder as I slipped out of the hall, but I had no real desire to execute intricate steps while hostile glares bored into my back.

A WEEK LATER, a somber-faced Guy interrupted my intimate supper with the duc de Longueville. "A special messenger has just arrived from the French court." He handed the duke a sealed letter.

Longueville broke the seal and read. For just a moment, he had the self-satisfied look of a cat with a mouse, but he hastily rearranged his features into solemn lines before he told us what the letter contained. "Anne of Brittany, queen of France, is dead."

An overwhelming sadness filled me. Queen Anne had been much admired, even loved, by my mother. I felt her loss on a deep and personal level.

"This provides a great opportunity." Longueville assessed me with a long, hard look. "The English king has two sisters, does he not?"

"You know he does."

"The younger is very dear to him, the flower of his court, and promised to Charles of Castile. But the elder, Margaret, is newly the widow of the king of Scotland. What could be more providential than that? Tell me all you know about her, Jane."

"She is regent of Scotland. Her young son is the king."

"Is she comely?"

"She was pretty as a girl, but I have not seen her for six years." A woman quickly lost her looks when she began bearing children.

"Was she as beautiful as her younger sister?"

"She had . . . a different sort of beauty." Margaret had been stocky as a girl. I suspected she'd grown heavier with age. Mary was a sylph and likely always would be. "Your Grace, you cannot think to marry Queen Margaret to the king of France."

"Why not? Alliances are formed by royal marriages, are they not? This one could bring peace for generations to come."

"But she has a duty to Scotland. She is *regent*."

He dismissed those responsibilities with a careless wave of the hand. "Some suitable Scots nobleman will be found to fill the post."

"Her son cannot leave Scotland. Would you deprive him of his mother?" Such separations were common, but that did not make them any less painful for those involved.

"She will have other children. King Louis' children."

"I should think," I said stiffly, "that you might give them each time to mourn before you force them into another marriage."

Incredulous, Longueville laughed at the very idea. "You are softhearted, sweeting. Let them commiserate with each other if they must grieve, but I would be surprised if that were necessary. Their earlier marriages were made for political reasons, and so will this one be." His words held no hint of sympathy for his bereaved monarch, his own distant cousin, let alone for my erstwhile playfellow Margaret Tudor.

"King James of Scotland was young and handsome, or so I have heard." I had also heard reports that he and Margaret had never taken to each other, that she'd been too strong willed to suit him, but saw no need to tell Longueville that.

"Until he was brutally slain by English troops at the Battle of Flodden," the duke said. Irritated, he rose from the table and walked to the coffer where he kept quills, ink, and parchment.

I had yet to follow the suggestion that I ask Longueville about his own experiences in battle. I did not think it would improve his temper to remind him of the ignominious defeat the French troops had suffered at what the English called the Battle of the Spurs. That, Harry had told me, had been all they'd seen of the French cavalry as they galloped away across the field at Guingates in an attempt to escape the victorious troops led by King Henry and his allies.

The longer I remained Longueville's mistress, the more I realized that he was no gallant knight and had never been. He might be kind to me, gentle with me, but he'd give me away in a heartbeat if he saw an advantage in it. If I did end up traveling with him to France, I would do well to remember that.

"Is Queen Margaret as unpredictable as her brother?" Longueville asked.

Mayhap I was concerned for her without reason, I thought. All I had to do to discourage the match was to tell the truth. "She is, and she has the Tudor temper, too. I remember once, when she was already styled queen of Scotland, although she had not yet gone north to consummate the marriage, she flew into a rage over a pair of sleeves."

At his lifted eyebrow, I explained.

"All the Tudors love fine clothing. You have seen that for yourself. After the death of Arthur, Prince of Wales, the entire family wore black, but as that summer wore on, the princesses were allowed a bit of color in their wardrobe. Princess Margaret acquired two sets of sleeves, one of white sarcenet and another pair in orange sarcenet. The orange sleeves were her favorite item of dress, and when they were accidentally left behind when the court moved from Baynard's Castle to Westminster, nothing would do but that

Queen Elizabeth's page of robes be sent back to fetch them. He was rewarded for doing so, but first he had to endure a tirade of abuse for forgetting them in the first place. A Tudor in a temper is a formidable sight, terrifying and ludicrous all at once."

"Even the Lady Mary has this failing?"

I nodded, though it felt disloyal to make the admission. "Even she. The princess has been known to scream and throw things in a manner more suited to a two-year-old child than a woman in her eighteenth year."

I hoped such tales might make the duke reconsider, but he seemed more set on his matchmaking than ever. I had, however, regained his goodwill. He asked for additional stories about Margaret's early life and in return spoke more freely in front of me, outlining his plan to approach King Henry to ask for his help in marrying off his widowed sister.

When I left the duke's lodgings, I went directly to the great hall. Word of Queen Anne's death had already spread among the courtiers but had created only a minor stir. Had the king of France died, that would have caused consternation. Since Louis was still alive, life went on unchanged. The dancing and dicing and games of cards continued, unaffected by the news from France.

I found Will Compton without difficulty, and relayed my information in a hurried whisper. He scarce seemed to hear me. He kept glancing toward the doorway, as if he expected someone to make an entrance.

"Will? Is aught amiss?"

He shook his head, but I did not believe him. A sense of foreboding settled over me when I saw Dr. John Chambre arrive. Even if I had not recognized his hawk nose and his habitually grim expression, he would have been marked as one of the king's physicians by his long, furred gown in royal livery colors.

He made his way directly to Will, but nodded to me in polite greeting. "Mistress Popyncourt. You look well."

Impressed that he'd remembered who I was, I thanked him for the compliment. When he started to follow Will from the presence chamber, I was struck by a sudden thought. I caught at his trailing sleeve. "Sir, a moment? May I speak with you privily?"

Here was one more person who might know something about my lady mother.

"You must wait and talk to him later," Will said, and hurried the doctor away.

I soon understood why they had been so distracted. The king had fallen ill again. For two weeks, as Dr. Chambre hovered and the queen set herself the task of nursing her husband back to health, the duc de Longueville could get nowhere near His Grace. His plan to negotiate for Queen Margaret's hand on behalf of King Louis fell into abeyance.

I shared his frustration, but not for the same reason. Now that I had remembered Dr. Chambre, I was anxious to speak with the royal physician but he was much too busy with his patient to have time for me. It was nearly a week later, after the king was well on his way to recovery, that the respected physician remembered my request and found his way to my lodgings.

Although Nan was a slow-witted girl, just bright enough to carry out her duties as my maid, I sent her away as soon as the doctor appeared. I had learned to be careful what I said when others might overhear.

He frowned. "It is customary to keep another female about during an examination, but I suppose you wish this kept secret." My blank expression had him narrowing his eyes. "You did wish to consult me on a private matter?"

Obviously he thought I was pregnant. Or worse, diseased. Heat

crept up my neck and into my face. "It is not . . . I did not . . . I only
wanted to ask you if you tended my mother during her last illness!"

"I have no notion who your mother was."

"She was Mistress Popyncourt. Joan Popyncourt. She joined
Queen Elizabeth's household in June of the thirteenth year of the
reign of King Henry the Seventh and traveled with the court into
East Anglia on progress. I am told she died that September at Collyweston."

"I was not yet at court then," Dr. Chambre said.

My spirits sank.

"Collyweston, you say?" He rubbed his chin as he considered.
"That was the home of the Countess of Richmond, King Henry
the Seventh's mother. The physician who attended your mother
was most likely Philip Morgan. At least he was the doctor who
looked after the countess during her final years."

The Countess of Richmond had been a force to be reckoned
with in my youth. She had written the rules and regulations
by which the royal nursery functioned. By the time I arrived at
Eltham, she'd only rarely visited, but I could remember how she'd
swoop down on her grandchildren, a scrawny figure in unrelieved
black. She had been very pious, always muttering prayers. And she
had not liked me. Once I had overheard her telling Mother Guildford that I should be sent away to a nunnery.

"Do you know where I might find Doctor Morgan?" I asked.

"In his grave, most like. Or mayhap he returned to his native
Wales." Dr. Chambre chuckled. "Some would say those two fates
are the same."

"I have been told my mother was ill before she ever came to
court."

His interest sharpened. "What ailed her?"

"Mother Guildford told me it was a wasting sickness, mayhap

consumption." The disease was common enough. It had killed King Henry VII and some thought it had been the cause of Prince Arthur's death, as well.

I thought I saw a spark of pity in the doctor's eyes, but it was gone too quickly to be certain.

"She was Sir Rowland Velville's twin sister," I added.

"Ah. I know Sir Rowland. But I fear I cannot help you, mistress. I was still a student when your mother died."

Dr. Chambre had already reached the door when I thought of one last question. "If it was the Countess of Richmond's physician who cared for my mother, would it have been the countess's confessor who gave her last rites?"

He paused, looking thoughtful. "I suppose it must have been."

"Do you remember who he was?"

A short bark of laughter answered me. "Oh, yes, Mistress Popyncourt. He went on to greater things. The countess's confessor was John Fisher. He's bishop of Rochester now."

My hopes of being able to question the priest dashed—one did not gain audiences with bishops easily, even minor ones—I thanked the doctor for his time. When he had gone I sank down on my luxurious bed, disconsolate. Even if I did convince the bishop of Rochester to speak with me in private, he would not tell me anything. He was not permitted to speak of what he heard in the confessional.

With that realization, I began to despair of ever learning more about my mother's time in England or her reason for bringing us here. Those few people who had come in close contact with her all seemed to be dead or in distant parts . . . or suffer from passing-poor memories.

To me she remained vivid. I could not understand why she had not made a deeper impression on all those who had met her. Even

if she had been dying—a thing I still found difficult to accept—
she should have been memorable. *Especially* if she'd been ill. If the
other ladies had shunned her, fearing infection, surely they should
recall doing so.

Unless she had deliberately effaced herself.

The air soughed out of my lungs. It appeared that there were
only two people left to approach who might know something—my
uncle and Lady Catherine Strangeways. To talk to either of them, I
would have to arrange for an extended absence from court.

Although I was not sure why, I was reluctant to put my questions in writing. Even if both of them could read and did not need
to share the contents with a secretary or a priest—something of
which I was not certain even in my uncle's case—it was far too
easy for letters to fall into the wrong hands.

Counseling myself to be patient, I continued to spend my days
with the Lady Mary and my nights with the duc de Longueville.

THE COURT HAD moved on to Greenwich Palace by the time the
next emissary arrived from France. The duc de Longueville met with
him and returned to his lodgings in an expansive mood. I had been
sitting near the window with my embroidery while Guy idly played
the lute. We both sprang to our feet when the duke came in.

"What news, my lord?" Guy asked. Even though the two men
were brothers, Guy never used the duke's first name. I rarely did
myself, and Longueville seemed content to be deferred to.

"The most excellent kind. The new envoy is here to arrange my
ransom. Talks have already begun with King Henry's representatives."

"Will matters be settled quickly, then?" I asked.

"That will depend upon our success at negotiating another matter."

"A marriage," I guessed.

"A marriage . . . between King Louis the Twelfth of France and the Lady Mary."

I sat down hard on the window seat, momentarily robbed of speech.

Guy voiced what I was thinking: "I thought Queen Margaret—"

"King Louis has heard that Mary is the most beautiful princess in Christendom. He sees no reason to settle for second best."

Heard from Longueville himself, I thought.

"Have you forgotten?" I asked. "The Lady Mary already has a husband. She was married by proxy years ago to Charles of Castile."

He dismissed that ceremony with a careless wave of one hand. "They have not taken final vows, nor has their marriage been consummated." The latter was what sealed the bargain. Until husband and wife slept together, they were wedded only on paper. With the cooperation of the church, such alliances—at least among princes—could easily be severed.

"What makes you think King Henry will go along with this plan?" I asked.

To my surprise, he told me.

More than an hour passed before I could leave the duke's apartments without arousing suspicion. When I did escape, I headed straight for the king's lodgings.

Hindered by long skirts, it took longer than I wished to race across one of Greenwich's three courtyards and reenter the palace through a side door to the great hall. Still, the shortcut had saved me some time. I paused only long enough to brush snow from my face and headdress and catch my breath.

A body stitchet of boiled leather is not designed to permit rapid movement of any kind, and mine was tightly laced. As soon as I had recovered sufficiently, I sped up the stairs that led to the king's apartments. I did not slow down as I passed through the great watching chamber and I ignored the guards standing at attention at regular intervals around the room. I all but ran through the curtained door that led into the king's presence chamber.

Seeing neither the king nor Will Compton, I slowed my pace only a little and advanced on the door to the privy chamber. A halberd appeared in front of me just before I could open the door, barring my way.

"You have no business in there, mistress."

I did not know the young man assigned to keep intruders out of the king's inner rooms. Frustration had my fingers curling into fists and my lips thinning into a flat, tight line. Nothing I could say would persuade him to let me in. It was his duty to regulate access to King Henry.

Forcing myself to smile, I removed the little dragon pendant my mother had given me so long ago and handed it him. "Give this to Sir William Compton and bid him come to me as soon as he may."

He held the small piece of jewelry up to examine it. "This is one of the king's emblems," he said. "A Welsh dragon."

That was exactly why I offered it. Outside of the royal family, few people had pieces of jewelry like it. Only my old friends from Eltham would know at once that a message sent with this little dragon had come from me and no other.

"What it is does not concern you, sirrah. Only that you deliver it to Sir William."

"I cannot leave my post, mistress." He returned the bauble to me.

I stamped my foot. He lifted an eyebrow, but did not relent.

I turned and surveyed the presence chamber, searching for any familiar face. There must be someone who could fetch Will out to me. I caught sight of Charles Brandon, recently elevated in the peerage to Duke of Suffolk, but doubted he would help. He was too full of himself.

During the campaign in France, the king and Brandon had become even closer than they had been before. Back in England again, King Henry had rewarded his boon companion with a title. The other gentlemen—Harry, Will, Ned, and the rest—were still high in the king's favor, but none of them had received any honors beyond a knighthood. There was now understandable tension between Brandon and the rest.

I considered asking Ned Neville or Nick Carew for help. Then my gaze settled on Harry Guildford. Although we had not spoken in weeks, I did not hesitate to approach him. I waited until he finished speaking with a gentleman in lawyer's robes before I tapped him on the shoulder.

"Jane!" Pleasure lit his face . . . until he remembered. His expression closed and he took a step back instead of greeting me with the customary kiss. "What do you want?"

Schooling my features to conceal how much his disdain wounded me, I asked if he would take a message to Will.

"Looking to couple with him now? I admit he's a well-set-up fellow, but I'd have thought you'd prefer Brandon. After all, he's a duke, too."

Harry's comment could not have been more hurtful. It was as if he had slapped me. I bit back a cry of pain and simply stared at him, eyes swimming with unshed tears.

"You brought ill feeling on yourself, Jane! How do you expect people to react when you fraternize with the enemy?" He glared at me, but our gazes locked for only a few seconds before he looked away. Ashamed of himself? I hoped so, but I did not count on it.

I longed to tell Harry the truth, but I did not dare. Bad enough he thought me a whore without adding spy to the list of my sins. Besides, I was sworn to secrecy. No one but Will and the king were supposed to know what I was about.

"I must talk to Will, Harry. It is important. Please. Tell him to come to my lodgings as soon as he can."

I'd thought he could hold himself no more stiffly, but I'd been wrong. He stared down his nose at me, aloof and condescending, but he agreed to deliver the message.

On my way out of the presence chamber I felt as if every eye was fixed upon me, censorious or, worse, speculative. I returned to my rooms, sent Nan away, and felt my lower lip start to quiver. Before I knew it, I was sobbing as if my heart had broken.

Guy found me like that, sitting on the floor, tears streaming down my cheeks, almost incoherent. He fell to his knees beside me and gathered me into his arms. I do not know what he said to me. His voice was simply a comforting murmur that slowly brought me back to myself.

"You are the only old friend I have left," I wailed, burying my face against his shoulder. I would have to go to France with Longueville. There was nothing for me here anymore.

"Shhh, Jeanne. It is not so bad as all that."

"It is. Everyone h-hates me for being with the duke. Even you do not approve."

"I do not hate you. I cannot." Very gently, he pressed his lips to mine.

It started out as a comforting kiss, but the moment he slid his arms around my waist and tugged me against him it became something quite different, something . . . magical.

My entire body tingled as I arched toward him, seeking to press closer. I returned his kiss, enraptured by the way his lips moved on mine. Longueville had never made me feel like this.

Abruptly, we both went still. He pulled back, slowly releasing me and helping me to my feet. "That should not have happened."

"No."

"I cannot regret that it did. I have dreamed of kissing you."

"Oh." I pressed my hands to my burning cheeks. "You should not be saying this to me."

He heaved a gusty sigh. "We will not speak of it again. My brother has the prior claim. Neither one of us wishes to betray him."

If only he knew! "We must pretend this never happened. Guy, I do not want to lose your friendship." I would be left with none save a half-wit maid and a self-absorbed princess if that happened.

"Friend is perhaps not the best word for what we have between us," Guy said, "but I do not want to lose you either. We will pretend." His mouth twisted into a wry grimace. "We are both good at that."

I took a step toward him, then stopped, shaking my head. "You should go now."

"I should."

Only moments after he'd left, Will Compton arrived. "This had better be important," he said by way of greeting. "King Louis' ransom envoy has arrived in England and talks have commenced to negotiate Longueville's release."

"Do you think I do not know that? Sit down. I will tell you what I have learned."

Will gave a low whistle when I'd completed my report. "The

French want a marriage between the Lady Mary and King Louis? Impossible! She is already married to Charles of Castile and will be sent to his court as soon as the final details are worked out."

"Before King Henry fell ill, it was his sister Margaret's name the duc de Longueville meant to propose as King Louis' bride, but now Louis wants Mary. She is younger. Prettier." I shrugged. "And perhaps he has heard of Margaret's temper."

"No one can deny that Mary is beautiful." Will helped himself to wine from my supply and filled two goblets, handing one to me. "But why would the French king think such a marriage might be possible?"

I hesitated, sipped the wine—a fine Canary—choosing my words with care. Longueville had given me a reason. "King Ferdinand of Spain is about to make a separate peace with France."

Will's breath hissed out on a curse. King Henry had gone to war against France with King Ferdinand, Queen Catherine's father and Charles of Castile's grandfather, as his ally. The negotiations for peace were supposed to be conducted jointly.

When Will began to pace, I understood his agitation. What I had just told him was not news anyone would wish to deliver to the king of England. Word that King Ferdinand had secretly changed sides would be a severe blow to King Henry's consequence. It would also affect his ability to secure favorable terms in his own peace with France. I did not need to say that it was the duc de Longueville's hope that King Henry would be so enraged by King Ferdinand's duplicity that he would rush into an agreement to marry his sister to King Louis. To jilt Ferdinand's grandson would be certain to strike Henry as the perfect revenge.

That the Lady Mary would be bartered to someone, no different from the king's goods or chattels, was not something I could stop, no matter how much I cared for her. There was little to choose, to my mind, between marriage to young Charles and old Louis . . . except that if my mistress was sent to France, I could accompany her there. While Will continued to pace and sputter in indignation, I let my mind drift. When all was said and done, perhaps a French marriage would suit me very well indeed.

10

King Henry did not want to believe me on the French reports of the new alliance between King Ferdinand and King Louis, but his own sources soon confirmed it. Once he was convinced that his father-in-law had betrayed him, he was eager to fall in with the duc de Longueville's suggestion. I accompanied the Lady Mary on the day she was taken into her brother's confidence. I watched her face as he told her she would one day be queen of France.

"I had not heard that Charles of Castile had conquered the French," she remarked, fiddling coyly with her pomander ball.

King Henry laughed. "Saucy wench! You know perfectly well that he has done no such thing."

"How else can I become queen of France?"

"By repudiating your marriage to Charles and entering into a betrothal with King Louis."

Mary toyed with one of the many rings she wore, a small one with a blue stone. "King Louis is quite old, is he not?"

"Fifty-two, I believe."

"The same age at which Father died."

"What are you thinking, Mary?" the king asked his sister.

"That I may not be queen of France very long if I marry an old man like that."

"Perhaps not, but you can do your country good service while he lives. You do not intend to be troublesome over this, do you?"

"I am yours to command," she assured him, but there was a look in her eyes that worried me.

"Good," said King Henry. "Now, for the present, you must tell no one about this change in plans. Your entanglement with Charles of Castile cannot be broken off just yet, not until the new alliance between France and England has been negotiated. To that end, you must behave in public as if you desire nothing more than to be queen of Castile."

He presented Mary with a portrait in miniature of King Charles and suggested that she carry it about with her wherever she went. She hugged it to her bosom all the way back to her own apartments. The way her face was working, I expected tears, but as soon as we were alone in her bedchamber, she burst into gales of laughter.

"Oh, this will be fun, Jane! I will fool them all."

"You seem remarkably calm at the thought of taking an old man into your bed."

"His age means that he is not likely to live long after the wedding. When he's dead, I will choose a man more to my liking for a second husband."

I eyed her warily. "What man?"

But she only shook her head and smiled mysteriously, refusing to give me a name. She did not need to. I was certain she was thinking of Charles Brandon, Duke of Suffolk.

"It is likely your brother will have his own ideas about your remarriage," I warned her. "If King Louis is considerate enough to make you a widow, what is to stop your brother from using you to seal some other alliance?"

"I will think of a way to prevent him," she assured me. "Now help me change my clothing. Tonight is St. Valentine's Eve and I must look my best for the lottery."

The church considered St. Valentine's Day only a minor holiday, but at court it was an excuse for a great deal of revelry. The names of every gentleman at court—and most of the noblemen, too—were written down on bits of paper. Then each lady and gentlewoman drew a name and that man became her companion all the next day. He was required to buy her a gift and behave toward her as did a knight to his lady. In the best tradition of courtly love, he would put her on a pedestal and worship her from afar—at least as far away as the lady wished to keep him!

We gathered for the drawing in the queen's presence chamber.

"I cannot wait to see what courtier will be my valentine," Bessie Blount whispered in my ear. "I hope he is well favored. And rich," she added as an afterthought.

"What man courts you will depend upon the luck of the draw." Hiding a smile, I turned to examine my embroidery by the light of the nearest candelabra.

"Do you think so?" Bessie worried her lower lip and her big blue eyes filled with concern. "I have heard that some ladies find a way to cheat."

"If those ladies are your betters, best make no mention of it."

"But it is not . . . ." She struggled to find the right word: "Sporting."

"Ah, Bessie. If you value fairness, you are in the wrong place."

"And if I value love? True love? Is that not what St. Valentine's Day celebrates?"

"True love, too, is in short supply at court."

It was in fashion for courtiers to say they had fallen in love with this woman or that, and to sigh after the unattainable, but it was all a game to them. Men pursued women to marry them for their fortunes, to win their favor and influence, or to entice them into coupling. None of those goals had anything to do with affection.

A fanfare sounded, announcing the beginning of the lottery. A huge wooden box, brightly painted, was carried in by liveried servants. The Lady Mary followed, seemingly distracted by something she held in her hand. She heaved a great sigh as she reached the table where the box had been placed. She murmured a single word: "Charles."

At my side, Bessie echoed the sigh. "See how she pines for her betrothed. Truly, she has fallen in love with his likeness."

It seemed the king's plan was working. I was the only one who realized that the princess's actions were all for show.

Mary dropped the little portrait of her betrothed, letting it dangle carelessly from a chain suspended from her waist. Then she dipped her hand into the box, drew out a name, and smirked. "I have chosen my lord of Suffolk for my valentine," she announced. "Now come all who would find their true loves. The lottery has begun."

When the Lady Mary pined in public for "Charles," it was not Charles of Castile she spoke of. She might stare at that miniature of the young king, but her thoughts were all for a different Charles— Charles Brandon, Duke of Suffolk. Mary continued to be infatuated with her brother's handsome friend from childhood.

If she thought she'd be allowed to marry Brandon someday, she was sadly mistaken, but I did not intend to tell her so again. She would realize soon enough that although the king might elevate one of his boon companions to a dukedom, he would not waste the hand of a royal princess on one of his own subjects, not when he could use her as a diplomatic pawn.

Urged forward by Bessie, I took my turn to dip my hand into the lottery box. The name I drew was Nicholas Carew. I had not expected to be matched with the duc de Longueville. His name had not been placed in the lottery, nor had the king's.

"Hard luck," Bessie commiserated, peering at the scrap of paper. "Nick is handsome but very poor."

"We will do well enough together . . . for one day." I had known Nick since he was a little boy, younger than I, at Eltham. "What name did you draw?"

She made a face. "The Earl of Worcester."

"He is wealthy," I reminded her.

"But he is older than almost everyone at court, except perhaps Sir Thomas Lovell, and married besides. And he has terrible bad breath. He always smells of onions."

"He can afford to give you a very nice Valentine's Day gift," I reminded her, "and is unlikely to demand much in return."

Mollified, Bessie left my side to return to her place among the queen's women. I shook my head as I watched her tuck the slip of paper into her bodice. She was smiling sweetly.

Had I ever been that innocent? I felt as though I should run after her with a warning to guard her virtue well if she ever hoped to catch a husband, wealthy or otherwise.

A low, venomous voice spoke from just behind me, tearing my attention away from Bessie Blount. "She's no better than a whore."

I did not need to turn to recognize the speaker as Meg

Guildford, Harry's wife. I also knew she'd meant me to overhear her comment.

"He was supposed to be mine," her sister Elizabeth whined.

I frowned. I had assumed Meg was talking about me—it would not be the first time she'd called me names, both behind my back and to my face. But surely her young sister did not mean she wanted to take my place as the duc de Longueville's mistress. Then I remembered the slip of paper I still held in my hand. It was drawing Nick Carew as my valentine that had made Elizabeth Bryan jealous.

Thinking to offer a trade, I turned toward them. Nick would most assuredly be happier that way, since everyone at court knew how besotted he was with Elizabeth. But before I could open my mouth to speak, the two sisters brushed past me, noses in the air. They twitched their skirts aside as they passed, as if they feared to do otherwise would dip them in muck.

It was a very unsatisfying Valentine's Day all around. Nick ignored me to stare at Elizabeth. Bessie's gift from her valentine was a caged bird, hardly what she'd hoped for. And even Charles Brandon was a disappointment. Well aware of the king's plans for Lady Mary, Brandon was careful to keep her at arm's length. His gift to her was unexceptional—a pair of embroidered sleeves.

WE WERE AT Greenwich again in April, having spent a few weeks at Westminster and another two at Richmond, when word arrived that the village of Brighton, on the coast, had been burnt to the ground by the French. The story spread through the court like wildfire and rumors fanned the flames. The news reached the duke's apartments in record time when Ivo Jumelle burst in without ceremony to blurt out what he'd heard.

Longueville, the Lady Mary, and I had met there to pass the

afternoon conversing in French. The princess had once been fluent in the language, thanks to me, but French had not been much spoken at court since the beginning of her brother's reign.

"They say an invasion force has landed," Ivo gasped out. His eyes were bright and his cheeks flushed. "Do you suppose they have come to rescue us?"

Longueville did not trouble to hide his displeasure. "What fool has launched an attack? He will ruin all. It is peace we need now, not war."

"I will go to my brother," the Lady Mary said. "The king will know what is truth and what is speculation."

When she had gone, the duke and I stared at each other in shared consternation. He had come to trust me in the months since he'd begun negotiating in secret with King Henry for a marriage between the Lady Mary and King Louis. More than once he had used me as a go-between with Henry.

As far as most people knew, the old alliance still held, even though King Ferdinand had indeed signed a treaty with France in March. Only in Henry's changed attitude toward his wife and queen, Ferdinand's daughter, had there been any hint of how incensed he was by this betrayal.

Changing policy to ally England with France was a delicate undertaking and one to which many in England would be opposed when they heard of it. I had been sworn to secrecy, one of only a select few in England who knew what was afoot. The others were Longueville and the king; the Lady Mary; Will Compton; Guy Dunois; and the king's almoner, Thomas Wolsey, newly consecrated as bishop of Lincoln.

"It may be much ado over nothing," I murmured. "You know how rumors exaggerate."

"There is something behind the tale. England and France are

still at war, for all the negotiating we have done," Longueville said.

I looked out through the window at a fine April day and wondered at how quickly such beauty could be marred. Many at court, the queen included, thought it a mistake to trust any Frenchman. This news would only reinforce their opinion.

Guy came into the chamber, the troubled expression on his face proof he'd heard the rumor.

"How bad is it?" the duke demanded.

"Bad enough, although it could be worse. The town of Brighton was attacked and burnt to the ground, but someone managed to light a warning beacon on the Sussex Downs to alert the neighboring villages. They sent archers to drive away the French rowing boats that were trying to land." Guy hesitated, then added, "Those ships were galleys that were flying Admiral Prégent de Bidoux's colors."

I felt the color drain out of my face. "Bidoux? The one they call Prior John?"

"You know the name, I see," Longueville said.

"I know it." It had been only a year earlier that this French admiral from Rhodes had last engaged our English fleet in battle.

"Sit down, Jane." Guy all but shoved me onto a stool. "You've gone the color of whey."

"Bidoux is a monster. A vile villain."

"In war—"

"No!" I would not allow Longueville to make excuses. "Your French admiral, this Bidoux, cut out the heart of an English lord to keep as a trophy! It was an atrocity not to be tolerated. Because of it, King Henry invaded France, hungry for French blood. He *settled* for taking prisoners of war."

"Bidoux is hailed as a hero in France." Longueville held himself stiffly, unwilling to admit to any fault.

"And he is reviled here as a devil. Do you think Lord Edward's friends have either forgotten or forgiven what happened to him? This raid will add fuel to the hatred all good Englishmen already feel toward your countrymen. Have a care, Your Grace. The king was not the only close friend Lord Edward had at court. Charles Brandon, the new Duke of Suffolk, is another."

"And so were you, I think," Guy said in a soft voice.

Longueville either did not hear him or chose to ignore what he said. "I am the king's guest. I am in no danger."

"I would not be so certain of that." I rose and stepped in front of him, forcing him to look at me. "Even if *you* are protected by your rank and position, the rest of your retinue is not. Keep Ivo close, my lord. Young as he is, he'd be easy prey." And Guy, I thought. He'd be a target, too. My heart tripped at what might be done to him if some of the king's courtiers caught him alone.

Longueville dismissed the danger as a minor annoyance. He'd convinced himself this was but a temporary setback in peace negotiations and nothing to be troubled about. No amount of argument on my part could convince him otherwise. When the king sent for him, he viewed it as a positive sign.

"You must have a care, too, Jane," Guy said when the duke had gone. "Those who sympathize with the enemy are often more hated than the enemy himself."

"How well I know it, but I doubt that anyone will attack one of the Lady Mary's gentlewomen with anything more lethal than sharp words."

His lips twisted into a wry grimace. "In your own way, you are as arrogant as the duke."

"What use is there in fearing shadows?" Brave words but inside I was quaking. Unwilling to acknowledge my anxiety, I swept out of the duke's lodgings, head held high. I went straight to my own rooms. I had entered the inner chamber before I realized there *was* someone lurking in the darkest corner. I gave a squeak of alarm before I recognized Will Compton.

"Did Longueville know about this attack on Brighton in advance?" Will's eyes were cold as ice.

"No. Longueville desires peace. He wants this marriage between King Louis and the Lady Mary to succeed. He hopes to arrange for a ceremony here in England with himself standing as proxy for his master. He called the raid the act of a fool."

"The king is furious."

"As he should be, but not with the duc de Longueville."

Will seized my upper arm in a painful grip. "Some may seek the most convenient target for their wrath."

"Do you count yourself in their number, Will?" I was trembling with fear, but I forced myself to challenge him. I glanced pointedly at his hand. I would have bruises where his fingers bit into my flesh.

Scowling, he released me, but he did not apologize.

"I lost the same friends you did to the French," I reminded him, remembering that before Lord Edward, there had been Tom Knyvett.

"And yet you do not hesitate to spread your legs for the enemy."

Fighting the instinct to shrink back and cower, I stood up straighter. "At the king's command! Since the night of the masque at Havering-atte-Bowe, I have been King Henry's creature and you, above all men, know it."

"You have taken pleasure from your duty."

"Mayhap I consider it my due, as I have had little other recompense!"

But Will Compton was no longer listening. He stood silent for a moment, and then began to laugh. Of a sudden, he picked me up and whirled me around, kissing me soundly on the lips before he set me back on my feet. "Ah, Jane! You are an inspiration."

"I—I am what?"

Still grinning, he seized me by the shoulders, bringing his face close to mine. His eyes danced with excitement. "Do you not see? By quarreling with you, my anger at the French was diverted into a safer channel. I exploded, but with fireworks instead of cannon fire. That is what the entire court needs—a means to vent their anger and frustration without doing any real harm."

I thought him mad. "I can scarce pick fights with each and every courtier."

"But the king, at my prompting, *can* invite the duc de Longueville and his bastard brother to compete in the May Day tournament."

With one last kiss, this one a resounding smack in the middle of my forehead, he left to set things in motion.

BY THE DAY of the tournament, I was almost ill with worry. No one would dare harm the duke, but Guy would be fair game. Nervous jitters attacked my belly and I felt an incessant dull pounding at my temples. Both were made worse by the noise and smell of the crowd of spectators.

From the purpose-built, covered grandstand that was the royal gallery, I had a clear view of the double tier of bare wooden benches, solidly but plainly constructed, that occupied the far side of the field. They could be had, for a price, by anyone who wished to attend the tournament. They were full to bursting with spectators gaping and pointing at the splendors of the king's new tiltyard.

Even in my troubled state, I could understand why they so admired the construction, which had been completed only a few days earlier. Inside the high wall that enclosed the whole were not only the lists with their wooden barriers and the tents of the competitors, but the gallery itself. At each end was a high octagonal tower—an octagonal stair turret, in truth—surmounted by pointed pinnacles of fanciful design. At their center the queen sat under her canopy of estate and in front of rich blue hangings embellished with gold designs. Cushions of cloth-of-gold padded even the lesser seats in her vicinity.

"Is it not splendid?" Bessie Blount whispered as the grand procession began. She'd chosen to sit beside me when others shunned my company. In spite of my jangled nerves, I could not help but smile at her simple delight in the spectacle.

"This is but a poor echo of the pageantry in old King Henry's time," I told her. "In those days, all the participants entered in fancy costumes and riding in pageant cars. They placed their names on a 'tree of chivalry' located near the head of the tilt. The tree was painted with leaves, flowers, and fruit, and beneath it, hung upon rails, were the shields of all the knights."

Once every jouster had been in costume, acting the role of Amadas or Lancelot or some other knight of olden times. The tournaments had been presented as allegories as elaborate as those in any masque. There was still pomp and ceremony, color and spectacle, but that element was missing. It was considered old-fashioned.

Footmen, drummers, and at least a dozen trumpeters came onto the field, along with forty mounted members of the king's spears and all the king's pages. The sun glinted off the gold chains the spears wore and the silver in their horses' trappings. The jousters, fully armed and with visors down, came next, challengers and answerers, each surrounded by gentlemen on foot who were dressed in satin and velvet. Tawny, scarlet, crimson, even silver and gold blossomed among the greater mass of gray and russet and servants' blue.

"I cannot tell one knight from the other," Bessie complained.

The gaily caparisoned mounts lacked heraldic devices, nor were there any to be seen on spear or helmet or breastplate. I could only pick out the duc de Longueville by the fluttering scarf he wore wound around his forearm. It was the one I had given to him as my favor only a few hours earlier. I had given Guy my little dragon pendant. I hoped it would serve as a good luck charm, a protection against injury.

"Mayhap it was deemed safest not to identify each knight," I murmured. During a mock battle, it would be far too easy to exact private vengeance on an opponent, to maim or even to kill.

"I have never attended a tournament before," Bessie confided. She'd been bouncing up and down with excitement since the moment she arrived and kept swiveling her head in order to see everything at once. "This is called a tiltyard. Is there an event called the tilt?"

"A tilt is any fight between a pair of competitors using lances."

I had to raise my voice to be heard above the noise. Interspersed with cheers and shouts were derisive catcalls aimed at the French jousters. Spirited wagering on the outcome of various matches also accounted for a good deal of racket.

"There will be four parts of the tournament," I continued. "First, opponents fighting on foot at the barriers, using swords across a waist-high wooden fence. Then hand-to-hand combat with a variety of weapons—two-handed swords and pikes and axes. The tourney is next, fought by small teams on horseback, with swords. And finally there is the joust between mounted knights with lances. Each knight will run several courses and dozens of lances will be broken before they are done." I could only pray no heads would be splintered in the process.

A sudden hush fell as two men dressed as hermits suddenly

appeared from the area underneath the grandstand, an area closed in to provide storage for jousting equipment between tournaments. The hermits bowed before the queen and waited for her to acknowledge them.

"Mayhap the fashion in pageantry has not passed away after all," I murmured, recognizing the king and Charles Brandon.

In truth, everyone knew who they were. And everyone pretended not to know. King Henry wore a white velvet habit with a hat of cloth-of-silver and a long silver beard made of damask. His companion, all in black velvet, sported false hair of similar color and design.

When enough time had passed for the crowd to admire his disguise and speculate about who he might be, the king threw off habit, beard, and hat to reveal shining black armor beneath. He tossed the garments to the queen, who caught them with apparent delight. Brandon did the same, gifting the Lady Mary. Her cheeks pink with pleasure, she accepted the robe and gave him a length of green ribbon. He kissed the bit of fabric and tucked it into the breastplate of the pure white armor revealed when he removed the black habit.

"The king looks very grand," Bessie whispered, "but does he not risk injury to participate?"

"He does, a lesson he learned early. The Earl of Kent, who was charged with teaching the young prince to joust, broke an arm just demonstrating the sport." Bessie's face paled and I hastened to reassure her. "His Grace is very good. He has trained in the lists since he was a boy of sixteen and he excels at breaking lances. There was a time when he would practice every day."

I had gone to watch him sometimes, with the Lady Mary. When they lacked real opponents, he and those companions his father approved—Harry Guildford, Will Compton, Ned Neville,

Charles Brandon, and the rest—had charged at detachable rings set on posts and tilted at the quintain, an effigy on a revolving bar.

"How do they decide who wins the tournament?" Bessie asked.

"The jouster's aim is to dismount his opponent, but that rarely happens. Next best is to shatter the lance on his head or body. The heralds keep the score sheets. Marks are awarded according to which parts of an opponent's armor are struck, even if the lance does not split. The helmet scores highest, closely followed by the breastplate."

She shuddered. "That sounds passing dangerous to me."

I had been struggling not to think about that aspect of things, glad of Bessie's questions to help keep my mind off my fears that someone dear to me might end up dead before the day was through. The throbbing pain in my head had subsided to a dull ache, but my stomach remained queasy.

"The knights break their lances across a high barrier to prevent collisions. They did not always do so. The contest was running *volant*—without lists—the day Ned Neville nearly killed Will Compton during a tournament."

Bessie's eyes widened. She was silent for a moment, then asked if the lances themselves were sharp.

"They are hollow, and fluted, and they have blunted points. They are designed to shatter on impact."

The force of two jousters colliding could shower long wooden splinters in every direction. They could blind a man. They could kill. While Will Compton had almost died at the hands of a good friend, I did not like to think what might happen when an opponent was filled with hatred and bent on revenge. Picturing Longueville and Guy in all their fine armor, lying side by side in a puddle of blood, I shuddered.

The tournament began to a roar of approval from the crowd.

All through the first two events men brandishing drawn swords shouted and whooped. The crowd cheered every time the flat of a sword clanged against armor. And as every hit reverberated, I shivered inside, thinking of what was to come.

When the tourney added horses to the mix, there was even more noise from thudding hooves and equine screams. The crowd greeted every foray by the king's team with enthusiastic cries of approval.

Although the ground was hard packed—a layer of sand deep enough to rake topped by a thick layer of gravel sealed with plaster—the horses stirred up great clouds of dust. It coated everything, spectators included. Throat clogged, vision obscured, I strained to see what was happening on the field and breathed a sigh of relief when I realized the tourney had concluded with no serious injuries.

The joust came next. Longueville rode out, matched against the king. He held his lance strongly braced in his right hand and charged without faltering. The horses raced toward each other, and within seconds both lances shattered with a crash like a thunderclap. I was certain I saw Longueville's armor bend from the impact, but he rode off as if nothing had happened.

Brandon took on Guy Dunois with a result nearly as spectacular. I let out a breath I had not been aware of holding when I realized that Longueville's half brother was no novice at this sport either. I should not have been surprised that Guy was competent. He was efficient, clever, and skilled at whatever he undertook to do. For just a moment, the memory of his kiss came to mind.

I quickly banished it by shifting my attention to Charles Brandon. There was something in Brandon's manner that I did not like. Lord Edward had been one of his particular friends in the old days, and Brandon was just arrogant enough to think he could use this tournament as an excuse to seek revenge. Would he? And would it be ruled an accident if he killed his opponent?

The challengers and the answerers were evenly matched. The king had taken care to assign knights of equal ability to each team. He had always preferred a fair fight in which to test his own mettle. Indeed, few things irritated him more than facing an unworthy opponent in the lists. I tried to take comfort from that knowledge, telling myself that I had no cause for alarm, but I could not quite quell my fears.

Lance after lance broke to loud applause and cheers. Once again dust filled the air, making it almost impossible to see the barriers. A part of me was grateful to be spared that sight. By then the wood was liberally caked with spatters of spilled blood.

"I thought there would be more falls." Bessie had been quiet for so long that I had almost forgotten she was there.

"Gentlemen warriors are trained from childhood to keep their seat. At Eltham, even as a young boy, King Henry was wont to practice leaping onto his horse from either side or the back while the horse was running. He could grab the mane of a galloping horse and jump into the saddle while wearing helmet, breastplate, and cuisses."

Only after close to a hundred lances had been broken did I begin to relax. The tournament was almost over. No one had been killed.

Then a soft, spring breeze carried Meg Guildford's venom-laced words to my ears: "Harry told me there were plans for a fight to the death. Only a direct order from the king put a stop to them."

"There is still the mêlée," her sister said in a cheerful voice. "Anything can happen then."

Seeing me cringe, Bessie leaned close to whisper, "What is a mêlée?"

"It is the general battle on horseback at the end of a tournament. Rival parties of knights fight using either long spears or blunted swords."

"Is it more dangerous than what has gone before?"

"It can be."

I remembered one time in the last reign when the mêlée had turned into a near riot. It had been necessary to call in the king's guard to quell it. I prayed matters would not go that far today.

"At most tournaments," I said to Bessie, "the rules are carefully laid down in advance and a marshall is present to enforce them. That prevents most serious mishaps and injuries."

Once again the king fought the duc de Longueville. Once again there was no clear victor. Then Guy rode out to face the Duke of Suffolk for a second time. I felt a chill run down my spine.

Charles Brandon was the most skilled jouster among the king's friends. Years of practice had made him a formidable opponent. When he'd been a young man, I remembered, participating in tournaments had kept him poor. That was no doubt why he'd decided to marry a wealthy widow rather than his pregnant mistress . . . or me.

The armor Guy wore had come from the king's own armory. I could not shake off the frightening notion that it might have been tampered with. There was no reason to think so. There had been no sign of trouble in the earlier bouts. The armor was cunningly jointed and padded. At most, even if a competitor took a solid hit from a lance or a sword, he should come away from a tournament with no more than a few bruises. But when Brandon and Guy took their positions at opposite ends of the course, my fingers strayed to my rosary.

A rare moment of absolute silence fell over the crowd. In the stillness, I heard Guy's visor slam shut. His warhorse, also borrowed from the king, pawed at the ground. Then there was nothing but the thundering of hooves as the two combatants galloped toward each other.

Wood thudded against metal. Guy's spear shattered into three pieces against Brandon's breastplate. A second later, Brandon's lance struck Guy's helmet just at the edge of the eye opening in the visor. Guy's head jerked back.

I was on my feet, my hands pressed tight against my lips to hold back a cry of distress. Had the visor been properly fastened? Even if the tip of the lance had not penetrated, if so small a thing as a splinter worked its way inside, it could do most terrible damage.

All around me spectators stood, cheering for the Duke of Suffolk. Shouts of "Finish him off!" and "Kill the Frenchman!" filled the air.

Guy swayed in his saddle but kept his seat. His horse carried him to the other end of the course and disappeared behind the row of tents set up for the combatants. Trembling, I sank onto my cushion.

Under cover of the noise, Bessie leaned close to my ear. "You should go to him."

I shook my head. "Women are not permitted to interfere in tournaments." Neither would it be a good idea to call more attention to myself when feelings ran so high against the French. Will's idea had worked, but only to a point. Many in the crowd still wanted blood.

"If you will not go yourself, then send one of the Lady Mary's pages to inquire after your friend." Kindhearted to a fault, Bessie found one of the boys for me. Under cover of the end of the tournament—without a mêlée—and the announcement that the Duke of Suffolk was champion of the day, a young lad in livery slipped away from the grandstand unnoticed.

While I waited anxiously for his return from the tents with news, Queen Catherine, who was the avowed enemy of all things French, announced that 114 lances had been broken that day. She presented Charles Brandon, Duke of Suffolk, with a jewel-encrusted gold ring.

Guy's reward was a visit from the king's surgeons and apothecaries.

"YOU ARE FORTUNATE not to have lost an eye!" I said to Guy as he lay on the field bed. He had been moved from Longueville's pavilion to the duke's lodgings, into the tiny, windowless cubicle he'd claimed for a bedchamber when he'd first taken up residence at Greenwich Palace.

Guy made no reply.

"His ears are still ringing," Ivo Jumelle said. "He cannot hear you."

"I intend to remain until I am certain everything necessary has been done for him."

I moved closer to the bed, noting that although it had the usual tester, ceiler, and bed curtains, the bedstead folded to make it portable. The duke had brought into captivity all the furnishings he'd taken with him on campaign.

Guy's face was a trelliswork of scratches, gouges, and bruises. There was swelling around both eyes and along the line of his jaw. I swallowed convulsively as I realized it was not just his sight that the lance had endangered. The wooden tip had slid upward beneath the visor, beneath the fringe of hair that covered Guy's forehead, nicking the center of that expanse. A tiny bit more force and it would have penetrated deeply enough to kill.

Without warning, I collapsed at the foot of the bed, my knees too weak to hold me upright any longer. With fingers that felt cold as ice I reached for Guy's hand.

"It distresses you that he is injured?" Ivo watched me with an unnerving intensity, head cocked to one side like a curious bird.

To show too much concern was unseemly, but I was strangely reluctant to release my grip. Then Guy squeezed my fingers and I forgot all about the boy's presence. Ivo was the duke's servant, no doubt some gentleman's son, but of little consequence himself.

Guy's eyes slitted open. His gaze caught mine and held. I stared back, trying to read his emotions, but the damage to his face made that impossible. When he finally spoke it was only to ask for something to drink.

After I helped him take several swallows of barley water, I settled myself on a stool pulled close to the head of the bed. "Sleep now, Guy." I told him. "Rest is the best cure for injuries."

"Your good luck charm kept me safe." His hoarse voice was gravelly but strong.

"Not safe enough."

"You must take it back. To protect you." To please him, I retrieved the dragon pendant from his discarded clothing.

"You need not keep watch over me."

"I know I *need* not. I wish to stay." I settled once more on the stool.

"The duke—"

"Longueville is with the king and has no need of me."

I hid my disgust. The duke had abandoned his half brother, who had bled and might have died for him. He was off carousing with King Henry and his companions, celebrating a successful afternoon in the lists. The enmity between English knights and French had been defused, as Will had predicted, by spilling blood. Guy's blood.

"Talk to me, then," Guy said. "Take my mind off the throbbing."

"Is the pain too great? The apothecary left a vial of poppy syrup."

"Have you ever had a bad tooth? I feel as if I have a whole head full of them."

I dosed him with poppy syrup first, then began to talk, recalling random memories of Amboise in our shared childhood. "It seems to me," I said, "that there was a constant parade of workmen coming and going along that winding road that led from the village up to the château."

"The workmen built that, too—a continuous circular ramp that runs all the way from town to castle, wide enough for wagons."

"The moat had no water in it," I recalled.

"King Charles's courtiers used it as a tennis play." He winced.

"Is the pain—?"

He waved away my concern. "It will pass, and already I grow sleepy. What else do you remember about Amboise?"

"Courtiers' houses lay clustered below the walls of the fortress. When I was very small, my father and I used to walk past them and make up stories about the people who lived there."

"I remember him, I think." Guy's words began to slur and I sensed that he would soon fall asleep. I smoothed his brow with one hand, relieved when the skin felt no warmer than was normal.

Amboise. What else *did* I recall? We could see Tours cathedral in the distance, off to the west, and the forest of Blois in the opposite direction. The main route to reach either was the river Loire. Water traffic had been as steady along that byway as it was on the Thames, with a constant procession of barges and ships bringing all manner of merchandise to the royal court.

"There was a zoo," I murmured. "I had forgotten that. King Charles kept lions in captivity. And once we went to see a rope walker perform on a rope strung between two towers of the château. He did somersaults and danced and hung by his teeth, all high above the ground."

I glanced at Guy, wondering if he remembered that day. He was deeply asleep. He lay with one arm flung wide and the other resting on his chest. His face, in repose, looked younger. Even the bruising seemed less severe.

Although I knew I should leave, I remained where I was, watching over him through the evening. Only once, when I heard low voices beyond the door, did I step away. Ivo was the only one there when I peeped out. Frowning, he was turning an oilskin-wrapped packet over and over in his hands.

"For the duke?" I asked in a whisper.

He shook his head. "For me. From my father. This is the first letter he has sent to me since we were captured, although I have written faithfully to him." Looking cautiously pleased, he broke the seal.

I left him in private in the outer room, where he and Longueville's four other attendants slept on pallets, to read his father's letter, but the door did not completely close behind me. A moment later I heard Ivo mutter something to himself, an oath, I thought.

I went to the door. "Ivo? Is something wrong?"

"No, Mistress Jane."

I studied his pale face. "Something is troubling you."

"It . . . it is just that my father has asked me to do something I do not wish to do." The paleness vanished beneath a wave of color. My questions plainly embarrassed him and he was too polite to remind me that what the letter contained was none of my business. I apologized for disturbing him and returned to Guy's bedside.

I stayed the night. There was no need, but it was no trouble and I doubted anyone would remark upon my presence in his room when my own lodgings were so near at hand. I fell asleep, head pillowed on arms resting on one side of the field bed.

I woke to discover that my headdress had fallen off. Guy's fingers rested gently on my hair.

11

The court moved from Greenwich to nearby Eltham in early May. Once I knew Guy would recover from his injuries, and could travel with us, I was happy enough to go. In our new lodgings I had, as before, two rooms for my own. When I was not on duty with the princess, I spent long, lazy afternoons escorting the duc de Longueville and Guy around the place where I had passed so much of my childhood. We ventured into every corner of the old redbrick palace, from the royal lodgings in the donjon in the inner court to the great hall to the grassy mount overlooking the moat where the royal swans glided, their collars glinting in the sun.

We promenaded along Eltham's tiled floors, pausing to gaze out the glazed windows toward the forested deer park that surrounded the place. We laughed and talked of inconsequential things. By mutual consent, we avoided visiting the tiltyard.

Early on a morning in mid-June, we three rode from Eltham to Greenwich together. There Longueville and Guy went aboard the barge already occupied by the king, the queen, and the princess. King Henry was a splendid sight in breeches and vest of cloth-of-gold and scarlet hose. He wore a whistle on a gold chain around his neck, the insignia of supreme commander of the navy. Beside him stood Queen Catherine, visibly pregnant.

I boarded a smaller barge, along with the lesser ladies of the court.

Even a small royal barge offered every comfort, from bread and cheese to stave off hunger to soft cushions to sit upon. The chatter of the other gentlewomen was loud and good humored as we set off for Erith, a village located on the Thames between Greenwich and Gravesend. It was home to a royal dockyard. Soon barges filled the river from one bank to the other, creating a magnificent pageant. The weather was perfect for such an expedition and for the launching of His Grace's great warship, the thousand-ton *Henry Grace à Dieu*.

"See that man standing with the king?" I overheard Meg Guildford ask her sister, Elizabeth. "He is the new ambassador from King Louis."

"Another one?"

"A significant one," Meg said. "Harry says he's too important to have been sent just to arrange a ransom, even for a duke."

"Why is he here, then?"

Meg whispered her answer, but I could guess what she'd said when Elizabeth gave a little squeal of excitement.

I moved away, standing apart so that I could watch the two sisters and also the men on the king's barge. The creak and slap of twenty-four oars and the steady drumbeat that kept the rowers' rhythm smooth and steady momentary blocked out the rise and fall of feminine voices. Small waves broke against the side of the barge as we moved through the water.

I had met the new ambassador from France earlier that morning. Meg was correct. He had not come to negotiate Longueville's ransom. He was in England to make a formal offer for the Lady Mary.

The negotiations had been conducted in secret for months, offer and counteroffer. The last I'd heard from Longueville, King Henry held firm, saying he would not sign a peace treaty or seal it with his sister's hand in marriage for less than 1,500,000 gold crowns; English control of Thérouanne, Tournai, and Saint-Quentin; and an annual pension of 50,000 ecus. King Louis had balked at those demands.

Carried on the freshening breeze, a female voice I did not recognize said, "I heard the king said he'd accept an offer of 100,000 crowns per annum if King Louis would take the older sister instead of the younger."

So, the "secret" was out. I wondered if the king himself had leaked the news in order to gauge reaction at court. Skirting the brazier where sweet herbs burned to mask the most offensive of the odors wafting up from the water's surface, I moved closer to Meg, hoping to hear what else was generally known.

A gust of wind caught at my skirts, making them billow perilously close to the embers. I had to twitch the fabric out of danger and sidestep, but neither sister noticed.

"I hear the queen of Scotland is not only willing but eager for the match," Meg said.

Elizabeth smirked. "I hear she's grown stout and coarse featured living in that heathen land."

"All the more reason not to be choosy," one of the queen's maids of honor chimed in. Several of them clustered close, a flock of brightly colored birds pecking at the crumbs of rumor.

"King Louis should have no cause to complain of her were she big as a sow," Meg said. "He is an old man, gouty and toothless."

"He is a *man*," Elizabeth countered. "He'll want the Lady Mary."

"But will she want him?"

"What does that matter? She will do her duty and wed as her brother wills. And why should she object to becoming a queen of France? France is a much more important place than Castile."

A gasp from one of the queen's damsels reminded Elizabeth that Catherine of Aragon's mother and then her sister Juana had been queens of Castile. To belittle them insulted the queen of England. Elizabeth flushed becomingly.

Meg simply surveyed the company aboard the barge to assure herself that none of the Spanish-born members of the queen's household was aboard. Her gaze rested briefly on me, then moved on. "The Lady Mary will do the king's bidding," she asserted.

"But will she not mind being bedded by a man old enough to be her grandfather?" It was the irrepressible, golden-haired Bessie Blount who asked. Together with the chestnut-haired Elizabeth Bryan, they outshone every other woman at court for beauty, saving only the Lady Mary herself.

"If she does, she will be clever enough to conceal her distaste. Besides, being so old and infirm means he will die all the sooner," Meg added callously, unknowingly echoing the Lady Mary's own philosophy. "Then she will be free."

I said nothing, but still I had my doubts about how much freedom the princess would have. Widowhood had not made Queen Margaret free, not when her name could still be bandied about as it had been during negotiations with France. A princess was a matrimonial prize and little more. I supposed all women were.

Someone's daughter. Someone's wife. Someone's mistress. Our connection to men defined all of us.

"Is the king of France a grandfather in truth?" Bessie had sidled closer to whisper her question to me.

"Queen Anne could produce no living sons for either of her royal husbands, but she gave Louis two daughters. The eldest, several years younger than the Lady Mary, has just been married off to François d'Angoulême, King Louis' heir. He is the king's cousin."

"I do not understand. If King Louis has a daughter, should she not rule after him? England had a queen once. Matilda. Or was it Maud?"

"Not in France." Overhearing the question, Meg broke in, happy to have the opportunity to parrot back another of the history lessons she'd learned from Harry. "Only kings are allowed to rule there and only sons can inherit a noble title."

Bessie glanced at me for confirmation. I nodded. In truth, matters were scarce better in England. A girl might inherit both lands and a title, but either her father or her guardian decided who she married and, once wed, her husband took control of both.

A short time later, we reached Erith and the *Henry Grace à Dieu*. We boarded the ship and were taken on a tour by the king himself. After we'd admired all five decks, High Mass was celebrated onboard. Festivities followed.

"The most magnificent pageant ever seen on the Thames," Guy said, joining me at the rail some time later. "That's what they are saying about our journey here today."

"I do not doubt it. I can never remember another time when every royal barge was on the water at the same time."

"And now the king has another vessel fit to wage war. She carries more than two hundred bronze and iron cannon. Remarkable," Guy said.

A sidelong look at his face revealed nothing but a bland countenance. "Surely peace is at hand."

"Is it? The king just let slip—intentionally, I am sure—that an English fleet set sail for Cherbourg last week. Their orders were to retaliate for the burning of Brighton," he added.

I looked up at the masts and spars rising above the deck on which we stood and then down at the gleaming cannons showing through the gunports below. So beautiful . . . and so deadly.

I told myself that the king would not be so foolish, not after all the months of negotiation, but I should have known better. A week later, we learned that on the very same day we'd gone to Erith with so much pomp and circumstance and good cheer, English troops landed just west of Cherbourg and burned down twenty-one French villages and towns.

SIX WEEKS AFTER the launch of the king's warship, the duc de Longueville and I watched the Lady Mary leave for the royal manor of Wanstead. Once there, she would officially repudiate her marriage to Charles of Castile. Members of the Privy Council would bear witness and convey the news of what they had seen to the king.

"The Lady Mary is nervous," I confided, "but she has rehearsed her speech many times. She will make no mistakes."

King Henry had written much of what Mary would say. Although he would pretend to be surprised by her words, he knew full well that she would charge Charles of Castile with breach of faith and say that evil counsel and malicious gossip had turned the prince against her. Claiming she had been humiliated, Mary would then refuse to keep her part of the bargain, rendering the contract null and void. She would declare that she was severing "the nuptial yoke" of her own volition, without threat or persuasion from anyone, and end by petitioning King Henry's forgiveness and affirming her loyalty to her brother.

"In all things I am ever ready to obey his good pleasure," I murmured, quoting from the speech I, too, had memorized. It was all diplomatic pretense, but it would clear the way, at long last, for a peace treaty between England and France.

Longueville swung away from the window, a scowl darkening his countenance. "I have misgivings about this proxy wedding between the Lady Mary and King Louis," he said.

Attempting to cajole him out of his ill humor, I ran my hand up the tawny velvet of his sleeve. The fabric felt soft and warm against my skin. "You do not have to assume all of the king's duties as bridegroom," I teased him. "Only say the words on his behalf."

He gave a snort of laughter. "It would be no hardship to swive the Lady Mary."

"My lord!"

Lost in thought, he barely heard my indignant protest. I could not fathom what ailed him. He should have been elated by the success of his negotiations. He had been angling for months for a ceremony here in England with himself standing in for King Louis.

"Your princess was married to Charles of Castile. A proxy wedding was celebrated then, too."

"Are you afraid negotiations will break down even now?" I asked.

"Everything seems to be within our grasp. We have the commission to sign a treaty of alliance and a marriage contract. King Louis has agreed to pay King Henry 1,000,000 crowns at the rate of 26,315 crowns twice a year."

"What does England give up, aside from her fairest lady?"

His smile was rueful. "The Lady Mary's dowry is 400,000

crowns, half to be in the form of jewels and apparel that go with her to France and half to be credited to the sum King Louis has agreed to pay your king. Mary will receive dower properties worth 700,000 ducats and will be permitted to keep them for the rest of her life, regardless of where she lives."

My eyebrows lifted of their own accord. Even the French, it seemed, expected their new queen to outlive the old man who would be her husband. I wished I could be so certain. Too many women, even queens, died in childbed. My mistress's future was far from secure.

Longueville continued to frown as he poured himself a goblet of wine. As an afterthought, he poured a second for me. "We have worked long and hard for this, Jane, but nothing is ever certain. What if your king changes his mind? If the proxy marriage to Charles of Castile can be set aside, so can this new one."

"King Henry has given you his word of honor."

A skeptical lift of both brows told me how little value that had.

"Well, then, what do you suggest?"

"It is consummation that makes a marriage final," he said slowly.

I choked on the sip of wine I'd just taken. "You cannot . . . *swive* the princess!"

"I had in mind a symbolic consummation, blessed by a priest." He saluted me with his cup and drank deep.

KING HENRY ROARED into his sister's bedchamber at Greenwich on the morning of Sunday, the thirteenth day of August, fury radiating from every pore. He strode past her cowering, bowing attendants and came to a halt directly in front of her, stance wide, hands on hips, and fire in his eyes. Solid and immovable as a mountain, he looked her up and down, giving a curt nod of approval as he surveyed her kirtle of silver-gray satin and checkered gown of purple satin and cloth-of-gold. Jewels sparkled at her throat, on her fingers, and in her hair.

"You are dressed and ready. Why are you not in the great banqueting hall? Your wedding guests have been waiting nearly three hours."

Only I was close enough to see the fine trembling of the princess's hands. Her voice was low but steady. She had rehearsed this speech, too, but unlike the repudiation of her betrothal at Wanstead, this time she had written it herself.

"Your Grace," she began, "while it is true I have sworn to yield to your good pleasure in all things, this treaty you have made with France offers me precious little for my pains."

For a moment I thought he was about to explode. "Pains?" he bellowed in a voice so terrifying that it sent everyone save the three of us scurrying from the chamber. "You will be queen of France! What more can you want?"

"I want to be happy!" Her voice was almost as loud as his, her temper as high. Just that quickly, she abandoned her carefully prepared arguments. "How can you not understand that? You married whom you loved. You wanted Catherine from the moment you first saw her when you were a boy of ten, and she was about to marry our brother Arthur."

He started to speak but she wagged a warning finger in his face. "In public you claimed that our father, on his deathbed, bade you marry her, but we both know that is not true. You wed her because no other woman would do. That she was a princess of Spain had naught to do with it."

His nostrils flared—always a warning sign—and his eyes narrowed to slits, inviting an unfortunate comparison to an enraged boar. That her words were nothing but the truth did not move him. If his sister refused to go through with the French marriage, it was his consequence that would suffer.

The Lady Mary's agitation was so great that she seemed unaware she might be in danger. No one else would dare lay hands on her, but her brother the king could beat her with impunity. I sidled closer, not daring yet to intervene but hoping I might be able to pull my mistress out of harm's way if King Henry tried to strike her.

"I have demands of my own," she announced. "We will negotiate now, or there will be no proxy wedding."

"The time for negotiation is past," her brother said through clenched teeth. "The treaty was signed six days ago. Your betrothal has been announced in London."

Greatly daring, she thumped him in the center of a chest covered in checkers of cloth-of-gold and ash-colored satin. "A very quiet announcement! No fanfare. No bonfires. No fireworks."

"And no demonstrations of protest," he muttered. "Be grateful for small favors."

"I have heard the terms of this treaty," the Lady Mary continued. "King Louis is to pay you a million gold crowns in renewal of the French pension he once paid our father."

The king nodded, a small, triumphant smile playing around the corners of his mouth. "Payments begin in September . . . by which time you will be in France."

She ignored that. "We are to keep Tournai and Thérouanne."

Another nod acknowledged those terms. This time the expression on his face was a smirk.

"And I am to be delivered to Abbeville in France at your expense." She sent a ferocious scowl in her brother's direction. "Like a parcel!"

"That is the way such things are done." The king had gained

a modicum of control over his anger and now attempted to cajole his sister into cooperating. "Come, Mary, all will be well. Old King Louis will not live long."

She'd have none of it. "But while he lives, I am his to command." A moue of distaste showed her opinion of that!

"Women are chattel under the law," the king reminded her. "The property of their fathers first and then their husbands."

"You are my *brother*."

"I am your *king!*" Temper building once more, he took a menacing step toward her.

My heart in my throat, I stepped between them. "Your Grace, I beg you be calm. No purpose is served by quarreling."

"I suppose I have you to thank for her knowledge of the treaty." King Henry gave me an ugly look that promised retribution.

"The terms are common knowledge, Your Grace." My voice dropped to a tremulous whisper. I cleared my throat. "The Lady Mary has a proposal for you, Your Majesty." Deliberately, I used the form of address just coming into fashion. King Henry was said to secretly prefer it to "Your Grace."

"Speak, then." He made an impatient gesture. "Your delay has already caused too much speculation among our guests."

"My request is a simple one," the Lady Mary said. "I will marry the king of France, I will be a dutiful wife to him, and I will bring honor to England by my every action . . . if you will give me your word that when King Louis dies, I may marry to please myself."

The king stared at her, momentarily taken aback by the demand. Then his eyes narrowed again, this time in suspicion. "Has any man had you? By St. George, if one of my courtiers has dared—"

"Do you think me a fool!" the Lady Mary snapped. "I value my honor as much as you do. More, mayhap, as I am loath to waste my maidenhead on an old man."

"Louis is only fifty-two," the king said with calculated nastiness. "He could easily live a decade more."

"Then I will be his faithful helpmeet for those ten years, but when I have done my duty, I want my reward."

In the distance, a bell rang the hour. A pained look on his face, the king regarded his sister, seeing in her stance, in her eyes, a reflection of his own stubbornness. Did he realize, I wondered, that it was his friend the Duke of Suffolk Mary thought to one day wed?

"Very well," the king said at last. "You have my promise."

His sister threw herself into his arms, kissing both his cheeks. Radiant with joy, she turned to me next. "You have borne witness, Jane. I am to be permitted to choose my own husband when I am widowed."

Although he seemed resigned to the bargain he had made, the king's impatience returned. "Now that we have settled your distant future, may we move on to present duties?"

"As you wish, Your Grace."

Her laughter was infectious. Even the king smiled faintly. He had always been fond of his younger sister. I was certain he hated the thought of sending her away forever, even as he gloated over the success of his negotiations with the French.

A short time later, I slipped into the back of the great banqueting hall, hung with cloth-of-gold embroidered with the royal arms of England and France, to join the others gathered to witness the wedding. All the principal noblemen of the realm were there, along with numerous foreign dignitaries invited by the king. I recognized several ambassadors and two papal envoys. The Spanish ambassador was conspicuous by his absence.

Heralded by fanfare, the king and queen entered. Queen Catherine, serene in her pregnancy for all that she still despised the idea of a French alliance, wore ash-colored satin and a little gold

Venetian cap. The king's clothing matched hers for color but was patterned in checkers of cloth-of-gold and satin. The whole was liberally appliquéd with jewels.

The Lady Mary came next, attended by several noblewomen of the realm. They were followed by the French delegation. The duc de Longueville's robes matched the bride's, as was the French custom. I remembered that from my childhood. The king and queen were supposed to appear in public as "a pair of brilliant jewels." I had more than once, though from a distance, seen King Charles and Queen Anne clad in identical colors.

Longueville's face was solemn, his expression a trifle strained. He must have guessed that something was wrong to cause such a long delay. I had not dared to warn him about what my mistress had planned. Neither did I intend to tell him anything of what had transpired in the Lady Mary's apartments. In this matter, I had only one loyalty, and that was to my princess.

The archbishop of Canterbury presided over the wedding ceremony, giving a long Latin address that few understood. One of the French envoys made a formal reply, after which the bishop of Durham read the French authorization for the proxy marriage. Then, holding the Lady Mary's hand in his, Longueville spoke King Louis' vows in French. She replied in the same tongue, her voice calm, clear, and sure. Longueville placed a ring on the fourth finger of her right hand and they exchanged a kiss, thus sealing the bond.

Once the marriage schedule had been signed, the formalities should have been complete, but Longueville's insistence that no way be left open to renounce this marriage had resulted in the addition of one more element. The whole company proceeded to a bedchamber. There, behind a screen, I helped the Lady Mary change into her most elaborate nightdress. When she was ready, she climbed onto the bed.

Longueville had also changed his clothing and now wore naught but a red doublet and hose. He rolled the latter up far enough to bare his leg to the thigh. That done, he positioned himself alongside his new queen. Delicately, she plucked at her skirt until one foot and ankle emerged. Carefully and deliberately, Longueville touched his bare leg to her naked foot. A shout of triumph went up from the witnesses as the archbishop declared the marriage consummated.

Smiling broadly, Longueville rose from the bed and led the crowd of spectators from the chamber. Only I remained behind to help the queen of France resume her checkered gown and a cloth-of-gold cap that covered her ears in the Venetian fashion. As soon as she was dressed, the celebrations resumed.

The Lady Mary had kept me awake most of the night before. Worried about her coming confrontation with her brother, she'd needed someone to talk to. The result was that I felt too exhausted to face the remaining festivities. I sought the peace and privacy of my own lodgings instead.

On my way there, I had to pass the duke's rooms. I could scarce fail to notice the unusual amount of activity within, nor could I stop myself from entering to investigate. I found Guy bent over a huge traveling chest, checking the contents against a list.

Curious, I came up beside him and peered inside. "These are Longueville's clothes!" I recognized the slashed taffeta doublet and the leather cape with the collar of marten.

"Why are you surprised? You knew he would leave when his ransom was paid."

"But . . . but I assumed he would accompany the princess . . . the *queen*, to France."

Guy refolded a black satin doublet and a pair of black hose and tucked them in around a casket covered in green velvet. "This evening the king will come here to drink French wine and sign the remaining legal documents, including one that states that the duke's ransom has been received. We leave for France tomorrow."

I could not take it in. I had not expected to be separated from Longueville and Guy so soon. I had assumed, foolishly perhaps, that they would remain with us during all our preparations and leave for France when we did.

"You will see him again soon enough." Guy spoke sharply, as if out of temper with me.

"That is not . . . I simply . . ." My voice trailed off and I made a gesture of helplessness, uncertain as to what I did mean.

"If you have nothing to contribute, I have work to do."

His curt dismissal hurt my feelings, but I did not let him see it. "I will leave you to it, then. How early do you depart?"

He gave a short bark of laughter. "When did you ever know the duke to rise before eight?"

Like the king, Longueville rarely went to bed before midnight, but those of us who *served* royalty often had to be up and about earlier, no matter how late we had stayed up the night before. By the hour of seven, when the morning watch of the yeomen of the guard relieved the night watch in the king's presence chamber, attendants on duty for the day with king, queen, or princess had long since dressed and broken their fast.

Still in disbelief that he had not told me personally of his leaving so soon, I vowed to rise before dawn the next day, to be sure I did not miss the duke's departure.

IN THE MORNING I had no difficulty locating the French party. The duke and his six servants were leaving with ten horses and a cart bearing presents to the value of two thousand pounds, including the gown King Henry had worn the previous day. Its value, Guy informed me, had been estimated at three hundred ducats.

"Presents for the king of France or for Longueville?" I asked.

"For the king, for the most part." But my question provoked a smile.

Although clearly impatient to be on his way, when the duke caught sight of me he left off giving instructions to young Ivo and crossed the courtyard. Drawing me a little aside, he bent his head and kissed me full on the lips. "I was disappointed not to find you waiting in my bed when I returned to my chamber last night."

"I was not certain I would be welcome."

My words were true enough, and he might have come in search of me, had he truly desired my company. But in all honesty, I had been glad to sleep alone. It was becoming more and more difficult to pretend to feelings I no longer had. I looked forward to returning to France, but not as the duke's mistress. I would be the queen's lady. I would not be dependent upon either Longueville or Guy.

"Ah, well," the duke said, "soon we will have all the time in the world. When you come to France, I will show you wonders."

"My duties to the new queen will keep me busy."

"Do you truly wish to remain in her service? I can offer you something better, Jane. At Beaugency."

It was as well that he chose to kiss me again, for I did not know how to reply. For months now, I had gone to his bed more from duty than desire. Like a wife, I thought, as Mary Tudor sprang to mind.

With a final clinging touch of lips to lips, Longueville left me, returning to his preparations for departure. I had thought to discourage his attention once we left England. I'd assumed he'd lose interest quickly. After all, he'd once offered to give me away. Now I was not so certain of that.

"You will like Beaugency." Guy still stood nearby. His sour expression had returned.

"He has a wife in France," I murmured. "He must go back to her." The statement sounded naive even to my own ears.

Guy shrugged. "The duchess does not care what he does or with whom he does it. Since she has already borne him four children, three of them sons, she considers that she has fulfilled her obligations as a wife."

Did that mean she had a lover of her own? I was not quite brave enough to ask that question, but I ventured another. "Where does she live?"

"At the French court when she can, or on the lands that came with her upon their marriage."

"At . . . court." I frowned. I was certain, then, to meet her when I arrived with the new queen. In spite of Guy's assurances, the prospect made me uneasy.

"I will not be at court or at Beaugency," Guy said without looking at me. "I plan to tend to my own lands." He started to turn away, but I caught his sleeve.

To my surprise, tears filled my eyes. "I have grown accustomed . . . I will miss you."

Guy reached out to caress my cheek, then took my face between his palms. "I want to remember you," he whispered. "The golden gleam in your eyes—"

"They are brown."

"With golden flecks, and your hair is the deep, rich color of ginger."

"It, too, is brown." But I had to smile. "What next? Poetry to the dimple in my lady's chin?"

He laughed, dispelling the last of the awkwardness between us. "You have no dimple."

An hour later, I watched the little cavalcade ride away, but I had the strangest feeling I had not seen the last of Guy Dunois.

➤ ❖

THE FRENCH KING sent gifts to his bride. Dozens of them, and a special attendant whose duties were to familiarize Queen Mary with French manners and customs and help prepare her trousseau—King Louis did not intend to permit his bride to arrive in France wearing Flemish fashions. There were lessons, fittings, sittings, too, since the king also sent his favorite court painter, Jean Perréal.

Perréal brought with him a portrait of Louis, the first Mary had seen. Instead of the elderly, sickly looking creature she had been led to expect, it showed a well-favored man of middle age. His face wore a sober expression but did not have the appearance of someone who was grievous ill. Nor did he look likely to die anytime soon.

King Louis' other gifts, borne into the great hall on a handsome white horse, proved more pleasing to the new bride. Two large coffers contained plate, seals, devices, and jewelry. First among the last was the chief bridal gift, the Mirror of Naples, a diamond as large as full-size finger with a huge pear-shaped pendant pearl the size of a pigeon's egg. King Henry at once sent it out to be valued. The experts reckoned it was worth sixty thousand crowns.

Shortly after the Frenchmen arrived, Mother Guildford returned to court. She had been appointed to take charge of Queen Mary's maids of honor. The new queen of France was overjoyed to have her, remembering her as a doting governess during the years she had been in charge of the nursery at Eltham. I was less enthusiastic, especially when she made a point of taking me aside to lecture me.

"Well, girl, you have ruined yourself. I always feared you would."

"I cannot see how. I am as high in favor at court as ever I was." Longueville's parting gift to me had been to ask that I be allowed to keep my private lodgings until I left for France. The king had agreed.

She stared pointedly at my belly. "No consequences?"

I pretended not to know what she meant, meanwhile struggling to hold on to my temper. Fortunately, Mother Guildford had too many other duties to bother much about me. There were to be over a hundred people in the queen of France's permanent household, some thirty of us female. Queen Mary also would take along her own secretary, chamberlain, treasurer, almoner, physician, and the like.

AFTER SEVERAL HECTIC weeks, we at last set out for Dover. Dresses, jewelry, and other goods came with us, transported in closed carts drawn by teams of six horses. They had fleurs-de-lis—the emblem of France—painted on the sides and were emblazoned with Mary's arms and her newly chosen motto, *La volantée de Dieu me suffit*— "To do God's will is enough for me."

Queen Mary traveled in a litter borne by two large horses ridden by liveried pages. The litter was covered in cloth-of-gold figured with lilies, half red, half white. The saddles and harnesses were also covered with cloth-of-gold.

I rode on horseback, as did many others. I was glad of it. Litters, even those padded with large cushions and hung with rich curtains, were devilishly uncomfortable. The carts called *charetas*, drawn by two or more horses harnessed one before the other, were even worse.

Once at Dover Castle, foul weather and high winds postponed our departure. Every time the storm abated, the wedding party prepared to embark, only to be turned back by the return of furious winds and lashing waves. There were occasional stretches of calm weather, but they lasted barely long enough for messengers to cross the Narrow Seas.

More than a week after our arrival in Dover, when one such lull gave promise of safe passage to France, I made my way through a scene of utter chaos in search of my mistress. I had to step around boxes and trunks and over garments made of cloth-of-gold and cloth-of-silver and other precious fabrics. We had been stranded for so long in Dover that, out of sheer boredom, Queen Mary had ordered all her new clothes unpacked. She had passed the time trying them on and admiring herself in the polished metal of an ornately framed mirror.

Now everything had to be packed away, and quickly, before the weather changed again—sixteen gowns, including a wedding dress, in the French fashion; six gowns in the Milanese style, with matching hats; and eight gowns of English cut. Each came with its own chemise, girdle, and accessories. The new queen also had fourteen pairs of double-soled shoes and hundreds of pieces of jewelry— gold chains and bracelets; carcanets of diamonds and rubies; pearled aiguillettes; golden, gem-studded frontlets; brooches, rings, and medallions.

I found the queen of France examining the contents of a golden coffer that stood open on a table in her bedchamber. A faint frown marred the perfection of her features. Mary Tudor might be accounted the most beautiful princess in Christendom—long golden hair, lively blue eyes, pale complexion, all flattered by a gown of blue velvet over a kirtle of tawny-colored damask—but just at present she was clearly out of sorts and still a little pale and wan from her reaction to the previous night's thunderstorm.

"Leave us," she ordered, dismissing the ladies-in-waiting hovering in the background. They left with ill grace. Sisters, wives, and daughters of noblemen all, they shot baleful glances my way in passing.

I ignored them, pretending to focus on the scattered contents of a small, ornately carved jewel chest. I was still accorded the courtesy title "keeper of jewels" and from force of habit counted two thick ropes of pearls, four brooches, three rings, and a diamond and ruby carcanet.

Only after the door closed with a solid thunk did I realize that Queen Mary had something to say to me that she wished to keep private. That did not bode well. "Your Grace?"

She heaved a heartfelt sigh, then took both my hands in hers. "There is no easy way to tell you this, Jane. It is hard news for both of us."

"What is, Your Grace?"

"You have been forbidden to travel with me into France. You must stay behind in England."

This announcement was so unexpected that at first I could think of nothing to say. I felt as if time had stopped, as if all my senses were wrapped in wool. Only after a long silence did I manage to stammer out a question. "But why, Your Grace?"

"The list of my attendants was sent to King Louis for approval. He crossed through your name."

Struggling to comprehend the enormity of this setback, and to conceal how badly it rattled me, I asked who else he had rejected.

"Only you, Jane." She squeezed my hands once and let go.

Bereft of that small comfort, the full impact of her words hit me with the force of a battle-ax. If I could not go to France with the queen, I might never discover the truth about my mother. I would be left behind, adrift and friendless. I would never see Guy again.

"I do not understand," I whispered.

"Nor do I." Mary spread her hands wide. "Henry thinks someone must have let slip that you were the duc de Longueville's mistress while Longueville was in England."

Although I allowed my outward demeanor to show little of my

reaction, beneath the surface my emotions continued to be chaotic. The numbness that had engulfed me upon first hearing the news had worn off. In rapid succession I felt a rush of helplessness, a wave of frustration, and, finally, the welcome surge of anger. I ruthlessly suppressed any sign of this last. It was all well and good for one of the Tudors to make a display of temper. A lowly waiting gentlewoman did not have that luxury.

I hid my distress as best I could. There was nothing I could do to change what had happened. All Longueville's fine designs for me, all my plans to investigate my past, had come to naught. And I would never see Guy again. I hastily pushed that thought away, and with it the deep sense of loss thinking it produced.

Taking my exterior calm at face value, the queen offered up what else she knew. "The king of France sounded most particular in his dislike of you, Jane. Has he any reason to mistrust you or your family?"

Surprised by the question, I almost blurted out what Guy had told me about the *gens d'armes* who had come looking for my mother. I caught myself in time. "I can think of none, Your Grace."

"It is what King Louis *said* when he struck your name off the list that makes me wonder. By one account, his words were these: 'If the king of England ordered Mistress Popyncourt to be burnt, it would be a good deed.' And then he claimed that you would be an evil influence on me and said you should not be allowed in my company."

"Burnt," I whispered. Everything inside me turned to ice at the word. The king of France did not just want me to stay in England. He wanted me dead.

"A second witness reports that King Louis told Henry's ambassador this: 'As you love me, speak of her no more. I would she were burnt.' Then the king claimed he acted only out of concern for my welfare and crossed out your name." Mary gave a disdainful sniff. With complete lack of concern for their value, she began to toss the scattered bits of jewelry back into the open coffer.

The sound of the lid slamming shut echoed in the stone chamber. It resounded in my thoughts, as well, and with a snap almost as loud, a piece of the puzzle fell into place. My name, in French, was the same as my mother's. Had Maman lived, she would be a woman barely forty, not yet too old to take a man of the duke's age into her bed. Had King Louis mistaken me for her?

"It appears I have been wedded to a tiresome old prude who meddles in the love affairs of his nobles," Mary grumbled.

I said nothing. My thoughts were still spinning. Mistress Popyncourt should be burnt? Lust did not lead to execution. The nobility of France were far more likely to honor long-term mistresses with important household posts than banish them.

I would she were burnt.

Burning was not the punishment for harlotry. It was a fate reserved for heretics, for witches, for wives who murdered their husbands . . . and for servants who killed their masters.

I felt myself blanch. A lady-in-waiting who poisoned her king fit into that last category all too well. I was certain I was right. King Louis had me confused with my mother, and he believed the rumor that she had poisoned King Charles.

I frowned. Louis had benefited from Charles's death. Why should he drive Maman out of France? Why would he wish to keep her away?

A logical reason was not so very difficult to imagine. He would do both if Maman was a threat to him, if she knew, mayhap, that *he* had poisoned King Charles. Had he tried, all those years ago, to blame her for his crime?

"If I please King Louis sufficiently, perhaps he will allow me to send for you later." Mary's expression brightened at the thought.

"I will pray for that outcome, Your Grace, but I think it most unlikely that the king will change his mind."

Even if he realized that I was not my mother, he would never allow me to set foot in France. He could not take the risk that Maman had confided in me.

12

ary Tudor, queen of France, left England without me at four o'clock on a chilly early October morning. During a brief respite from the wind and rain, the English fleet caught the early tide. I watched them sail away, numb from more than the cold. I do not know how long I stood there, but when I turned away, the king was watching me.

Our paths crossed again later that same day. He stopped to glower down at me as I made my obeisance. He spoke in a voice too low for the courtiers hovering nearby to hear. "You disappointed me, Jane. I had hoped you would remain with my sister and send reports back from France."

"Your Grace?"

When he continued on, I took several steps in pursuit. He stopped, looking back at me over his shoulder. His face was terrifying easy to read—annoyance, impatience . . . and the promise of retribution if I angered him further.

"I have no place at court now that your sister is gone, and nowhere else to go."

Until that moment, he had given no thought to my plight. A speculative light came into his eyes as he looked me up and down. It was the same look I'd seen on his face when he'd first examined some Mantuan horses he'd been sent as a gift.

He was assessing the benefits of *acquiring* me!

In haste, I dropped my gaze. I had only moments to think of a way to divert his attention before he proposed something I did not want to agree to. He always strayed when the queen was great with child . . . and he always sent his mistresses away as soon as he was allowed back into his wife's bed. If I was not to go to France, I wanted to *stay* at court. What other home did I have?

Inspiration obliged me. I managed a credible sniffle, then a sob.

The king gaped at me. "Are you crying? Stop it at once."

Pretending to struggle against my emotions, I spoke in a choked voice. "I cannot help myself, Your Grace. I have served you loyally and well. I sent word to you of everything the duke said. But I . . . *care* for him. We were to be together in France. He would have treated me with honor."

Plainly discomfited by the notion, King Henry gave my shoulder a few awkward pats.

"I do not mean to trouble you with this, Your Majesty. You have so many more important things to do. Perhaps I should go to my uncle, my only living relative. Surely he will take me in."

"To Velville? In Wales?"

"We . . . we are not close. He has never shown any particular affection toward me. But he is all the kin I have." I let my voice trail off and tried to look pathetic.

"That will not do." The king's smile was magnanimous. "You must stay here. Forthwith, you will enter the queen's service."

THE COURT WAS at Eltham Palace throughout October. Catherine of Aragon believed in keeping her attendants busy and I was glad of it. If she resented having me thrust upon her, she did not show it. That made adjusting to my changed circumstances easier, as did Bessie Blount's friendship. I invited her to share the double lodgings the king had generously allowed me to keep.

In the middle of the month, King Henry received a letter from his sister. She complained bitterly about her new husband. King Louis had dismissed all of her English ladies and menservants except for a few of the youngest maids of honor. In particular Mary lamented the loss of Mother Guildford.

What the king replied to this I do not know. I was not in his confidence. I took heart, however, from the fact that a number of English gentlemen would soon be in a position to see for themselves that their princess was well treated. A great tournament was to be held in Paris to celebrate Queen Mary's coronation. The Dauphin had issued a challenge to English knights to come and fight. Harry Guildford had already left, leading a detachment of yeomen of the guard. So had Charles Brandon. Of the king's closest friends, only Will Compton remained in England.

Will had wanted to go. He had been prevented by the sudden onset of pains in his legs, a condition that manifested itself just before the knights were to leave from Dover. He had been unable to walk for a week.

"Some say Compton was bewitched," Bessie confided in a whisper as we sat side by side in the queen's presence chamber to work on yet another altar cloth.

"What nonsense," I replied.

She cast a wary eye on the other ladies in the circle, then lowered her voice even more. "Elizabeth Bryan told me that her sister, Meg Guildford, heard a rumor that the Duke of Suffolk used sorcery to prevent Compton from traveling to France. They are great rivals, as you well know, and equally impressive in a tournament."

"What nonsense," I said again. "And how foolish of someone to spread such a story at court." The talk might cause trouble for Charles Brandon, but as Duke of Suffolk he was a very powerful man. Accusations against him would likely cause even greater difficulty for the person who invented the tale, if he—or she—were ever identified.

My next stitch went askew. My mother must once have been in a similar situation. The accusation that she'd poisoned King Charles might have been difficult to prove, but it would have been even more difficult to refute, especially for someone who possessed neither title nor wealth as protection.

On the last day of October, I returned to my lodgings a little earlier than usual. I had been excused from my duties with the queen in order that I might pack for the next day's move to Greenwich Palace. We were scheduled to remain there for the remainder of the year. When I entered the outer chamber, I made no particular effort to be silent, but my footfalls made no sound on the rushes. The two people in the inner room remained unaware of my presence. I heard Bessie's soft laugh and a murmured response that was clearly masculine.

I started to back out as quietly as I had come in, but froze when Bessie's guest spoke a bit more loudly and I recognized his voice. It was the king. I knew I should leave, and quickly, but surprise held me immobile.

"Say you will come to me when I send for you, sweet Bessie.

Mere kisses are not enough for me any longer. I must have all of you."

Her reply was too faint for me to make out, but I doubted she was refusing him. I heard a rustle of fabric, then silence.

"Oh, Your Grace," Bessie cried. "You must not. Not here. Jane could come in at any moment!"

"Jane will not betray us, my little love."

No, Jane would not, I thought bitterly. Not when Bessie was the only one who had never reviled me for giving myself to a foreign duke. And not when King Henry provided everything I had.

Was this why he had allowed me to stay at court? Did King Henry think Bessie Blount would benefit from having someone older and wiser to guide her in the art of being a great man's mistress?

Slowly, I backed out of our lodgings and settled myself on a nearby window seat to wait for the king to leave. He did so a few minutes later.

"Bessie?" I called, entering our rooms once again.

"Here."

I found her on the bed, lying on her back and staring up at the ceiler.

"The king wants you," I said.

Her pink cheeks flamed rose red. "You saw him leave."

"I heard you talking just before that." I climbed up onto the high bed and sat beside her, tucking my legs beneath me.

"What am I to do, Jane? He says he will send Sir William Compton to fetch me. That all I have to do is follow where Compton leads. But, Jane—I do not know how to . . . what to . . . I am a *virgin!*" The last word emerged on a wail of distress.

"Do you wish to lie with the king?" I asked.

"Oh, yes!" She sat up, a dreamy look in her eyes and a shy smile tilting up the corners of her rosebud mouth.

I surveyed her with a critical eye, then leaned closer and sniffed. Bessie used a light marjoram scent, but beneath it I caught a whiff of sweat. "The king was raised with very high standards of cleanliness. There is a bathtub here at Eltham. Avail yourself of it before we leave for Greenwich. And find a soap made from olive oil, not one of the ones the laundresses use."

Her eyes widened. "But . . . but is that not unhealthy? To immerse one's self in water?"

"It has not hurt the king, nor the princess . . . the queen of France. Nor has careful attention to their teeth." My former mistress had the most even teeth of anyone I knew and took particular pride in the fact that they were the color of ivory. She owned no fewer than three sets of tooth cloths and picks. "Further, you must put on your newest clothing after you bathe, and beneath all your other garments, wear a little piece of fur next to your skin."

"Why?"

"To attract any vermin to that one spot." I touched the side of my bodice. "I have one here. It is a practice the king follows, as well." All of us who were educated at Eltham did the same.

Impulsively, Bessie embraced me. "I would be lost without you, Jane. How am I ever to thank you?"

"Be happy," I said before I thought.

When she beamed at me, I bit back all the warnings crowding into my brain. She was willing, I reminded myself. And even if she had not been so enthusiastic about going to the king's bed, what choice did she have?

What choice did any of us have about anything?

IN DEFERENCE TO the queen's sensibilities, the king chose to use Will Compton's house in Thames Street for his first assignation with Bessie Blount. This took place in early November, shortly after the move from Eltham to Greenwich.

In spite of dismal weather, Bessie and I left the palace on the pretext of a trip to London to visit the shops. Our presence was not required by the queen and in theory we were free to go where we wished, but it seemed a poor ruse to me. If not for my growing fondness for Bessie, I most assuredly would not have ventured out on such a day.

After a cold, damp five-mile trip by wherry, we were hustled up the river stairs, through a back door, and along a passage to a bedchamber. A fire blazed in the hearth, giving off welcome warmth. A dozen quarriers had been lit—square blocks of beeswax with a wick, similar to those that illuminated King Henry's chambers at court. A luxurious, fur-trimmed robe for Bessie to change into had been left on the bed.

Relegated to the role of tiring maid, I helped her out of her damp cloak and the elaborate court dress beneath, removed her headdress, and brought her water for a last wash before she donned the sumptuous robe. I brushed her long, golden hair till it shone, and then produced a mixture of white wine and vinegar boiled with honey with which she could freshen her breath.

When all was ready, we had naught to do but wait for the king to arrive. Bessie kept a tight hold on my arm, her hand icy with last-minute nerves. I had told her all I could to help her through the afternoon. The rest was up to King Henry. As soon as His Grace arrived, I left them alone together, following the sound of voices to Will's hall.

"Come, Jane, join us in a game of chance." Will had already suborned the two yeomen of the guard who had accompanied the king into playing with him. They sat on stools around a small gaming table, tankards of ale at their elbows and coins at the ready to wager.

"Without the knight marshall of the household to oversee matters?" I asked in mock horror. "I am not sure I can trust you not to cheat."

Will took no offense, only grinned at me and used one foot to push the remaining stool in my direction. "We need no official to bring us cards or act as bookmaker."

"Perhaps I prefer dice." The queen, for all that she was very pious, gambled with as much fervor as everyone else at court. I meandered closer. "The knight marshal's dice are brought to the table in a silver bowl. Did you neglect to furnish yourself with one?"

Will shuffled cards, his pride pricked by that sally. He lived well for a simple country knight, and if the rumors I had heard were true, he was building a veritable palace for himself in the Cotswolds. After Charles Brandon, King Henry favored Will Compton above all men and had given him many gifts to prove it.

"You may choose the game, Jane. What will it be? Mumchance? Gleek? Click-Clack? Imperial? Primero?"

I pretended to give the matter deep thought, but I'd been lucky of late at primero and hoped to be so again. Compton dealt three cards to each player. I looked at my hand and calculated quickly. In primero, each card had three times its usual value. Hiding my smile, I settled in to play. An hour later I had won all the two yeomen of the guard had to wager and was in a cheerful frame of mind.

"A pity you cannot afford to play for higher stakes," Will commented as I raked in my winnings. "You will never grow rich wagering pennies."

"Nor will I be reduced to selling my clothing."

The two yeomen of the guard laughed and wandered off, no doubt to rid themselves of all the ale they had consumed. Left alone with Will, I felt a sudden awkwardness descend. I could not help but wonder how long the king usually spent disporting himself with a mistress, but that was not the kind of question I could ask, not even of an old friend.

I sent a sidelong glance his way and discovered that he was staring at me intently. I quickly looked away, a frown on my face. I picked up the cards and idly began to shuffle them.

"The king hoped at least one of his own people would remain in France," Will said.

I stifled a laugh. "I do not know why he expected me to continue to spy for him. Or how. I would have been hard pressed to send intelligence back to England."

"Had you other plans?" Will's voice was so smooth and uncritical that I almost confided in him.

I caught myself in time, lest a desire to do other than King Henry's bidding be misconstrued as treason. "If I had not been refused entry in the first place, I would doubtless have been sent home with the rest of the French queen's English household." In spite of Mary's passionate and tearful protests, not even Mother Guildford had been allowed to remain at the French court.

"You were fond of Longueville." It was not a question.

"I was. So was the king," I added, in case this, too, should be misunderstood.

"And when you came to England, years ago, it was from France."

"I was born in Brittany." I grew tired of reminding people of that but they never seemed to remember. "My mother was one of Duchess Anne's ladies." I looked up at last, into sympathetic, even pitying hazel eyes.

"You must have been disappointed, then, not to be allowed to go with the Lady Mary."

"Has the king assigned you to test my loyalty?"

The blunt question surprised a laugh out of him. "No, he has not. Be of good cheer, Jane. You may yet have your heart's desire. King Henry has been talking of a meeting with King Louis come spring. If the entire court travels to France, the queen will perforce take all her ladies with her, even you."

I smiled and pretended to be pleased by the notion, but all I could think was that the king of France thought I should be burnt. I did not dare go back, not even under King Henry's protection.

"HE WAS SO gentle with me, Jane. So tender." Bessie whirled around in a circle, her face wreathed in smiles.

"I am happy for you," I said.

"And I think I pleased him." She blushed becomingly. "He praised my eyes and my hair and my breasts."

"Bessie." I caught her hands in mine and waited until she looked at me. "You must never forget that King Henry takes mistresses when the queen is with child and he is denied her bed. When he can return to it, he will lose interest in you. He is, in his way, a faithful husband."

Her smile was one of pity. "But he is mine to keep for a while," she said. "How many women can say they have bedded the king of England?"

IT WAS LATE November when Meg Guildford sought me out at court with surprising news. "Harry's mother desires your company, Mistress Popyncourt," she said. Her mouth was pursed with disapproval, making her look as if she'd just bitten into a lemon.

I dropped my needle in surprise. "She has returned to England?"

"She has. Will you come with me or not?"

I went. Mother Guildford was in full spate when we arrived at the double lodgings Meg and Harry occupied at court, complaining to Meg's sister, Elizabeth, of King Louis' many sins. She did not even pause for breath when Meg and I entered the room.

"He suffers from gout and God knows what else. Both hands and feet are crippled, and he can barely keep his seat on a horse. He needs the help of three servants to get him into the saddle. He is confined to bed for days at a time, and he is the most nervous fellow you would ever want to meet."

"The king's portrait showed a pleasant enough countenance," I interrupted, remembering a strong face, weather beaten and sagging a little with middle age, but with striking features—large eyes and a long, thin nose.

"That was painted years ago. Now he looks a decade older than he is. Swollen cheeks. Bulbous nose. Decayed teeth. He is plagued by a catarrh, and he gulps his spittle when he talks. They say he was a tall man once, but you would not know it to look at him now."

"I gather you did not get on with him," I murmured.

She rounded on me and I heard both sisters suck in their breaths. Then, surprising all of us, Mother Guildford laughed. "You have changed little since I saw you last, Jane Popyncourt."

"Have you news of the Lady Mary?"

"The queen of France, you mean."

"Yes. The queen of France."

"Only what all hear, that she sits beside her new husband's bed, tending to him with loving kindness as he receives envoys from England." Her face was a study in conflict, her dislike of King Louis at war with pride in Mary Tudor. "He sent me away on the day after the French wedding ceremony. Said I meddled."

"That was nearly two months ago. Have you spent all this time traveling home?"

"On King Henry's orders I went no farther than Boulogne, in case I should be called back. I spent weeks waiting there, hoping King Louis could be persuaded to change his mind. That foul old man! I should have heeded the omens."

"The storm before you sailed, do you mean?"

"That one and the other tempest that struck when our ships were in the midst of the crossing from Dover. The fleet was scattered. The ship we were aboard ended up grounded on a sandbank."

"My poor lady," I murmured. "How terrified she must have been of the thunder and lightning."

"That was the least of it," Mother Guildford declared. "Her Grace was lowered into a rowing boat to be taken ashore, but even that small craft could not land. One of her entourage had to carry her through the surf in his arms. The queen of France! She arrived damp and bedraggled, hardly an auspicious beginning."

"I am sure her new subjects took the weather into consideration. We have heard that there were pageants to welcome her and much rejoicing that the war was at an end."

"The French put on a passable display," Mother Guildford grudgingly admitted. "Both the Duke and the Duchess of Longueville came to greet their new queen," she added, slanting her eyes in my direction. "The duchess is a striking woman. Very handsome. She and Longueville seemed most affectionate toward each other, as is only to be expected after such a long separation."

That her comments failed to provoke a jealous reaction seemed to increase the old woman's animosity toward me. She went on to provide elaborate descriptions of the journey to Abbeville and the official wedding ceremony held there, waxing vituperative and vitriolic once more about her dismissal from the queen's service.

"Only a few minor attendants and six maidens too young to have had any experience at court remain with Queen Mary," she complained. "I was replaced by a Frenchwoman, a Madam d'Aumont, about whom I know nothing."

Mother Guildford's litany of grievances was still going strong when I excused myself to return to my duties with Queen Catherine. Belatedly, she remembered that she had sent for me. She slid a sealed letter out of one of her long, loose sleeves.

"The Duke of Longueville's man sends you this." She fixed me with a gimlet-eyed stare, no doubt hoping for some telling reaction when she handed it over.

I thanked her politely and carried the letter away with me.

I stopped at the nearest window alcove after leaving the Guild-fords' lodgings and broke the seal, noticing as I did so that it showed signs of having been tampered with. I was not surprised, nor was I alarmed. Guy must have known that anything he wrote to me could be read by others.

He had written on the tenth of October, just before Mother Guildford's departure from Abbeville. He began by expressing his sadness that I had been denied the opportunity to visit France. He made no mention of how the duke felt about that development. Then he said that it would be some time yet before he could travel to Amboise.

I read that sentence again. Amboise, not Beaugency, the duke's home, nor yet Guy's own lands, but Amboise, where I had hoped to go to ask questions about my mother. Did he mean to ask them for me?

A rustle of fabric had me hastily refolding the letter before I finished reading it.

"You are ill advised to fraternize with the French," said Mother Guildford. "If you have the sense God gave a goose, you will live righteously from this day forward. No good ever comes of illicit love, nor yet from seeking to live above your station."

"I am no longer in the schoolroom, madam, nor under your control. And I am no longer convinced that you have my best interests at heart."

"Ungrateful girl!"

"Hardly a girl any longer, madam. And not best pleased to have been lied to."

"What are you going on about now?"

"You, madam. You told me Queen Elizabeth's ladies from my mother's time had scattered, and you implied that most were dead. In truth, a goodly number of them now serve our present queen. *And* you must have known the name of the priest most likely to have heard my mother's confession, for he went with your husband to the Holy Land and died there with him." Once started, I could not seem to stop myself. "Was my mother really ill when she first came to court, or was that another lie?"

The look of panic on Mother Guildford's face brought my tirade to an abrupt end. Bereft of speech, I watched as her eyes rolled up and her knees buckled. She landed in an ungainly heap at my feet.

Kneeling beside her, I called out for help. In short order she had been tucked into bed and a physician had been called to look after her. When Meg ordered me to leave, I did not argue, but I was puzzled by what had just happened. What had I said to cause such an extreme reaction?

Brooding, I returned to the queen's presence chamber, where I was scolded for neglecting my duties. Many hours passed before I was able to finish reading the letter Guy had written to me more than a month earlier. When I did, a frisson of fear snaked through me.

The explanation for his delay in leaving for Amboise was both simple and terrifying. He intended to remain at the French court in order to participate in the tournament being held to celebrate Queen Mary's coronation. He hoped to acquit himself better this time.

THE TOURNAMENT HAD originally been planned to last three days. In actuality, it stretched out over a much longer period because of delays caused by rain. The first event was held on Monday, the thirteenth day of November. Over three hundred contestants, fifty of them English, participated. Among them were Charles Brandon, Harry Guildford, and Ned Neville.

"Ten challengers were led by the Dauphin himself," I heard someone say as I entered the queen's presence chamber at Greenwich the day following my encounter with Mother Guildford.

"—held at the Parc des Tournelles in Paris."

"The old palace there was the Louvre, but it is in such bad repair that no one uses it anymore."

"—interrupted by heavy rains."

"Suffolk wore small red crosses all over his armor, for St. George and England."

"They all did."

The king, seated on the dais with the queen, raised his hand for silence. "The news from France is good. I received earlier reports, but now I have a letter giving details. On the first day of the tournament, my lord of Suffolk ran fifteen courses. Several horses and one Frenchman were slain but none of our good English knights took any serious injury."

For a moment I lost my breath. One Frenchman slain? I prayed with all my heart that it had not been Guy. I did not consider for a moment that it might have been the duc de Longueville. If he had been injured or killed, the king would have said so.

Bracing one hand against a window frame, I forced myself to

listen to King Henry, who was now reading from a letter. It gave an account of the bouts fought on the eighteenth of November.

" '—divers times both horse and man were overthrown. There were horses slain, and one Frenchman was hurt that is not likely to live.' "

Yet again, word of an unidentified Frenchman. Did the English competitors care so little for life that they could not even be bothered to name their victims?

"My lord of Suffolk ran only the first day," the king continued, squinting to decipher the tiny letters on the page, "because there was no nobleman to be put against him, only poor men at arms and Scots. Many were injured on both sides, but of our Englishmen none were overthrown nor greatly hurt except a little upon their hands."

There was more, but my attention wandered. Around me I could see that the lack of names troubled others among the queen's ladies. That their husbands or lovers or sons might be hurt "a little upon their hands" was a concern to them. Injuries, even small ones, could all too easily lead to death.

My gaze darted back to the king when he laughed. He joked with Compton but ignored the queen. There had been a certain coldness between them since he'd first learned of King Ferdinand's betrayal. No one could hold a grudge like King Henry. I doubted that the queen would regain his favor fully until she gave birth to his heir, and that event would not occur for some months.

If the queen knew about Bessie, she pretended not to. Tonight, once again, it would be Bessie who shared the king's bed. I would be the one to accompany her to their rendezvous and ready her to receive him. Then I would wait with Will Compton in a drafty antechamber until it was time to escort Bessie away again. Wait . . . and worry.

It did not matter where I spent the night. I doubted I would sleep even if I had our soft feather bed all to myself. My thoughts would keep circling back to the unnamed Frenchman who had died in the tournament. Were there more dead by now, more "poor men at arms and Scots" who did not deserve to be mentioned by name?

And was one of them Guy Dunois?

IN DECEMBER, ELIZABETH Bryan married Nick Carew at Greenwich Palace. I was there, as part of the queen's entourage, for Catherine attended the wedding even though she was hugely pregnant. The king was there, too. So were Harry Guildford, at last returned from France, and Mother Guildford, fully recovered from what she now termed a mere dizzy spell.

My friendship with Harry had been strained for some time, both because his wife did not like me and in consequence of my liaison with the duc de Longueville. In spite of that, I hoped he might be willing to answer questions about his time in France.

My first opportunity to speak with him came when the dancing commenced. I singled him out during a lull between pavanes and motioned for him to join me in an antechamber.

"Does this mean you missed me?" he quipped.

"Try not to be any more foolish than God made you!"

He sobered instantly. "What is it, Jane?"

"The Frenchmen who were killed or gravely injured—was one of them Guy Dunois?"

"No. Dunois was hale and hearty the last time I saw him."

My relief was so great that I had to brace my hand against the nearest tapestry-covered wall for support.

"Are you ill?"

"No."

"Are you with child?"

"No!"

The baffled look on his face might have been comic if I had not been so full of other emotions. "Both Dunois and Longueville took part in the jousting. Once again, your duke acquitted himself well."

When I did not respond, his eyes narrowed. He gave a low whistle. "So that's the way of it. It is not the duke you pine for, but his bastard brother."

"I am not pining for any man!"

Holding both hands up, palms out, he backed away from me, a huge grin splitting his face. I caught his arm. We did not have much time. Someone would come looking for us if we remained here long, most likely Harry's wife. "Did he send any message to me?"

"Dunois?"

I glared at him. "Yes, Dunois. He offered to undertake an . . . errand for me in France."

Harry scowled at that. "I could have carried out any commission—"

"It was to do with my mother," I said in haste. I had not told Harry Guildford a great deal about my inquiries into my past, but I had mentioned them months before.

"I know nothing of that, but I think someone said that Dunois left Paris as soon as the tournament was over."

When Harry returned to the dancing, I remained where I was awhile longer. In the dimly lit antechamber, I attempted to collect my thoughts. I was relieved of my concerns about Guy's survival, but was left to wonder when and how he would contrive to send word to me of what he found at Amboise. I supposed that was where he had gone, unless the duke had sent him on an errand elsewhere.

It did no good to speculate. Either Guy would write to me again or he would not. In the meantime, I had no way to leave court, let alone make the journey to France to join him, even if I dared risk entering that country while King Louis reigned. The best thing I could do was concentrate on living the life I had. I would serve the queen and stay, as much as possible, in the background. With that I could be content . . . for now.

Returning to the festivities, I wandered aimlessly about the hall, listening in here and there to conversations. Much of the talk continued to be about the French tournament.

"In the tourney, Suffolk nearly killed a man and beat another to the ground and broke his sword on a third. He—"

"I hear the Dauphin dropped out because he broke a finger."

"Our knights fought on despite injury."

"—an attempt by the French to embarrass the Duke of Suffolk by substituting a German in the foot combats."

I had already heard that tale, told by Charles Brandon himself, and I was not surprised to come upon him telling it yet again.

"Of a sudden I found myself facing a giant, hooded to conceal his identity. He was a powerful German fighter who had been substituted for a Frenchman, but I did not know that then. All I could see was a mountain of a man charging straight at me. By sheer strength, I fought off the attack, seizing the fellow by the neck and pummeling him so about the head that the blood issued out of his nose."

"And was the French deceit revealed?" Bessie Blount asked in a breathless voice. She stared up at the Duke of Suffolk, her face full of admiration for his prowess.

By her side stood the king, looking less impressed and a trifle annoyed that he had to share her hero worship.

"The German was spirited away before his identity could be

discovered, but we learned the truth later. And in the tournament as a whole, Englishmen were victorious. None was killed and few were injured." Brandon affected a sheepish look—all for show!—and drew back his glove to show Bessie the small injury he'd sustained to one hand.

I continued on, my thoughts having once again strayed to Guy Dunois. I paid little attention to my surroundings until a great commotion drew my gaze to the dais where the queen sat. For a moment I could make no sense of what I saw there. Then both dismay and pity filled my heart.

The queen was in labor . . . and it was much too soon.

13

racing myself, I slipped into the room that had been intended for a nursery. The queen was just as I had seen her last, as if she had not slept or eaten or even prayed, although I knew she had. She had aged a decade in mere days and she was already nearly six years older than the king. Still as a statue, she sat by an empty cradle, head bowed, hands clasped in her lap. A week earlier, she had been delivered of a tiny scrap of a son who had lived only a few hours.

As I approached, she spoke, but not to me. "You must love me, Lord, to confer upon me the privilege of so much sorrow." Her eyes were closed, but tears leaked out at the corners.

When King Henry and Queen Catherine had last lost a son, the entire court had gone into mourning. This time, King Henry made no show of grief. He seemed utterly unaffected by the loss, treating it like another miscarriage. Discounting his wife's suffering, he acted as if the child's premature birth was her fault. Her father's betrayal had altered his devotion, and her failure to give him a living son now widened the divide between them.

The king ordered that preparations for Yuletide go forward as if nothing had happened. He continued to welcome Bessie into his bed, only now he did not seem to care who knew. Evenings were filled with music and dance, and the king's boon companions organized snowball fights to pass the daylight hours.

By the time New Year's Eve was nigh, however, the queen's state of mind had begun to concern even the most insensitive of courtiers. "The king must renew relations with her," Charles Brandon said bluntly. "He needs a son."

"Queen Catherine would never turn him away from her bed," I said stiffly. No matter how callous his behavior toward her had been!

"Nevertheless," Harry Guildford said, "Charles here thinks we need a special disguising, one that will both surprise and please the queen. We have devised a night of revelry designed to win Her Grace's favor and lighten her spirits."

I regarded Brandon's participation with skepticism. He was all but illiterate in his letter writing and had no talent as a poet. I'd read one poor attempt he'd sent to the Lady Mary. A child of seven could have done better. The king, at seven, had.

But Brandon surprised me by suggesting several clever ideas for the queen's entertainment. In the end, I agreed to act as a go-between to the queen's steward and chamberlain to make certain that all would go smoothly.

On New Year's Eve, word was sent to Queen Catherine that the evening's festivities required her presence. Never one to shirk her duty, she allowed herself to be dressed in her finest clothing and sat down to sup with a better appetite than she had shown since she lost her child. If she was disappointed that the king did not share the meal with her, she gave no sign, but whether that was from indifference or stoicism was impossible to tell.

I slipped out of her bedchamber while she ate and hurriedly assumed my costume, an intricate garment of blue velvet in the Savoyard fashion, worn with a bonnet of burnished gold. As soon as food and table both had been cleared away, the queen's steward announced that a troupe of poor players had come to her door and craved her indulgence that they might perform for her. After a slight hesitation, she gave her permission and the great double doors swung open.

Minstrels and drummers entered first, all clad in colorful motley. Next came four gentlemen dressed as knights of Portugal and, last, four ladies, faces hidden by elaborate masks.

"Such strange apparel!" The queen seemed much taken with our costumes. If she recognized the tallest of the knights as her husband, she did not let on.

When the music began, we danced, performing intricate steps to delight the queen and her ladies. The chamber was lit only by torchlight, adding to the romance of the performance. A pity I was paired with Charles Brandon. Harry and Nick Carew danced with their wives and the king partnered Bessie Blount.

"It has been a long time since I held you in my arms, Mistress Popyncourt," Brandon whispered in my ear.

"I do not recall that we ever danced together," I lied, unwilling to be reminded that once I had found him appealing. "But then I danced with all the young men at court, so I suppose you were one of them."

"Ah, Jane, such a pity you did not turn out to be wealthy."

"Would you have wed me for my money, then?"

"I thought to marry you for your powerful kin, but it was not to be." What sounded like genuine regret in his voice distracted me for a moment from the words themselves. When I comprehended what he had said, I frowned.

"Sir Rowland Velville is scarcely a great magnate and seems unlikely ever to be one. Only you appear capable of rising so far and so fast."

He took my comment as a compliment and I had sense enough to say no more. If he held me a little too tightly when we came together in the movements of the dance, forcing my body to rub against his, I pretended not to notice.

When at last it was time to remove our masks, the king approached his wife with cap in hand and threw off his visor with a flourish. A look of genuine surprise on her face, the queen rose from her chair, clapping her hands in delight.

"You have given me much pleasure," she said, speaking to him alone, "in this goodly pastime." Taking his face in both hands she kissed him full on the lips.

The courtiers cheered and applauded.

Laughing, Queen Catherine, arm linked through her husband's, came down off her dais to thank each of us for entertaining her. She affected further surprise as each dancer in turn unmasked. Her smile faltered a bit when she recognized me. I had never been one of her favorites. But when she came to Bessie Blount, I saw something else, something far more ominous, flicker in her eyes.

Face taut, she managed a graceful compliment and passed on to Elizabeth Carew. Bessie shot a panicked glance my way. The queen *knew*.

That night and the next and the next, King Henry slept with his queen, leaving Bessie to sob into her pillow, convinced that His Majesty was through with her. "She pleases him better than I do," she wailed.

"He needs a son, Bessie. That is all it is. If you want him, he'll come back to you. Be patient, and above all do not rail at him for his neglect. He cannot bear to be criticized."

WE HAD BARELY settled in at Eltham, where we were to celebrate Twelfth Night, when word came from France that King Louis was dead.

My first reaction was relief. I no longer had to fear for my life if I left the safety of the English court. Even better, with a new king on the throne in France, the prohibition against my journeying to that country could be lifted. I knew little about the new king, François I, except that he was young and yet another Longueville cousin, but I thought I might even find myself welcome at the French court.

I did not rush straight to King Henry to ask permission to leave England. It would be at least six weeks before the French succession was settled. By custom, the widowed queen must spend that length of time in seclusion. If, at the end of it, it was certain that Mary was not with child by the late king, her brother would doubtless demand that she return to England. If she was carrying Louis' heir and gave birth to a boy . . . clearly it was too soon to make any plans.

A memorial service was held for King Louis at St. Paul's, in London. That was the extent of royal mourning in England. In fact, King Henry commanded that *The Pavilion on the Place Perilous*, the masque we had been rehearsing for Twelfth Night, go on as planned . . . with one change. Bessie Blount's role was given to another.

Once again, I consoled my bedfellow while she wept.

"He is through with me, Jane. I know it! He has taken away my part in the pageant to please the queen."

"Perhaps, but not for the reason you imagine. Your part has been given to the imperial ambassador's wife."

"What difference does that make?"

"Think, Bessie. Why include her? She's nobody."

"She's married to an ambassador." Bessie sat up and dried her eyes. "You think the king is trying to sweeten him?"

"King Henry must already be thinking of new alliances he can make by using his sister as a pawn. The Imperial ambassador is the ideal candidate to act as a go-between to reopen negotiations for Charles of Castile." So much for Henry's promise that Mary might choose her own husband when Louis died!

I was certain my interpretation of the king's motives was correct when the Imperial ambassador himself was also invited to participate in the masque, replacing Harry Guildford. Teaching two foreigners their roles was a challenge. By the time the pageant wagon, carrying a pavilion made of crimson and blue damask surmounted by a gold crown and a rosebush, rolled into the hall, I felt as nervous as if this were my first disguising.

We ladies were hidden behind the draperies while the "lords," portrayed by the ambassador, Nick Carew, Charles Brandon, and the king, manned brickwork towers at each corner. Six minstrels perched on the stage as well, and more armed knights—members of the King's Players—marched alongside. Two of the Children of the Chapel preceded the pageant wagon and by means of musical verses explained what was to come.

It was an ambitious endeavor. Never before had anyone attempted to hold a tourney indoors. Granted, it was a small one, but it still required a show of skill extraordinary in the extreme. The four knights were attacked by six "wild men" appareled in "moss" made of green silk. Master Gibson had created strange and ominous-looking weapons for them to carry and I had painted their faces so that when they scowled they showed most terrible visages.

After a heroic struggle, long enough to have everyone in the hall cheering for their champions, the four knights drove the wild men away and it was time for the ladies to descend from the pavilion to dance with them. Once again, masks were the order of the day, but we wore our hair long and loose. Bessie's beautiful golden tresses would have been immediately recognizable. I took note of the queen's quietly satisfied smile as she realized that her rival was not among the dancers.

Bessie, by her own choice, had remained in our lodgings. If she could not dance with the king, she said, she did not want to join in the revels at all.

We unmasked after several dances and, as usual, everyone affected to be surprised that the king was one of the knights. In short order after that, we all returned to the pavilion—four ladies and four knights—to be conveyed out of the hall.

Once the silken draperies were drawn closed, the quarters were cramped. I was unsurprised when Charles Brandon took advantage of the enforced intimacy to run his hands over my breasts. I ignored the overture.

When the pageant wagon came to a halt some distance outside the great hall, we all climbed off. Meg and her sister had been delegated to escort the ambassador and his wife back to the queen's presence, and I meant to go with them, but as I straightened from smoothing my skirts I realized that Brandon had taken the king aside. They seemed to be arguing.

Curious, I lingered, pretending that I had a rush caught on my shoe.

"I swear on my life," I heard Brandon say, "that if you send me after her, I will do no more than bring her home to you."

"On your life be it," replied the king. Impatience, and mayhap some stronger emotion, creased his face into a frown. He waved

Brandon away, looked around for the yeomen of the guard assigned to him, and saw me instead. "Jane."

"Your Grace." I hastened to make my obeisance.

He studied my face. He had caught me off guard and I had no time to conceal what I'd been thinking. "My sister . . . confided in you? You know what man it is she wishes to wed?"

Keeping my eyes averted, I nodded.

"Brandon?"

"Yes." I wavered, then whispered, "She will be most distressed if you do him any harm."

A beringed hand appeared in front of me. I took it and he lifted me up, obliging me to meet his troubled gaze. "She was always a great one for reading the romances," he murmured. "*The Romaunt of the Rose, The Romance of Bertrand*—"

"*The Canterbury Tales. Ogier the Dane*," I contributed, hoping to lighten his mood. "*Legenda Sanctorum*." The last was a collection of saints' lives, translated into English. The Lady Mary's copy, which had come to her from her grandmother, was bound in red velvet with a silver clasp.

A reluctant smile blossomed on the king's ruddy face. "You always were quick witted, Jane. It is no wonder my sister is so fond of you. You will be glad of it when she returns, I have no doubt."

"I will, Your Grace." Of that much, at least, I was certain.

IN LATE FEBRUARY, word reached the English court from Paris that the widowed queen of France had married Charles Brandon, Duke of Suffolk.

The king was furious. The king of England, that is. The new king of France, François, had not only approved of the match but facilitated it, mayhap in part to tweak the nose of a fellow monarch.

For months after that no one knew for certain if King Henry would allow his sister and the man who had been one of his closest friends to return to England, or what kind of reception they would receive if they did. I suspected the king's anger stemmed not so much from being outmaneuvered as because he had lost a marriage pawn. He truly loved his sister, and his admiration of Brandon went back to the days when his father was still king. I could not imagine that even Henry Tudor would hold this grudge forever.

In the interim, however, those around him kept their opinions to themselves. It was not a good time for me to ask permission to travel to France.

By May Day, matters seemed to have resolved themselves. The Duke and Duchess of Suffolk were on their way home and would arrive within the week. The entire court was in high spirits as we rode out from Greenwich, the queen's ladies all mounted on white palfreys. We traveled two miles into the country early on May Day morning. "Robin Hood" had invited the king and queen to a banquet in the greenwood.

After some pageantry and an archery contest, we adjourned to a special arbor fashioned of boughs and covered with flowers and sweet herbs. It was large enough to contain a hall, a great chamber, and an inner chamber, and in this setting, the "outlaws" and their ladies served a breakfast of venison and other game washed down with wine.

When he had eaten, the king rose and moved among his guests, stopping near me to engage a member of the new Venetian embassy in conversation. "Talk with me awhile," the king invited, speaking in French. "I am told that you have met the new king of France. Is he as tall as I am?"

The ambassador seemed taken aback by the question but recovered quickly. "There is but little difference, Sire."

"Is he as stout?"

"No, he is not."

"What sort of legs has he?"

"Spare, Your Majesty."

"Hah!" The king, pleased by this answer, pulled aside the skirt of his doublet and slapped a hand on his thigh. "Look here! I have also a good calf to my leg."

Curious as to what that had been about, I sought out Will Compton and repeated the conversation I had overheard. "Is there some reason he singled out the Venetian?" I asked.

"The best of reasons. The fellow leaves on the morrow for France. He can now be counted upon to tell the new French king what he has observed in England, in particular the splendor of the court and the physical prowess of King Henry."

"I would have thought King François knew all that already. He has met any number of English noblemen, including the Duke of Suffolk." The sour expression on Will's face reminded me that he had never been fond of Charles Brandon. "Is there any word yet of when the king's sister will reach England?"

"Any day now."

"And what reception will she be given?"

Will made a derisive sound. "What sort do you imagine? She has already sent all the jewelry she got from old King Louis to her brother as a bribe and Brandon has agreed to pay a huge fine for marrying her out of hand. They'll be welcomed back with open arms."

"JANE!" THERE WAS no mistaking the delight in Mary Tudor's voice as she entered the room I shared with Bessie Blount. She rushed into my arms and hugged me tight. "Is it not wonderful! I have my Charles at last."

As Will had predicted, in the end there was little trouble over the clandestine marriage. The queen of France and her new husband arrived in Dover and were escorted to a private meeting with King Henry at the royal manor of Barking in Essex. Then they came to Greenwich to be remarried by an English priest.

"I am delighted to see you so happy, Your Grace." Both Bessie and Nan, the tiring maid we shared, slipped out of the room, leaving me privacy for our reunion.

"Do not be so formal with me, Jane. We are old friends, you and I. And although I will always bear the title Queen of France, I now think of myself as plain Lady Suffolk. Why, we are very nearly equals."

"Scarcely that."

"Nevertheless, you are my dearest Jane and from now on I command you to call me Mary when we are alone."

"I would be pleased to, and even more pleased if you will allow me to rejoin your household."

At once her smile dimmed. "Charles is . . . we—" She broke off with a rueful laugh. "We are *poor*, Jane. Almost everything we own is now pledged to the king. We will have to go to Charles's country house in Lincolnshire when the court leaves on its summer progress because we can live there more cheaply. It would not be fair to take you in when I must dismiss so many others."

Seeing my crestfallen look, she took my hands in hers. "We are *friends*, Jane. And I am certain you do not wish to leave the court. I do not wish to myself. Only having my dear Charles with me will make our exile to the country bearable."

Hiding my disappointment, I changed the subject. We talked for hours. I told her about pageants and petty rivalries at court. She recounted her adventures as queen of France, skimming over her marital duties and the long days of solitude after King Louis' death. Those weeks shut up in a dark room, wearing white and expected to keep to her bed had nearly driven her mad, but her only respite had proven nearly as nerve-wracking as the isolation.

"The new king visited me," she confided. "He is a handsome fellow, except for that huge nose of his, and he knows it. He tried to take liberties."

"I thought he was newly wed."

"So he is, to a lumpish girl named Claude, my stepdaughter. And he has a mistress, the young wife of an elderly Paris barrister." She gave a light laugh, but it conveyed no pleasure.

I shifted closer to her on the padded bench we shared and helped myself to a slice of candied apple from the bowl she held in her lap. The treat had been a gift to Bessie from the king. "How did you deal with him?"

"I told him the truth, that I loved Charles and wished to wed him. Then I burst into tears and said that I did not trust my brother to keep his promise. It was not at all difficult after that to convince the king of France to help us. It was a chance, you see, for him to score points against Henry. They are like little boys, the two of them, setting themselves up as rivals."

"Little boys with great power," I reminded her. "If you had returned unwed, your brother would have found some way to thwart your plans."

Color flooded Mary's face and her hands curled into fists. "Henry will not make decisions for me ever again!" I caught the bowl just as she was about to hurl it across the room.

When her temper cooled, I asked after the duc de Longueville.

"Oh, Jane, what you must think of me!" She fumbled in the purse suspended from her belt and produced a letter. This time the seal was unbroken.

I waited until I was alone to read Guy's missive. It was short and to the point and written on Longueville's behalf: Should I choose to leave England, King François had no objection to my presence in France.

SEVERAL DAYS PASSED before I found an opportunity to speak privily with King Henry. It was evening and, as usual, there was music and dancing. The king partnered me in a pavane. I waited until the dance was done, then placed one hand on his forearm when he tried to take his leave.

"Jane?" Mild annoyance shimmered just beneath the curiosity in his voice.

"Sire, I have a boon to ask." I spoke quickly, fearing we'd be interrupted. The music had already started up again.

Thunderclouds darkened his expression before I was halfway through my request. My heart sank. I had been too hasty. I should have waited longer. And I should have approached him through channels, perhaps recruiting Will or Harry to speak on my behalf.

"You wish to go to France?" His voice was dangerously quiet.

"A visit only, Your Grace. I lived there once, you know."

Mentally kicking myself for reminding him that I was not a native Englishwoman, I clamped my lips tightly together. To say more would only make matters worse.

"Do you still miss your lover?" Again the silken tone was deceptive, but I knew how I must answer that question.

"No, Your Grace. I do not." It was, after all, the truth.

The king shook his head, his eyes full of suspicion. I did not dare remind him that when Mary was wed to King Louis he had *wanted* me to go to France.

"You are forbidden to leave England," King Henry said. "You

will not go to France or to any foreign land unless I give you leave."

"Yes, Your Grace." Repressing a sigh, I made my obeisance and backed away. Tears swam in my eyes but I refused to let them fall.

EVERY SUMMER THE king went on progress. The route varied so that he could visit different subjects each time. The houses he would stay in were announced well in advance. When I realized that the upcoming progress would pass near Fyfield, the house belonging to James Strangeways and his wife, I made plans of my own. Not all the answers I sought were to be found in France.

James Strangeways's wife had been born Lady Catherine Gordon, the daughter of a Scottish nobleman, and had been married off by King James IV—the same James who later married Margaret Tudor, the same James killed at Flodden Field—to the pretender, Perkin Warbeck, in the belief that he was the rightful heir to the English throne. Lady Catherine had accompanied her first husband when he invaded England and had been captured. Instead of being imprisoned, however, she had become one of Queen Elizabeth of York's ladies, just as my mother had.

She and my mother, so I had been told, had befriended each other.

I had seen Lady Catherine at court when I was a child, and she had assisted with the preparations for Princess Margaret's wedding to the Scots king, but I did not think I had ever spoken to her. Certainly she had never sought me out. Still, I hoped she would agree to talk to me.

I was curious about her, aside from her connection to my mother. As I recalled the story, she had been kept apart from her husband, but otherwise well treated. She'd stayed at court even after Warbeck's execution. Following Queen Elizabeth's death, she had married Strangeways, a gentleman usher to the king, and been granted the rural manor of Fyfield in Berkshire. Since then, Lady Catherine had remained in the country.

To leave the progress and travel to Fyfield, I was obliged to ask permission from the queen's chamberlain to visit "an old friend." To my relief, he made no difficulty about my going. As far as the chamberlain was concerned, my absence meant he had one less body to provide with food and shelter. I borrowed a groom and horses for Nan and myself from Harry Guildford and set out over wretched rural roads.

I had not written to say I was coming. I was not certain Lady Catherine could read, and I wanted my business kept private. That meant I could not be certain she would be at home when I arrived. I could, at least, be certain of her hospitality. Country landowners always kept open house for gently born travelers. I was made welcome as soon as I identified myself, and within an hour of my arrival was sitting in the parlor with my hostess.

Lady Catherine's slender figure had become plump since I'd last seen her, but she was still pretty, and she had an air of placid contentment about her. She waved me toward a stool near her chair and ordered her hovering maidservant to bring barley water and comfits.

"It is rare that anyone from court comes to visit me here at Fyfield," she remarked.

"The king is on progress and staying nearby."

She chuckled. "Not so very close or I should have been obliged to house excess courtiers."

I smiled at her observation, thinking it must be a great imposition to have the king visit. No one would dare tell him they did not want his company, but being his host entailed considerable expense.

There was food and drink and entertainment while the king was in residence and then the cost to clean up the mess the court left behind.

"Is it curiosity that brought you to me, Mistress Popyncourt? Did you wish to see what had become of me?"

"Curiosity, yes, but not about you. Or, not only about you."

"Mistress Popyncourt," Lady Catherine repeated, abandoning a piece of fine embroidery for the collar of a shirt to peer into my face. "I remember you now. You serve the Lady Mary, do you not?"

"I did, madam, but when she went to France to marry King Louis, I became one of the queen's maids of honor."

Her eyebrows, already arched, shot higher. "A bit long in the tooth for a maid, are you not?"

"And you, madam, are much younger than I expected." She could have been no more than fifteen or sixteen when she wed Perkin Warbeck. Either that or the country air was exceptionally beneficial to preserving a youthful appearance.

"You left the progress to travel here on your own," she observed. "Why?"

"You knew my mother. Lady Lovell told me that you befriended her when she first came to England."

"Say rather that she befriended me." Lady Catherine's unlined face showed no emotion, but her eyes lost their welcoming gleam. "You were a child in those days, but you must have known how incensed the court was by my first husband's ingratitude. He'd dared try to escape his velvet shackles."

Uncertain how to respond, I held my silence. I had seen Perkin Warbeck after his capture. I remembered that he'd tried to escape a second time and had been executed for it. Even if she had not loved him, he had been her husband. She'd shared his defeat and his disgrace.

After a moment, Lady Catherine continued speaking. "My first marriage lasted four years. I wed in good faith, and Richard, as I called him, believing he was the prince he claimed to be, was a gentle and loving husband. I accepted that we could never live again as man and wife after our capture. I even understood the reasons when King Henry ordered his death. But there was always a part of me that wondered what my life would have been like had he been what he claimed, if he had won the support of his people and deposed the upstart Tudor king."

"You would have been queen of England."

Her smile was sad. "Most of the time, I am convinced I had a lucky escape."

"There do seem to be . . . drawbacks to being wedded to a king." Thinking of the Lady Mary, of the Lady Margaret, and of Queen Catherine of Aragon, I sighed.

The maid returned bearing a heavy tray.

"The queen is again with child," I said as she set out food and drink. "A babe that, God willing, will be born in February." King Henry had already taken Bessie Blount back into his bed.

The door closed behind the servant with a solid thunk. Lady Catherine reached for a seed cake. Our eyes met as she took the first bite. She chewed thoughtfully, then took another. "What do you want to know about your mother?"

"She died only months after coming to court. I had been separated from her, sent to the royal nursery at Eltham. No one I have talked to seems to have known her well enough to tell me how she spent her last days."

"And you want to learn more." She pondered this, consuming the second seed cake. "Well, I will tell you what I can recall, but I do not believe it will be of much help to you."

"I understand that it was a long time ago, that memories—"

"Oh, I recall that year well enough! How could I not. Everyone regarded me with suspicion, and yet I was obliged to go along on progress with the rest of the court."

"Maman died at Collyweston."

"The Countess of Richmond's house." Lady Catherine nodded, looking thoughtful. "Oh, yes. I remember the king's mother well. She traveled with the court most of that summer. We left London in late July, as I recall, and stopped first at Stratford Abbey."

She closed her eyes, the better to let her mind drift back to that time.

"We visited Havering, and were at Sir James Tyrell's house, and at Mr. Bardwell's. Those were in Essex." She frowned. "One or two fine old castles, and then on to Bury St. Edmunds. Thetford. Buckingham Castle. Norwich. Sir William Boleyn's place in Norfolk. Blickling Hall, I believe it is called. Then Walsingham and King's Lynn. We visited Sir Edmund Bedingfield's widow at Oxburgh Hall. Newmarket. Ely. Cambridge. Huntingdon. Peterborough." She ticked the towns off on her fingers, one by one.

"You have an excellent memory." Impatient, I fought the urge to tell her to skip ahead to Collyweston.

"At times I think memories are all I have left to me." Her eyes popped open and she trilled a light, self-deprecating laugh. "You must not feel pity for me. I am quite content to live in the country. Here I am ruler of my own little domain." She reached for a third seed cake.

"What of Collyweston?" I prompted her.

"That was the next stop. The king stayed three days, then went on to Drayton in Leicestershire and one or two other places. Queen Elizabeth and her ladies remained at the Countess of Richmond's house for two more days before joining King Henry at Great Harrowden in Northamptonshire."

"And my mother succumbed to her illness during that five-day stay?"

"Your mother fell ill and died right after the king left his mother's house."

My breath caught in my throat. My surprise must have shown on my face, because Lady Catherine narrowed her eyes at me. "You were told something different," she murmured. "What was it?"

"That my mother was dying even before she came to England, wasting away from some illness no one could cure."

"Nonsense. There was nothing wrong with her that I could see. She was cheerful and energetic in spite of the rigors of being on a royal progress. She had begun to make friends with some of the other ladies, and she even seemed to have won the approval of the king's mother."

"The Countess of Richmond took note of her?"

"She did, and was most distressed when your mother died." Lady Catherine frowned. "A bad mushroom, someone said. Food poisoning." She shrugged.

"Did anyone else fall ill?"

"Not that I recall, but then the English are not overly fond of mushrooms. The French dote on them, or so I am told."

"Maman was not French," I murmured. "She was Breton."

Lady Catherine did not seem to be listening. "No doubt your mother gathered the mushrooms herself and mistook one for another. That happens all too often in the country. I am obliged to take the utmost care that I do not mix in the wrong herb by accident when I prepare medicines in my stillroom."

I HAD MUCH to think about when I rejoined the royal progress. Lady Catherine's account of my mother's death was vastly different from Mother Guildford's, but I could think of no reason why

Mother Guildford should try to prevent me from learning the truth . . . unless Maman's sudden illness and death had not been a case of *accidental* poisoning.

When the progress ended and the court was once more at Greenwich, near enough to London that I could consider confronting Harry's mother with what I had learned, I found myself strangely reluctant to do so. I wished I had someone to confide in, someone with whom I could discuss what to do next, but the habit of secrecy was strong, as was my fear of trusting the wrong person. What if I was right? By revealing my suspicion, I might alert the killer, and I might be the next to die.

Foolish imaginings! I told myself that I'd thought of murder only because Maman had been accused of poisoning King Charles. Lady Catherine had not questioned the cause of my mother's death. The refusal of other ladies to tell me what they could recall likely stemmed from guilt over the shabby way they'd treated a newcomer. They'd not have wanted to remember that! And Mother Guildford's lie? Well, she had been raised in the Countess of Richmond's household. Could I believe this just an example of misguided loyalty? Rather than let the slightest blame fall on the king's mother for a death that had occurred at her house at Collyweston, Mother Guildford might have invented the tale of a wasting sickness, thinking that would cause less consternation.

I was not altogether satisfied with this explanation, but in the end it had to suffice. The queen's new pregnancy was a difficult one. She kept all her attendants fully occupied in the months that followed the progress . . . right up until the birth of a daughter the king named Mary, after his sister.

The Duke and Duchess of Suffolk had been forgiven for their clandestine marriage. King Henry now directed all his anger at

King François instead. He had been even more furious when he heard that his rival had won a great military victory at Marignano, near Milan. The French, taking advantage of the peace with England and Spain, had invaded Italy.

On the twenty-first day of February, the three-day-old princess was christened. I did not attend the ceremony. Instead I traveled to Suffolk Place in Southwark, where Mary had taken up residence to await the birth of her own child. The mansion faced the Thames and had its own private quay, but the winter had been a brutal one and the river had once again frozen solid. I rode across the ice, then made my way to the house on foot, passing two gardens and a maze en route.

I entered the great hall by way of a goodly porch of timberwork hung with cloth of arras without and cloth-of-gold within. The hall boasted fireplaces in every corner and twenty-four torches in wall sconces—I counted them. But only three were lit and the hearths were cold. I shivered in spite of my fur-lined cloak and three wool underskirts.

Mary Tudor awaited me in her bedchamber, where a cheerful fire blazed in the hearth. Great with child, she sat on a cushioned window seat, warmly wrapped in furs against the draft.

"How does my new niece?" she demanded as soon as she saw me.

"Even now she is being carried to the font, the silver one brought from Canterbury."

Mary's hand drifted to her swollen belly. Her cheeks were flushed, her eyes bright, but I could not tell if the high color came from fever or excitement. Her child was due in less than a month. "Tell me what she looks like."

"The princess is but three days old. She looks like most other infants at that age."

"Charles says her hair is red."

"That is true, but what other color could it be, given her parentage?"

We shared a smile, and Mary reached up to touch one of her own red-gold locks. "Will my child take after me, I wonder, or have dark hair? Oh, it does not matter. I will love him either way, but I do wish he would hurry up and be born!"

"You must be patient."

"You were always better at that than I," she lamented.

If only she knew! Ever since the king's refusal to let me visit France, I'd behaved as ever I had, joining in the dancing and revelry, waiting on my royal mistress, passing the rest of the time with card games and dice and fancy needlework. But beneath my calm demeanor my frustration had built to the screaming point.

"I find little pleasure these days in planning wardrobes or listening to music," I said, "or even in helping Harry and Master Gibson with the disguisings."

"I would be happy to be able to join in any of those pastimes." Mary's peevish tone reminded me that, in spite of her avowed desire for my friendship, she had no wish to listen to anyone else's troubles, not even mine.

"Forgive me. I am out of sorts." I stared out the window behind her at the Thames, striving for calm. Boats being useless on ice, people had taken their horses and carts out onto the frozen river. A few enterprising souls had even set up booths to sell food, and dozens of children had bound animal shinbones to their shoes with leather thongs to go sliding on the ice. Some used iron-shod poles to help them stay upright.

"Has there been any further news from France?" Mary asked.

"Nothing." I had learned that the duc de Longueville had fought at the great battle of Marignano, but I had received no direct word from Guy or of him. Had he survived the tournament only to be slain in a French war? I could only pray that he had not been one of the five thousand Frenchmen who had lost their lives to achieve King François's great victory.

"What word at court of my sister?"

"Nothing new. Queen Margaret is still in Northumberland."

The queen of Scotland had been obliged to flee from that country the previous September after unwisely choosing a second husband for herself. Her marriage to the Earl of Angus, a Scot with dynastic ambitions, had turned the other noblemen of Scotland against her. They'd taken away her regency and her children and had been keeping her a virtual prisoner in Edinburgh until she'd managed to escape.

"I heard Margaret almost died giving birth to a daughter."

"So I am told, but she is recovering. She has sent word to your brother that she wishes to come to court."

"And will he allow it?"

"Who is to say? King Henry is not happy about her marriage. He talks of having it set aside."

Mary started to speak, then fell silent. If her sister's marriage could be annulled, even after the birth of a child to that union, then so could her own. It was a fear that must always haunt her.

14

In his role as Master of Revels, Harry Guildford brought together his usual lieutenants to plan Queen Margaret's entertainment. Officially, Master Gibson was his second in command but, as he had so often in the past, Harry asked for my suggestions. Once again, I was to play an active, if unacknowledged part in the proceedings.

"We have until the first of May," Harry Guildford announced one morning several weeks after my visit to the Duchess of Suffolk. "Queen Margaret will not travel south until then. When she does, her brother wishes to give visible proof of his affection and forgiveness. I am inclined toward gentlemen dressed in Turkey fashion and carrying scimitars."

"It is already early March," I reminded him, "and surely King Henry will want something original." This presented a problem. There was very little that had not been done before. Neither the Fortress Dangerous nor the Rich Mount were novelties any longer.

"Build a bigger castle," Master Gibson suggested, "one twenty feet square and fifty feet high. The ladies within will be the object of an entire tournament instead of a simple mock combat."

"We should need to stage such a thing out of doors," Harry mused.

"And why not?" Gibson's eyes gleamed. "The ladies would be delighted by such a spectacle, would they not, Mistress Popyncourt?"

"Must it always be ladies hidden within a mountain or a castle?" I ran my hand over a sample of velvet Gibson had brought with him. "Do you remember the pageants when the queen married Prince Arthur? There was a pageant wagon in the shape of a castle with four towers, but instead of ladies, each one contained a singing child."

"There must be beautiful women somewhere," Harry objected. "The king expects it."

"As does every other gentleman at court," Gibson agreed, "and the more outrageously clad, the better."

Harry laughed. "Eight damsels, I think, in a castle, drawn in on a wagon pulled by eight burly, costumed servants. Two will be garbed as a golden lion, two as a silver lion, the third pair as a hart with gilt horns, and the fourth team as an ibex."

"What if we add a second pageant wagon?" Master Gibson suggested. "It will carry a ship in full sail manned by eight gentlemen dressed as knights. It will drop anchor near the castle and the knights will descend by means of a ladder and approach the ladies."

"Still nothing new." I grew tired of their debate. I had lost my enthusiasm for pageantry.

They ignored my comment. "The audience will think this is all that is in store for them. Some will even begin to chatter among themselves as the knights try to gain access to the ladies. Flattery will fail. So will the threat of force. But then, just as everyone expects the knights to storm the castle, a third pageant wagon will be pulled into the room."

"The mountain?" I intended sarcasm but was not really surprised when Master Gibson nodded.

"I can paint it a bright Kendall green this time and adorn it with banners. It will open to reveal yet another band of knights. They will fight with the knights from the ship. After the battle, the winners will compel the ladies to surrender, descend from the castle, and dance."

They were still sketching out ideas when I slipped quietly away. Neither noticed my departure.

Halfway back to my lodgings, I caught sight of a familiar face and my heart stuttered. "Ivo?"

It was plainly Ivo Jumelle, Longueville's page, only he had finally grown into his feet. He was taller than I was now, and his chest and arms had filled out, giving the impression of considerable strength.

"Mistress Popyncourt," he greeted me after an awkward moment when he seemed torn between acknowledging me and taking flight. "You look well."

"And you, Ivo. I did not think to see you again, at least not in England."

"I have a place in the retinue of the new envoy," he said with no little pride in his voice. "We have come from King François with gifts for the baby princess."

I walked with him toward the royal apartments. "Did any of the duke's other servants come back with you?" I held my breath.

"No, mistress. I have not seen them since the duke left to fight at Marignano."

"Did . . . did Guy Dunois cross the Alps with him?"

"I . . . I suppose you would not hear."

"Hear what, Ivo?" I felt cold all over, as if the life was slowly draining out of me. I stopped him at the top of a staircase, catching his arm and tugging until he turned to face me. He tried to avoid my eyes, but I would not allow it. "What have I not heard?"

"I do not know that it was Guy, mistress." He squirmed in my grasp and looked everywhere but at my face. "I only heard that it was one of the duke's brothers. It could have been Jacques."

"What happened!" I had both hands on his arms now. I'd have shaken the information out of him had he not been too big for me to move.

"He was killed!" Ivo's voice broke. "The duke lost a brother in the Battle of Marignano! Not his full brother, who is a priest. It was one of his father's bastards, but I do not know which one."

"I must find out," I said, half to myself. "If need be, I will go to France without the king's permission."

I was standing at the top of the stairs when I suddenly lost my footing. I felt myself falling and heard the horrendous crack of a bone breaking as my arm struck the stone steps. A moment later, everything went black.

When I regained consciousness, I was lying on my own bed. Worried faces hovered over me—Bessie, Harry, and Will Compton.

"According to the king's surgeon, you are most fortunate," Bessie said. "You broke your arm when you fell, but the bone has been bound tight and he says it will likely heal in time."

I looked down at my arm. Lead plates had been tied around it to keep everything in place. It throbbed with pain. So did my head. Gingerly, I lifted my good arm to feel the lump beneath my hair.

"He used the large hollow root of comfrey as a bonesetter and packed it around the straightened bone," Bessie continued. "He said you must not try to lift anything for at least two months."

I did not want to think very far ahead. "Did he leave anything for the pain?" I asked.

Harry produced a vial of poppy juice, and when I had swallowed a dose, I sank back into pain-free oblivion. While I slept, Bessie, Harry, and Will sent word of my accident to Suffolk Place.

The Duchess of Suffolk did not respond at once. On the eleventh day of March she gave birth to a son. As soon as she was advised of my condition, however, she asked Queen Catherine if she could spare me and, with unflattering speed, I was transported from Greenwich to Southwark.

As I began to recover, I realized that I had been gifted with an opportunity I should not waste. I was no longer at court. No one would notice if I also left Suffolk Place. At first I thought I might manage to travel all the way to France, but I soon realized I would not be able to leave the country without a passport, not unless I could afford a hefty bribe. That it was still March was a further deterrent. For a safe crossing, I should delay at least until May.

I would find a way to go there. I was determined upon it, and not only to discover more about my mother. I had to find out what had happened to Guy. I did not want to believe he was dead. I prayed it had been his brother Jacques who had been killed in battle.

Frustrated in my desire to cross the Narrow Seas, I soon conceived an alternate plan. Whether I succeeded in finding my way to France or not, I doubted I would ever have a better opportunity to take another journey. This was my best chance to visit my uncle, the one person my mother was most likely to have confided in when she first came to England.

"What better medicine than to be reunited with my only remaining family member?" I argued when Mary reminded me that I was not yet fully healed.

"But Sir Rowland is in *Wales*," she objected. "The journey there is long and arduous even for someone in the best of health."

"I am not ill, Mary, only afflicted with a bulky set of bandages, and since it is my left arm that is broken, I can still control a horse."

"You'd do better in a litter."

"A litter requires too much fuss and too many men and horses and is both slower and more uncomfortable than traveling on horseback. I am a good rider." I had learned to manage a horse at Eltham and had since ridden in processions, on progresses, and to hunt.

"The roads are frozen," Mary protested, "where they can still be found at all beneath the snow."

"And when spring comes in earnest, the roads will be even worse, a quagmire."

Throwing up her hands in defeat, she insisted that I take along four sturdy Suffolk retainers as protection.

I SET OUT for Wales in late March. Little can be said of the journey itself except that it was unpleasant. We rarely managed to travel more than ten miles a day and were obliged to stay in the guesthouses provided by priories and monasteries along the way, there being few reputable inns. Nearly two weeks after leaving Southwark, I reached the island of Anglesey in North Wales.

My first glimpse of Beaumaris Castle left me awed and speechless. It stood at one end of Castle Street, partially surrounded by a water-filled moat. Set between the mountains and the sea, its stone walls looked impenetrable, but the guards let me pass through the gates on the strength of my claim that my uncle was the constable.

It was a huge place, but a question to a passing maidservant was sufficient to locate Sir Rowland. He was in the mews with his falcons and hawks.

I cannot say he was pleased to see me.

He was also cup-shot, and this appeared to be no new condition. His eyes had the redness, his physique the flabbiness of a confirmed tippler. When I'd last seen him, just before the king embarked on his invasion of France, he'd gained weight. He'd no longer been the premiere jouster he once was. But I was shocked by how dissipated he'd become in the less than three years since then.

"Are you my charge now, to go with the new annuity?" he demanded when I greeted him and reminded him of who I was.

"I know nothing of any pension," I said, wrinkling my nose at the smell of bird lime and giving the hooded hawks on the nearest perch a wary look. Such birds were trained to catch and kill their prey. Their talons were sharp and deadly. I was relieved when Uncle, muttering to himself, escorted me out of the mews, across a courtyard, and into his own lodgings.

"Agnes!" he bellowed. "We have company!"

A small, plump wren of a woman popped out of an inner room. I would have thought her Uncle's housekeeper had he not slapped her on the rump as he passed.

"Jane is my niece," he announced. "Find her a place to sleep."

When he'd stumbled out again, Agnes eyed me curiously. She did not appear to be in awe of me, for all that I had dressed in court finery for my arrival at the castle.

"I fear I have descended upon you without warning, madam."

"Mistress Dowdyng," she said, introducing herself. "I am a

widow. What escort have you?" She spoke English, but with a Welsh accent.

"Four henchmen and a maid," I answered. Mary had provided a sturdy young woman named Nell to look after me.

Agnes Dowdyng showed me to a small, drafty bedchamber, and I suspect she intended to abandon me there, but when I shrugged out of my cloak, she saw my bandaged arm and the sling that supported it. "You are injured, Mistress Popyncourt."

"A small accident. The bone is healing nicely."

She peered into my face, her brow wrinkling and her gaze intense. "You are too pale. Lie down and rest. I will find your maid and send her up with a light supper."

I was asleep within moments.

The next day, I attempted to speak to my uncle, but he avoided me. He'd had a great deal of practice doing so. I could count on my fingers the number of times in the last eighteen years that we had exchanged more than a few words with each other.

Left with only Agnes to talk to, I set about making an ally of her. She was, as I had guessed, my uncle's mistress. With her sympathy and support and the promise that I would leave as soon as I was satisfied, I at length persuaded Uncle to agree to listen to my questions.

He watched me through narrowed eyes as I entered the room he used for conducting business. With ill grace he waved me toward the uncomfortable-looking bench that was the only place to sit besides the Glastonbury chair he already occupied. A half-empty tankard of ale sat in front of him on the table.

"What is it you want to know?" Impatience simmered beneath the question. He took another swig of the ale while he waited for my answer.

"Why did my mother leave France?"

"I've no idea. She never said." He scowled so hard at my injured arm that new furrows appeared in his forehead. "I say, let the dead past stay dead."

"Why are you here in Wales and not at court?" I asked.

"The king sent me here." Bitterness laced his words.

"It is an important post, is it not?"

"It was a way to get rid of me."

"Why should he want to?"

"His minions said I was too quarrelsome, that I could not control my temper, but I suspect there was another reason." He looked at my arm again, but still did not remark upon my injury.

If he did not want to talk about himself, I had no objection to returning to other questions. "Do we have kin still in Brittany?" I asked.

He drained the tankard before he answered. "Our mother died long before my sister brought you here."

"But surely there were a few Velvilles still alive at that time. Aunts. Uncles. Cousins. I—"

The tankard slammed down onto the table with a crash. I jumped and pressed my lips together to hold back the spate of questions. Anger simmered behind his dark brown eyes, but I did not think it was aimed at me. For several interminable minutes he sat there, lost in thought. Then he turned his head and glared at me. "I suppose you will not be satisfied until you know everything."

"You suppose correctly. I want to know why Maman did not return to Brittany, to her family."

"The Velvilles wanted no part of her, or of me."

"Why not?"

"Because they were no kin to us and they knew it."

"I do not understand."

A sneer replaced the scowl. "Use your head, girl. It is perfectly plain. My mother was a young wife who betrayed her husband and gave birth to twins."

I could feel my eyes widen. "How do you know this?"

"Because she told us, your mother and me! How else do you suppose? We were very small, and she was dying, but I remember. Oh, yes. I remember." He started to lift the tankard, realized it was empty, and rose to refill it from a cask in the corner of the room.

"What of *her* family, then?"

"She never spoke of them. I've no idea who her people were. I do not even know what surname she had before her marriage. What does it matter? Your mother did not go to them. She came to England."

"Why?"

He shrugged. "For the same reason I stayed—to be with our father."

His answer so startled me that I could not think of a single thing to say.

"Speechless?" He laughed and drank deeply from the brimming tankard. "So you should be. She meant to tell you. I suppose she died too soon."

"Tell me what?" My voice sounded hoarse, but was audible enough.

"It is a simple story." He flung himself into the chair and stretched his long legs out in front of him. "There were a goodly number of Englishmen living in exile in Brittany, unlikely ever to return to their homeland unless the Duke of Brittany—Duchess Anne's father—decided to renege on his pledge of protection and turn them over to King Edward. They were shuffled about from castle to manor to château until, when one particular English exile was about fifteen—a very foolish age—he met a beautiful young gentlewoman. They conceived a passion for each other, a love that would not be denied even though the gentlewoman was married. After the young man was moved to another place, his mistress discovered that she had conceived." He drank again, deeply, and his eyes began to go bleary.

I rose, unable to sit still any longer. My thoughts whirled. I was not particularly upset to learn that he and my mother were illegitimate, or that their father had been an Englishman. It was the Englishman's name that concerned me. The obvious choice seemed impossible. I planted my good hand on the table and leaned across it to assure that I had my uncle's full attention. "Who was your father?"

"Have you not guessed?" He snickered into his tankard. "He went by the title the Earl of Richmond when he was in exile, but by the time his legitimate children were born, he was King Henry the Seventh. A pity he could not have married your grandmother," he added sourly. "If he had, I'd be king of England now."

"This cannot be true." King Henry VII my grandfather? King Henry VIII and Mary and Margaret my uncle and aunts? No wonder Maman had hesitated to burden me with her secret.

"Why not?" Suddenly belligerent, Uncle half-rose from his chair. "The old king refused to acknowledge me in public, but he knew who I was. Why else bring me with him to England when I was but a boy?"

Staring at his face, I suddenly saw King Henry's features there. The eyes were a different color, brown not blue, but they were deep set like the late king's. Uncle Rowland also had the same long thin nose, high cheekbones, and thin lips. All he lacked was a wart on his cheek and he'd have been the image of his father.

"He *should* have acknowledged you!"

"Oh, aye. He should have." He subsided, drank, and let out

a gusty sigh. "He did not dare. Think back, Jane. You were only a child, but you remember Perkin Warbeck. There were other challenges to the throne. Even if he'd been married to your grandmother, he'd not have wanted his English subjects to know. Especially if he'd married her! Another potential challenge to the throne? God forbid!"

His voice full of bitterness and resentment, he rambled on about "this godforsaken outpost" and how little he had to show for his royal blood.

"Be grateful," I snapped when I could bear no more. "Royal blood is a deadly inheritance, and well you know it." Imposters were not the only ones King Henry—my grandfather—had executed. If Uncle's secret ever came out, he risked the same fate. My hand crept to my throat and I swallowed hard. "When old King Henry was alive, I often felt I was not quite servant, not quite family. Now I know why."

"For all the good it will do you!"

"Does . . . does the present King Henry know about you? About me?"

Uncle shook his head, but his gaze had once more fixed on my broken arm. "How were you injured?"

"A fall down a flight of stairs at Greenwich. An accident."

"Are you certain of that? There are others who know about us. Not the king, but people who might wish to eliminate us all the same."

"There was no one nearby when I fell who could possibly mean me any harm."

"You were alone? Mayhap a thin rope, stretched across the top of the stairs—?"

"I was talking to a young man. A friend."

For the first time, I wondered what had become of Ivo Jumelle. I had not seen him again after my fall. I assumed he'd gone for help, but for all I knew, he'd run off in a panic.

"Never be certain of anything, Jane."

"You have had too much to drink, Uncle. You grow fanciful."

"I drink to forget that I live in fear for my life." He suited action to words. "I am safe only here, far from court."

"Who at court would wish you harm?"

"I have enemies. Those who fear I might one day try to claim the throne."

He had enemies because of his temper, I thought, not because he was Henry Tudor's bastard son. It was the Tudor temper, I realized. Thank God I had not inherited that!

"What enemies?" I asked after Uncle had taken another swallow. "Who knows your secret?"

"Our secret now! Knowledge is no boon, Jane. It will make you more vulnerable to harm."

"Nonsense," I said brusquely. "It is ignorance that puts me in danger, if there is any danger. I ask again—who knows?"

"Brandon," he muttered. "Your great and mighty Duke of Suffolk, God rot him."

"Charles Brandon? How could he? He wasn't even born when King Henry the Seventh took the throne."

"His uncle was one of the king's men in Brittany. Sir Thomas Brandon knew. I am certain he told his nephew. That's why the younger Brandon came sniffing around you, years ago, before he married that London widow."

What Uncle said made a discouraging kind of sense. Learning our family secret could account for Charles Brandon's sudden interest in me. He had been looking for a wealthy bride. It had not taken him long to realize I would be of no use to him, I thought ruefully. If my heritage were known, whatever man I married, whatever children I bore, risked being perceived as threats to the Crown. At the king's whim, we could be showered with lands and titles or imprisoned in the Tower as traitors. On the other hand, as long as no one knew I was King Henry VII's granddaughter, I would never have any inheritance at all. No wonder Brandon had abandoned his courtship!

"Did anyone else know?" I asked.

His eyes were bleary when he looked at me. "Anyone who was with the young Henry Tudor during his exile in Brittany."

"They *all* knew you were his son?"

"They all suspected. How could they not? I looked a great deal like him."

"That is not proof of anything," I said. "Ned Neville and King Henry the Eighth look much alike, but Ned is not the king's brother."

Uncle quaffed more ale. "She was murdered, you know. Your mother."

"Murdered? No. That is not possible."

"Murder has been done before to secure the Crown. I have had a long time to think about it. I did not realize it then, but now I am certain that she was killed because she was King Henry's daughter."

If what he'd already told me had been difficult to accept, this defied belief. "Who do you think killed my mother?" I demanded.

"The king's mother was responsible."

"Elizabeth of York?" Confused, I struggled to follow his logic.

"Not our present king's mother. I mean my father's mother— Margaret Beaufort, the old Countess of Richmond. It was at Collyweston that your mother died. The countess's house." Uncle wagged a finger at me. "I see that skeptical look, but I know what I know. Someone told the countess that her son had fathered a daughter in Brittany and that your mother was that child. Mayhap she thought King Henry *had* married our mother. Mayhap she just wished to eliminate even the slightest threat to the succession. Whatever drove her, she had your mother poisoned at Collyweston."

"But . . . but Maman was her granddaughter!"

He seemed so convinced his accusation was true that I began to wonder if he was right. Shortly after my mother's death, the countess *had* become much more pious, even wearing a hair shirt next to her skin. Had she been seeking forgiveness for the sin of murder?

"If she killed Maman, why did she not seek you out and kill you, too?" I asked, fixing on the biggest flaw in my uncle's theory.

"It is not easy to kill a trained knight."

It is with poison, I thought. Then another realization struck me.

"Surely if what you say is true, she'd have ordered me slain, as well."

"Not so long as you were ignorant of your heritage."

"So you have been protecting me all these years?"

He winced at the skepticism in my voice, then forced a laugh. "Think what you will. I know what I know."

I tried to convince myself that this was a tale told by a drunkard, an invention. Except for the part about King Henry being my grandfather. The more I looked at Uncle Rowland's face, the more I knew that much was true.

I sank back down on the bench, too confused to think of any other questions to ask. We sat there in silence, save for the sound of Uncle lifting the tankard and swallowing. And then a question did occur to me.

"How did she know? The Countess of Richmond—who told her about Maman?"

Uncle shrugged.

"Who told her?" I shouted at him, on my feet once more. "You must have some idea!"

Grudgingly, he gave me a name. "I warrant it was Sir Richard Guildford. He was with the king in exile in Brittany, but he was in service to the countess originally."

Harry's father. The same Sir Richard Guildford who had written to his son that he wished to go on a pilgrimage to the Holy Land because he had a great sin on his conscience.

"He's dead now," Uncle said, "and so is the countess. But I am certain there are others who'd like to see our line end. Be very careful, Jane, when you return to court."

I LEFT WALES the day after I heard my uncle's story. Although I was convinced that he believed everything he'd told me, I was still uncertain as to how much of it was true. I could not understand why, if the countess had been responsible for my mother's death, she had allowed my uncle to live. Surely, as a man, he posed more of a threat to the succession than any woman.

Uncle claimed that Henry VIII did not know he had a half brother. If that was true, why had he sent my uncle to Wales? At least an answer to that question was not hard to come by. Uncle had always been difficult to get along with, and the older he got, the more quarrelsome he became. He'd never been popular at court. Why wouldn't the king seize on any excuse to send him away?

So, if King Henry did not perceive Sir Rowland Velville as a threat to the Crown, was anyone really trying to kill him? Was anyone trying to kill me? By the time I returned to Suffolk Place, I had convinced myself that neither one of us was in any danger. Too much drink had addled my uncle's mind. The people who wanted him dead were figments of his imagination.

Traveling to Wales and back had taken well over a month. It

was already the third week in April in the year of our Lord fifteen hundred and sixteen by the time I returned to Suffolk Place.

"Was your uncle any help?" Mary asked when she came to my chamber to welcome me from my journey. "Did he know why your mother left France?"

I shook my head, suddenly struck by the enormity of what I had learned. Mary Tudor, Duchess of Suffolk, although she was five years younger than I, was my aunt. The king was my uncle.

"A wasted journey, then. What a pity. You should have stayed here and been comfortable."

"Has Queen Margaret arrived yet?" I asked. Margaret Tudor, Queen of Scotland . . . another aunt.

"She is expected to enter London on the third of May," Mary said. "I wonder how much she will have changed." Margaret had been fourteen the last time we'd seen her and Mary only eight.

I wondered if the two sisters would find they had much in common. They both had new babies, as did the queen. I supposed that would give them something to talk about. I doubted Margaret would have anything at all to say to me.

As Mary cheerfully continued to describe plans for the reunion of her siblings, I realized that my uncle's secret was the one thing I could never share with her. Nor could I ever reveal his suggestion that the Countess of Richmond had been responsible for my mother's death.

I'd spent much of my return journey and since thinking about that accusation. It was possible my uncle was right. The countess had been fully capable of doing whatever was necessary to reduce the number of potential claimants to the throne. She did, after all, orchestrate her son's return to England and make sure he had sufficient allies to defeat King Richard III. She'd also arranged the marriage between her son and Elizabeth of York, to ensure that the succession would go unchallenged. If she had discovered that the king had another child, an *older* child, she might well have acted precipitously to eliminate that threat.

And Uncle was right. Sir Richard Guildford was the most likely person to have told her who Maman was when she was at Colly-weston. A casual comment, perhaps. Not realizing that Maman had a twin brother, the countess had acted in haste to remove a poten-tial threat. And then? Guilt? Regret? There was evidence of both in the countess's sudden increase in religious fervor and Sir Richard's pilgrimage. He'd have known he shared some of the blame.

I doubted I would ever know the full truth. Both Sir Richard and the countess were dead.

I responded absently to Mary's comments while I considered Mother Guildford. She had gone out of her way to discourage my questions and make me think no one knew more than she was tell-ing me. She had lied when she'd implied that Maman died of con-sumption. Did that mean she know Maman's real heritage—and mine, too? Had she had a hand in the murder herself? Or had she only learned of it later from her husband?

I wanted to confront her, to demand the truth, but I knew bet-ter than to do such a foolish thing. She was a strong-willed woman. She'd never admit to any wrongdoing. She might even try to get rid of me, to protect her late husband's reputation.

I could not tell anyone, I realized. My secret was too dangerous. My uncle and I might be in real danger if the truth came out.

Although my arm was still sore, it had mended adequately to allow me to return to Queen Catherine's service a few days before Queen Margaret was scheduled to arrive. As soon as I was settled, I asked after Ivo Jumelle. Not because I thought he'd seen anything suspicious when I fell, but because I hoped he might have heard something more about Guy.

"The envoy he served has been recalled and took the young man away with him," Harry Guildford told me.

"He was not here very long." I stepped close to Harry, following the pattern of a complicated dance that was to be part of a masque to entertain Queen Margaret.

"Ran off in fear, no doubt, after hearing that King Henry is talking of another invasion of France."

"Why? I had not heard that France has done anything to provoke an attack."

"King Henry sees the new French king as a rival since they are so near in age and physical prowess. François acquitted himself well in his war in Italy. Now Henry is determined to prove himself the better commander."

I thought that a very foolish reason for starting a war. Then it occurred to me that I might disguise myself as a soldier and travel to France that way. The possibility so distracted me that I faltered in the steps we were rehearsing.

Harry caught me around the waist and lifted me high. "Pay attention," he cautioned me. "If one of us puts a foot wrong, we'll all go tumbling down."

I tried to concentrate, but it was difficult. I discarded the idea of dressing as a man, but only because I'd had a better idea. I'd thought of a way to persuade King Henry to send me home to Amboise. All I had to do was find a way to speak with him in private.

That would be a problem. The king could meet privily with anyone he wished if *he* chose to arrange the assignation. For me to whisk him behind an arras or into an empty antechamber would not be as easy. He was always surrounded by counselors, courtiers, or guards.

"By the saints, Jane!" Harry stopped the practice and waved the others away. "What ails you? If Bessie Blount were here, I'd bring her in to replace you even if it is the last moment."

"She will be back soon enough," I said. "In the meantime you must make do with me." Bessie had left court to visit her mother, who was ailing, while I was in Wales. A pity, I thought. Her absence deprived me of the easiest means of access to the king.

Then it struck me. There *was* a way to get King Henry alone. I might not be able to enter the royal bedchamber in Bessie's company, but I could contrive to be invited there in her place.

15

I considered trying to arrange a rendezvous with the king during a pavane or a galliard, but the movements brought partners together only briefly before drawing them apart again, making conversation difficult. I would flirt, then, I decided, but save my more devious machinations for the bowling green.

King Henry was fond of tennis, loved to joust, and excelled at games of chance, but he was also an enthusiastic bowler. The bowling alley was a turf-covered area bounded by hedges. Ladies usually watched the play from a gallery, but I chose to cross the close-shaven grass to a vantage point much nearer the players. I stood in the shadow of the tiltyard wall to observe the king and three of his companions play at bowls. The steady clack of wood on wood and the occasional bursts of applause were interspersed with sounds of low conversation and laughter from the players.

Stooping, the king balanced the first of two heavy, highly polished wooden balls called "bowls" on his palm and sighted the stake at the far end of the alley. His target was called a "mistress." Dipping his right knee, he made his cast. A cheer went up from the spectators when it came to rest a scant inch from where he'd aimed it.

Charles Brandon bowled next, then Will Compton and Ned Neville, who were on the opposing team. All four of them took turns casting while Nick Carew kept score on a tablet and awarded points based on whose bowls ended up closest to the mistress.

After the first match, which the king won handily, I stepped into the alley. "Your Grace, your game is dull."

King Henry turned, glowering. "Dull, mistress? When your king is playing?"

"Ah, me—I misspoke. What I meant to say is that it could be made much more interesting." I sidled closer to him and daringly brushed one hand across his sleeve. I could feel the other players, the scorekeeper, and the pages who handed out the bowls all staring at me, but I ignored them, just as I ignored those few courtiers and ladies in the gallery. The queen was not among them. I had made sure of that before I began my play.

"Interesting in what way?" King Henry asked. He was more intrigued than irritated now, as I'd hoped he would be.

"You might make use of a *real* mistress," I suggested, glancing toward the stake that bore that name, then back up at the king through lowered lashes.

Charles Brandon caught my meaning first and responded with a burst of ribald laughter. "A worthy target indeed!" he declared, slapping his thigh as he chortled. "And also, mayhap, the prize for the winner."

"I am told that at some foreign courts noblemen play chess with courtiers as the pieces," I said when King Henry's eyes narrowed speculatively. "Would it not be a fine new game to substitute a living woman for a mistress made of wood?" Sauntering casually down the length of the alley, I positioned myself in front of the far stake.

Inside, I was shaking like a leaf in a windstorm, but that only made me try harder to maintain a surface calm. I could afford no hesitation, no appearance of second thoughts. I put my hands on my hips and called out, "Come, gentlemen. Send your balls my way."

In appreciation of the risqué invitation, all four players responded with good-natured laughter. The king obliged me. His first cast was a good one and the second bowl very nearly struck my foot. When Brandon took his turn, I moved at the last moment, distracting him, and his first bowl skimmed past me and into a hedge. The second curled around to lie next to the king's two attempts.

"A kiss for the winner," I called, and I managed to affect Ned's aim by lifting my skirts above my ankles. His cast went wildly astray.

Will Compton glowered at me as he prepared to take his turn. I was beginning to enjoy myself. For the rest of the match, I kept up a steady flow of banter, using as many words with double meanings as I dared. I had always known that the king had a low sense of humor, but I had never catered to it before.

When the game was over, it came as no surprise that His Grace had won. He advanced upon me to claim his prize. "Come share a kiss, Your Majesty," I called, and smiled invitingly. I grasped his broad shoulders as our lips met and clung to them afterward to keep him close while I whispered in his ear. "If we were in private," I promised, "I would be willing to share so much more."

I meant the idea I'd had to spy on the French, but I knew full well that was not how the king interpreted my words. From the look in his eyes, he would soon send for me.

"WILL, WAIT! YOU go too fast."

Slowing his long strides, Will Compton cast a contemptuous look over his shoulder. "You were the one in a great hurry only a few hours ago. You set out to capture the king's attention and now you have it. I wish you joy of it!"

Although I winced at the acid in his tone, it was far too late to change my mind. We were already in the privy gallery. At the far end lay the door that led to the king's bedchamber.

"I cannot run in these shoes," I protested when Will resumed his brisk pace. The cork-soled crimson velvet pantoufles on my feet were backless slippers more decorative than sturdy.

"Kick them off, then." Radiating impatience, he stopped to glare at me. "You were wont to go about in stocking feet when we were younger."

"Why are you so wroth with me?" Hands on hips, I stood my ground on the rush matting that covered the floor of the privy gallery. "It is not as if the king has never before sent for a woman, nor are you unaccustomed to escorting such females to him."

"God's bones, Jane! Have you no shame? Had you not thrown yourself in his path, the king would be with the queen this night, as he should be, endeavoring to get a son on her."

"It is barely twelve weeks since his daughter's birth," I protested. "The king always turns to other women when his wife is with child and, as you well know, it is customary to allow a high-born lady several months to recover after she is delivered of a living child."

We had stopped beneath a portrait of Henry VII. The bright

green-and-gold-striped silk curtain usually drawn in front of portraits to keep the paint from fading had been pulled back to reveal a frame of black ebony garnished with silver and the canvas it contained. Will gestured toward it. "He'd be ashamed of you, Jane. He treated you as another daughter, favoring you above all the other gentlewomen at court."

"And he died without making provision for me." Staring at the portrait, I found it difficult to keep the bitterness out of my voice.

It was a good likeness, better than the one at Richmond. It had been painted before illness inscribed lines of pain into my grandfather's face. The artist had accurately depicted the unsmiling lips, the pronounced cheekbones, and the straight, thin, high-bridged nose. He'd also given him the same autocratic air he'd so often exhibited in life. The portrait showed the unusual blue-gray color of the king's eyes, as well, as large and deep set as I remembered them. For a moment I imagined a look of stern disapproval in his gaze.

Hastily looking away, I caught sight of a peculiar expression on Will Compton's face. Lips pursed, brow furrowed, eyes troubled, his earlier irritation had been replaced by confusion. "What are you up to, Jane?"

"Why do you care?"

"I should like to make sense of your behavior. After all, if it is only that you miss having a man in your bed, that lack might easily have been remedied, and in ways that would have given you more pleasure than a few nights as the king's mistress."

"The pleasures of Pleasure Palace?" I quipped.

Will's lips twitched.

I *had* taken pleasure at Greenwich with the duc de Longueville. He had been my first lover, my only lover. I glanced apprehensively toward the door to the king's bedchamber.

Taking a deep breath in an attempt to quell the fluttering

sensation in the pit of my stomach, I managed a tentative smile. Will had been an ally in the past. A friend. We had known each other for eighteen years. He could help me now, or hinder me. I could allow him to believe me wanton, even promise to share my favors with him . . . or I could tell him as much of the truth as I dared.

"I have need to speak privily with him, Will," I blurted out. "That is all I want, just to talk."

He frowned.

"This was the only way I could think of to arrange a private meeting given my standing. I had to _pretend_ I wanted him to bed me."

Will's frown rearranged itself into an expression rife with suspicion. For a moment I feared he would call the guards. He was responsible for the king's safety. If he perceived me as a threat—

"He expects to swive you, Jane. He does not take kindly to being thwarted."

I breathed a sigh of relief. Will _was_ still my friend. His concern was for my well-being.

"You need not remind me of His Grace's temper. I will be careful."

We covered the remaining distance to the end of the privy gallery without further speech. A yeoman usher, resplendent in scarlet livery, stood waiting to open the door. I hesitated on the threshold. What if I had miscalculated? Would the king insist upon taking me to bed even if I was not willing?

I repressed a shudder at the thought—in light of our blood relationship.

The door opened and I passed through.

Henry was waiting for me, a light in his eyes that told me Will's concern was well founded. "Ah, Jane." He opened his arms and the loose robe he wore gaped open, too.

Averting my eyes from the nakedness beneath, I kept my gaze

on his face. *My uncle's face*, I reminded myself. Younger than I he might be, but he was my grandfather's son, just as Sir Rowland Velville was.

"I have thought of this often, Jane," the king murmured.

If he had been anyone but who he was, I might have been tempted. It *had* been a long time since I had enjoyed a man's embraces. He poured wine and offered me the cup, spoke gently and in a coaxing tone. And in his eyes, I could see the spark of genuine interest. I was not just any female body. He knew who I was and he wanted me.

"Your Grace—"

"It must be Henry when we are private like this. I like to hear my name whispered soft and sweet."

But I shook my head. Setting aside the goblet, a beautiful thing of crystal chased with gold, I faced him. "I have deceived you, Your Grace. I came to you under false pretenses."

Brow knit in consternation, eyes narrowing, he regarded me warily. "What are you saying, Jane?"

"Forgive me, Sire. I could think of no other way that would allow me to speak with you in absolute privacy." I went down on my knees before him, head bowed, praying that he would not throw me out of his bedchamber before I could plead my case.

He seized me by both elbows and jerked me upward. My head whipped back but I ignored the sharp flash of pain in my neck and the even more agonizing ache from his grip on my barely healed arm. My eyes met his angry gaze and held there. I knew I had only seconds to explain myself.

"Let me go to France!" I blurted out. "I will gather intelligence for you and warn you of King François' plans."

His already ruddy skin flamed redder. At any moment I expected his eyes to shoot flames as he gave me a hard shake.

"P-please, Your Grace! Hear me out! I have an excuse to go, one no one will question. My mother left the court at Amboise, and France, under mysterious circumstances. My inquiries into her past will allow me to move freely, to stay as long as you need me to—"

He released me so suddenly that I stumbled. To prevent a fall, I caught myself on a nearby cupboard, using my left hand and jarring the newly healed bone once again. For a moment the pain was so intense that I could not speak.

I saw the king's brow furrow and realized he had forgotten that I had been injured. For a breathless moment we stared at each other. Then he turned his back on me. I did not need to see his face to know that he was still angry. The set of his massive shoulders told me that.

"Leave now," he ordered as he stalked away.

Backing toward the door, I strove to control my emotions. I wanted to rail at him. I feared I was about to burst into tears. My head was bowed, eyes on the floor, but I heard the swish of fabric when he turned.

"Wait."

I froze. Slowly, I lifted my head to look at him. He was still furious with me, but there was something else in his eyes, something that made me shiver with dread.

"You deceived me, Jane."

His voice had gentled, but I was not fooled into thinking he had mellowed toward me. "I crave your pardon, Your Majesty." I dropped my gaze again, but it was too late.

His ornate, gilded slippers appeared on the rush mat in front of me. He lifted my chin using the side of one hand. Candlelight reflected off the big ruby he wore on the second finger and I stared at it, noticing for the first time that the gold band was etched with dragons. Why had I never realized what that meant? Mother's pendant, the one thing she had left behind for me, had been crafted in the shape of that same royal emblem—the red dragon of Wales. I wondered if the pendant had been a gift to her from her father.

"You might persuade me to change my mind," the king murmured.

His tone left no doubt about how I might do so. He was still irritated with me, but he'd remembered why he'd ordered me brought to him in the first place.

"I cannot do that, Your Grace."

"Cannot? Or will not?" Before I could answer, he shot more questions at me. "Do you fancy yourself in love with the duc de Longueville? Is that the real reason you want to leave England?"

"No, Your Grace, I do not love him, nor do I pine for him. Indeed, I have had no communication whatsoever with him since he left England."

His hard stare bored into me, but I had told him the truth and he could see that. A slow smile overspread his features and I swallowed convulsively. This interview had not gone at all the way I'd planned and I had a feeling matters were about to get worse.

"Then you are free to share your favors with whatever man you choose." The king all but purred the words. "Come, Jane, we will—"

"I cannot." To reinforce my refusal, I took a step back.

Before I could retreat farther, he caught my right arm in a bruising grip. Once again his voice went cold while his eyes filled with the heat of anger. "You dare deny your *king*?"

"I must deny my *kinsman*!"

He dropped his hand as if touching me had burnt him. "Explain yourself."

"We cannot become lovers, Your Grace. It would be a sin." His implacable expression prevented me from stopping there. With a sinking heart, I told him the rest. "You are my uncle, Sire. My mother was your half sister."

The blank, unblinking stare that greeted this news frightened me far more than his earlier show of temper. I did not know whether to say more or hold my tongue. Either course seemed full of risk. In a whisper, I added, "Your father sired bastards, Your Grace, during his exile in Brittany."

Abruptly, the blue eyes came into focus again. "Bastards? More than one?"

"Twins, Your Majesty."

"Velville," the king muttered, and I knew he must be making the same comparisons I had, seeing his father's features in my uncle's face.

King Henry sank into an upholstered chair and waved me onto a nearby stool. For a long moment he simply stared at my face, looking there for the heritage I'd claimed. Whatever he found, it made him contemplative.

For the moment, his anger seemed to have passed, but I did not trust his uncertain temper. I waited for him to speak first.

"So, Jane, you are my niece, even though you are older than I am." It was not a question. He had accepted my claim.

I answered him anyway. "So I am told, Your Grace."

"By whom?"

"Sir Rowland Velville, my mother's twin brother." I related the tale as my uncle had told it to me, omitting only Uncle's speculations about my mother's murder.

When I had finished the story, the king sat thoughtfully stroking a recently barbered chin. I waited in an agony of suspense, knowing I had taken a huge risk. I'd had no choice but to confess, but that was little consolation when my own life, and that of my uncle, would be forfeit if King Henry decided we were a threat to his throne.

"You went to Wales with my sister's connivance." This seemed to amuse him.

"She knows nothing of—"

A wave of his hand cut short my attempt to defend the Duchess of Suffolk. "I know full well you would not have told her. You never meant to tell me."

"No, Your Grace. And my uncle would not have shared his secret had he not been in his cups."

A derisive snort greeted that comment.

"I never guessed, although your father was always kind to me," I said. "He treated me more like family than a servant, but I never thought to ask why."

A sudden change in his expression silenced me. I bit my lip. Had I said too much?

Then he rose and with a cold stare and steely voice said, "You will never speak of this again. Swear it, Jane. On your life."

"I swear." With all the courage I could muster, I looked up at him, letting him see the sincerity in my eyes.

His gaze bored into mine, assessing, weighing, judging. The smile that blossomed on his face had nothing of humor in it. "You will do one more thing for me, Jane."

"Anything, Your Grace."

"You will say nothing at all of this night. Ever. If the rest of the court believes that you gave yourself to me, you will not disabuse them of that notion."

THAT LAST PROMISE cost me dearly. Those among the queen's ladies who had been friendly no longer spoke to me. Even Bessie Blount, when she returned to court just before Queen Margaret's arrival, believed that I had replaced her in the king's bed. The look of reproach in her eyes made me think of a puppy that had been kicked by a heartless master.

Harry Guildford's scorn was the hardest to bear, but I kept my word to the king. How could I not? He held my very life in his hands. In the end, I was replaced with Bessie Blount in the masque. Before I had the chance to renew my acquaintance with Margaret Tudor, Queen Catherine dismissed me from her service. I packed up all my belongings—pitifully few for a life spent at court—and sought shelter at Suffolk Place. Even there, news of my folly preceded me.

"Charles informs me that you have bedded my brother," Mary said when I was shown into her presence. I could not tell if she was horrified or amused. Her expression gave nothing away.

"I cannot speak of it."

Her brows lifted.

"I cannot, Mary. I beg you, do not ask me about the king."

"How disappointing." Her smile was rueful. "I had hoped for details."

The next few days passed pleasantly enough, often in the nursery of Mary's young son, another Henry. I had not given up the hope that I might be allowed to leave England, but if I tried to cross the Narrow Seas without permission, I knew that the attempt would most assuredly lead to my arrest. Instead, I once again broached the subject of a place in the Suffolk household. My request was met by silence. I looked up from my embroidery to find that Mary was avoiding my gaze.

"Charles says we must retire to the country again after the entertainments to welcome Margaret are done. We spent more money than we should have to celebrate our son's christening."

I waited, but I could guess what was coming.

"I cannot take you with us, Jane. Nothing has changed in that regard. But I will write to the king on your behalf, reminding him of all your years of service to our family. He must settle an annuity on you. I shall tell him so."

She was as good as her promise and within the week King Henry sent word that I was to go to Will Compton's house in Thames Street at a certain day and time. Without much enthusiasm, I caught a wherry from the quay at Suffolk Place and bade the boatman take me across the river to Compton's water gate. A servant let me in and conducted me to the same chamber where Bessie had first bedded the king. My spirits dropped even lower as I entered. I wondered if Will was about to ruin what little was left of our friendship with an offer to set me up as his mistress. I stopped short when I realized that the room's only occupant was not Will Compton.

"Your Grace." I made the deepest obeisance I could manage.

"Jane. Rise."

King Henry was smiling. I did not trust that look. He gestured toward a stool while he settled into a chair. There were comfits set out on the table between us and he selected a sugared almond while I sat and arranged my skirts. When he offered the box to me, I shook my head.

"Will you take these, then?" He offered me two papers.

At first I did not understand the significance of either. Then I realized that one was a letter of credit, such as travelers use to convey money from one country to another. The amount was £100, a goodly sum. My heart began to beat a little faster. I'd heard that the king's council had finally talked him out of his plan to invade France, that peace was again a possibility, but I had not dared let myself hope he would change his mind about letting me leave England.

I looked at the second document. "This is written in Latin. I cannot read it."

"It is a 'protection,' issued for one year under the privy seal at Greenwich—a form of letter of passport designed to give the bearer free passage between London and Calais. I have reconsidered your offer, Jane. If you still wish to journey into France, you have leave to go. In return I expect regular intelligence about King François. Your friend the duc de Longueville can provide you with entry to the French court. You parted on good terms, did you not?"

I remembered Longueville's promise to set me up as his mistress at Beaugency. "We did, Your Grace."

"Then you should have no difficulty persuading him to help you." His tone of voice and the wink that went with it told me plainly that he expected me to bribe the duke with my body.

Bitterness welled up inside me, but on the surface I was careful to display only what King Henry expected to see: gratitude and submission. "Of course, Your Grace."

"If you allow the rumor that you were my mistress to spread, that may smooth your way to higher things." There was a sly look in his eyes as he made the suggestion.

"Yes, Your Grace. No doubt it will." The bitterness turned to simmering anger. Rumors of King François' satyrlike appetites had reached the English court within a few months of King Louis' death. "How am I to deliver the intelligence I gather for you?"

"It will be only natural that you speak, from time to time, with the English ambassador. In addition, you may write to your good friend the queen of France." Seeing my momentary confusion, he chuckled. "My sister Mary, not Queen Claude. What would be more natural than for you to share your experiences with your former mistress? Compton will supply a code for you to use."

Although I thought it doubtful the king of France would confide in me, even if I did gain access to his court, I told King Henry what he wanted to hear. Then I asked where King François was at present.

"Still in Lyons."

I had no intention of going there, for it was a goodly distance from Amboise, but King Henry's next words changed my mind.

"The duc de Longueville is also in Lyons," he said, "along with a bastard brother."

He claimed he did not know which one.

THREE WEEKS LATER I arrived in Lyons. I traveled there in the retinue of a Genoese merchant, Master di Grimaldo, who had been visiting a cousin in London—the elderly banker Francesca de Carceres had married. Now di Grimaldo had business with the king of France. I did not inquire into its nature. I was too happy to have found an escort for my journey.

The last part of the trek was through mountainous terrain that seemed most foreign to me. Master di Grimaldo held the opposite opinion. "This countryside reminds me of parts of my beautiful Italy," he told me, "and surely Lyons is the most lovely of all French cities."

It did boast fine stone houses, well-ordered streets, and bustling businesses. Built on a strip of land between two rivers, it was a natural center of commerce.

Master di Grimaldo had been more than kind to me on the journey. He had provided me with food, shelter, and lessons in the workings of the French court. The organization of the royal household was similar to what I was familiar with in England, but not exactly the same.

I did not plan to seek an audience with King François. In truth, I hoped to avoid him entirely. But to locate the duc de

Longueville and, I hoped, Guy Dunois, I knew I would have to brave the court.

That prospect seemed daunting at first. The *maison du roi* included more than five hundred individuals and the queen's household over two hundred. The king's mother also had her own retinue, as did the one child Queen Claude had so far produced, a girl named Louise. The princess had been born at Amboise the previous August, only a few days after her father won the great battle at Marignano.

More unsettling than the sheer numbers was the presence of hundreds of men of a military bent. From the Garde Écossaise to the companies of archers, to the *gentilhommes de l'hôtel*, uniforms and armament were everywhere at the French court. So were the *prévôt de l'hôtel* and his staff. With his three lieutenants and thirty archers, the *prévôt* was the one responsible for investigating and punishing crimes committed within a five-mile radius of the king's person. The *gens d'armes* who had searched for my mother and arrested my old governess had likely been members of this band. Until I had talked to Guy, I was wary of coming to the attention of the current *prévôt*.

I had convinced myself that Guy was still alive. In all the months since Ivo Jumelle had told me that one of the duke's half brothers had been killed at Marignano, I had clung to this belief, but now that I had reached Lyons, doubts niggled at me. Had I come all this way for nothing? Would I end up obliged to spy for King Henry after all?

Access to the royal court proved surprisingly easy. It appeared that anyone who was decently dressed—and I wore my finest clothing for the occasion—was allowed in. When I accosted an archer, he directed me to the rooms the duc de Longueville used to conduct business connected to his post as governor of the province of Dauphiné.

The antechamber reminded me of Guy's workplace in the Tower of London, even to the smell of the marjoram flowers and woodruff leaves in the rushes. Several gentlemen were assembled there, apparently awaiting the duke's arrival. Only one displayed any interest in me, and then only after I told the duke's secretary my name. Such a startled look crossed the fellow's long, horselike face that I might have pursued the matter had the curtains behind the secretary not been pushed apart at just that moment.

Guy Dunois appeared in the opening. My awareness of everything and everyone else faded away. My world narrowed until it included only one other person. My eyes locked with Guy's, and I saw in those blue-green depths a reflection of my own longing, my own dreams.

I do not remember leaving the antechamber, but by the time I found my voice, we were in the inner room with the curtains closed behind us.

"I feared you were dead," I whispered as Guy drew me into his arms. "We heard the duke had lost one of his half brothers."

"Jacques."

Before I could tell him I was sorry for his loss, he was kissing me—deep, drugging kisses that left me in no doubt about how he felt. "I'd have come for you," he whispered, holding me closer. "I'd have found a way to return to England. I've been here at court seeking a place in the next embassy."

"No need now." I touched my fingertips to his lips, cutting off any further explanations. "I came to you."

He lowered his head, as if to kiss me again, then stopped. "How? Why?" His voice was hoarse, choked with emotion, but before I could reply, it changed. His next words were accusing: "I heard you ask for the duke."

"How else was I to find you?" I broke free and backed away, but

I knew he had no reason to believe me. We had been separated a long time. He'd had no communication from me. I'd had no way to acknowledge those two brief messages he had sent to me.

Letters singularly lacking in any hint of deeper feelings for me, I reminded myself. I should be the suspicious one. In all the time we had been apart, anything could have happened. He might even have acquired a wife.

I took a deep breath and looked away from him. The chamber was sparsely furnished—a bench, a table, a chair. Papers sat in neat stacks on the tabletop, with quills and ink near at hand for the secretary. I thought of the petitioners waiting just beyond the curtain. Clearly the duke was expected.

"I do not want to see Longueville," I said.

"You planned to come to him. He promised to establish you at Beaugéncy."

"You *know* the only reason I wanted to visit France back then. I wanted to learn the truth about my mother."

"Then?" he echoed. "And now?"

"I came to find you."

A slow, satisfied smile overspread his features. It lasted but a moment before consternation replaced it. "You cannot stay here, not if you truly wish to avoid Longueville."

"I do."

"Then come with me."

I went willingly and a short time later found myself in a tiny cubicle of a room that was clearly Guy's bedchamber. The only place to sit was on the camp bed.

"I do not know where to begin," I said. "I have so many questions."

"I can guess some of them." Guy produced a bottle of wine and two cups from a chest and poured generous portions, then sat beside me. "You want to know what happened when Longueville and I returned home, and why you were not permitted to accompany the new bride to France."

"I know why. Or rather, I think I do. I believe King Louis confused me with my mother. She and I shared the same name."

"Jeanne," Guy murmured. I liked the way it sounded when he said it. "It is possible. Longueville asked for an explanation, but the king never gave him a satisfactory answer, only some nonsense about his fondness for the Duchess of Longueville. King Louis said it was not meet for the duke to set his English mistress up at court when his wife was already there."

"Longueville never intended to do so. He meant to establish me at Beaugency."

Guy shrugged. "And I do not believe that King Louis was particularly concerned about Longueville's wife or how she would feel about your presence in France. But it is pointless to argue with a king."

In other words, Longueville had not cared enough to risk the king's displeasure. I was not surprised. I doubted that the duke had ever thought of me as more than a convenience.

"Have you learned any more about why my mother left France?" I asked abruptly. "There must have been some reason King Louis did not want her to return."

"Nothing. It was a long time ago. Even though King François has kept many of King Louis' retainers, few of them were also at court so long ago as King Charles's reign. I went to Amboise, but no one there could tell me anything about Sylvie Andrée." At my blank look, he added, "She was the governess the *gens d'armes* took away.

"Perhaps the *prévôt*—"

"He is new. He knows nothing of Sylvie Andrée or Jeanne Popyncourt."

I sighed.

"Will you return to England once you are convinced there is nothing more for you to discover here?"

I set my cup on the floor amid the woodruff-scented rushes and sent a slow smile his way. "That was not my only reason for the journey. I also wanted to know if you . . . if *we*—"

He cut short my stumbling effort to ask him if he loved me by pulling me into his arms and kissing me again. His cup fell to the floor, spilling its contents, but neither of us noticed.

"There is so much I have to tell you," I gasped when he allowed me to come up for air.

"Later."

We did not speak again for a long time.

Unlike his half brother, Guy was a considerate lover. He made sure of my pleasure before he took his own. And when we were spent and lying naked together in his narrow bed, I felt no shame, no confusion, only wonderment.

"It would be best if no one at court knew you were here," he said when we finally rose and began to dress. Once again he assumed the role of my tiring maid.

"Do you plan to keep me hidden?"

He did not smile at my teasing. I felt a flash of alarm when I saw a look of concern cloud the clear blue-green of his eyes.

"I will not go back to the duke. You need have no fear of that!"

"It is not the duke alone who would threaten our happiness. This court is a dangerous place for any woman. Have you somewhere to stay in Lyons until I can arrange to leave Longueville's service?"

"Master di Grimaldo has offered me lodging and I accepted for a night or two, being uncertain what I would find at court. He is a respectable gentleman," I added as Guy's eyes narrowed, "and looking forward to returning to his wife and seven children in Genoa."

Satisfied, Guy spirited me away from court by a series of back ways and escorted me to Master di Grimaldo's lodgings. Only when we were in sight of the place did he tell me the one thing he had been holding back. "I did discover something odd during my inquiries, Jane."

"Information about my mother?"

He shook his head. "This matter concerned your father. He owned land between Orléans and Salbris. I was able to visit the region only briefly. I had scarcely arrived when I was ordered away to join the duke's forces in support of the king's effort to conquer Milan."

"Papa owned property in France? Neither he nor Maman ever spoke of it."

"It is possible your mother did not know. From what I was able to learn, the purchase was made with a business partner only a few months before your father's death."

I frowned at that. "I wonder if Papa made a poor investment, spending his fortune on land that could not turn a profit. That might explain why Maman and I were obliged to accept charity from King Henry."

"We will find out," Guy promised. "As soon I can make arrangements, I will take you there. We will visit your father's estate on our way to Amboise."

16

Three days later, Guy and I left Lyons, traveling overland as far as Roanne, where the Loire becomes navigable, then boarding a longboat with a cabin for the next part of the journey. A *sapinière*, a raft made of fir trunks, conveyed our horses and the henchmen Guy had hired for protection on the journey.

The Loire flows northward, and we might have gone all the way to Amboise by water, but our destination was somewhat short of there. "It never occurred to me to ask my uncle about Papa," I confessed as we sailed past vineyard after vineyard on a fine June day. "I do not think they ever met."

Idly, I watched the wind turn the sails of a windmill perched on the crest of a hill. I felt a curious contentment, in spite of all that remained unsettled. No doubt this was due to spending my nights with Guy. I had agreed to pose as his wife on our journey, for safety and for convenience.

"He was Flemish," Guy remarked after a time.

We both knew that did not necessarily mean that Papa had been born in Flanders. The term was loosely used to refer to anyone who hailed from the lands controlled by Burgundy—Franche-Comté, Luxembourg, Hainaut, Picardy, Artois, the Somme towns, Boulogne, Belgium, and the Netherlands. The Burgundian court spent time at equally far-flung locations from Bruges and Lille to Brussels and the Hague.

"He was a merchant," I said after another long lull in conversation spent enjoying the warmth of the sun on my face and the sight of the blue water of the Loire lapping against banks of golden sand. "He met my mother when she was in the household of Anne of Brittany. She was fifteen when they were married. They loved each other very much."

Guy slid an arm around my waist as we stood at the door of our cabin. Poplars and willow trees now dotted the landscape. On the river, dozens of other boats plied the water, as they had all along the way. I abandoned speculation and relaxed against him, too happy to allow worries to intrude on my peace of mind for long.

At Orléans we resumed our journey by road. I noticed that several other vessels had also put passengers ashore. I thought one man looked familiar, but I could not think where I might have seen him before. There was nothing particularly remarkable about his long, narrow face or his clothing. Unable to remember, I dismissed him from my mind.

Guy had friends living just outside Orléans and chose the comfort of their manor house over a room at an inn or beds in an abbey guesthouse. We were made welcome, even though the family was away from home, but the housekeeper, knowing that Guy was not married, took care to install us in separate wings of the house.

It was just as well, I decided, settling into a sinfully soft bed. After several long days of river travel and the even longer journey that had gone before, I was so exhausted that I fell instantly asleep.

I was roused sometime later by the smell of smoke. At first I thought I was dreaming. I'd had nightmares more than once about King Louis' declaration that I should be burnt. Then I began to cough, and realized that this was real.

Opening bleary eyes, I fought against a confusion of my senses. The room should have been full dark. I had snuffed out the candle before getting into bed, there had been no fire in the hearth, and the shutters had been closed against the dangerous things that live in the night air.

Flickering light showed beneath the door. Fire!

I rolled out of bed, landing awkwardly. Although I fought to stay on my feet, I ended up in a heap on the floor. Pushing myself up on my hands and knees, I realized of a sudden that the air lower down was less smoke filled and easier to breathe than that above. Remaining as I was, I started to scuttle toward the door.

I stopped at the sight of flames licking along the edges of the wood. The fire beyond was leaping higher and higher, cutting off any possibility of escaping that way.

The bedchamber had two windows, both opening onto a courtyard, but it was a long way to the ground. *Fool*, I chided myself. Any injury I sustained from a fall was less likely to be fatal than burning to death. Pressing myself even closer to the floor, I crawled toward the casement.

Curls of smoke seemed to chase me across the room. I tried holding my breath, but that only made my eyes water. Making a mask with the hem of my chemise filtered out the worst of it, but it was almost impossible to press the linen over my mouth and nose and crawl at the same time.

I began to wheeze. My progress slowed. I resorted to traveling like a snake, inching along on my belly, but I began to despair of ever escaping.

Then my hand struck the chest beneath the window. All I had to do was find strength enough to stand up and open the shutters. With an effort of will, I hauled myself onto the chest and lifted the latch. Cool air greeted me, and a shout from below.

"Jump, Jane!" Guy was there in the courtyard, both arms lifted toward me. "Jump and I will catch you."

I dragged one leg over the casement, then the other, thankful neither bars nor glass panes blocked the way. My chemise snagged on something, but I tugged until I heard the linen rip. The crackle of flames behind me overcame my fear of letting go. Trusting in Guy's promise, I hurled myself out and away from the burning building.

My weight took us both to the ground, jarring the arm I had broken only a few months earlier, but one look over my shoulder banished any thought of complaint. The entire chamber was engulfed in flame. Had I hesitated, I would be afire, too.

Guy's arms tightened around me. He buried his face in my throat. "By all that is holy, Jane. I do not think I could have borne to lose you."

Embracing him in return, I murmured incoherent words of thanks . . . and of love . . . but we had no time to indulge in tender exchanges. The entire house seemed likely to go up in flames. The blaze was already well past the point where it could have been contained by a few buckets of water.

We made our way to the stable, found the henchmen Guy had hired, and led our horses to safety. Some of my packs had been left with the mule and I hastily dressed in the first clothes I found. We spent the remainder of the night in a nearby field, watching the manor house burn. It was destroyed utterly, but at least there was no loss of life.

The next morning, after a brief return to Orléans to buy clothing and supplies to replace what we had lost, we set off again on the road south. Still dazed and disoriented by the night's terrors, I did not realize for some time that the hired guards who escorted us were more numerous than they had been when we set out from Lyons. At least three more burly specimens had been added to their ranks.

"Do you expect to encounter robbers?" I asked Guy.

"I no longer know what to expect." He turned in the saddle to study my face.

I forced a smile. He was not fooled, but I could tell that he was hesitant to speak. "What troubles you, Guy?"

"Have you any notion how the fire started?"

I shook my head and told him what little I remembered. "An ember?" I suggested. "Or someone careless with a candle?" Accidents with fire were not uncommon, although most people took sensible precautions to prevent them.

Guy continued to stew about it as we rode, the steady plodding of horses' hooves the only sound in the morning stillness. Belatedly, I came to the same conclusion he must already have reached: It might *not* have been an accident.

"In early March, at court," I said slowly, "I fell down a flight of stairs and broke my arm. I was unconscious for a time and had difficulty remembering afterward what had happened."

His breath hissed in sharply. "So this is the second near-fatal accident you have suffered. Was anyone nearby when you . . . fell?"

"I had been talking with Ivo Jumelle when I lost my footing."

"Jumelle!" The anger in his voice seemed out of proportion and he required several minutes to bring himself under control and speak calmly. "I told you that your father bought land with a partner, Jane, but I neglected to tell you his name. It was Alain Jumelle, Seigneur de Villeneuve-en-Laye et de Saint-Gelais, a member of the minor nobility. Ivo Jumelle is his youngest son."

"Are you saying *Ivo* tried to kill me? But why? And how would his father know I had returned to France?"

"Why? After the reports of your death and that of your mother, Alain Jumelle laid claim to all the lands he and your father had purchased together. That you are still alive means he may now have to give up a considerable portion of his current wealth. As for how he knew you were no longer in England—Alain Jumelle was one of those waiting in the duke's anteroom at Lyons for an audience with Longueville on the day you came to the French court."

I gasped. "A horse-faced fellow?"

Guy nodded.

No wonder he had reacted with such surprise upon hearing my name. And then I remembered something else, the man with the long, narrow face I'd seen disembarking in Orléans. He'd seemed familiar to me. Now I knew why.

Alain Jumelle had been in the duke's antechamber in Lyons. He'd been a stranger to me, but he'd known who I was as soon as he heard the name Popyncourt.

THE LAND MY father had purchased with Jumelle included a fine manor house. The entrance gate had been set into the center of a thick wall ten feet high and was wide enough to admit a cartload of hay. We rode through into a large and spacious courtyard at least an acre square. When a groom rushed out of the stables to our right to take our horses, I glanced nervously at Guy.

"What if Alain Jumelle is here?"

"We will throw him out."

"But he is still half owner of the place. And what if the servants are loyal to him?"

"Then we will throw them out, too. He tried to murder you, Jane. That is grounds to call for him to forfeit everything in your favor. Besides, we have might on our side." Behind us, swords rattled in scabbards as our hired henchmen dismounted.

Guy strode up to the entrance to the manor house and called out in a loud, carrying voice. "This is Mistress Jane Popyncourt come to reclaim her inheritance from her father. All those who wish to remain in her service will be generously rewarded."

By the time we had climbed the eight steps leading to the door, it had been flung open to reveal an aged crone, her hair snowy white and her blue eyes faded and bulging. I stared at her. That small mole above her right eyebrow seemed familiar, and the way her front teeth protruded over her lower lip.

"I know you," I murmured as she led us inside. There was no sign of Ivo or his father, or of anyone else.

"I was your governess, child," the old woman said, "till your mother came and took you away. And a good thing she did, too."

"You are Sylvie Andrée, the woman the *gens d'armes* arrested?"

"They were not just any ordinary soldiers," she said with a cackle. "Sent by the king's *prévôt de l'hôtel* they were, to question me about a crime at court."

Finding it suddenly hard to breathe, let alone speak, I croaked out a question: "What crime?"

"Why King Charles's murder, of course. Done in with a poisoned orange, he was."

"That is a foolish rumor," Guy snapped. "You should not repeat such things."

She wagged a gnarled finger at him. "Your elders know better, boy. Do you think me a fool? I know what I know and what I know is that King Charles's enemies killed him and then covered up the crime."

I leaned forward and placed my hand on her forearm. "Was my mother the king's enemy?"

"Why bless me, child! Whatever gave you that idea?"

"You were questioned," I reminded her. "They came looking for my mother and they took you instead."

"Ah, well. That is the way of things."

I exchanged a look with Guy, both of us wondering if the old woman's wits were wandering. "Why were they looking for my mother?"

"Have you not guessed?" She gestured with her free hand to indicate the luxury that surrounded us—fine tapestries, ornately carved chests and chairs, Turkey carpets, and Majolica vases. "The almighty Alain Jumelle, Seigneur de Villeneuve-en-Laye et de Saint-Gelais. He told King Louis she was to blame. Well, she did hand King Charles that orange, that's true enough, but how was she to know it was poisoned?"

"Jumelle wanted my mother out of the way," I said slowly, "so that he could claim lands that should rightfully have been hers. She feared he would be believed, so she ran before the *gens d'armes* came."

"Jumelle had the new King Louis' ear." The old lady nodded sagely. "Your mother was right to be afraid, right to run. But when she left all of a sudden, that convinced King Louis that she was guilty."

"Then King Louis was not responsible for King Charles's death either?"

"Oh, no. No one knows who killed him. I myself suspect the Italians. They are experts in the use of poisons, you know."

"If you knew so much about the king's death at the time," Guy said, humoring her, "why did you not speak out?"

"Do you think me a fool?" she repeated. "I said I knew nothing of any of it, and they believed me because I had been in the Popyncourt household only a short time. They let me go and I came back here, to Master Popyncourt's lands."

I exchanged a look with Guy. Sylvie seemed harmless enough, but she also appeared to be somewhat simpleminded.

"You came back here, even knowing that Jumelle would be your new master?" Guy asked.

She tapped the side of her nose. "I let him think he'd bought my silence. And then, once word came that you and your mother were dead, there was no reason for him to worry about what I knew."

"Her story makes sense," I told Guy after Sylvie had gone off to roust the other servants and give them orders concerning fresh linens and hot food. "Parts of it, at least. I suppose that, years later, Alain Jumelle heard my name in connection with Longueville's."

I was remembering that Ivo had told me he wrote home regularly but rarely had any reply. I remembered, too, how he had looked at me after he'd received a letter from his father. I wondered what it had said about me.

"I'd not have thought young Ivo capable of murder," Guy said.

"A reluctant killer." I frowned, considering. "It was only when I said, in his hearing, that I would return to France, even without King Henry's consent, that he acted to stop me."

"Do you suppose Alain Jumelle had you confused with your mother, too? And yet, why would they suppose Longueville would take an old woman for his mistress?"

I stared at a tapestry showing a hunting scene. The border was filled to bursting with flowers in a multitude of varieties. "She would have been only a year or two older than he. And nothing else explains King Louis' contention that Jane Popyncourt should be burnt. If Maman *had* conspired to cause King Charles's death, as Alain Jumelle made King Louis believe, then that would have been her fate." I shuddered at the thought.

Guy wrapped his arms around me. "You are safe now." Turning me in his arms, he lowered his head and kissed me. "Safe with me."

I came to believe him when days turned into weeks and no one troubled us. Guy consulted a man of law and brought formal suit against Alain Jumelle to claim not only my inheritance, but reparations in the form of the other half of the property. While we waited for the outcome, Guy instructed me in the proper management of a country estate. During the warm summer nights, he taught me other things.

It was late July before our peace was shattered by the arrival of an urgent message from Beaugency.

FROM MY MANOR house to Dunois Castle in Beaugency was but a few hours' ride. We arrived less than a day after receiving word that the duke was on his deathbed. Longueville had not been wounded at the battle of Marignano, but he had fallen prey to that other battlefield killer, the flux. His recovery had been slow and incomplete, with frequent relapses, each one draining his strength more than the last. A year after the French victory over Milan, his defeat at the hands of this insidious illness seemed imminent.

I'd not have recognized my former lover. His skin had a ghastly grayish pallor. His once luxuriant black hair lay in dull, lank clumps and some of it had fallen out. His physicians had been dosing him with tincture of gold given in wine, but it did not appear to have done him any good.

Longueville looked first at Guy and then at me. He managed a faint, ironic smile. "Would you have come to see me, Jane, if I were not dying?"

"Your Grace, you must not talk that way!" Tears sprang into my eyes, blinding me. I had never loved this man, but for what we had shared and lost, I grieved. I moved to the side of his bed and took one of his thin, wasted hands in mine. "You are young yet and strong. You must not lose your will to live."

He snatched his hand away and his voice turned querulous. "Spare me your pity! I am neither a child nor a fool."

Behind me, I heard Guy move closer. He did not touch me, but just having him near gave me strength. "You asked us here for a reason," I reminded the duke.

It had come as a shock to realize that Longueville knew I was in France, but it had not taken much thought to understand how. By filing a lawsuit against Alain Jumelle, I had brought myself to the attention of the local gentry, and Beaugency was not that far distant from my father's holdings. I wondered how exaggerated the story of our takeover of the manor house had become.

Ignoring me, Longueville now turned to Guy. "I have sent for a lawyer to make my will. You will receive nothing."

"I did not expect anything, Your Grace. I have never expected anything."

"And that is why you have been so valuable to me." His voice grew fainter with each word and his eyes drifted closed.

"He needs to rest now," a hovering physician whispered.

I started to move away, but clawlike fingers curled around my wrist, preventing my retreat. I looked down into the duke's dark eyes and froze at the cold calculation I saw there.

"I have news for you, Jane. The king wants to meet you."

My mouth went dry. "King François?"

More death rattle than laugh, the sound he made contained

nothing of humor or goodwill. His grip tightened and he tugged me closer, until my face was only inches from his and I could smell the fetid stench of illness on his breath.

"I told him all about you, Jane, what you like, how talented you are. He likes to hear such tales from his friends. He likes it when they share."

A chill passed through me and I felt my face blanch.

"He knows how you won permission to leave England, too." Another dry, rattling cackle issued from his thin, cracked lips. How had I ever thought that mouth appealing? "A warning, Jane. He will want to know what it was like to bed King Henry."

I sensed rather than saw Guy's shock. Too late to silence Longueville, I stood immobile, my hand still held prisoner in his, as he pounded more nails into my coffin.

"Give King François every detail, Jane. And then demonstrate what you did for one king to the other. Do that, and he will be inclined to be generous with you. He likes his mistresses lively but submissive. A few weeks, a few months, and you will have earned his gratitude. Your father's lands, jewelry, mayhap even a wealthy courtier for a husband."

When the duke had finished showering me with unwanted advice, I tugged my hand free. He lacked the strength to hold me. He watched me back away from him, his smile a death's-head, and I wondered if this had been his idea of petty revenge because I had turned to Guy and not to him. It did not matter. When I reached the door, I fled.

Guy followed me out, his face grim. He took care not to touch me. "Is it true? Were you King Henry's mistress?"

"Guy—"

"Answer me!"

I wanted to tell him the truth, but did I dare? Guy did not want to hear that I had bartered my body for passage out of England, but would he be any happier with the knowledge that I had agreed to gather intelligence against France? And how could I explain the king's failure to bed me without breaking my solemn oath never to reveal my mother's parentage?

I could lie.

I was beset by a terrible temptation. I could claim the king of England was well nigh impotent and repeat that story to the king of France if he should ever ask.

Drawing in a deep breath, I met Guy's eyes. "I have had only two lovers in all my life and have no desire ever to take a third."

The hard lines of his face softened. When he took my arm, his grip was firm but gentle. We left Dunois Castle and the village of Beaugency riding side by side. During the journey home, I told him everything, even the name of my mother's father.

I expected some overt reaction to this news, but Guy merely nodded, accepting it as calmly as he had the rest of my story.

"Shouldn't you be more impressed—or appalled—that I have royal blood in my veins?"

"So do I," he reminded me. "It matters very little when it is the result of being born on the wrong side of the blanket. That your connection to the King of England is unacknowledged makes it even less important. Then again, I am glad you had a good argument to convince King Henry to change his mind about making you his mistress." He reached across the distance between our horses to take my hand and squeeze it.

"And the spying? That does not disturb you?"

He shrugged. "You are not an English agent now and I can scarcely object to a lie when it brought you back to me."

I regarded him warily. "What if I am lying to you now?"

"Are you?"

"No, but—"

Abruptly, he brought our horses to a stop and turned in the saddle to face me. "The past shapes our lives, Jeanne, but it doesn't have to rule them. If our trust in each other is strong enough, we can make what we will of the future."

Guy was a good man, I thought. The best man I had ever known. When we were children, he had taught me how to play card games and climb trees and he'd made me laugh. As an adult, I was still learning from him. And he could still make me laugh.

"I am not certain I deserve you," I told him.

He chuckled. "We both deserve all the happiness we can find."

My horse shifted restlessly. I would have ridden on, but Guy brought his hand up to my face, lifting my chin until I was staring straight into his eyes. "Are you certain you do not want to return to England? You have friends there. And family, even if you cannot claim your royal aunts and uncle."

I shook my head. "The king would be a dangerous kinsman to have, acknowledged or not, and friendship cannot truly flourish at any court."

Neither could love.

THE DUKE DIED on the first day of August.

The summons to Amboise came some four weeks later. King François had at last returned to his château on the Loire. Awaiting him had been a petition from the Seigneur de Villeneuve-en-Laye et de Saint-Gelais, complaining about the usurpation of his estates. According to Alain Jumelle, his lands and manor had been unlawfully seized by Guy Dunois. He begged King François to settle the matter.

I would have relished a confrontation with Jumelle in front of the king, but that was not to be. Guy and I saw no sign of Ivo's father as we waited in an anteroom of the palace.

"What is taking so long?" I fidgeted on the bench we shared and craned my head to try and see into the inner room.

The lawyer Guy had hired to sue Jumelle had told us that the king of France customarily devoted the late morning, after he had eaten alone in his *salle*, to audiences with both deputations and individuals. By midafternoon, he was always out of doors, walking or riding in the open air or engaged in a game of tennis or a hunt. Then he stayed up late, enjoying revels and dancing, much like his brother king in England.

It was already late evening, and still we waited.

Just as a distant clock struck nine at night, one of the king's minions appeared and announced he would escort me to his liege lord. Guy rose to accompany me. He was told to sit down, the order reinforced by armed guards. The king had sent for me alone.

"You know what he wants," Guy warned.

"I know what he thinks he wants." I hoped I sounded more confident than I felt. "I will persuade him otherwise."

Guy caught my arm. "Do you suppose it would make any difference to him if we were married?"

"It would not matter in the slightest to King François, but it would please me mightily."

Leaving him with that thought and a quick kiss, I sallied forth into battle. I squared my shoulders and took deep breaths, telling myself that the king of France could not be any more difficult to deal with than the king of England.

I was wrong.

King François would take anyone's breath away. Tall, broadly built, he was, as Mary Tudor had described to me, a most pleasant

and charming man. His voice was low and agreeable, his countenance had a certain rugged appeal. His eyes were hazel in color, a
good match for his luxuriant chestnut-colored hair, which he wore
long. He was clean shaven.

"We are pleased to welcome you to our court," King François
said, taking my hand.

He stood alarmingly close.

"I am pleased to be here, Your Grace." My stomach clenched
with nervousness at the lie, but I was prepared to use every skill
I had learned at Pleasure Palace to secure my rightful inheritance
and still keep my honor.

"I am told you were an . . . intimate of King Henry."

Forcing a smile, I put a little distance between us before I answered. "I was given a great honor as a child, Your Grace. I was
installed in the royal nursery to be a companion to the royal children and help them learn to speak French. King Henry the Seventh
was well aware that all civilized people prefer to converse in that
tongue."

This was not what he'd expected me to say.

"I am an intimate of the Lady Mary—your pardon, the queen of
France—and her brother and sister were like siblings to me. I am
older than King Henry and so I knew him as a young boy."

*Let him think me too long in the tooth to suit him. And let him know
that I have heard all about his lecherous overtures to Mary Tudor when
she was in seclusion during the six weeks following King Louis' death.*

Some things could not be spoken of aloud for fear of drawing
unwanted attention to them. I chattered on for fully a quarter of
an hour about the young King Henry, recounting escapades fifteen
years or more in the past. Whatever stories King François might
have heard about me, he could not now be certain that I had been
the king of England's mistress.

At length, he ran out of patience. "Why did you come to France, Mistress Popyncourt?"

"It was time to return home." I made it sound as if this were the simplest thing in the world, as if I knew nothing of wars or politics. "I would have come much sooner, Your Grace, but for some inexplicable reason King Louis took exception to that plan." I sighed. "Indeed, he sent most of the queen's household home again."

"Louis must have had more reason than that to single you out."

I hesitated, but only for a moment. I had hoped to avoid mentioning the rumors that had surrounded King Charles's death, but there was no help for it now. It might all come out anyway, if I ever had to face Alain Jumelle in a court of law.

I presented my case to the king in a logical fashion, telling him everything Guy and I had uncovered concerning Jumelle's perfidy. I kept to myself the secret of my mother's birth, and I made no mention of the promises I had given King Henry.

The fact that Maman had fled to her brother in England annoyed King François, but there was nothing remarkable about Sir Rowland Velville being there. A number of Bretons had accompanied Henry Tudor when he sailed across the Narrow Seas to seize the English throne. More than a few had stayed.

"King Charles died of an apoplexy," he said when I finally stopped speaking.

"So I have always believed, Your Grace. My mother fled only because she felt threatened. At that time, no one could have known that King Louis would marry Queen Anne. Without the assurance of the queen's protection, Maman must have been sore afraid."

A grunt answered my comment. Either he did not care, or he was preoccupied with some other aspect of the situation.

"I am certain she would have returned, bringing me with her, had she lived long enough." That was another outright lie, but the king did not challenge it.

"Why did you come here now, Mistress Popyncourt?" he demanded.

"To discover the truth about my mother, Sire, and to recover my inheritance from my father."

"Not to resume your liaison with the duc de Longueville?"

"No, Sire." That, at least, was true.

"And now that you are a woman of property, will you stay in France?"

This was the difficult moment, I thought, even more fraught with danger than warding off the king's lecherous advances. Indeed, he seemed to have lost interest in making love to me.

"There is more to hold me here than the land, Your Grace," I said carefully. "I felt affection for the late duke, but what I share with his half brother is much deeper than that. We wish to marry."

"He has no place at court," the king reminded me. "*You* could, if you chose." A flicker of his earlier amorous interest reappeared, but it was not strong enough to seem threatening. I remembered how he had helped Mary Tudor wed Charles Brandon. I prayed he still possessed that chivalrous streak.

"If it please Your Grace, I should like to live with my husband on the land my father owned."

To my own surprise, I had found contentment living in the country. Like Lady Catherine at Fyfield, I had discovered that there was more to life than the struggle to stay afloat in the dangerous waters at court.

Lifting my bowed head, I dared meet the king's eyes. "The Lady Mary was my mistress for many years and is still my friend. She has told me of your generosity and kindness to her in the days after King Louis' death, and of your understanding and compassion when she confessed to you her desire to wed the Duke of Suffolk. You helped her to find great happiness, Your Grace. Dare I hope you might do the same for me?"

The king of France looked at me askance. And then he began to laugh.

"Boldness becomes you, Mistress Popyncourt," he managed to say, still laughing, "but you must not make a habit of it."

"Mayhap it would be safest then," I suggested, "if I removed myself from Amboise."

"Go." He made a shooing motion. "Wed your lover and settle on your estates. You'll have no more trouble from the Jumelles."

I fled before he could change his mind, found Guy, and left the king's house, even though by then it was late at night. As we rode toward home, I told Guy everything that had transpired in the king's bedchamber. By the end of my account, he was smiling broadly.

"I can almost feel sorry for His Grace. He will never know the joy I have found in your company."

I grinned back at him. I understood now why Maman had told me so little. I had been too young to be burdened with her secrets. She'd wanted to protect me. Perhaps that was even why Uncle had remained silent all these years. I had been safe as I was, but until I met Guy again, I had lived only half a life. The most real part of being at court had been the masques I'd helped create and sometimes performed in. My belief that I was part of a family there? That had been an illusion.

But at last I had found true happiness. I had come home. I had reclaimed the part of my heritage that mattered most. I had found Guy again and my love for him felt right. I had no doubts about our future. I would not forget the people who had been part of my life for so long. I would write to Mary Tudor and to Harry Guildford and think of them often with great fondness. But the friend who mattered most to me was also my lover and soon would be my husband.

I'd once thought of Greenwich as the Pleasure Palace. Now I knew better. True pleasure combines happiness and contentment with passionate love. No place can provide that. Only a person is capable of bringing all those things into another's life. The man who had brought them into mine rode beside me through the night. Dawn found us on our own land again and we followed its golden light all the way home.

AUTHOR'S NOTE

ane Popyncourt was a real person. She was French, or perhaps Flemish. She was in England by 1498, in the royal household at Eltham and teaching French to the two princesses, Margaret and Mary Tudor, through daily conversation. In 1513–14, when the duc de Longueville was awaiting payment of his ransom in England, comfortably lodged at court, Jane became his mistress. When King Louis XII of France struck Jane's name off the list of Mary Tudor's gentlewomen, he declared that she should be burnt. Why he thought so is not clear. At some point Jane was one of Catherine of Aragon's maids of honor. She finally left England in May 1516, taking with her a gift of £100 from Henry VIII. After the duc de Longueville's death later that same year, she remained in France and corresponded regularly with her former mistress, Mary Tudor, who had by then married Charles Brandon, Duke of Suffolk. As late as 1528, Jane was still alive, still living in France, and apparently had influential friends at the French court.

Everything else I have written about Jane Popyncourt is my own invention and an attempt to explain the mysteries that surround her. I have portrayed other real people in this novel with as much accuracy as I could. They may not have had the same relationship with Jane that I have given them, but their interaction with other historical figures agrees with what modern scholars know of them.

For those who want to read more about the court and courtiers at the time of Henry VII and Henry VIII, I suggest Mary Louise Bruce's *The Making of Henry VIII* and Alison Weir's *Henry VIII and His Court*. Both books were invaluable to me in writing this novel, as was Simon Thurley's *The Royal Palaces of Tudor England*. For a complete bibliography of my sources, please consult my website at www.KateEmersonHistoricals.com.

I did fudge two historical facts. One is the date of the French raid on Brighton. Most sources say only that it occurred in the spring of 1514, but I did find one that specified it took place in May. For dramatic purposes I needed to have the French attack before May Day. The other is the amount spent on the duc de Longueville's upkeep in the Tower of London. An account of royal expenses indicates that holding the duke and six others cost £13 6s. 8d. but does not specify how long a period was paid for with that amount. I hope I may be forgiven for taking these small liberties with historical accuracy.

I've also used a bit of poetic license in writing about the Valentine's Day lottery. A description of a later Valentine's Day at court indicates that the men drew the names, not the women, and that gifts were given by both parties. The gifts did, however, include such items as spaniels, caged birds, embroidered sleeves, smocks, lace, and artificial flowers.

Some purists may object that Jane's vocabulary sounds too "modern" and contains anachronistic words. For this I make no apology. The real language of early Tudor England would be littered with annoying period words like " 'tis" (the contraction "it's" was not yet in use), while lacking the richness of later sixteenth-century speech. And, of course, much of the dialogue would be in French. Consider *The Pleasure Palace* my translation of Jane Popyncourt's memoirs.

A WHO'S WHO OF THE EARLY TUDOR COURT

Beaufort, Margaret (Countess of Richmond)(1443–1509)
Margaret Beaufort gave birth to the future King Henry VII when she was only fourteen. She conspired to put him on the throne of England and to arrange his marriage to Elizabeth of York. She set up the rules that governed the nursery at Eltham. Late in life she became extremely pious.

Blount, Elizabeth (c. 1500–1540)
A "damsel of the most serene queen" from about 1513, Bess Blount was Henry VIII's mistress and the mother of his acknowledged son, Henry FitzRoy (1519–1536). She married twice, had six more children, and was back at court as Lady Clinton when Anne of Cleves was queen.

Brandon, Charles (1485?–1545)

Starting as a page to Prince Arthur, Charles Brandon advanced steadily at court. He was sewer to Henry VII circa 1503, master of horse to the Earl of Essex from 1505, esquire of the body to Henry VII in 1507, and had developed a close personal friendship with the future Henry VIII before 1509. He was knighted in 1512, created Viscount Lisle in December of that same year, and elevated in the peerage to Duke of Suffolk in 1514. He married the king's sister in mid-February 1515. His matrimonial history up to that point included three earlier "marriages" and an annulment, and he wed yet again after Mary Tudor's death.

Brandon, Sir Thomas (1454?–1510)

Charles Brandon's uncle, Sir Thomas was master of horse to Henry VII, with whom he was in exile in Brittany and France.

Bryan, Elizabeth (Lady Carew) (c. 1495–1546)

At court with her mother, one of Queen Catherine's ladies, Elizabeth Bryan married Sir Nicholas Carew in December 1514. She was at court for most of Henry VIII's reign and considered one of the most beautiful women there.

Bryan, Margaret (Lady Guildford) (d. by 1527)

Older sister of Elizabeth, Margaret Bryan married Sir Henry Guildford at court in May 1512. She participated in many of the masques and revels her husband produced. She died sometime between 1521 and 1527.

Carew, Nicholas (c. 1496–1539)

Squire of the king's body, then groom of the privy chamber to Henry VIII, Nicholas Carew was probably in Prince Henry's household as early as age six. He married Elizabeth Bryan in December 1514. He was not knighted until 1520, but he was already a champion jouster by 1516. He was executed for treason in 1539.

Catherine of Aragon (1485–1536)

The daughter of Ferdinand of Aragon and Isabella of Castile, Catherine of Aragon was sent to England in 1501 to marry Henry VII's oldest son, Arthur, Prince of Wales. Arthur died soon after their marriage and Catherine spent the next seven years on the fringes of the English court and in near poverty. When Henry VIII succeeded his father, one of his first acts was to marry his brother's widow. During the early years of Henry's reign, theirs was a successful and harmonious marriage. When the king left England to make war on France, he named Catherine as regent. Although she had expert help from the Earl of Surrey and others, she was the one who ordered troops to defend England against the Scottish invasion that ended with the Battle of Flodden and she had a hand in negotiating the peace that followed. When she failed to give King Henry a son, he divorced her.

Chambre, John (1470–1549)

One of six physicians and five apothecaries to the king, Dr. Chambre served both Henry VII and Henry VIII. He first came to court in 1507.

Compton, Sir William (1482–1528)

William Compton was a ward of the king after his father's death in 1493 and entered royal service at that time as a page to Prince Henry. To King Henry VIII he was groom of the bedchamber, groom of the stole, and chief gentleman of the bedchamber. He was knighted in 1513 and married by 1514 to Werburga Brereton,

Lady Cheyney, a wealthy widow. He used her fortune to rebuild Compton Wynyates. His house in Thames Street in London was reportedly used by the king for assignations with at least one mistress, and in 1510 Compton himself was at the center of a scandal involving the married Lady Hastings. Earlier that same year he was almost killed in a tournament he and the king had entered in disguise.

Denys, Hugh (d. by 1516)

Hugh Denys was Henry VII's groom of the stole. His wife, Mary Roos, was a member of Queen Elizabeth's household and later joined that of Queen Catherine of Aragon. Mrs. Denys was still alive in 1540, by which time she had been widowed a second time.

Gibson, Richard

Richard Gibson was actively involved in every revel, spectacle, and tournament at court from 1510 to 1534. He was a yeoman tailor by profession, but he was also one of the King's Players under Henry VII and their leader from 1505 to 1509. This troupe of players did not travel other than with the court and each received an annual salary of twenty marks plus livery and rewards for performances. Gibson was made sergeant of tents and sergeant at arms for the journey to France in 1513. He went on to become principal costume designer and producer of revels, working with Sir Henry Guildford, the king's master of revels, as his deputy, and with William Cornish, director of the Children of the Chapel and designer of masques and pageants. Gibson was responsible for obtaining material from the wardrobe, renting houses to serve as workshops, contracting the services of whatever household departments were needed, hiring artists and artisans to make costumes, properties, and pageant wagons, and arranging for their transportation. He also made jousting apparel and trappings for the horses and decorated banqueting houses, some of which he helped construct.

Goose, John
"Goose" was Henry VIII's fool when Henry was Duke of York.

Gordon, Lady Catherine (d. 1537)
Married to Perkin Warbeck by command of James IV of Scotland as part of the attempt to overthrow Henry VII, Lady Catherine ended up as a prisoner of the English king. She was placed in Elizabeth of York's household, where she became a favored lady-in-waiting, and when Henry VIII became king she received several grants of land in Berkshire. In 1510 she married James Strangeways, a gentleman usher of the king's chamber. After Strangeways's death she married twice more, both times to minor courtiers.

Guildford, Henry (1489–1532)
Although there is no record of Henry Guildford at court before 1509, he may have been one of the children of honor in the Duke of York's household at Eltham, where his mother was the Lady Mary's lady governess. Guildford was knighted in 1512. He served the king as master of revels and became master of horse in 1515. He married Margaret Bryan at court on April 25, 1512.

Guildford, Sir Richard (1450–1506)
Father of Henry and husband of "Mother Guildford," Sir Richard was deeply in debt at the time of his death in Jerusalem, where he had gone on pilgrimage. The previous year he had lost his post as controller of the king's household due to poor management of

money and had spent six months in the Fleet before being released by the king's order. He was pardoned just before he left England.

Henry VII (1457–1509)

From 1471 until 1485, Henry Tudor was in exile in Brittany and France. Little is known of his exact location or his companions before 1483. In 1485, he defeated Richard III to seize the throne of England. He married Elizabeth of York (1465–1503) to strengthen his claim.

Henry VIII (1491–1547)

The second son of Henry VII and Elizabeth of York, Henry was Duke of York until the death of his older brother, Arthur. He then became Prince of Wales. He succeeded his father to the throne in 1509 and immediately married Arthur's widow, Catherine of Aragon. In 1514, Henry VIII was twenty-three, stood six feet two inches tall and had a thirty-five-inch waist and a forty-two-inch chest. He was an athletic man, especially fond of tennis and jousting, at which he excelled. He was known to love his younger sister dearly and take great pleasure in her company. He was the first English monarch to adopt the style "Your Majesty" in preference to the traditional "Your Grace."

Orléans, Louis d', second duc de Longueville, Marquis of Rothelin, Count of Dunois, and Lord of Beaugency (1480–August 1, 1516)

On the death of his older brother, the first duke, in 1515, Louis d'Orléans inherited the title. At that time he was the captain of one hundred gentlemen of the king's horse. He had been married for ten years to Jôhanna of Baden-Hochberg (1480–1543) and had four children by her, the youngest born in 1513. Longueville was captured at the Battle of the Spurs and sent to England as a prisoner of war to wait for his ransom (100,000 crowns) to be paid. While there he took a mistress, Jane Popyncourt. After the death of Queen Anne, he took an active role in negotiating the marriage of Louis XII of France and Henry VIII's sister Mary, and served as proxy bridegroom at the wedding at Greenwich Palace. The next day, his ransom having been paid, he left for France. He was high in favor with both Louis XII and his successor, Francis I, both of whom were Longueville's distant kinsmen. He was a combatant at the Battle of Marignano and reportedly lost a brother there. He died of unknown causes at Beaugency on August 1, 1516, having made his will the previous day. Although Jane Popyncourt left England for France in late May 1516, it is not known whether they were reunited. The story that he set her up at the Louvre and lived with her there for many years has no basis in fact. Not only did he die only a few months after she arrived, but in 1516 the Louvre was a ruin. The court, when in Paris, resided at Les Tournelles.

Pole, Eleanor (Lady Verney) (b. c. 1463)
As Lady Verney, wife of Sir Ralph (c. 1452–1528), Eleanor Pole served both Elizabeth of York and Catherine of Aragon. She was one of Elizabeth of York's favorite ladies. As the daughter of one of Margaret Beaufort's half sisters, she was also a cousin to Henry VII and his children.

Popyncourt, Jane (d. 1528+)
Records place Jane in England in 1498 as a French-speaking damsel assigned to teach the princesses that language through "daily conversation." Nothing is known of her background. Some records identify her as French, others as Flemish. During the duc de Longueville's stay at the English court as a prisoner of war, she

became his mistress. Her name was struck off the list of Mary Tudor's attendants at the last moment by King Louis XII, who made the comment that she should be "burnt." She remained at the English court, participating in masques and serving as a maid of honor to Queen Catherine, until May 1516, at which time she received a gift of £100 from King Henry and left England for France. She corresponded with Mary Tudor for some years thereafter and sent gifts to Mary's children. She is last heard of in 1528, when Mary asked Jane to use her influence at the French court on Mary's behalf.

Radcliffe, Eleanor (Lady Lovell) (d. 1518)

Both Sir Thomas (1453–1524) and Lady Lovell were at court during the reign of Henry VII and the first part of that of Henry VIII. Lovell was constable of the Tower from 1509 on and one of the leaders of the army that marched north to defend England from Scottish invaders in 1513. He retired from court in 1516.

Salinas, Maria de (d. 1539)

Considered Queen Catherine's closest friend by 1514, Maria de Salinas replaced her cousin, Maria de Rojas, as one of Catherine's ladies in 1503. She was naturalized in 1516, shortly before her marriage to William, tenth Baron Willoughby d'Eresby. She had one child, Catherine, who became the ward of Charles Brandon, Duke of Suffolk, upon Willoughby's death in 1526. In 1533, after Mary Tudor's death, Charles Brandon married Catherine Willoughby.

Tudor, Margaret (1489–1541)

The oldest daughter of Henry VII and Elizabeth of York, Margaret was married off to James IV of Scotland in 1503. She was willing to marry Louis XII of France, but he wanted her sister. Shortly after that marriage was contracted, Margaret chose her own second husband, Archibald Douglas, Earl of Angus, by whom she had a daughter, Margaret, born in England in early 1516. In May of that year, Queen Margaret was reunited with her brother and a tournament was held in her honor at Greenwich, but their relationship was a prickly one. She did not remain at the English court.

Tudor, Mary (1495–1533)

Younger sister of Henry VIII and Margaret Tudor, the Lady Mary was for some years betrothed to Charles of Castile. She repudiated that marriage in order to wed Louis XII of France. She was eighteen. He was fifty-two. She is said to have been in love with Charles Brandon, Duke of Suffolk, before she left England and to have made her brother promise that she could choose a second husband for herself when Louis died. She may have helped this outcome along by encouraging King Louis to stay up late and join in the revels celebrating their marriage. Once widowed, she married Charles Brandon in Paris sometime before February 20, 1515. They were remarried at Greenwich, with her brother's blessing, on May 13, 1515. Mary and Jane Popyncourt were lifelong friends and corresponded with each other after Jane left England for France in 1516.

Vaux, Joan (Mother Guildford) (c. 1463–1538)

A protégée of Margaret Beaufort, Countess of Richmond (Henry VII's mother), Joan Vaux married Sir Richard Guildford as his second wife. She was in the household of Elizabeth of York and later became "lady governess" to Mary Tudor. She was again one of Margaret Beaufort's ladies in 1509. By 1510 she had retired and was living on a small pension in a house in Blackfriars. That same year she inherited a second house in Southwark from Sir Thomas Brandon and leased it back to Brandon's principal heir, Charles Brandon. Lady Guildford was called out of retirement to travel to France with Mary Tudor in 1514. Her dismissal by King Louis, along with most of Mary's English attendants, on the day after the French wedding ceremony, caused a furor. In particular, Mary objected to sending her "Mother Guildford" away. Upon her return to England, Lady Guildford resumed her retirement. She was granted two pensions by the king totaling £60 per annum.

Velville, Sir Rowland (1474–1535)

Contemporary records say nothing of the rumor that Sir Rowland Velville was the illegitimate son of Henry VII by a Breton lady, but his descendants in Wales have always maintained that this was the case. It is certainly possible, and the king's failure to acknowledge him is not particularly strange given the climate of the times. King Edward IV's illegitimate son, known as Arthur Wayte during his early years and Arthur Plantagenet only later in life, lived at court under four successive English kings without having his parentage particularly remarked upon. What is certain is that Velville was a mere boy when he accompanied Henry Tudor to England. He lived at court, was knighted in 1497, and was an obsessive jouster. Velville participated in more tournaments than anyone else at the court of Henry VII. He was also known for his short temper. In 1509, he took up his duties as constable of Beaumaris Castle in Wales. His relationship to Jane is my own invention, an attempt to explain why she, of all the girls in France, might have been selected for the honor of teaching French to two English princesses.

READERS CLUB GUIDE

Introduction

Young Jane Popyncourt comes to England from France in 1498 when she is eight years old to be a companion and French tutor to the two daughters of Henry VII. When her mother dies shortly thereafter, Jane becomes a regular member of the royal court.

But all that changes when the duc de Longueville arrives in 1513 as a French prisoner of war. Accompanying the duke is Guy Dunois, a childhood friend of Jane's who will help her discover the truth about her past and her mother's mysterious death.

The chemistry between Jane and Longueville is strong and soon leads Jane to become his mistress. Her new intimacy with the duke makes her privy to French political secrets, and King Henry VIII enlists her as a spy. She is hesitant to engage in this kind of deception, but when she learns the duke has only lustful feelings for her, she uses their relationship to return to France to uncover the secrets of her mother's last days and her reasons for fleeing France when Jane was just a child.

As Jane makes her way to France, she discovers the perfidy that has cost her family their ancestral lands. Now all she has to do is use the skills she honed in the royal court to win over the king of France and persuade him to award her her rightful inheritance.

Discussion Questions

1. Jane learns about her royal connection as an adult, but there are earlier clues to her secret lineage. What are some hints that Jane is "not quite servant, not quite family" (308) to the Tudors?

2. Jane confesses, "For some reason the other girls among the children of honor had never taken to me, and I had always felt more comfortable spending my free time with the boys" (76). Do you think the other women at court treat her fairly? Why or why not?

3. Secret or mistaken identities abound in the novel, from Perkin Warbeck, the executed "pretender to the throne" (24), to Jane's own royal lineage. What threat do "royal bastards" (10) and imposters pose to the crown? Do you think that Jane's mother was murdered because of her royal blood? Why or why not?

4. Jane slowly learns the difference between lust and love over the course of the novel. When does it become apparent that her relationship with Longueville is based solely on "a storm of passion" (100)? When does Jane's love for Guy first come to light?

5. "Friendship cannot truly flourish at any court. Neither could love" (352). Are there exceptions to Jane's statement? Which characters seem to have found love or friendship at court? Do their attachments seem genuine? Why or why not?

6. Jane outwits two kings who try to seduce her: Henry VIII and François. Compare Jane's strategy with each king. How does she sidestep their advances? Which strategy seems more successful?

7. What do you think of Longueville's character? What is his approach to courtly love, sex, and marriage? Is he a villain in the novel? Why or why not?

8. "True pleasure combines happiness and contentment with passionate love" (358). How does the Pleasure Palace fail to live up to its name? Where does Jane finally find true pleasure?

9. Jane realizes that in the English court, "Everyone around me knew exactly who they were and where they belonged" (92). Do you think a person's lineage and social standing are as connected today as they were in the Tudor era? Why or why not?

10. Almost all of the characters of *The Pleasure Palace* were actual members of the Tudor court. Which historical figures especially came to life as you read the novel?

Enhance Your Book Club

1. Set the mood at your book club meeting by playing music from the Tudor era. You can find music files at www.tudorhistory .org/topics/music/midi.html.

2. Challenge your book club to a match of bowling, Tudor-style! You can use croquet balls or softballs as "bowls," and a wooden stake as a target, or "mistress." Whoever throws the bowl closest to the mistress wins the match.

3. Using the descriptions of dress in *The Pleasure Palace* for

inspiration, draw a member of the Tudor court in full costume. Try your hand at sketching Jane in her velvet gown, or Henry VIII in his brocade doublet and jeweled codpiece.

4. The Tower of London, "a palace as well as a prison" (85), is a key setting of the novel. Research the Tower's fascinating history. You can learn about the prisoners, treasures, and folklore of the Tower at www.camelotintl.com/tower_site/index.html.

Questions for the Author

1. **Why do you think contemporary readers are still fascinated by Tudor England? What is it about that era that captures our imaginations?**

The Tudors and their times have always made interesting reading, starting with the gossip-filled dispatches of sixteenth-century foreign ambassadors. Hundreds of books have been written about Henry VIII and Elizabeth I and Shakespeare, but there were many other people in Tudor England who led remarkable lives. It would be hard *not* to be fascinated by them.

2. **Why did you choose to write a novel about Jane Popyncourt, an actual member of the Tudor court? Why not invent a character from scratch, or build a novel around a historical figure with a better-known past?**

I've had an interest in the real women of the sixteenth century for a long time, particularly those who are not as well known as some of their contemporaries. What drew me to Jane as a character were the mysteries surrounding her. Why was she chosen to come to England and join the royal nursery? Why did King Louis forbid Jane—and only Jane—to accompany Mary Tudor to

France? Why did he say she should be burned? The challenge I gave myself was to work out reasonable fictional answers to those questions while sticking to the facts that *are* known. Inventing a character from scratch would probably have been easier, but not as much fun. Initially, I did consider using Henry VIII's sister, Mary, as my protagonist. I decided against it for two reasons. First, other novelists have already written her story. Second, there was less scope for invention in her life, since so much of it is well documented.

3. *The Pleasure Palace* is meticulously detailed, from costumes and banquets to masques and battles. How did you go about researching the Tudor court for this novel?

I've been reading about Tudor times since I was in high school and I started accumulating books on the subject at about the same time. I still read everything I can get my hands on and have file folders stuffed with notes on all sorts of arcane subjects. Fortunately, since many other people have been fascinated with the era for such a long time, there is a great deal out there. Biographies are a particularly rich source of information. For anyone who is interested, there is a list of some of the sources I used for this novel at www.KateEmersonHistoricals.com.

4. Holiday celebrations, from the Twelfth Night banquet to the St. Valentine's Eve lottery, play a big role in *The Pleasure Palace*. Which holiday traditions from the Tudor era do you wish were still in practice today?

I think it would be fun to have a Lord of Misrule or a King of the Bean at Yuletide. The only problem is that you'd also have to have a very large household. With the small families most people have these days, the tradition wouldn't work quite so well.

5. According to your Author's Note, Jane Popyncourt might have been French or Flemish. Why did you decide to make your heroine Breton-Flemish, a sort of combination of the two?

I wanted to account for the confusion, and also for her surname, which didn't strike me as particularly French. As for the Breton half, Jane's mother almost had to be from there in order to make the connection to the future Henry VII work.

6. The games and tournaments of the court punctuate the plot of the novel. What were some of the challenges in describing these spectacles on the page? Which games do you think you would have enjoyed playing or watching, if you had lived in Tudor England?

The biggest challenge (and my editor will vouch for this) was deciding what to cut. I found so much information on tennis and bowls and masques and tournaments, all of it fascinating to me, that I found it difficult to choose which details to include and which to leave out. My original manuscript contained way too much description of pageant wagons and costumes and the like. I think I would have enjoyed watching most of the spectacles, but the only one I'd have wanted to participate in would have been the dancing.

7. "Courtly love" is common throughout the novel—many affairs occur, and lovers are easily replaced. Do you see any similarities to romance today, or has the battle of the sexes changed dramatically since Henry VIII's lifetime?

Some things never change. People fall in and out of love, suffer heartbreak, and make life-altering decisions based on physical attraction. The difference in Tudor times was that young people were more likely to give in to family and religious pressure to marry someone chosen for them, opting for economic and social stability over romantic love.

8. Two murder mysteries remain unsolved in the novel: King Charles of France and Jane's mother, Jeanne Popyncourt. Why did you leave these suspicious deaths open-ended?

The rumors I mention surrounding King Charles's death really were bandied about. He died in a rather bizarre way and no one can be certain what happened. Even so, I suspect his death was an accident, caused by that blow to the head. Jeanne Popyncourt's death, on the other hand, being fiction, gave me the chance to make sense of several odd historical facts: What happened to Jane's parents when she came to England? Why is there a Jane Popyncourt listed in the household accounts of Elizabeth of York when Jane was sent to the nursery? Why did Sir Richard Guildford go on a pilgrimage to the Holy Land at a time when such journeys by Englishmen were extremely rare? And finally, why did Margaret Beaufort, King Henry VII's mother, take a vow of chastity, dress like a nun, and wear a hair shirt during the last part of her life?

9. Your Author's Note reveals that you invented the uncle-niece relationship between Sir Rowland Velville and Jane Popyncourt, two historical figures. Were there other imaginative connections you considered while planning this book?

I looked at several possibilities, including having Henry VII bring Jane to England because she was his natural daughter. For that to work, however, Jane would have had to be much older. Whoever Jane really was, there must have been some reason why she was selected, and the most likely was that there was a family connection to some prominent figure at court.

10. Have readers seen the last of Jane, or do you think you will revisit this character in another book?

I've said pretty much all I wanted to about Jane and left her at a good place in her life. However, since no one knows exactly when she died, it is always possible she might make a cameo appearance in a future novel.